Praise for the Sophie Katz novels of

KYRA DAVIS

SEX, MURDER AND A DOUBLE LATTE

"Part romantic comedy and part mystery,
with witty dialogue and enjoyable characters,
Sex, Murder and a Double Latte is the perfect summer read."
—*The Oregonian*

"A thoroughly readable romp."
—*Publishers Weekly*

"A terrific mystery. Kyra Davis comes up with
the right mix of snappy and spine-tingling,
and throws in a hot Russian mystery man, too."
—*Detroit Free Press*

PASSION, BETRAYAL AND KILLER HIGHLIGHTS

"A witty and engaging blend of chick lit, pop culture,
and amateur-sleuth whodunit [that] will appeal not only to
female readers but to any mystery fan who has an
offbeat sense of humor.... Laugh-out-loud funny."
—*Barnes & Noble.com*

"Davis' snappy dialogue [is] funny all the way."
—*Publishers Weekly*

"Davis spins a tale full of unexpected turns and fun humor...
keeps readers guessing till the very end."
—*Romantic Times BOOKreviews*

KYRA DAVIS

OBSESSION, DECEIT

AND REALLY DARK

CHOCOLATE

RED
DRESS
INK
™

OBSESSION, DECEIT AND REALLY DARK CHOCOLATE

A Red Dress Ink novel

ISBN-13: 978-0-373-89553-3
ISBN-10:   0-373-89553-4

www.RedDressInk.com

Printed in U.S.A.

To my readers. Your letters and e-mails of support
and praise never fail to inspire and motivate me.

ACKNOWLEDGMENTS

I want to thank my wonderful editor, Margaret Marbury, for all of her help and encouragement, and Police Chief John Weiss for helping me with this book's ending. I also want to thank my stepbrother, Chris Sullivan, my mother, Gail Davis, and my stepfather, Richard Sullivan, for taking care of my son while I wrote this novel. Last but absolutely NOT least I want to thank my son, Isaac, for being my biggest fan and greatest motivator. Isaac, I love you with all my heart and soul.

Why sleep with the enemy when you can screw 'em?
—*C'est La Mort*

IT'S NOT OFTEN THAT AN OLD FRIEND AND MENTOR ASKS YOU TO SEDUCE
her husband. I suppose it was the bizarre nature of the request
that made me want to do it. Or perhaps it was because I
knew that Melanie O'Reilly was at least partially responsible
for my becoming a novelist. Or maybe I just agreed because
I thought it would be a good way to get my mind off my
ex-boyfriend, Anatoly Darinsky.

Whatever. The point is that after years of very sporadic
contact Melanie invited me to lunch and asked if I would
do her a big favor. My initial assumption was that she wanted
me to donate some money to one of her favorite organizations or charities—the Salvation Army, the Symphony, the
Boy Scouts…what have you. It even occurred to me that
she wanted me to attend one of those five-hundred-dollar-

a-plate dinners to support Flynn Fitzgerald, the majorly right-wing Contra Costa County congressional hopeful whose campaign was currently employing her husband, Eugene. The last really would have been a huge favor since I disagreed with almost everything Fitzgerald stood for, but for my favorite former writing professor I would have done it. But this...this one came out of left field.

It seems that Eugene had not been the same since he and a few of his evangelical buds had returned from a Moral Majority road trip, an excursion not unlike the MTV Rock the Vote road trip, except this expedition involved more Jesus talk and less talk of body piercing. Melanie was convinced that the Jesus van had doubled as a magnet for wayward sluts, and that her husband had been nibbling on the forbidden fruit.

But I digress. *My* mission had nothing to do with Jesus, nor was I supposed to emulate the Virgin Mary. My mission was to tempt Eugene by behaving like Mary Magdalene during her party years. Melanie explained that I was the only "younger woman" friend who had never met her husband. At thirty-one I wasn't sure I still qualified as a younger woman, but it was true that I had never met Eugene O'Reilly. I was supposed to have gone to their wedding but a bout of strep throat put an end to those plans.

I wasn't going to sleep with him, of course. Apart from the fact that this was only a fact-finding mission, one look told me that the man's weight had to be somewhere *under* one hundred and twenty pounds. If a guy looks like Brad Pitt I'll willingly compromise my political ideals in exchange for a little face time, but when confronted with a conservative who's twice my age and skinny enough to make me feel fat, I emphatically refused to cross the party line.

I'd simply be testing him: if Eugene O'Reilly wanted to play "break the commandments" with me I would simply ditch him and report back to Melanie. If he resisted my charms, all was right with the conservative world.

I took one more sip of the lemon drop I had been nursing while scoping him out from my seat in the darkened corner of the Antioch bar, screwed up my courage and then crossed the room to Eugene.

"Is this seat taken?" I pretended not to notice the way my short red dress rode up when I climbed onto the bar stool.

The man didn't even bother to look up from his Scotch and soda. "Not that I'm aware of."

So far so good—still, I couldn't help but feel a little hurt. I mean really, when an older man doesn't bother to give you the time of day after you stick your boobs in his face you have to question your own sex appeal.

I tried to discreetly glance at myself in the mirror behind the bar. No major pimples, and as far as I could tell I didn't have food in my teeth. My hair was a little out of control but no more than usual. My father was African-American and my mother had curly hair that was typical of her Eastern European Jewish ancestry, so when it came to my hair "a little out of control" was the best-case scenario.

I rested my elbow on the bar and tried another tactic. "I've never been to this place before."

"Mmm." He took another sip of his Scotch and casually looked around the room. I caught a glimpse of his hands, which seemed to be one of his few saving graces. They were big and strong…I'm into hands, but they need to be attached to a body that is at least a little appealing. Anatoly had great hands, and arms, and shoulders…but I wasn't going to think of him right now or ever again. I was over Anatoly. Really.

"I don't usually go to bars," I said, bringing my focus back to the task at hand, "but tonight I just had to get out of the house. You ever feel like that? Like you just need to go somewhere no one knows you and forget your troubles?"

Eugene looked at me for the first time. "What are you trying to forget?"

I hesitated. I hadn't really worked this story out in my head yet. "Oh, you know…family stuff."

He nodded and turned his attention back to his Scotch.

"My younger brother dropped a big bomb on the whole family today," I said quickly. In reality, the only sibling I had was a younger sister, but he didn't need to know that.

"Oh?" His disinterest was palpable.

"Yeah…it turns out he's ga…a homosexual."

Eugene snapped his head back in my direction. "I'm so sorry."

"It gets worse," I said, encouraged by the reaction. "He has a boyfriend and they're going to Massachusetts to get married."

"No!" Eugene put his glass on the bar with a thud. "Did anyone see this coming?"

I shook my head and looked away. "He was always such a good kid. He consistently made the honor roll, played lots of sports in high school…he even got a full scholarship to Syracuse University."

"Syracuse is a good conservative town."

"I know! That's why everyone in the family was so happy

when he decided to go there instead of to the other university he was accepted to—" I leaned over and lowered my voice to a tremulous whisper "—UC Berkeley."

Eugene exhaled loudly. "Clearly he made the right choice. But something must have gone wrong. Something must have happened to make him lose his way."

"Yes, but what? Here we all thought he was busy studying and partying it up with a bunch of nice Republican fraternity brothers, and as it turns out he was spending all his free time campaigning for…for…" I dropped my head in my hands in what I hoped looked like a display of grief rather than an attempt to hide a smile "…for Hillary Clinton!"

"My God! Your parents must be devastated."

"Oh, they are, and so am I. I keep replaying the whole sordid event in my head." I glazed my eyes and pretended to relive the moment. "I'm eagerly awaiting his arrival with my parents at their place, he walks in the door, and before you can say 'Green Party' my whole world is turned upside down!"

Eugene put a hand on my arm. I held my breath and waited for him to use his thumb to stroke my skin or to somehow make the gesture more intimate, but he released me quickly, leaving me with nothing but the sense of being comforted by a well-meaning stranger.

"You need to have faith that your brother is going to be okay," he said in a tone that was much gentler than what I was expecting. "People sometimes make mistakes, but with the love and the guidance of a good family many find their way back to the path of righteousness. You can't give up on him."

I looked up into Eugene's eyes, expecting to see some kind of mad religious fervor, but all I saw was sincerity and conviction. He waved the bartender over. "Sir, I'd like another Scotch and soda and the lady needs a drink as well." He turned and smiled at me. "Put it on my tab."

I ended up closing the place with Eugene. I kept waiting for him to make a move on me, but everything he did seemed to be motivated by a desire for companionship. He sucked down a countless number of cocktails, and while the alcohol definitely made him more talkative, it didn't make him more flirtatious.

"This country's going to hell in a handbasket," he said as he stumbled to his feet and tried unsuccessfully to help me put on my coat. "Immorality is everywhere—on the TV, radio, don't even get me started about the Internet."

"Tell me about it," I said as I gently guided him out of the bar and into the warm night. "There's this Web site, www.womenserotica.com—it's despicable. I go on it every day to read the new entries and I'm horrified every time."

"Exactly what I'm talking about!" Eugene slurred, too drunk to pick up on my sarcasm. "How are we suppose-ta raise children with good solid Christian values when they're continually confronted with evil temptations?"

I nodded gravely. "I'm having a hard enough time just trying to shelter my cat from the filth they've been promoting on *Animal Planet!* Do you know that they had a whole show on elephant sperm?"

"My God!" Eugene shook his head. He looked at me in a blatant attempt to focus. "You realize that you're not fit to drive."

My lips curved into an amused smile. "And you think you are?"

"No, no. I'm gonna walk back to my hotel. I live in Walnut Creek. I'm jus' here on business, my hotel's only a mile away," he slurred.

"It's two in the morning, kind of late for a long walk."

"Normally I'd take a cab," Eugene conceded, "but tonight I need fresh air. You're not the only one who had a bad day, ya know."

I spotted a park bench on the other side of the street. "Why don't we sit down for a while and talk? Like you said, I can't drive and you're obviously not in any big hurry to get to sleep, so you might as well hang out with me and talk while I sober up."

Eugene nodded and followed me to the bench. Out of the corner of my eye I saw a green SUV parked at the end of the city block. Other than that, the area had already been deserted. The vehicle probably belonged to one of the bartenders closing up. I sat down on the bench and patted the seat next to me, but Eugene hesitated.

"Sophie, you're a very nice girl and you're very beautiful…but I'm married."

"I saw the ring."

"My wife's been impossible lately, but I believe in the sanctity of marriage," he said matter-of-factly. He sat down next to me and gazed at me with bloodshot eyes. "I *practice* what I preach."

I felt myself soften toward him instantly. "I respect that, Eugene."

"That's the *real* problem with the world today," he said, grandly gesturing out into space, "no one ever means what they say anymore. They're all a bunch of bloody hypocrites. Moral corruption is everywhere, Sophie. Everywhere. Look!

Look at that!" He jumped to his feet and picked up a dis-carded candy wrapper featuring a cartoon sea animal. "We now have sponges promoting deviant behavior!"

"Eugene, I think maybe we should get you a cab so you can sleep this one off."

"Damn furry freaks if you ask me!"

How did Melanie end up with this man? I mean, he was honest and honorable, but his view of the world was incredibly whacked. I stood up and smiled at him sympatheti-cally. "I think it's time for me to head home. I have a long drive ahead of me."

"But you've been drinking."

"I switched to soda water a while back, you probably just didn't notice—" *because you were too drunk to notice anything* "—because soda water can look like vodka and tonic."

Eugene nodded. "Let me walk you to your car."

I shrugged and waited as he staggered to his feet. I thought I heard the sound of an engine start up a ways behind me on the otherwise quiet street. We walked in silence for the three blocks to my car. I'd decided to be cheap and forgo the nearby garage, which meant that I had been forced to park a bit off the main strip. When we got to my Audi I turned to Eugene and put a hand on his shoulder. "Can I please give you a ride back to your hotel? It's really no trouble."

He shook his head and rubbed his eyes. "I wanna walk."

I suppressed a giggle. "I really think you should let me drive you."

"No thanks, Sophie." He lifted my hand to his lips and kissed it gently. "It's nice to know there are some decent people out there. You give me hope."

And with that he stumbled off. I watched him until he turned the corner before getting into my car. I felt sorry for him. I wasn't sure why he seemed so dejected, almost disillusioned.

I sighed, fastened my seat belt and turned the key in the ignition.

Just then I heard a quick series of loud bangs and the sound of a car screeching away.

My heart stopped. I quickly checked my rearview mirror, but there was no one on the block. The commotion had happened on one of the streets nearby.

Eugene.

Obviously the smart thing to do would have been to stay in the car and call 911 on my cell phone, but common sense temporarily abandoned me. I jumped out and ran to the street corner where I had last seen Eugene. As soon as I rounded the corner there he was, lying on the sidewalk, motionless. Blood was seeping through his previously white dress shirt.

I could see lights being turned on in the surrounding buildings as some of the residents tried to figure out what was going on. I sprinted to Eugene's side and kneeled down. His eyes were at half mast and I heard a gurgling coming out of his throat.

"Eugene, it's Sophie. Eugene, can you hear me?"

"Goddamned furry shit," he muttered.

"Eugene, you're delirious, just stay calm and I'll get an ambulance." But even as I said the words I heard the distant wail of sirens.

I also heard Eugene take his final breath.

2

People expect so much from the individuals they bear
a fondness for. That's why I focus my energy into being
as disagreeable as possible.
—*C'est La Mort*

"THANK YOU SO MUCH FOR COMING." MELANIE GESTURED FOR ME TO SIT
on her tan leather couch as she settled herself into an overstuffed armchair.

I sat down and stared blankly at the wall behind her. It
had been three days since I called Melanie to tell her that
she was a widow, and this was the first time since that awful
event that I had seen her. I took three Advil before driving
from San Francisco to her Walnut Creek home and now,
forty-five minutes later, I still had a headache.

"Can I get you anything?" Melanie asked. "Johnny,
Fitzgerald's personal assistant, brought me a lovely fruit basket

the other day. I could cut up a few pieces and some cheese if you're hungry. Or how about a cup of tea?"

I shook my head mutely. Migraines and food didn't mix.

There were a few moments of silence. Melanie squeezed her knees causing her linen pants to take on the quality of wrinkled paper. "I don't really know what to say."

"Maybe there's nothing *to* say."

Melanie winced. "You think less of me now."

"That's what you're worried about?" I asked, surprise overwhelming my discomfort. "What I think of you? How can that possibly matter at this point?"

"Your opinion has always mattered to me, Sophie. You were a very special student…my favorite, really." A sad smile played on her lips. "I am so proud of all of your accomplishments. I understand that *C'est La Mort* hit the *New York Times* bestseller list in its first week! I like to think I played a small part…."

"Melanie, your husband's dead. Your fanatically conservative, crazy, good-hearted and loyal husband is being embalmed right now."

"I know." Her voice was so soft I could barely hear her, and her rapid blinking seemed to imply that she was holding back tears, but her grief didn't do a lot to alleviate my indignation.

"I've spent the last few nights awake berating myself for agreeing to entrap him. I can't *believe* he spent the last minutes of his life with me and all I did was lie to him."

"You always told me you were a good liar," she tried to joke.

"I'm a great liar! And I enjoy it, but now all of a sudden lying seems ugly and…wrong! I spent all of three hours with your husband, and I know damn well that this was not a man who would have ever compromised his beliefs by cheating on you. What I don't understand is how could you even suspect him of something like that?"

Melanie ran her hand over the loose skin that draped from her neck. "I did know him, but something had changed. Eugene didn't like secrets. He always said that a husband and wife should tell each other everything.

"Let me give you an example," Melanie said, apparently noting my incredulity. "Last year Eugene was trying to organize a boycott against *The Da Vinci Code* in keeping with the request of the Vatican. But I really wanted to see what all the fuss was about so I went ahead and bought the book, and once I started reading it I couldn't put it down! I was just finishing up the last chapter when Eugene walked in on me. It was awful. At first I thought it was because he thought that reading it against the Vatican's advice was a sin and that *was* clearly a problem for him, but what hurt him the most was knowing that I had tried to hide it from him. He saw that as a betrayal."

"Not telling him that you were reading a book that everyone and their brother had already read was a betrayal?"

"I know it sounds extreme, but that's just the way Eugene was." I could have been mistaken, but I thought I heard a note of respect in her voice. "Lately I could tell that something was bothering him and yet he wouldn't talk about it. It was so unlike him, and even though I couldn't imagine him cheating on me I didn't know what else it could be. We all make mistakes, and I thought that maybe he wasn't as immune to temptation as I thought he was. I wouldn't have left him, Sophie, I just wanted to know what I was dealing with. But now…now, he's gone…."

Fresh tears trickled down the pale skin of her cheeks and I felt the unwelcome pang of guilt. I shifted in my seat, unsure if I should offer an apology, condolences or just get up and leave.

Melanie was right. I did think less of her. The dynamics of our relationship had changed so much over the past twelve years. She had started as my writing professor and then quickly become my mentor. When my father died I completely fell apart and Melanie had helped me pull myself together. After I graduated from University of San Francisco we had stayed in contact, meeting for coffee every few months. During our visits I began to see Melanie for who she really was: an intelligent, kind and altruistic woman with a lot of insecurities. Eventually she took a teaching position at Saint Mary's College in Moraga and our visits became semiannual occurrences. That was my fault. It just seemed like every time she suggested we get together I had something else I had to do. When she got married to Eugene and moved to Walnut Creek our visits became even less frequent, although she never forgot my birthday or failed to congratulate me when one of my books hit the stands. I often thought of her but rarely picked up the phone to tell her so. I assumed that she was happily occupied with pursuits that didn't involve me; perhaps mentoring another young writer. But looking at her now it was hard to admire her. For once it felt like I was the stronger one, the one with the most common sense, which was really scary since common sense isn't always my strong suit.

"I didn't want him to die, Sophie."

I took a deep breath and forced myself to reassess the situation. Who the hell was *I* to give *her* grief? She didn't give me a hard time when I told her I was getting a divorce after only two years of marriage, nor did she take issue with the content of the novels I wrote even though I knew they flew in the face of many of her religious beliefs. I leaned forward so I could take her hand. "Of course you didn't want that, Melanie. I know that."

"It never occurred to me that we would end this way."

"It was just one of those awful random twists of fate," I said. "He was in the wrong place at the wrong time. No one could have foreseen this."

"Yes, a random drive-by shooting." Melanie said the words slowly, as if trying to convince herself of them. "Or at least that's what the Antioch police are saying."

I pulled back in surprise. "You think they're wrong?"

"They don't know everything."

"What else is there?"

"It's just a feeling I have." Melanie tucked a gray-streaked lock behind her ear. "As I said, Eugene was keeping something from me and he was so agitated and distant during the past few weeks. Definitely not himself."

"Okay, but to assume that his recent attitude change had something to do with his death?"

"Thing is, he wasn't just upset, he was nervous. All of a sudden he started looking over his shoulder when we'd be out in public. He'd double-, then triple-check the locks. For a while I thought that maybe he'd had an extramarital affair with a stalker, like Michael Douglas in that awful movie with the rabbit. In retrospect I feel terrible for thinking that, but still, something was wrong and I'm afraid that maybe, just maybe, that *something* got to him…." Her voice faded away once more.

"Melanie, you need to talk to the police about this."

"I can't! What if he was involved in something he shouldn't have been? Reputation was everything to Eugene. If I did something to besmirch his name now, his memory would be tarnished—I just couldn't!"

But testing him to see if he'd make a drunken pass at a woman half his age was okay? I bit back the remark and tried to smile reassuringly. "Eugene wasn't involved in anything that he felt was immoral or unethical. I'd bet on it."

"Sophie, forgive me for saying this, but you spent one evening with the man. You're not in the position to make that statement."

"Okay, fine. Let's say you're right. What are you going to do? Are you going to keep this information to yourself even if it means that the person who killed your husband might get away with it?"

"Sophie, I need one more favor."

"Are you kidding?"

"I understand you're dating a private detective. The newspaper mentioned it right after your brother-in-law's killer was captured."

My heart fell to the bottom of my stomach. I wasn't supposed to be upset by references to Anatoly anymore. He was an idiot. A commitment-phobic, womanizing, egocentric idiot…with an incredible body and a sexy half smile that sent tingles down my spine and straight into my nether regions.

"Is he discreet?"

"Hmm?" I said absently as I briefly entertained a multi-orgasmic memory.

"Is he discreet?" she asked again. "Can I trust him to keep any information he digs up out of the hands of the media?"

"Are you saying you want to hire him?"

"I want to find out what happened to my husband, but I don't want people to know that I've enlisted a detective outside the police department. This whole thing is getting enough publicity without making things worse."

"Ah, right. The thing is, Anatoly's really expensive. For a case like this he'd charge you at least ten thousand dollars." I wasn't exactly lying. Anatoly had quoted that price to me before. Of course that was only because he was trying to piss me off.

Melanie's eyes fluttered at the figure. "He must be very good at what he does." She nodded resolutely. "I'll pay it."

"Really?" Note to self, those who possess American Express Platinum Cards cannot be scared away by high prices. "But…um…I don't think Anatoly's available."

"I see." Her disappointment was palpable. I should have probably just put her in touch with Anatoly. No doubt he'd take the case and I could stay out of the whole thing. But for some reason I didn't really believe that. I was the one who found Eugene. He'd want to talk to me about that. In fact he'd probably spend a lot of time questioning me, coaxing me to go over every detail and nuance. One thing would lead to another and before you knew it I'd be cuddled up in bed with my commitment-phobic Russian love god, sipping espresso. I just couldn't go there again.

"Maybe you don't need a detective," I suggested. "Maybe you just need someone trustworthy who's sneaky, good at networking and knows how to craft well-worded, probing questions."

"Someone sneaky?" I could hear the hope creeping back into her voice. "You?"

"*And* good at networking," I said a bit defensively. "I could talk to a few people…just try to get a sense of whether or not your fears are founded. If they are, then we could call a P.I. to do some more digging. But if Eugene's problems can be explained by the typical stresses of working on a campaign then you'll leave it to the police to find the person responsible for what happened."

"So this would be a preliminary investigation…a fact-finding expedition, as it were?"

"Exactly."

Melanie nodded slowly. "I suppose we could do that. Are you up for it?"

I hesitated and thought about what exactly I was up for. A couple of years ago the very idea of using the amateur sleuth tactics I wrote about in my novels in a real-life situation would have been laughable. But within the past few years I had been stalked by a serial killer and my sister's husband had been killed. I had been instrumental in solving both crimes and I got some satisfaction out of knowing I helped. Furthermore, solving crimes was often a rather enjoyable activity. Kind of like playing Clue with live psychotic actors. Well okay, it wasn't a lot of fun when people were trying to kill you, but the rest of it wasn't so bad. Plus, for reasons I couldn't quite put my finger on, I felt compelled to help Melanie with this. Logic told me that Eugene's death was probably a random act of violence. If that was the case

I could talk to a few of his co-workers, tell Melanie she was imagining things and leave it at that. Melanie could rest easy and I would never have to talk to Anatoly again. That was a good thing. I nodded eagerly. "I'm up for it."

Melanie offered me a shaky smile. "Very well. Should we start the questioning now?"

"You mean of you?"

"Yes. I assume there's information that you'll need from me."

"Um, yeah…okay." I quickly tried to formulate a few passably intelligent questions. "Who was Eugene closest to on the campaign?"

"I'm not sure I know the answer to that. He was very close to Flynn Fitzgerald, perhaps more so than most of the other strategists and consultants. Fitzgerald's media consultant, Maggie Gallagher, was a friend. We had her and her husband over for dinner a few times. Eugene was also an old family friend of Fitzgerald's top political strategist, Rick Wilkes."

"Had he complained about any problems at work?"

"No. Well, he was frustrated that Anne Brooke is always neck and neck with Fitzgerald in the polls. Considering her character, she should be trailing far behind by now."

I took a deep breath. A lot of very unpleasant information had come out about Anne Brooke since she announced her bid for Congress. And if the Republicans had run someone who was a moderate, Brooke's career would have been political toast. But the Republicans had given their endorsement to Flynn Fitzgerald, a man who was just to the right of Pat Robertson. Although Contra Costa County citizens were definitely more conservative than their Bay Area neighbors, they were understandably reluctant to vote for a man who had blamed single mothers and "queers" for the downfall of our society. Unless Brooke was caught making out with Fidel Castro, she could probably prevent Fitzgerald from getting a double-digit lead on her.

"Anything else?" I asked. "Was he having problems with any of his coworkers? Or anyone at all, for that matter?"

Melanie shook her head. "Eugene was opinionated, and that sometimes rubbed people the wrong way, but in the end most found that he had a good heart. He had a subtle charm that tended to transcend political differences."

I smiled slightly. I had been exposed to some of that charm. It had been nice to meet a man who had really believed in something, even if his beliefs differed from mine.

"Tell you what," I said as I pushed myself to my feet. "I'll find a way to talk to some of the people he saw or worked with regularly and see if I can find out anything."

Melanie swallowed hard and looked up at me from her seat. "Do you want me to introduce you to anyone? Because—"

"You don't want people to know that you're looking into Eugene's death...or rather his life," I finished for her. "No, I don't need introductions, but if anyone in his circle invites you to a social event and you can find a way of bringing me along without it looking suspicious, give me a ring."

Melanie flashed me a relieved smile. "I can do that." She got up and walked me to the door but hesitated before opening it. "There's one more thing I was hoping you could help me with."

"You're pushing your luck."

"I just wanted to know what—" Her voice caught and she looked down at the floor. "What were Eugene's last words?"

There were two ways to go with this. I could tell her the truth, that her husband's last words had been "Goddamn furry shit," (which was either evidence of the fact that he was completely delirious or that he truly had a problem with sponges that wore pants) or I could lie.

"Tell Melanie I love her," I said confidently. "His last words were tell Melanie I love her."

"Really? But wait…" Melanie's mouth turned down at the corners. "Are you sure he said Melanie?"

"You really need to get over this jealousy thing. He wasn't cheating."

"I know, I know," she said quickly. "It's just that he so rarely called me Melanie. He always referred to me by my pet name."

I swallowed and looked away. "Well, it was kind of a stressful moment, I could have misheard him. What's his pet name for you?"

"Curly. He loved my curls." She held up a lock of wavy hair that would have been flat as a board without the help of her stylist.

"I'm sure that's what he said. There was a lot to take in at that moment."

For instance, I could have heard "furry" when in fact what he said was "curly." My mentor and former professor could be a Goddamn curly shit.

I popped in the latest Gorillaz CD and turned over in my mind all the things I had just learned, which wasn't a lot. With traffic it took me over an hour to get back to San Francisco. Even if I had misheard Eugene, it didn't mean anything other than that he was in pain, delirious and pissed off at his wife. (Melanie wasn't capable of violence.) Besides, I was ninety percent sure that I *did* hear him correctly. Eugene had been cursing someone named Furry. Which, of course, raised another question: was Eugene the adulterous type after all? Wasn't it possible that someone who was dorky enough to call his naturally straight-haired wife "Curly" might also be dorky enough to call his mistress "Furry"?

But what kind of woman would sleep with a man who called her Furry? No, Eugene had to have been delirious. It didn't really matter; this entire mess was much ado about nothing. I decided to shelve the whole thing until tomorrow and spend this time on more productive activities like cursing at the traffic.

My cell phone rang just as I was contemplating the best way to stir up a little road rage.

"C'est Sophie."

"Hello, Sophie, it's Melanie. I just thought of a social event that you could attend where you would meet almost all of Eugene's friends and coworkers."

"And what would that be?"

"His funeral."

I felt the beginnings of another headache coming on. "Melanie, I can't interrogate people at a funeral."

"Of course not. I just thought you might be able to meet a few people and make connections. If someone happens to volunteer something useful you can pursue it at a later date."

Gee, that sounded like great fun. Melanie would be busy receiving all of Eugene's friends while I walked around by myself trying to initiate conversations with grieving strangers.

"If I come I want to bring a friend...actually, I want to bring

Leah." My sister was one of maybe ten Republicans who actually lived in San Francisco. If nothing else she'd be able to help me come up with topics of conversation that would play well with the politicians Eugene used to hang with.

"Then bring Leah," Melanie said. "But...do you think she'll be comfortable standing quietly by your side while you ask people about Eugene?"

I tried to imagine Leah doing anything quietly. "I'll bring my friend Mary Ann, too. That way Leah will have someone to complain—I mean *talk* to, no matter what."

"I think I met Mary Ann once. Is she the pretty girl with the long curly hair?"

"That's her."

"Very well, bring them both. And Sophie?"

"Yes?"

"Thank you."

I smiled and beeped at the idiot who had just cut me off. How many times had I said those words to Melanie? I owed her a lot, but I was fairly sure that when this was over we would finally be settled up.

I would rather burn in the fires of hell than spend eternity in heaven listening to a bunch of religious zealots say I told you so.
—*C'est La Mort*

IT WAS LIKE A BLACK-AND-GRAY SEA OF ST. JOHN AND BROOKS BROTHERS suits. I looked down at my own dark brown Old Navy dress as Mary Ann, Leah and I found seats in one of the rows toward the front, and then eyed their designer black dresses with undisguised resentment. "I thought you said earth tones were the new black when it came to mourning."

"They are," Mary Ann said slowly, "but being in mourning and attending a funeral are different things."

"Oh?" I regarded her skeptically. "Don't people come to funerals to mourn?"

"Really, Sophie." Leah let out an exasperated sigh.

"People mourn on their own time. They come to funerals to get *credit* for mourning. There's a huge difference."

I nodded thoughtfully. "I see your point."

"I didn't expect them to have an open casket," Mary Ann whispered. "Gosh, it's so sad," she added, tugging at the ends of her hair. "And look, they put way too much blush on him."

"Is anyone sitting here?" I looked up to see two men, both wearing the prerequisite gray suit. The one who had spoken was probably in his late thirties and was smiling down at Mary Ann. Or at least his mouth was smiling. His eyes were far too red to twinkle. He seemed fairly calm at the moment, so I wasn't sure if the redness was due to a morning of crying or a night full of drinking. Still, he was cute in a teddy bear kind of way. His hairline was receding but he had a healthy tan that hinted at a love for the outdoors and a pug nose that automatically gave him a youthful air, despite his conservative attire. The other man was younger, taller and maybe in his mid-twenties. His dishwater-blond hair was cut a little too short for his round face and he was fidgeting with the knot in his tie in a way that made me think he wasn't accustomed to wearing one.

Mary Ann scooted over enough to make room for them. The older man nodded his appreciation and slid in first; the younger sat at the aisle and pulled out the prayer book in front of him.

"I'm Rick," the older said, presumably addressing all of us, although I noticed that his gaze lingered a little longer on Mary Ann. "And this is Johnny."

"Hi there!" Johnny chirped, then immediately looked a little abashed as if his tone had been too cheerful for the occasion.

"I'm Mary Ann," she said, "and this is Sophie and her sister Leah."

"Sophie…" Johnny looked at me and his eyes widened with recognition. "You're that novelist…the one who found him!"

"Yes, that's me."

Rick did a quick double take while Johnny kept talking. "It must have been horrible. The newspaper said you didn't see the crime actually happen, but surely you must have seen *something,* the make of the car driving away, perhaps? It doesn't seem possible that someone could do something like this and not leave any evidence behind."

"Probably not, but if there was an eyewitness it wasn't me."

"So it's true, all you really saw was Eugene," he said glumly. He looked like a kid who had just been forced to witness a Harry Potter book burning.

"I can't imagine what that was like for you," Rick said. "You must have been terrified and—"

"Did you know Eugene well?" I asked, cutting him off before he could miscast me in the role of innocent damsel in distress.

"I spent time with him every day. I'm Flynn Fitzgerald's main strategist. Johnny here is Fitzgerald's personal assistant."

So he was *that* Rick! Perfect! Networking made easy.

"Flynn Fitzgerald?" Mary Ann asked. "He's a writer, right? I think I might have read one of his books a long time ago. Didn't he write about parties and socialites?"

Rick knitted his brow and studied Mary Ann as if trying to determine if she was joking.

Leah cleared her throat awkwardly. "Mary Ann, you're thinking of F. *Scott* Fitzgerald."

Rick nodded in agreement. "I actually love F. Scott Fitzgerald. I just reread *Tender Is the Night* last month."

"He was a great writer." I patted Mary Ann's knee. "But I'm fairly sure he doesn't need an assistant or strategist."

"Why not?" Mary Ann asked innocently.

Even sitting several feet away I could tell that Johnny was working hard to stop from giggling. "Well, for one thing, he's dead, Mary Ann," I explained.

"Oh!" Mary Ann put a gentle hand on Rick's arm. "And you loved him! So much loss in such a short time! When did Scott pass away?"

For a second Rick just looked stunned, but then his expression changed and it was clear that he was amused despite himself. "I never actually met F. Scott Fitzgerald," he explained. "Just Flynn Fitzgerald. The one running for the House of Representatives."

"The man Eugene worked for!" Mary Ann smacked her hand against her thigh, the whole situation becoming clear to her. "That would explain how you knew Eugene."

Rick broke out into a full grin. "Yes, that would explain it. Were you acquainted with Eugene?"

Mary Ann shook her head, causing her perfect chestnut curls to bounce around her face. "No, I'm just here to support Sophie."

"That's a shame. Eugene would have liked you."

She cocked her head to the side. "What makes you say that?"

"Eugene liked sweet, compassionate, genuine people."

Mary Ann blushed slightly. "That's one of the nicest compliments anyone's ever paid me."

"They're flirting," Leah whispered in my ear. "They're flirting at a funeral."

I glanced over at our three other companions. Johnny was engrossed in the Bible and Rick had his head bent toward Mary Ann in a rather intimate fashion. I could make out that he was telling her about Eugene, but his voice was too low for me to really eavesdrop effectively. I would grill Mary Ann later. I shrugged and turned to Leah. "I had sex after your husband's funeral," I whispered.

"That's different. You were bereaved, and bereaved people can have sex after a funeral. It's a coping mechanism."

"But I wasn't all that bereaved…."

"Well you would have been if my husband hadn't been an adulterous parasite. The point is that you and Bob were family, and any person who's related to the deceased is allowed to have sex with someone after the funeral."

"Melanie actually told me about this guy. Eugene was a friend of Rick's family, which means they were almost related, so he should be able to *almost* have sex…or at the very least flirt."

Leah clucked her tongue in disapproval. Just then a distinguished-looking couple walked down the aisle toward the front row where Melanie was sitting. The man was in his early forties, and was wearing a perfectly fitted, very expensive-looking suit. The woman on his arm was about ten years younger, dressed equally well, with sandy blond hair coifed in an elegant updo.

"There's the boss man and the missus," Johnny said, finally looking up from his reading. "I should probably sit with them. Never know when Fitzgerald might need his personal assistant."

"At a funeral?" Leah asked skeptically.

Johnny shrugged. "Maybe he'll need me to provide him with Kleenex."

I started to laugh but checked myself when I noted that Johnny wasn't joking. He jumped up and took a place at Fitzgerald's side.

"Johnny's very enthusiastic about his job," Rick noted.

"Clearly," I said, but I didn't have a chance to add more since the priest had just taken his place at the pulpit.

The funeral consisted of one long-winded speech after another. Flynn Fitzgerald spoke, as did his speech writer, who claimed to have been close to Eugene. Neither of them said anything that would make me think someone would want to kill the man they were eulogizing. It was a full hour into the service before the priest called up Rick Wilkes. Rick walked to the front of the room and adjusted the microphone. His initial statements were basically the same as everyone else's, just reworded. I was beginning to drift off when Rick started talking about Eugene's previous vocations.

"Eugene excelled at everything he did. My father continually told me that Eugene was one of the best agents in the FBI, and everyone working on Fitzgerald's campaign can tell you that he was a star...."

"Did you know about that?" Leah asked in a hushed voice.

"No!" I said a little too loudly. The woman in front of us shot me a mean look and I slipped down lower in my seat.

"I can't believe Melanie didn't tell me," I said in a much softer whisper. "If he was in the FBI, he could have been dealing with any number of unsavory types."

"Maybe Melanie didn't think it was important because he wasn't that kind of agent," Mary Ann whispered. "Maybe he was like a…a travel agent for the FBI."

Leah started giggling and the woman in front of us shot us another glare. We all fell into silence as Rick continued to wax poetic.

When the service was over I tried to get a moment with Rick, but he was whisked away by other friends. I tried again during the wake at Melanie's house, but while he took pains to check in with Mary Ann a few times, he never got more than a few words out before someone else took him away to discuss something. Flynn Fitzgerald was equally unavailable.

I was fiddling with my necklace while listening to Mary Ann and Leah discuss the wisdom of serving fondue at a buffet when Johnny sidled up to me, offering me a glass of wine. "I have a confession to make," he said with a sheepish grin. "I've read every one of your books. I just finished *C'est La Mort*. You're one of my favorite authors."

"Thank you, that's sweet," I said, referring to both the compliment and the wine.

"I'm an author, too, you know."

"Really?" I asked. "What have you written?" My eyes sought out Melanie. She was in the middle of a group of women engaged in what looked like a friendly but somewhat somber conversation.

"I haven't actually written anything, but I do have a book. It's all up here." He tapped his forehead with his index finger.

I managed not to roll my eyes. I had long since lost track of how many people (from lawyers to waiters) had told me that they were really writers at heart. As far as I was concerned that claim didn't mean a lot until you *wrote* something. It was a detail that most of these unrecognized "authors" didn't seem to be willing to address.

"I was a computer science major in school," Johnny babbled. "But computers aren't exciting. I mean, can you see me as a computer geek? Not my thing. I'm still amazed I didn't flunk out due to intense boredom. Then I got my master's in poly sci and somewhere along the line I said to myself, hey, I can write political thrillers! I still think that's my true calling, but for now I'm a personal assistant. I love my job and Fitzgerald's great, but I don't think I want to go into politics. I want to be a writer like you, or maybe a journalist."

I wrinkled my nose ever so slightly. Johnny was a spaz. Maybe he could write scripts for the *Wiggles* or something.

"Look at poor Melanie. I feel so bad for her. I bet she's feeling kind of alone. Maybe I'll invite her to come to church with me on Sunday. I'm not Catholic, but maybe she'll come. It might make her feel better. Just look at her standing in the corner by herself! Doesn't she look sad?"

"By herself?" I looked back at Melanie. Sure enough, she had managed to extricate herself from the crowd and was now enjoying a rare moment of solitude.

"Leah, hold this." I turned and handed my glass to my sister, who was standing a few feet behind me as she and Mary Ann continued to chat about the buffet.

Johnny started to say something but I ignored him and

made a beeline for Melanie, who greeted me with a fragile smile. "Sophie, thank you so much for being here."

"Don't you think you should have mentioned that Eugene was in the FBI?"

"Is it relevant?"

"Of course it's relevant! What if someone whom he investigated while at the bureau decided to get revenge? Maybe that's why he's dead!"

Melanie shook her head. "Eugene hasn't worked for the FBI in over twenty years. If someone wanted revenge, they would have gotten it by now."

"Are you sure? I mean, come on, Melanie, my theory has to be as good as the one you have."

"I don't really have a theory."

"My point exactly."

Melanie sighed and rubbed her eyes. "I know, I know. I've given you nothing to go on. I suppose I'm not thinking straight these days. It's just that nothing seems to make sense anymore."

"Melanie," I said, cutting her off, "I just need to know if Eugene was involved in anything or anyone else that might have led to his death. Is the FBI thing the only bit of information you were keeping from me?"

"That's it…really."

"Why don't I believe you?"

Melanie gave me a pained look before turning her attention to a couple of well-wishers who apparently had no qualms about interrupting our conversation. I marched back to where Leah and Mary Ann were standing. Johnny had moved on.

"I can't believe you just handed me a wineglass like I was hired help," Leah spat.

"Sorry, I wanted to catch Melanie while she was alone, and I knew that was probably going to be my one and only opportunity to do so today." I checked my watch. "Let's get out of here. It's getting late and I'm not finding anything out."

"Fine with me," Leah said. "Liz isn't expecting me for another few hours, but I like the idea of showing up early to make sure she's not doing anything she shouldn't. I think her boyfriend may be stopping by for the occasional visit while she's watching Jack, which is completely unacceptable. I will not have Jack exposed to his babysitter's love life."

Yes, God forbid Jack be exposed to a healthy relationship between a man and a woman. Given a frame of reference he might come to understand how romantically challenged his mother and aunt really are.

"If you're worried about your babysitter why didn't you leave Jack with his grandma?" Mary Ann asked.

"Mama's on a three-week cruise to Baja with her Jewish seniors' group," I explained.

"Baja?" Mary Ann repeated. "Wow, that sounds like a fun vacation."

"Yes," Leah confirmed. "Sophie and I have been enjoying it immensely. Now, let's get our coats, shall we?"

"Did I just overhear that you were leaving?"

We all turned at the sound of Rick's voice.

"We have to get back to the city," Mary Ann explained.

"I see, well it was good to meet you." He looked deep into Mary Ann's eyes. "Thank you so much for talking to me. You made today a little more bearable."

"It was good to meet you, too," I said, although it was exceedingly obvious that he wasn't talking to me. "I know this isn't the place to ask for a professional favor, but I recently pitched an idea to…um…the *National Review* for an article dealing with the inner workings of political campaigns," I lied. "I'd love to interview you for it…and Flynn Fitzgerald, of course."

"The *National Review?*" Rick shifted his weight back on his heels. "That's a fairly conservative periodical."

"Yes, I guess it is." And Microsoft is a *fairly* big computer company.

"Forgive me if I'm out of line, but Johnny was just telling me about your books. He said they were quite good, but he also said that your protagonist is a committed Democrat. I had assumed that you were a Democrat, as well."

"Um…yes, I am, but a very conservative one."

Rick cocked his head. "You must be if you're writing for the *National Review.*"

"I'm like the John McCain of the Democratic party."

"Really?" Rick sounded incredibly skeptical.

"Yes, I really think we should lower the income tax and I just love the idea of…school vouchers."

"Is that so? Do you have children?"

"No, she has a nephew, my son Jack," Leah said, eyeing the door longingly. "He'll be attending Adda Clevenger Junior Preparatory and then I plan on sending him to the Bay School of San Francisco. I've spoken to people in the admissions offices of Harvard and Yale and everyone agrees that a Bay School education will be beneficial."

Rick nodded appreciatively. "How old is your son?"

"Two. I'm truly sorry, Rick, but I have to pick him up

now. Do you think you could give my sister your card so she can contact you later to set up an interview?"

"An interview?" Johnny had just popped up from nowhere. "Are you going to interview somebody? Are you researching one of your books? Can I help? I would love to help you research an Alicia Bright novel!"

"I'm actually writing an article for the *National Review,*" I muttered. I *should* have said that I was researching a book. That would have been a much easier lie to pull off.

"So you're a journalist, too? That's so cool!" Johnny gushed. "Who do you want to interview? Can I help?"

"This article is about the campaign process, so I'd love to talk to any of the top people on Fitzgerald's team. You know, the people Eugene worked with."

"I suppose I could help you with that," Rick said, pulling out his card and pressing it into my hand. "Even when I'm out of the office I always check my messages."

"Good to know." I smiled at my companions. "Shall we?"

"Bye!" Johnny called after us.

When we got out to the car I threw my arms around Leah's neck. "Thank you so much for coming to my rescue. All that stuff about making college plans for your two-year-old was perfect."

Leah broke away and looked at me. "I didn't make that up. My son's going to Harvard. Yale's just his backup."

"Oh…right, of course." I bit my lip as I got behind the wheel of my car and waited for Mary Ann and Leah to get themselves settled. I love my nephew, but I didn't see him going to Harvard so much as I saw him going on Ritalin.

I dropped Mary Ann off first and then started toward

Leah's babysitter's family home, which was conveniently located across the street from Leah's. "How's work?" I asked as I idled my car at a stoplight.

Not long ago Leah had been a stay-at-home mom married to Bob Miller. Now Bob was dead, which should have been sad except he had been such an incredibly awful and emotionally abusive man that pretending to be mournful over his early demise was kind of like shedding tears over the retirement of stone-washed jeans. So no one blinked an eye when Leah quickly pulled herself together, sold her large Forest Hill home for $3.4 million dollars, along with most of Bob's things and bought a $1.6 million two-bedroom in Laurel Heights. She used some of her excess cash to get herself set up as a freelance special-events coordinator. Her Junior League friends helped out by funneling business her way, and it quickly became apparent that Leah was born for the job. Whether it was a corporate retreat or an elaborate birthday celebration for a debutante's shih tzu, my sister managed to make the event an elegant affair to remember.

"Work's fine," Leah said as she adjusted the clasp of the new Tiffany charm bracelet she had recently bought herself. "I'm currently planning the retirement dinner for Delcoe's CEO. I've convinced them to have it at the Marines' Memorial to honor the years he spent in the service." She paused a moment before changing subjects. "Do you realize that today was the first time I've seen Melanie since Dad's funeral? Odd that it would take another death for our paths to cross again."

I didn't say anything. I didn't like thinking about Dad's funeral.

"You almost never talk about Melanie anymore," Leah added.

"Melanie and I have both been busy living our lives in different towns and in different social circles. We still talk on the phone every once in a while and she's still important to me." I opened the moon roof to give us a little more fresh air. "You're probably wondering why I agreed to investigate Eugene's death for her."

"I know why you're doing it," Leah said, "although I seriously doubt *you* know why you're doing it."

"What is that supposed to mean?"

"It means that the reasons that you have allowed your relationship with Melanie to fade into the background of your life are the exact same reasons why you continue to care about her so much. But of course you can't examine any of that because that would require you to revisit painful memories that you've pushed into your subconscious."

I gave Leah a questioning look as I turned onto her block. "Again, I have no idea what you're talking about."

"Exactly my point. Aha! That's Liz's boyfriend's car! That's why that little harlot asked if she could watch Jack at her parents' house, because she knew Bruce would be welcome there! And to think I bought her line about wanting Jack to be able to play with their new puppy! Let me out here. I swear, if either of them so much as has the top two buttons of their shirts undone I'm going to have them arrested for indecent exposure in front of a minor."

"Mmm, that will go over well in a city that allows men to parade in G-strings during Carnival."

Leah glared at me right before she shot out the door to

scare a couple of overeager teenagers into a life of abstinence. As I drove home I made a halfhearted attempt to make sense of what Leah had said but quickly gave up the effort. Leah was a lot crazier than I was, so it seemed foolhardy to take her psychobabble seriously.

When I got back to my neighborhood I began the arduous task of looking for parking. After fifteen minutes with no luck I finally accepted the fact that I was going to have to give Anatoly's block a go. Anatoly lived all of three blocks away from me, and over the past two months I had spent an exorbitant amount of time trying to avoid him. I would never make that mistake again. From now on if a man lived so close that it would make honoring a restraining order a challenge I would not get involved with him. I turned onto his block and, as Murphy's law would have it, there he was at the other end of the block, crouched over, examining the front of his Harley.

It occurred to me that maybe this was why I hadn't heard from him. It wasn't that he had moved on, it was that he had been standing on his corner in the hopes that I would eventually drive by and pick him up.

But if that was the case he should have noticed my car by now, and he definitely had not. He was too absorbed with his tire.

I slowed the car from ten miles an hour to two. Something about Anatoly's crouched position reminded me of certain things he used to do to me. *Just drive by.* If I stopped and talked to him I was bound to do something stupid, or he would do something that would make me feel stupid, and then I would be thrown into a downward spiral of lost pride and low self-esteem.

But of course, there was a parking place just a few feet in front of him.

Beads of sweat dampened my brow. I had two seconds to figure out what was more important to me—my dignity or parking. My God, it was like *Sophie's Choice.* Of course, if I lost my dignity I could always turn to my friend Smirnoff for some much-needed comfort. But if I gave up the parking spot I might be stuck driving around my neighborhood for days, and there would be no solace since there are laws about drinking before you parked your car.

I took a deep breath and made the only logical choice by pulling into the empty space. Anatoly looked up as I did so and I felt his eyes boring into me. *Here it comes. This is the part where he walks up and tells me that we should put our differences aside and indulge in safe, casual, early-evening sex.*

Anatoly nodded in greeting as I pulled up on the emergency break and then returned all of his attention to the bike.

Okay, self-esteem gone.

I got out of my car. *Turn around and walk away.* I walked over to him. "Nice tire. Do you usually come out here to pay homage or is today a special occasion?"

"Someone hit my bike while it was parked here. The front fairing is seriously damaged."

"I hate it when people try to screw with my fairing."

"This is going to cost me at least twenty-five hundred dollars."

"Seriously?" I tapped the part that he was examining. "It's a flimsy piece of metal. How can that possibly add up to twenty-five hundred?"

"It's not just a piece of metal, it's the front fairing."

Two months. We hadn't spoken in two months and he wanted to complain to me about his fucking fairing? I felt my hands ball up into fists. "Well, good luck with this." I turned and started to walk away.

"Doesn't that hurt your palms?"

I slowly pivoted. "Excuse me?"

He had straightened up and was wearing that little half smile of his. "Whenever you're angry you make a fist, and I've always wondered if your nails dug into your palms. They're long enough that it seems like they should."

"This is something you think about?"

"Occasionally I wonder."

"Huh, what else do you wonder about?"

"Lately, I've been wondering how you are."

"I'm fine." I waited a beat before adding, "If that's really been on your mind so much you could have given me a call."

"I didn't think you wanted me to call."

"Why would you think that?" I asked.

"Because you told me not to."

"Oh…and you listened to me?"

"Didn't you want me to?"

Of course I hadn't wanted him to. I had wanted him to fight for me, to ask me to come back to him and to tell me that he was hopelessly in love with me and couldn't live without me. "Yes, I wanted you to listen…I'm just surprised that you did."

Anatoly nodded, then looked down at the bike again. "My insurance won't cover this."

And we were back to the fairing. "I'm sure one of your clients will give you an advance if you ask them to."

"Business has been slow lately." Anatoly stuffed his hands into his leather jacket and smiled wryly. "I don't suppose you know anyone who needs a private detective."

Shit. This was the moment of truth. Was I a good person or a selfish bitch who would rather avoid a potentially uncomfortable social situation than give a man in need the opportunity to make a living? "I don't know anyone who needs a P.I." Selfish bitch it was.

"Not a single person?" By the tone of Anatoly's voice I could tell he wasn't really asking a question but underscoring the desperate state of his finances.

"Not a soul. All of my friends' significant others have been annoyingly faithful lately."

"Ah, well." Anatoly shrugged and then looked me over carefully. "You look good."

"Thanks."

"Really good."

And here comes that self-esteem again.

"There's one more thing I've been wondering about."

"Oh?"

"Last time we talked you said you wanted more of a commitment."

"I did say that."

"That was two months ago and we've both had some time to think."

I felt my heart pick up in speed. He had reconsidered. He wanted to be in a relationship with me. Suddenly I saw my future and it was filled with emotional growth!

"I've missed you, Sophie," he said, taking a step forward. "If you were willing to let go of this idea of improving on what was already a good thing, we could go back to the way things were."

And we were back to feeling like shit. I stepped forward and ran my finger across his pecks. "Anatoly?"

He smiled his sexy half smile and leaned in closer. "Yes?"

"Take your front fairing and stick it up your ass."

I don't mind asking the tough questions. I just don't
want to hear the answers.
—*C'est La Mort*

"SO LET ME GET THIS STRAIGHT," DENA SAID SLOWLY. "MELANIE WANTS
a private dick and Anatoly wants more clients, but you're not
going to get them in touch with each other."

"That's right," I said. We were sitting in the back room
of Dena's store, Guilty Pleasures, and I had just finished
telling her about everything that had gone down with both
Melanie and Eugene and my little run-in with Anatoly and
his front fairing. Beyond being my favorite supplier of
sensuous flavored body oils, Dena was also my best friend
in the world and had been since high school. Normally
she'd be the first person I'd call after an awkward exchange
with an ex or if, say…the husband of my old mentor was

shot right after I made a pass at him, but she had been off attending a bondage-wear trade show in Amsterdam.

"Sophie, this is insane. It was one thing to play detective when your own life was at risk or when your sister was falsely accused of killing that asshole husband of hers, but to do it just so you don't have to answer a few casual questions for Anatoly…"

"Nothing's ever casual when it comes to Anatoly. Every exchange I have with the man is emotionally volatile and nerve-racking. Except for the sex, and according to Anatoly the sex we've had has been nothing but casual."

"So this is about avoidance?" Dena crossed her toned lambskin-clad legs and ran her fingers through her short dark hair. "Are you sure the real reason you're not telling Anatoly about this gig is because you're pissed at him and you don't want to help his business?"

"Of course not," I shot back, but Dena's brown Sicilian eyes were skeptical and I knew I couldn't carry off the lie. "Okay, fine. Maybe I'm a little pissed. Why should I refer clients to him or help him in any way after what he did?"

"You know, I'm still not really clear on what exactly he did that was so wrong."

"Are you kidding me? We had been dating for almost a year, Dena. A year! And it wasn't like I was looking for a ring. You know I don't want to get married again. I don't even want to live with someone. I like my space too much, and besides if I moved a guy into my place how would that make Mr. Katz feel? He might think I was trying to replace him."

"Please tell me your relationship with your cat is vastly different from your relationships with the men you date."

"Obviously it's different—I *trust* my cat. But we're getting off the subject. The point is that all I really wanted out of Anatoly was for him to fess up to being my boyfriend and to agree to be monogamous, but he couldn't even do *that.*"

"But he wasn't actually sleeping with other people while you guys were together, right? He just didn't want the option taken away from him."

"Well, yeah, but who the hell wants to give her boyfriend that kind of option?"

"Me for starters," Dena said. "If he has the option that means I've got it, too, and that can only be a good thing. You see, men are like See's candy lollipops."

"Excuse me?"

"See's candy lollipops, Sophie. I like the chocolate pops the best, and nine times out of ten that's what I'm going to buy when I want something sweet. But every once in a while I have a craving for butterscotch or vanilla, and if that's what I'm craving that's what I'm going to have. Why should I limit myself to only sucking on chocolate when I can suck on so much more?"

"But the only guy I wanted to suck on was Anatoly! Wait—can I change that to lick? I don't really like…you know…sucking on anyone."

"Lick him, suck him, saddle him up and ride him like a bronco if that's what you want to do, he certainly doesn't seem to be stopping you. He just doesn't want to emotionally commit. So stop obsessing on words like *boyfriend, girlfriend* and *monogamy* and use him as a GBC."

"GBC?"

"Glorified Booty Call. A guy you sleep with who also occasionally takes you out to a nice dinner."

"I don't think I could use Anatoly as a GBC at this point. There are too many emotions involved."

"Emotions? Sophie, when you say *emotions* do you mean you care about him or…you don't love him, do you?"

"No," I said quickly, "but for a second there I thought maybe I was sort of *falling* in love with him. I mean, I hadn't hit bottom yet but I could have gotten there pretty quick."

"But he drives you nuts!"

I shrugged. Everything had been so perfect for a while. After the first six months of dating I had kind of figured that Anatoly *was* my boyfriend. I just assumed that the reason Anatoly wasn't dating other women was because the nature of our relationship would have made doing so inappropriate, not because he hadn't been able to fit infidelity into his schedule. Despite what Dena seemed to think, it wasn't always what someone did or didn't do that was important; it was *why* they did or didn't do it. Clearly he hadn't felt as strongly about me as I had felt about him. I suppose one could argue that I didn't have the right to be angry with him just because he didn't feel what I wanted him to feel, but I couldn't help it. He had no right *not* to love me, particularly when there had been so many times in which he'd treated me as if he had.

Dena wiggled a pen between her fingers and sighed. "Sophie, men are good for a lot of things, and they're also a nice accessory to wear to the opera. Kind of like an expensive bracelet or wrap. But when it comes to emotional stuff they do nothing but disappoint. That's why we all need girlfriends. If you're having a crisis and need a shoulder to cry on, call me. If you want to get off…well you can call me for that, too, since I am the one who sells vibrators, but if you're craving a penis that *isn't* battery-operated, then that's the time to call a man. Live by those rules and you'll never get your heart broken."

"So you're not a big believer in the whole 'better to have loved and lost' thing."

"You were in love with your first husband and you lost…well maybe you didn't lose him so much as you threw him out, but the point is you gave your heart away once and it didn't work out. Why give it away again to a man who's stupid enough not to want it?"

I laughed softly. Dena was the only person I knew who could be callous and supportive at the same time. I glanced at my watch and winced. "I've gotta go. Rick Wilkes managed to get me an interview with Flynn Fitzgerald this afternoon and I'm supposed to meet him at his Pleasant Hill campaign headquarters in about forty-five minutes."

"Rick's that guy Mary Ann met at the funeral, right?"

"That's the one."

"I can't believe my uptight little cousin allowed some man to put the moves on her at a funeral," Dena said. "I wish I could have seen that."

"It's probably best that you weren't there."

"How come?"

"Well, it was in a church and it would have really sucked if you had stepped inside and burst into flames."

Dena grinned. "Get the hell out of my office before I smack you."

★ ★ ★

When I stepped inside Fitzgerald's campaign headquarters I couldn't help but be a little disappointed. I had expected to be confronted with a scene reminiscent of the trading floor on Wall Street, but instead no one looked harried or stressed, and the only multitasking going on involved stuffing envelopes while talking on the phone. The room was unimpressive, too. Fluorescent lights, gray carpets: a far cry from the elitist image Fitzgerald had been unintentionally projecting to voters.

"Hi, Sophie!"

I nearly jumped out of my skin. Johnny clearly had a knack for being able to sneak up on me.

"Wow," he said, looking down at his watch. "You're right on time! It's four o'clock on the button."

"I didn't want to be late." I treated him to a disinterested smile. I had the uncomfortable feeling that Johnny's effusive babbling was his way of flirting.

"But you're not early, either! That's pretty impressive considering you came from Frisco. You timed it perfectly!"

"Mmm-hmm, Johnny? It's *San Francisco*. Never, *ever* Frisco."

Johnny laughed as if I had made a great joke. "Oh, right, Frisco is like the *F* word for you city people! Too funny! Do you think that there's a name that New Yorkers hate? Like do the people upstate call it *York* or *'ork…*"

"Johnny, I don't mean to be rude, but could you let Fitzgerald know I'm here?"

"I'm fairly certain he already knows," said a deep, friendly voice.

I turned to see Flynn Fitzgerald flashing his perfectly

straight white teeth. He had to look up to make eye contact with me, which surprised me since even with the three-inch heels I was wearing I only came to five-eight. But he carried himself well, giving him the illusion of height.

He gave my hand a firm shake. "Did you have any trouble finding the place?"

"No, I just…followed the scent of victory," I said with a smile.

Fitzgerald released a chuckle.

"I'll call and confirm your appointments for tomorrow," Johnny said to his boss. "Have a good interview!"

"Thank you, Keyes," Fitzgerald said, addressing Johnny by what I assumed was his last name. He then led me to the back of the main room and into a small office. "Thank you so much for coming." He gestured for me to sit.

"I think I'm the one who should be thanking *you*," I said as I draped my jacket over the back of my chair. "You're the one doing *me* a favor."

"Don't be ridiculous." Fitzgerald closed the door before sitting down behind his particle-wood desk. "Politicians should always be grateful when a journalist takes the time to talk to them. You'd be surprised how many reporters write articles without ever bothering to question the person they're writing about."

"Thank you, but this article isn't so much about your campaign per se as it is about campaigning in general." I took a small notebook and pen out of my purse. "I thought we could start by discussing how you divide up responsibilities among your top staff."

"We all wear a lot of hats around here. I have a media consultant who spends an enormous amount of time editing my speeches, a speechwriter who spends hours talking to the press, and so on and so forth."

"So everyone here is a jack-of-all-trades?"

"You could say that."

"It must be hard with Eugene gone. I mean, with the workload."

"O'Reilly was a wonderful man and his absence will be sorely felt. However, I have an incredible staff and they'll rise to the occasion."

"What was Eugene responsible for?"

Fitzgerald's smile tightened. "As I said before, we are all responsible for a little bit of everything."

"But what did the bulk of his responsibilities entail?"

For a moment Fitzgerald didn't answer and I had the horrible suspicion that he had just figured out that I wasn't there for the reasons I had claimed. Perhaps it was the knee-length leather skirt that was giving me away. Only Ann Coulter could pull off right-wing shtick in leather. The rest of us needed to wear pastels or risk being called out as imposters. But then Fitzgerald's expression softened and he leaned back in his chair. "Eugene was a researcher. But every campaign is run differently, as I'm sure you'll discover if you talk with Anne Brooke. Have you made an appointment to speak with her?"

I shifted slightly in my seat. The idea had never occurred to me. "I'll be speaking to her soon."

Fitzgerald lifted his eyebrows. "So she agreed to an interview? I wasn't sure if she would since, as you probably know, the *National Review* has the unjust reputation of being somewhat biased."

Shit, I had just walked into a trap and an obvious one at that. "I told her the same thing I told you. This article is less about the politics involved in the campaigns and more about the campaigns themselves." Fitzgerald nodded but didn't say anything. "Plus, I told her I was impressed that she had the courage to speak out against the cigarette tax, despite its popularity within the Democratic Party."

"Right, the cigarette tax. It may be the only issue Brooke and I agree on. That and Robert Louis Stevenson, the school she chose for her son. I went there myself. However, I do find it odd that a woman who refuses to support school vouchers would send her son to a private boarding school."

"Guess she has her reasons." I didn't know enough about Brooke and her son's situation to be able to comfortably comment further. "Are you and your wife planning on sending *your* children to Robert Louis Stevenson?"

Fitzgerald frowned and looked down at his desk. "We haven't been blessed with children, though we are planning on adopting."

"I'm sure you'll be a wonderful father," I said, unsure if that was true. He was being nice and appeared to have some gentlemanly qualities, but my gut told me that he wasn't a spare-the-rod kind of guy.

"Thank you. Getting back to Brooke, she's run a very good campaign so far, but then again I expected nothing less. She's a very calculating woman."

I hesitated, choosing my words carefully. "I'm not sure her campaign has been all that great. Since it began she's had to spend more time explaining her previous affairs and drug use than talk about her positions, and then one of her campaign workers threw himself out of the fifteenth-story window of her campaign office. I've got to think it's a bad sign when the people who are supporting you start killing themselves."

If Fitzgerald was amused he showed no sign of it. "What happened to that boy was tragic."

"What happened...*to* him?"

"He was only twenty-two, much too young to die," Fitzgerald replied. "It was just an awful thing."

"But it didn't happen *to* him, he did it *to* himself."

"The loss of a life is a tragedy under any circumstances. As for Brooke, she wouldn't have to defend her reputation if she would just live a moral life. Don't get me wrong, I have nothing against the woman personally. In fact I pray for her every day."

I tried to imagine how these little conversations would go. *"Dear God, please help Anne Brooke get her priorities straight and decide to become a stay-at-home mom sometime before November."*

"She's cheated on her last husband three times that we know about, and when O'Reilly told me about her aborted pregnancy..." Fitzgerald stopped short. I couldn't be positive, but I thought I saw him flinch.

"*Eugene* told you about that?"

"Yes, well, I can't be the first to know about everything, can I?" He laughed, but it sounded forced. "I think he read about it in some periodical."

"So he found out about it after it came out in the press."

"I don't really remember. Are you going to be comparing Brooke's campaign and mine?"

"Yeah, sure. Eugene told me that the workers on this campaign had become sort of an extended family, if you will. That everyone really looks out for one another."

"Yes, everyone here is very close."

"It certainly seemed that way at Eugene's funeral. Rick Wilkes gave a beautiful eulogy and so did…um…who was that woman who spoke? The one who said she met him during this campaign?"

"Maggie Gallagher. Gallagher is my media consultant. She and O'Reilly bonded immediately. I think their Irish heritage played a role in that."

"Is Gallagher here today?" I was following Fitzgerald's lead by referring to her by her last name. In California pretty much everybody called one another by their first name, but clearly Fitzgerald had a preference for surnames.

"No, her husband is having surgery so she'll be out for the next two days."

"How awful. Is he going to be all right?"

"He'll be fine, he's had severe back pain for years and Gallagher finally convinced him to get a laminectomy."

A bad back usually translated into a bad sex life. Plenty of people had been driven to adultery for lesser reasons. In her eulogy Gallagher said Eugene had been a father figure to her, but maybe she had a Freudian thing going on.

"O'Reilly hit the nail on the head when he compared us all to a family," Fitzgerald continued. "Family unity is definitely what this campaign is all about. Politicians should take the principles and values they nurture within their homes and apply them to their work environment and their policies. That's why character is so important."

Fitzgerald was beginning to sound like one of his commercials. "Campaigning must be incredibly nerve-racking. There's so much on the line," I said. "I remember Melanie telling me a few weeks ago that Eugene was a bit on edge. How do you and your staff deal with the stress?"

"I find that prayer helps."

The phone rang and Fitzgerald smiled apologetically before picking up.

I studied him while he proceeded to mutter a series of *I-sees* and *interestings* into the receiver. There was something about him that I didn't trust—something about his hair. It was as if all that pomade was hiding something, maybe even the beginnings of a bald spot. I had always felt that men who tried to hide something as innocuous as hair loss were also likely to go to great pains to hide all of their other issues and faults.

"Ms. Katz, I'm so sorry," Fitzgerald said as he hung up, "something's come up and I'm afraid I'm going to have to cut this interview short."

"I think I have all the information I need for now, but if I have any further questions…"

"Just give me a call." He rose from his seat and waited for me to do the same. "I'd be happy to help in any way that I can."

Funny, he didn't look happy. He looked nauseated. Whatever had "come up" couldn't have been good. "Okay," I said, "then maybe you could help me get an appointment with Maggie Gallagher and Rick…"

"Of course. I'm sorry to rush you out like this, but the mayor of Orinda is under the impression that I'm scheduled to meet with him this afternoon, although I would have sworn that meeting was tomorrow. But that's politics for you. No one's ever on the same page."

"Totally understand." I stuffed my notebook in my purse

as he escorted me out of his office. Johnny was sitting at a desk right outside the door, clicking off his computer. "Did you have a good interview?"

"It was fine," Fitzgerald said a bit too quickly. "Are you leaving for the day, Keyes?"

"I was going to, but if you need me to stay, I can. I don't mind staying."

"No, you go enjoy your evening," Fitzgerald said. "Perhaps you can escort Ms. Katz to her car."

"Sure thing, boss!" Johnny looked a little too excited about the task.

"Wonderful. Ms. Katz—" Fitzgerald turned to me one last time "—it's been a pleasure."

Fitzgerald disappeared back into his office, leaving me in Johnny's incapable hands. I took one look at his dippy grin and started booking it toward the elevator. "You don't need to escort me to my car," I said over my shoulder as Johnny struggled to keep up with me. "It's really not necessary."

"I insist!" Johnny said. He jumped onto the elevator with me and eagerly pressed the button that would bring us to the ground floor. "That interview was shorter than I expected."

"I had thought it was going to be longer, but as it turns out Fitzgerald forgot about an appointment with the mayor of Orinda."

"The mayor of Orinda? He doesn't have an appointment with him today."

"Apparently the mayor wrote down the wrong date." The elevator doors opened and I started race-walking toward my car.

"But I'm the one who confirms Fitzgerald's appointments, and I don't know anything about any appointment with the Orinda mayor today or even this month." Johnny's voice was getting a little panicky. "I *couldn't* have forgotten something that important. Oh, jeez, what if I did? No wonder Fitzgerald looked kind of mad when he came out of the office. What if I messed up? I'll be in so much trouble!"

"I guess you might be," I said, not really caring. We had reached my car and I was desperately fishing for my keys.

"You want to join me for my dinner plans tonight?"

"No." I knew it was rude to be so blunt, but clearly Johnny wasn't good at picking up on subtlety.

"How come?"

Subtlety definitely wasn't his thing. "Look, Johnny, you seem like a really nice guy but…"

"I'm actually meeting Rick Wilkes for dinner at Max's Opera Café in Frisco and was hoping you could join us! You know, the one on Van Ness. He's taking me out for my birthday—it was my birthday yesterday. Maybe you could bring your friend Mary Ann. I think Rick really liked her."

"You're meeting Rick Wilkes?" This could be helpful. I needed to talk to Rick, and if I could get him in a social setting (other than a funeral) he might be a little more chatty than if I set up a formal interview. "What time's dinner?"

Johnny beamed. "Six-thirty. Do you think Mary Ann will come? Rick would really like that."

"I'll give her a call," I promised. "Nice of you to invite us to your birthday dinner," I added. "Especially since we're all *just friends.*"

"No problem, it'll be fun!" He looked down at his watch. "I guess I should let you go. I want to change before dinner. I want to look good for you, my new lady friend." He winked at me before turning and heading off in the opposite direction.

Ew. I always attracted the winners.

I called Mary Ann on my way back to the city and she quickly agreed to dinner. I had a feeling that she was as interested in Rick as he was in her, which surprised me a little. Men were always asking Mary Ann out but she rarely said yes. Despite her naiveté she was pretty discerning when it came to the opposite sex.

Getting back to the city took far longer than I had anticipated. I was hit with a major Frappuccino craving but couldn't find a Starbucks (a problem I hadn't had since 1994). Then I hit rush-hour traffic, there was an accident on the Bay Bridge, yada, yada, yada.

When I finally arrived in my neighborhood I only had fifteen minutes to spare before getting to the restaurant. I thought about just going straight to dinner, but I needed to feed my cat and my feet were screaming to be freed from the designer torture devices I had confined them in.

I ran upstairs to my third-floor, two-bedroom flat, and went straight to the bathroom, then rushed into the living room, where I pressed the play button on my answering machine and sat down on the arm of my sofa as I began to unbuckle my strappy sandals.

"I know what you're really up to, Sophie," a voice began. I did a quick double take. The voice wasn't normal. It didn't even sound fully human. Someone had left a message on my machine using a voice synthesizer.

"You know what they say, curiosity killed the cat," the

caller continued, "and that would be a shame…because I do…love…cats."

And that was it. The whole message.

I looked down at the one shoe I still had on and tried to make sense of what I had just heard. "Curiosity killed the cat," I repeated. Was that a death threat or a donation request from the SPCA?

Where was my cat?

My heart jumped to my throat. Where *was* Mr. Katz?

In a flash I was on my feet, my gaze quickly moving from the window seat to the couch to the love seat. Not there. Not under the coffee table or under the dining table.

I opened my mouth to call out to him, but I was too scared to actually make a sound. He had to be here, he just had to be!

With one shoe still securely on my foot I hobbled into the kitchen. No Mr. Katz. Okay, no need to panic yet. He could be asleep in my bedroom, or in the guest room. I lived in a flat, not a mansion. I just needed to check the other rooms.

But of course even that wasn't necessary. If Mr. Katz was home and able to walk I could get him to come to me. I reached out and, after sending up a quick silent prayer, pressed down on the electric can opener.

I squeezed my eyes closed. "Give him to the count of ten, Sophie," I whispered to myself. "One, two…"

I felt something soft against my ankles. I looked down at Mr. Katz, who was nuzzling me and swishing his tail in anticipation of his next meal.

"Oh, thank God!" I dropped to my knees and tried to scoop him up in my arms. He evaded me and jumped up on the counter instead. He cast one eager glance toward the can opener, then narrowed his kitty eyes and glared down at me accusingly.

"I'm sorry, I'm sorry, I really do have wet food," I assured him, my voice shaky with relief.

Mr. Katz didn't look convinced.

I got up and pulled a can of Fancy Feast from the cupboard and waved it in front of him. "See, it's all good. I have food and you're here, safe and gluttonous as always. No need to freak."

I emptied half the can into his food bowl and then hurried back to my bedroom to change into a cute but much more comfortable pair of Munros, conscious of the fact that my car could be towed any minute.

The call had been a prank. That's all. Although, the last time I had gotten a prank call it had been a serial killer playing the joke….

But this was different. Serious psychos killed cats, they didn't love them. Everybody knew that the best way to identify which child was most likely to grow up to be a serial killer was to figure out which one liked to torture animals (which didn't bode well for my nephew, but that was a different issue). The point was, I had nothing to worry about.

I just wish the caller hadn't known my name.

5

When it comes to men I prefer the strong silent type.
The ones who speak annoy me.
—*C'est La Mort*

BY THE TIME I GOT TO MAX'S, MARY ANN, JOHNNY AND RICK HAD
already arrived and were waiting at a table, Mary Ann and
Rick enjoying a glass of cola and Johnny a glass of what
looked like Scotch.

"Hey, sorry to keep you waiting. I had to change and, um,
feed my cat. My sweet, very *curious* cat."

I gauged Rick's and Johnny's reaction. I couldn't think of
a single reason why either of them would have left that
message on my answering machine, but then again I couldn't
think of a reason why anyone else would, either.

Rick barely even seemed to hear me. He was too busy
ogling Mary Ann. Johnny, on the other hand, reacted the
way he always did, eagerly. "You're a cat person! I should

have guessed, you *look* like a cat person. I mean not like a crazy old cat lady or anything, but like you have it in you to provide an animal with care and affection. I've always wanted a pet but I'm allergic. But I can always take a Claritin if you want to introduce me to your pussy."

As soon as he said it his eyes widened with embarrassment and Rick burst out laughing. "I didn't mean your—I would *never* say that! That's the word my last girlfriend used. For her cat! I really am talking about cats!" He dropped his head in his hands. "I'm seriously messing this up, aren't I?"

"You're just a little nervous," Mary Ann said, giving him a kindly pat on his shoulder. "I think it's sweet. Don't you, Sophie?" She shot me a pleading look. Mary Ann was a little more sympathetic to the embarrassment of others than I was.

"It's sweet," I said grudgingly as I took my place at the round table between Johnny and Rick. "But you don't need to be nervous, after all we're all *just friends here,* remember?"

Johnny removed his head from his hands and flashed me a relieved smile. "Thanks for understanding. I get a little tongue-tied around beautiful women, and when that beautiful woman happens to be my favorite author, well, I'm done for."

A young waitress approached our table and handed me a menu. "Would you like another Scotch?" she asked, looking down at Johnny's now-empty glass.

Johnny nodded eagerly. "That'd be great. It was the Macallan 18." He pushed his chair back and smiled down at me. "I need to use the boy's room. Be back in a minute."

I watched his back retreat and shook my head in wonder. "Is he *always* like this?"

"Not quite this bad," Rick said with a laugh. "He honestly

is very nervous. He's a huge fan of your work so he's star-struck. Plus, what he said was true, he has a habit of getting tongue-tied in the company of a woman he's become inter-ested in. Give him a chance, he'll calm down."

"Without the help of medication?"

"Yes, without medication. He's a little naive and inexperi-enced, but he's a good guy and he's sort of like a little brother to me. I'm trying to be a mentor to him at work."

"How nice of you to take him under your wing!" Mary Ann said. "And taking him out for his birthday was nice, too."

"A whole bunch of people from the office took him out for drinks on his real birthday yesterday but I had other plans. This is my way of making it up to him and apparently I'm being rewarded for my good deed." He leaned in a little closer to Mary Ann. "I'm glad you're here. I didn't think it was right to ask for your phone number at a funeral, but I'll admit that I wanted to."

Mary Ann blushed prettily and took a sip of her cola. She really did like him, which was understandable since he was kind of likable. Unlike…

"I'm back!" Johnny sat down at my side. "Miss me?"

I bit my lip to prevent myself from answering honestly.

After I consumed two chocolate martinis Johnny went from being insufferable to being vaguely annoying.

I had been hoping that Rick would switch to alcohol at some point, since I needed his lips loose, but he and Mary Ann steadfastly stuck to soda. He did seem a little drunk, though, but it was Mary Ann that was causing the intoxication. When one of the singing waiters (all the waiters at Max's Opera Café sing, thus the name) approached the mike in order to perform a rendition of a Broadway show tune, Rick would turn his eyes to them politely, but the rest of the time he kept his focus on my friend as she devoured Max's signature Meaty Lasagna. I had hoped to discreetly control the conversation so that I could get everyone talking about Eugene without having to ask pointed questions. I realized that discretion would not be mine when we got to the point of ordering dessert without a single word about Eugene.

I waited for Mary Ann to finish telling us all about the features, advantages and benefits of Lancôme's Juicy Tubes before asking pointed question number one. "How long ago did you two first meet Eugene?"

"Huh?" Rick was preoccupied with Mary Ann's juicy lips. "I've known him most of my life. He worked with my father when they were in the FBI."

"I didn't meet him until I got the job with Fitzgerald," Johnny said. "He was always nice to everyone on Fitzgerald's team, just a really swell guy." He laughed. "Did you hear that? I just used the word *swell*. Does anyone use that word anymore? Well, I guess I do, don't I? Let's see if I can use it again. These bread sticks sure are swell."

It took everything in me not to use one of the swell bread sticks to whack him on the head. "What did he do between leaving the FBI and joining Fitzgerald's team?" I asked, angling my body away from Johnny and toward Rick.

Rick fiddled with his fork. "Aren't you friends with Melanie?"

"We're like family," I confirmed.

"Then how come she never told you any of this?"

A damn good question. "When I say *family* I mean she's like a favorite aunt. I love her to death but I don't see her all the time. For the most part Melanie and I have been out of touch since she moved and married Eugene. I never got the full scoop and asking her now feels a bit insensitive."

"Poor Melanie," Johnny sighed. "I think she just wants some company. She's such a nice lady. Kind of reminds me of my mom."

"I bet she'd like your mom," Rick mused. "They're both religious and passionate about reading. Maybe you should introduce them."

"Great idea! I take my mom out to lunch all the time," Johnny explained. "I think I'll ask Melanie if she wants to come with us next time. She could probably use some more friends. Don't you think so, Sophie?"

"Yeah, sure, great idea." I tried to imagine the kind of parents that would have produced a man like Johnny. No, better not go there. I turned back to Rick. "So, anyway, you were telling me about Eugene's work."

"Yes." Rick flashed Johnny a sympathetic smile. I think it was pretty obvious that he was striking out. "Eugene worked on a lot of political campaigns," he explained. "He had so many areas of expertise, but I personally think his greatest strength lay in his research ability." He smiled fondly. "The man should have been a librarian."

"Wait a minute. What kind of research?" I sat back in my chair as a new realization hit me. "He dug up the dirt."

"Excuse me?" Rick dropped his eyes to his food. Johnny just looked confused.

"Fitzgerald hired him to be an operative of sorts," I said,

"to get the goods on the competition. In this case the competition would be Anne Brooke."

"Eugene and everyone else working for Fitzgerald have the same basic job," Rick said a bit too sharply. "To convince the voters to put their faith in our candidate…no, more than that, our job is to make them *love* Fitzgerald. Tearing down the opposing candidate isn't going to do that."

"Are you telling me that Fitzgerald *didn't* hire Eugene to dig up dirt?" I asked incredulously. "Because while dissing Brooke may not, in and of itself, score Fitzgerald enough votes to win, it does seem to be enough to keep things in a dead heat."

"Eugene may have stumbled onto a few details regarding Brooke's personal life," Rick hedged, "but I don't think any of Brooke's past indiscretions are important enough to seriously affect the polls. Fitzgerald is managing to give Brooke a run for her money because of his proposed policies and positions on the issues. I know that people in San Francisco see him as a conservative extremist, but you have to remember that people in Contra Costa County see San Francisco as a beacon of *liberal* extremism. Fitzgerald's family-values platform strikes a chord with the folks he wants to represent."

"Fitzgerald really does have a lot of great things to say about family," Johnny piped in. "He knows God and family are the most important things, but he's not one of those dowdy politicians who thinks the only way to have fun is to take the wife to a church picnic in the beige family Oldsmobile. He drives her there in a green Sportrac! It's like he's the *cool* evangelical husband who knows how to live it up!"

"Give me a break," I scoffed. "Brooke's personal reputation is so bad it's even made the *San Francisco* papers. If voters liked Fitzgerald so much he'd have a huge lead on Brooke, but as it stands now he's never been ahead by more than three points, which is within the margin of error for most of those polls. Brooke may be more liberal than what the people of Contra Costa are used to, but they're more comfortable with her love of labor unions than they are with Fitzgerald's hatred of contraceptives. Based on his positions he should be *losing* this race. The only way he's going to win is if Brooke self-destructs, which she seems to be doing,"

"I wouldn't go so far as to say she's self-destructing," Rick mumbled.

"I would," Johnny said. "You'd have to be pretty self-destructive to marry that broccoli guy! You do know she's married to the guy who wrote *Broccoli for Life*. Can you imagine how much gas he must have? I know, I know, it's a gross thing to think about, but it's funny since—"

"She was arrested for drunk driving at seventeen," I said, completely ignoring Johnny and holding up my fingers to count off Brooke's faux pas. "When pressed, she admitted to taking all sorts of drugs in college, she had an abortion at the tail end of her first trimester when she was in her early thirties, and a former coworker from her private-sector days is claiming that she slept with her boss in exchange for promotions and raises. Furthermore, we know that she cheated on her previous husband at least two times. This woman makes Clinton look like a poster boy for moral behavior. And now there are accusations that she cheated on her taxes and broke one of the fifty million rules regarding campaign fundraising. But no one knew any of that stuff before she announced her run for Congress. Now, look me in the eye and tell me that Fitzgerald didn't hire Eugene to dig that information up so it could be leaked to the media."

Rick swallowed hard and evaded my obvious attempts at eye contact. "Brooke's problems have helped our camp," he said begrudgingly, "but that has nothing to do with Eugene or what he did for the campaign."

Just then a large group of waiters materialized carrying a huge piece of chocolate cake and singing a perfectly harmonized version of "Happy Birthday."

"You guys did this for me?" Johnny asked. "This is *great!* Isn't this great?"

No, it wasn't great. Rick was lying to me; I was sure of it, which meant that I was right about the dirt-digging stuff. Some of the accusations floating around about Brooke were so bad that if anyone was able to prove them she would most likely lose her freedom right along with the election. If Eugene had been able to prove that she had done something really awful she might have felt the need to shut him up quickly. Ruthless political ambition mixed with a healthy dose of survival instinct. It was a dangerous combination. And one that scared me, a lot.

The rest of the evening passed without any more revelations. Johnny continued his pathetic attempts to flirt with me and Rick and Mary Ann became more and more enamored. We eventually parted ways after Mary Ann and Rick exchanged numbers. I gave my number to Johnny as well, but only because he said he might be able to convince Maggie Gallagher to agree to an interview. All I wanted to do was go home, curl up in front of the television. But any hope I had of achieving a state of calm went out the window when I saw Anatoly sitting on my doorstep.

"You lied to me," he snapped.

"How is that possible?" I quibbled. "I haven't been talking to you."

"You spoke to me for five minutes the other day, which is apparently all the time you needed. Did it ever occur to you that the reason I wasn't ready to commit was because you were so rarely honest with me?"

I blinked in surprise. "That's the reason?"

"No, but if it was it would have been a logical one."

"I think I hate you."

Anatoly's mouth turned up slightly at the corners. "Another lie."

"Why are you here?"

"Your friend Melanie O'Reilly called me."

"What! Why?" The pounding in my temples increased in force. "How the hell did she even get your number?"

"I'm listed in the phone book under private detectives. That is my vocation if you recall."

"Yes I *recall*," I emphasized the last word to underscore my feelings about his condescension, "but Melanie doesn't need a private detective. She has me."

Anatoly lifted his eyebrow. "Explain to me how this is helpful."

"Isn't it obvious? I've been gathering information for her!"

Anatoly took a step forward and put a hand on each one of my arms. "I know I've said this before, but since you never listen I'll say it again. You are not a detective. You are a writer. You have no business running around the city trying to solve murders."

"I'm not trying to solve a murder. I'm just doing a little research." I unlocked the door to my building and tried to close it in Anatoly's face, but he was too quick for me and scooted into the lobby.

"I'm not in the mood for this, Anatoly," I snapped. "If you want to talk to me you call me. You do not get to just show up at my place unannounced."

"I called your home and cell. You didn't pick up."

"Bullshit." I reached into my purse and fished for my cell phone. "I've had this on all day and you didn't...oh." I looked at the words "one missed call" printed across the screen of my Nokia. The restaurant had been a little noisy. "So you phoned," I grumbled. "You still shouldn't have come over without talking to me first."

"We can talk now," he said. "Melanie told me that Flynn Fitzgerald hired Eugene to get the goods on Anne Brooke."

Melanie told *him* that? "Tell me something I don't know."

He crossed his arms and leaned his back against the wall of mailboxes. "I think there's a chance Eugene's death might be politically motivated."

"Really?" I tried to swallow my panic. Hearing that idea vocalized by someone else gave it a validity that I didn't want it to have.

"Melanie offered me a significant sum of money to look into Eugene's death. She said she wanted to hire me before but you told her I was unavailable."

"You *aren't* available...at least not emotionally."

"I'm going to take the case," Anatoly said.

"You are?" Maybe this was a good thing after all. He was forcing the issue of my talking to him, anyway, so now I could give him the information I had collected so far and start focusing on my next book. And if I did have to talk to him, this was the way to do it, in my lobby while he was being too obnoxious to be attractive.

"But I'm going to tell her I have one condition," he continued. "I don't want you involved in the case at all. You are not to question people or research Eugene O'Reilly's death in any way."

I blinked in disbelief. "Excuse me? What gives you the right to tell me that I *can't* be involved?"

"Sophie, in the past few years you've ticked off several people and a few of them have been murderers."

"So I've had a few guns pointed at me. You even pointed a gun at me once."

"You were wielding a broken bottle at the time."

"It wasn't a rock-paper-scissors game. There was no need for you to trump me."

Anatoly shook his head in annoyance. "What I'm saying is that you have been very lucky. You have behaved stupidly in extremely dangerous situations and yet you have managed to stay alive."

"Which is more than they're going to be able to say about you unless you change your tone."

"This time you may need more than luck," Anatoly said, completely ignoring my threat. "If the motivations for this killing can somehow be traced back to Eugene's actions in the FBI, or worse yet, his position on Flynn Fitzgerald's campaign, then Eugene's death isn't so much a murder as it is an assassination. As dangerous as it is to antagonize serial killers, it's even more dangerous to antagonize professional assassins. I may not be able to protect you this time."

I laughed bitterly. "What the hell are you talking about? The closest you've ever come to protecting me is when you put on a Trojan!"

"This is too dangerous, Sophie. Let me handle it."

"And what makes you more qualified to handle this than me? Oh, let me guess, it has something to do with the Y chromosome."

"No, it has to do with my service in the Russian and Israeli armies."

"Being a mercenary doesn't make you more qualified to deal with professional killers."

"First of all, I'm not and have never been a mercenary. I was a citizen of both countries at the time of my service. Second, *of course* it makes me more qualified! What the hell do you think a mercenary is?"

I leaned forward and looked him in the eyes. "I told Melanie that I'd help her and that's what I'm going to do."

"Getting me to take her case is helping her. You're done now."

"Um, I don't think so."

Anatoly glared at me. "You're making a big mistake with this, Sophie."

"If that's true it's my mistake to make. I've already interviewed Flynn Fitzgerald and his top adviser, and I have an appointment to interview Anne Brooke." Okay, that last part was a lie but he didn't need to know that. "I'm in this now. If Melanie wants to hire you, fine, she can do that. But if you actually plan on solving this case and not just bilking her for thousands of dollars for no reason, then you might want to start working with me instead of treating me like a spoiled five-year-old."

"It would be easier to treat you like an adult if you'd start acting like one."

"This from the man who three months ago bought a bunch of lawn chairs to use for his living room furniture."

"They're comfortable!"

"They are so not comfortable. I'm going upstairs now."

Anatoly smirked. "Is that an invitation?"

"Yes. I'm inviting you to walk out of my building before I call the police."

"The police?" Anatoly laughed. "Are they still taking your calls?"

"Out!"

Anatoly shook his head resignedly. "There's nothing I can do to convince you to stop investigating this case, is there?"

"Nope."

"Fine." Anatoly yanked the door open. "I'll call you about the information you've gotten so far and accompany you to your interview with Anne Brooke."

"You're not going on that interview."

"If you don't invite me I'll tell her people about the time you signed a petition supporting the death penalty, and then you know she'll refuse to see you."

"You wouldn't dare."

Anatoly raised one eyebrow and then strolled out onto the street, leaving me seething in frustration.

It wasn't until I was back up in my apartment that I

realized that I had just insisted on doing something that I didn't want to do.

I cursed under my breath and plopped myself down on the love seat where Mr. Katz was sleeping. What if the cat message on the phone had been a death threat after all? What if the caller was actually Eugene's killer and now he had decided that I was going to be his next victim? I should call Anatoly right now and tell him I'd changed my mind.

Then I thought about the smug expression he would be wearing if I did that.

No. I couldn't back out now. There were very few things in this world that were worth risking your life for. Pissing Anatoly off was definitely one of them.

6

Politicians are like cartoon characters. With a few charming one-liners and a lot of corporate support, they persuade people to excuse their violent and stupid behavior and learn to love them.
—*C'est La Mort*

"DID I HEAR YOU CORRECTLY?" MARCUS ASKED AS HE RAN HIS FINGERS through my hair, his handsome brown face scrunched up in confusion. "You are going to investigate Eugene O'Reilly's murder, even though you don't want to, and now Darth Vader is threatening your cat?"

I sighed and studied Ooh La La through the mirror in front of me. One of the things I liked about the salon was that the stations were far enough apart and the music just loud enough so that you were able to converse with your hairstylist without worrying about being overheard. That and the fact that they served free cappuccinos and mimosas.

"I didn't say he was Darth Vader, although now that you mention it, the synthesized voice did kind of have a Darth Vader-like quality, so who knows? It's as likely as anything else at this point. But he didn't threaten my cat. Whoever called really likes cats. He was emphatic about that," I said. "And I do want to investigate this. I just don't *think* I want to."

Marcus shook his head hard enough to make his short, well-groomed dreadlocks jiggle. "You lost me."

"What I'm saying is that I want to do it more than I don't want to do it. I just have to figure out why that is."

"I thought you were helping out your mentor."

"That was the original excuse, but I'm not sure that holds up anymore. She asked me to get her in touch with Anatoly so she could hire him to investigate. I was the one who suggested that I do my amateur-sleuth thing. So technically Anatoly was right when he said that my obligation to her ended as soon as he took the case."

"*Technically* he was right? Honey, he was *completely* right. He was *absolutely* right. Pick any positive adverb, place it in front of the word 'right' and that's pretty much what Anatoly was."

"Fine," I said through gritted teeth. "But I'm still not going to stop investigating this case."

"Because you want to."

"Yes."

"Even though you don't think you want to."

"Don't ask me why, but I feel like I need to do more for Melanie than what I've done for her so far." I tried to turn to face him but Marcus held my head in place, so I was forced to talk to the mirror. "Besides, if I stop investigating now

Anatoly will think it's because he told me to stop. I can't give him the satisfaction."

"So you're proving a point."

"Kind of."

"You realize that's insane."

"No, it's not," I insisted. "Do you remember what you told me right after I caught my dear ex-hubby screwing that dancer?"

"I said that he was an asshole."

"Yes, but you also said that someday I would be an incredibly successful and famous writer and I would be able to flaunt that success in front of Scott. You said he would suffer every day of his life because he would know that he blew his chance to reap the rewards of my accomplishments and that I would gain an enormous amount of satisfaction from that."

Marcus grinned. "And look at you now. *C'est La Mort* was on the *New York Times* bestseller list for five weeks straight. I am wise and all-knowing."

"No, you're *not* because Scott fell off the face of the earth so I have never had the chance to rub it in his face. He's probably living like a king in some third world country where they have legalized gambling and women waving around I-will-hook-for-food poster boards. Living well is only a good revenge if those you're trying to get revenge on *know* you're living well."

"And this is pertinent because…?"

"Because I don't repeat my mistakes. I'm seriously pissed at Anatoly and I want to show him that I'm better at his job than he is. This is my chance to make him miserable and I just can't pass up an opportunity like that."

"Okay, right now you're putting out a 'Kathy Bates in *Misery*' kind of vibe."

"I'm not crazy!" I snapped. "But I'll admit that maybe I sound…well, a little bit less than sane. If I were to give one of my characters this motivation, *Publishers Weekly* would tear me apart. That's why you need to help me come up with a good cover story. Melanie has left me five messages asking me to leave this whole investigation to Anatoly and I have to find a way to change her mind about that."

"But aren't you too busy for these kind of games? Shouldn't you be writing a book or something?"

"Well, yeah. But, Marcus, did it ever occur to you that investigating this case is going to *help* me write my next book? What better way to research a cozy mystery than to start volunteering as a real-life amateur sleuth?"

"This has nothing to do with research."

"Of course it doesn't, but if anyone else asks me about this, that's what I'm going to say. There! That's my reason. Or does that sound dumb?"

"Don't underestimate yourself, you're way past dumb, now you're moving toward idiotic." Marcus plugged in a curling iron. "Honey, think about what you're getting yourself mixed up in. You said it yourself, this murder could have been politically motivated. Eugene could have pissed off the wrong Democrat."

"Don't be ridiculous," I said with more conviction than I actually felt. "Democrats don't kill people."

"Are you sure about that?" Marcus asked as he parted my hair at the side. "Maybe this is the party's new strategy for getting the support of the NRA. And then there's that cat message. Sounds like code-speak to me and code-speak is something government agents are likely to use. You know how they talk—" he bent down so he was ear level and said in a low, dramatic voice "'—the eagle has landed—shoot the moon.'"

"What the hell are you talking about?"

"It's from an old Sean Penn movie…at least I think that's how it goes. Nonetheless, the cat thing probably means that you're dealing with a politician who's coveting the support of fanatical animal rights organizations, and as it so happens, Ms. Brooke recently announced that she's going to write a big ol' check to help save a few endangered toads. You could be dealing with the next Stalin!"

"I probably should reserve judgment on Anne Brooke until I meet her, but I have to say, she doesn't really strike me as the Stalin type."

"She bears certain similarities," Marcus said as he attacked my split ends with his sparkling silver clippers. "I saw her interviewed on Channel Two Morning News…."

"Didn't you tell me last month that you were going to start dedicating your mornings to reading your favorite authors?" I asked.

"That was the plan, but *somebody* absconded with my Lee Nichols book before I had a chance to read it."

I winced. "I guess I told you I was going to return that last week, huh?"

"Yes, you did, and I'm very cross about it. But back to Anne. I saw the interview, and girlfriend's definitely on the paranoid side. She was complaining about being mistreated by the media, which you know is just another way of saying that she wants to *control* the media. Also, Stalin paid lip service to the teachings of Lenin, and in this interview Brooke actually quoted the lyrics of a song by Lennon from his *Imagine* album or something. And to top it all off, I heard that Brooke's insurance carrier is State Farm."

I wrinkled my brow. "Why is *that* important?"

"Are you kidding? Honey, where do you think Stalin sent all those poor peasants? To the State Farm!"

"Not the insurance company, you dork!"

"Still, it's a sign."

I watched as little snippets of my hair fell on the cream marble tile floor. "I'm going to do this, Marcus."

He released a heavy sigh. "I don't know why I continue to fool myself into believing that you'll ever take any of the advice I give you. You wouldn't be you if you suddenly became rational."

"Rational? This from the man who just likened the Beatles' lead singer to the founder of the Communist Party?"

"Johnny wrote a whole song telling people to imagine a world where there wasn't any religion and everybody shared everything—basically just a rockin' version of *The Communist Manifesto*. But seriously, I worry about you, Sophie. I hate the thought of anyone hurting even one chemically treated hair on your head."

"I won't get hurt. I can do this…with a little help from my friends. Can I count on you to help me with this marginally important mission?"

Marcus stopped cutting my hair and pretended to consider the question. "Will I help you put your life in danger for no good reason whatsoever? Hmm, I'm going to go with no."

"Will you at least help me think of a reason to give Melanie for my continued involvement?"

"Tell her...oh, I know! Tell her that while Anatoly *is* a great P.I., he's also a recovering alcoholic and that you need to work with him in order to make sure he stays on the sobriety wagon."

"Hey," I said slowly, "that's good! But what if she talks to Anatoly about it?"

"Tell her that he just recently joined AA and that he doesn't want anyone to know. As I see it, she'll either fire him, in which case your revenge will be taken care of and you can relax, or she'll ask you to keep tabs on him, which means that you'll have to stay on the case, which is what you claim is your unconscious desire."

"Marcus, that's genius!"

"Of course it is. My smile isn't the only reason they call me brilliant."

The minute I left Ooh La La I was on the phone to Melanie. It was surprisingly easy to convince her of Anatoly's alcoholism and it wasn't much harder to get her to agree to my continued participation in the investigation. I suspected that she had hired Anatoly out of guilt. She wasn't comfortable with the idea of putting me at risk by asking me to investigate a murder. But guilt aside, I think deep down she wanted me to be involved. Melanie was a private person, and furthermore she wanted people to think fondly of her deceased husband. She knew that if Anatoly or I discovered information that would cast Eugene in a negative light, I would do everything in my power to make sure that information stayed out of the papers, even if that meant withholding information regarding a criminal act from the police. Perhaps Anatoly would do the same without my urging, but she didn't know that.

So, as far as I was concerned, it was a win-win. I could help a woman in need while simultaneously sticking it to my chauvinistic ex. I was certain that *Ms.* magazine would be proud.

A little competition never hurt anyone…with the notable exception of the losers.
—*C'est La Mort*

"THESE NAPKINS SMELL FUNNY."

I gave Leah a weird look before taking a sniff of my own cloth napkin. Four days had passed since I had told Marcus I was going to continue to investigate Eugene's violent death, and now I had just made the same declaration to my sister as we prepared to have brunch in a new restaurant located in downtown Pleasanton.

We had chosen this place for two reasons. One, she was contemplating whether the restaurant was suitable for a bridal shower she was coordinating, and two, in a few hours I would be meeting with Anne Brooke in her nearby Livermore campaign headquarters. I had finagled the appointment by posing as a freelance journalist for *Tikkun* magazine, a famously liberal Jewish publication. I didn't actually read *Tikkun* (I was turned off by the magazine's lack of fashion tips and celebrity gossip), but I knew enough about the causes they championed to convince Brooke and her people that I was writing for them. The best thing about the appointment was that Anatoly knew nothing about it. I had asked him to meet at Boudin in Fisherman's Wharf this afternoon so we could come up with a new game plan. By the time he figured out that I wasn't going to be showing up it would be too late for him to do anything about it.

"Stop thinking about Anatoly and tell me what you think of that smell," Leah said.

"They smell like fabric softener, and how did you know I was thinking about Anatoly?"

"You had that wicked look in your eye," she said with a disapproving sigh.

"I wasn't having wicked thoughts, at least they weren't wicked in the way you're implying."

"Whatever. I'm not going to recommend this place to my client unless the management is willing to switch to a lavender wash. And I have very mixed feelings about this china. Why are they serving continental cuisine on plates with fleur-de-lis accents?"

"To remind the customers that they serve French toast?" I suggested. I actually liked the restaurant. It was light and airy and the hostess had mistaken me for the instructor on her workout video. "Melanie doesn't think that Eugene's time in the FBI has anything to do with Eugene's murder," I continued, hoping to circumvent a conversation about the restaurant's flatware. "She said that Eugene did most of his work behind a desk and the little fieldwork he did was undercover. So with maybe one or two exceptions, the bad guys Eugene helped put away don't even know that he was the reason for their misfortune. Plus, as she pointed out, if a man wants to return to a life of crime after being released from prison he's not going to hunt down the officer who arrested him. Instead he'll steer clear of the cops and the feds and hang out with those who are more supportive of his nefarious activities."

"Mmm-hmm, fascinating. You do realize that French toast is about as French as McDonald's fries, don't you?" Leah took another look at the fleur-de-lis china and clucked her tongue in disapproval.

I should have known better than to have tried to change the subject on Leah. It had always been an unspoken rule in my family that Leah and Mama were the ones who got to control the conversations, and my father (when he had been alive) and I were the ones responsible for placating them. "Leah, no one is going to notice that the pattern on their plate doesn't reflect the cultural origins of the omelet on top of it," I responded reasonably.

"They won't consciously notice it, but they may very well walk away thinking the event wasn't quite perfect," Leah said. "People don't have to be consciously aware of something in order to react to it. Isn't that what subliminal advertising is all about?"

Couldn't argue with that logic. I studied my bread plate with new interest. Were these fleur-de-lis sending me subliminal messages? Would I leave here with the urge to hand out cake to the proletariat while wearing Yves Saint Laurent's newest fragrance?

"Speaking of being motivated by your unconscious," Leah said, "you've told me that you're going to continue to help Melanie figure out why Eugene was killed, but have you come to terms with why it's so important to you that you help her?"

"Yes, I've figured it all out." I launched into the whole spiel I had given Marcus, emphasizing my need to show up Anatoly. "He was so condescending when he told me that I was to have nothing to do with this case. Now I'm going to show him that his low opinion of my investigative abilities is totally off," I explained. "I can get to the bottom of this whole thing faster than he can. After I've beaten him at his own game I'm going to waltz off into the sunset without him, and eventually, when it's too late, he'll realize what he lost when he gave me up."

Leah stared at me for a full minute before speaking. "You're like a psychological case study," she finally said.

"Okay, enough." I rested my elbows on the table, ignoring her look of disapproval. "You obviously have a theory as to what's motivating me to do all this, so why not just tell me what it is?"

Leah looked away and I watched as she fought some kind of silent internal struggle. "You need to figure this out yourself."

"What? *You* are going to keep your opinions to yourself? Have you been possessed by a nonjudgmental alien?"

"I wasn't going to tell you this," she said slowly, "but I'm going to therapy now."

"Really? But you've always said that the only therapy you would ever engage in was the kind that involved an Amex and a Nordstrom shoe sale."

"Jo-Jo changed my mind," Leah explained. "You remember Jo-Jo, don't you? She's one of the women from the Junior League. She's thirty-nine years old and up until recently she's never been in a relationship that has lasted more than two weeks. A while back she started seeing this therapist who helped her realize what she was doing wrong, and now, after less than two years of weekly sessions, she's managed to get a plastic surgeon to propose to her. Now Jo-Jo's looking forward to a lifetime filled with love, security and free liposuction. As soon as I found out I made an appointment with the same therapist and he said that I need to let the people in my life figure out their own problems."

"So you think I have a problem?"

"Too many to count. But my therapist also thinks that I push people away by being too critical of them, so I'm not going to criticize you until you're out of hearing distance."

"I'm fairly sure that telling me I'm 'like a psychological case study' is a criticism."

"I slipped, sue me." She gave an approving smile to the waiter as he served her a warm plate of ricotta cheese pancakes and me a seafood breakfast casserole.

"So what's the goal here?" I asked. "To see this therapist until you get an M.D. to marry you?" I took a large bite of my casserole. Not good. Maybe this would be an ideal time to start my next diet.

"I don't need to marry a doctor," Leah said. "A lawyer would be okay, or even a dentist. Dental insurance is so pricey these days and it never covers the cosmetic stuff."

"And you think *I* have issues," I muttered. "Need I

remind you that you were a married woman not too long ago and you hated it?"

Leah blinked in surprise. "I couldn't stand my husband but I loved being married. I loved being part of a family unit, I loved showing off my ring, and I took comfort in the knowledge that I had crossed 'get married' off my to-do list. If I could just be married without having to actually have a husband, my life would be perfect."

"I guess you could become a lesbian and do the whole civil-union thing." I forced myself to take another bite of my food. Leah's pancakes looked so much better.

"I've considered it," she said, "but I have a feeling that being married to another woman would be even harder than being married to a man. What if I married a woman who was like me?"

"My God," I gasped, truly horrified by the idea, "that would be unbearable."

"Yes, it would be," she agreed with an amused smile. "Too much of a good thing."

We both laughed, but our moment of harmonious sisterly love was cut short by the ringing of my cell phone.

Leah glared at my purse. "Really, Sophie. The only people who keep their cell phones on in expensive restaurants are clueless teens and the nouveau riche."

"It could be important," I protested, not bothering to point out that she wasn't exactly old money. "It's Melanie," I said once I had fished out my phone. "Would you prefer if I took this outside?"

"Or at least in the ladies' lounge," Leah said, pointing toward the restrooms.

I got up and made my way to the ladies' room, wondering what Emily Post would say about cell phone/bathroom etiquette. "Hi, Melanie," I said as soon as I was standing outside one of the stalls. "Everything okay?"

"I think so," she said carefully. "I just received the strangest call from Flynn Fitzgerald."

"Oh?"

"Yes, at first I thought he was just calling to see how I was holding up, but as the conversation progressed it became clear that he was really calling to find out about you."

"Me? What did he want to know?"

"How long we've been friends, if you had published any other articles dealing with politics or had dealings with any other publications. That sort of thing. He seems to be under the impression that you work with the *National Review.*"

I braced myself against the sink. "Please tell me that you didn't tell him otherwise."

"I surmised fairly quickly that you had made up that story as a way to get an appointment with Fitzgerald, but I may not have covered for you very convincingly."

"What do you mean?"

"When he first suggested that you were writing for that publication, I laughed. I laughed a lot, Sophie."

Shit! "If Fitzgerald calls again, tell him that we met for tea or whatever and that now you realize that I've moved politically to the right. Tell him that I couldn't stop gushing about the opportunity the *Review* has given me."

"I'll tell him."

"Fantastic, thank you, Melanie. I'm sure no harm was done. In the meantime, do you think you could help me get in to see Maggie Gallagher? I've been trying to reach her, but she never returns my calls."

"I'll try, but I don't know if I'll be much help. Maggie and I have never been close. I'm not even sure if she likes me very much. She was more Eugene's friend."

"Really? But how can anyone not like you?"

"I'm sure there are a slew of reasons," Melanie said modestly, "but I have no idea what specifically caused Maggie to be so distant with me."

"Huh." I briefly considered the possibility that Maggie's dislike of Melanie had something to do with an inappropriate fondness Maggie might have had for Melanie's husband. It certainly was something worth checking out. "Listen, Melanie, I'm having brunch with Leah right now so I should get going, but thank you for telling me about Fitzgerald."

"Of course, Sophie. Enjoy your meal."

I clicked off and studied my reflection in the mirror. So what if Fitzgerald knew that I had lied to him? It wasn't like he was a suspect. Still, the idea made me more than a little uneasy.

When I got back to the table Leah had almost finished her pancakes and was looking more than a little irritated.

"Sorry about that," I said as I took my seat. "But I had to take that call."

"Of course you did. It was Melanie after all," Leah snapped. Then she paused and some of the irritation slipped from her countenance as she met my eyes. "Sophie, I'm not going to tell you what your problems are, but I am going to make three suggestions."

"I can't wait to hear this." I looked down at my plate. I

wasn't going to eat my casserole. It wasn't even good enough to feed to my cat.

"Start thinking about why Melanie became important to you in the first place," Leah suggested, "and then think about why you don't have any photos of Dad hanging up in your apartment."

"I don't hang photos," I said a bit too quickly. "I keep them in albums."

"Albums that can be easily stored out of sight," Leah pointed out.

The waiter walked by and I got his attention long enough to ask for our check. "I have to get to Livermore," I said, smiling apologetically at Leah.

"Right," Leah said dryly. "I'm sure your sudden need to leave has nothing to do with avoidance. But you can't go without hearing my third suggestion."

"Uh-huh." I sent a beseeching look at our waiter, who was now across the room totaling up our tab. I was pretty much done with this conversation. "If your client wants the bridal shower here, tell her not to order the seafood casserole."

"Don't change the subject. You need to drop your vendetta against Anatoly," Leah said. "If he's not willing to commit, you should definitely walk off into the sunset without him, but it's better to do it now instead of later. You don't need to show him up."

I turned back to her with surprise. "Since when have you had a problem with revenge?"

"I don't have a problem with it. I just don't think you should use it as an excuse to stay close to someone. Especially if you happen to be in love with that someone."

"I'm not in love with Anatoly!"

"I see. Just because you think about him all the time, get agitated every time you hear his name and can't get past the fact that he won't commit to you, that doesn't mean you're in love with him, right?" The waiter came back with our check and Leah tossed an Amex card at him without even looking at it. "Like I said, Sophie, you're a walking case study."

"Leah, you know how you're going to start criticizing me behind my back, rather than to my face?"

"Yes?"

"Well, I'm about to make that task easy for you." I stood up, turned my back to her and walked out.

By the time I was on the elevator going up to Anne Brooke's top-floor campaign headquarters I was in a better mood. I had spent my life not listening to Leah and I saw no reason to change that pattern now. I was not in love with Anatoly. Furthermore, I knew why I was on this case, and it didn't matter if my reasons were logical or not. They were still my reasons, and if I wanted to show Anatoly up that was my prerogative. And I wasn't insisting on staying on this case just so I could be close to him. If that were true I would have told him about this interview rather than trick him into going to Boudin.

The elevator opened, and I put on my most winning smile and was all ready to charm the Brooke campaign workers when I spotted him.

Anatoly's hands were jammed into the pockets of his leather jacket, a large camera case dangled over his shoulder, and he was engaged in a seemingly casual conversation with Anne Brooke.

That son of a bitch. How had he known? I took a steady-ing breath and tried to walk (rather than march or stomp) over to where they were talking.

Anatoly's eyes met mine and the right corner of his mouth turned up. "So," he said, his Russian accent making the word sound sexier than it had any right to be, "the reporter has arrived."

"Ah, you must be Sophie Katz." Anne Brooke held out her hand for me to shake. "I've just been speaking to your pho-tographer. I didn't realize your article would include photos."

"It was a last-minute decision," I said through gritted teeth. "Just one of those extraspecial surprises."

"I was telling Anne how I like to sit in on the interviews," Anatoly explained. "That way I get a better sense of the subject's personality, which, of course, helps me decide how I want to photograph them."

"I didn't actually get Ms. Brooke's permission to have an extra person sit in on our interview," I said. "I'm sure she would feel more comfortable if you waited outside."

"Don't be ridiculous. I have no problem with Anatoly sitting in on the interview, and please call me Anne. We're all very casual here."

I nodded and tried to pretend to be okay with Anatoly's latest little maneuver. I looked around the rest of the office and examined the other occupants. People were definitely dressed more casually than they were at Fitzgerald's camp. However, they did seem more frazzled if that counted for anything. Dark circles seemed to be in vogue and everyone had a phone glued to their ear and a keyboard under their fingers (except for a few who were writing the old-fashioned way).

Anne was the only one of the lot who looked at all collected. Her blue suit was neatly pressed and managed to flatter her fit figure without being too clingy or in any way risqué. Her hair was done in a perfect French twist, and the pearl-and-sapphire drop earrings matched her bracelet. I suspected that she had the same dark circles as the rest of her team but she was much more adept at covering them up. She led us through two adjoining rooms (all filled with workers) and then into a private small conference area. She gestured for Anatoly and me to take a seat in two padded folding chairs and then pulled up a much more inviting-looking office chair for herself.

"So you're here for *Tikkun,*" Anne said. She chose to sit next to me rather than across the table, thus sandwiching me between her and Anatoly. The move was probably intended to reinforce her I'm-just-one-of-the-people image but it made me a bit uncomfortable. "I love that magazine." She gave me a curious look. "Are you Israeli? Sephardic, right? I find the Sephardic traditions to be so beautiful. Very spiritual. I once visited a kibbutz."

"I'm not Sephardic," I interrupted. "My mother's family is Ashkenazic of Eastern European decent. I owe my dark skin to my father, who was African-American."

"What a wonderful combination!" Anne said, clearly happy with this information. "I always like to point out to people that if we were truly an integrated society we would all be multiracial."

Yes, that's why my parents slept together, they were trying to improve society. But I kept my sarcasm to myself and instead tried to redirect the conversation. "Actually," I said slowly, "I was more interested in how your campaign works. You see—"

"The campaign Fitzgerald has been running has been very negative, and it seems that this is a new trend among Republican candidates," Anatoly said, totally cutting me off. "I think *Tikkun* is interested in hearing how Democratic candidates are handling the attacks and what they think of them. Isn't that right, Sophie?"

I glared at him.

"Ah, the attacks." Anne nodded her head solemnly. "Here's the reason Fitzgerald is playing dirty—he doesn't have anything positive to say about himself. He wants to keep all the focus on alleged, and frequently false, accounts of my past indiscretions. He thinks it's his only chance of winning, but the voters see through it. That's why I'm ahead in the polls."

According to yesterday's *Contra Costa Times* she was ahead by four percentage points. It was that kind of lead that lost Al Gore the presidency.

"I've read some of the transcripts from his speeches," I said carefully, "and while he does talk a lot about the importance of character and high moral standards, he keeps most of the focus on himself. In the speech he made at the Antioch senior center last week he didn't mention you at all."

"No, but he's been more than happy to comment on my personal life when the press brings it up to *him,*" she replied. "And how do you think the press got that information? I'll tell you how. It's been leaked from his camp. He won't admit to it but it's common knowledge that he hired someone whose only duty was to tarnish my reputation!"

"Do you know specifically who in his camp has been investigating you?" Anatoly asked.

"It was Eugene O'Reilly. You've probably heard of him, he was killed in a drive-by shooting on the evening of that senior center visit you mentioned. An ironic end for a major gun advocate. I have friends who've spoken to him at various social gatherings and they all tell me that he was obsessed with finding fault with others. If he wanted to find fault he should have looked at his employer. I'm certain that Fitzgerald is not the choirboy he pretends to be. But Mr. O'Reilly wasn't interested in exposing the hypocrisy within his own camp. He just wanted to destroy those who disagreed with his opinions. I don't mean to speak ill of the dead, but he was an awful, awful man. He had no scruples whatsoever."

I had to bite my tongue in order to keep from protesting. I may have only met Eugene that one time but he was *not* awful. Although, the *Da Vinci* thing was a little obnoxious, but that had been Melanie's problem, not Anne's. "How can you be sure it was Mr. O'Reilly?" I asked.

"For one thing, he used to be an agent in the FBI, which makes him the only trained investigator who worked for Fitzgerald that I know of, and secondly…well let's just say that people have told me that he was asking a lot of inappropriate questions about me."

"Inappropriate in what way?" Anatoly asked.

"Questions about my marriage and the like. He used various pretenses in order to contact several men whom I've shared friendships with at one point or another. He approached my old friend William in a bar with a story about how he was having an affair with a married woman. In reality the only married woman Eugene was ever involved with was his own wife. I'm sure he was hoping his lie would encourage William to let something sordid slip about the relationship he used to have with me, not that there was anything sordid about it," she added quickly. "We were just friends."

Why didn't I believe that? "So Mr. O'Reilly was really poking his nose where it didn't belong. I suppose things are easier for you now that he's gone."

Anne swallowed hard and she leaned back in her chair. "I'm not glad that he's dead if that's what you're asking. I'm not a monster no matter what Fitzgerald would have people believe."

"That's obvious," said Anatoly. "But I think what Sophie was getting at is that if the man on Fitzgerald's team who was investigating you is no longer around, you will now have the luxury of focusing on the issues that you're so passionate about rather than having to defend your personal life."

"Of course I want to talk about the issues," Anne said. "But that doesn't mean I'm glad Mr. O'Reilly is dead. What happened to him was just…horrific." Anne said the last word with feeling, and she paused for a moment as if to consider its truth. "It also perfectly demonstrates why gun control is so important," she continued with considerably less emotion. "No one should have the means to randomly kill someone on the street. It also demonstrates why we need to reach out to the urban youth. If we spent more money on our schools and made it possible for parents to find safe low-income housing…"

I tuned out. Whether or not she was willing to admit it, Anne Brooke's life was a lot easier without Eugene around. But would she really have someone killed just so she could cover up a few affairs?

Anatoly crossed his ankle over his knee and smiled at her benignly. "You have some wonderful ideas. I wish you were running for Congress in *my* district."

This from the man who had voted for the Terminator.

"I'm also impressed with how you're able to stay so well informed about the goings-on in your opponent's camp."

Anne shifted uncomfortably. "What do you mean?"

"What I mean is that not only do you know that Eugene O'Reilly was the person Fitzgerald enlisted to research your past, but you also know a lot of personal details about O'Reilly himself."

Anne laughed but it sounded forced. "You give me too much credit. I know very little about Mr. O'Reilly, just what I've heard through the grapevine, from William and from the newspapers."

"You seem very confident that Eugene's confession to William about his having an affair was false," Anatoly pointed out. "And you know his position on gun control. You even seem to have some insight into what he was like as a person. You said that he was an awful man with no scruples. Surely you didn't make that assessment based solely on the little bit of information William was able to share with you."

Anne's eyes narrowed. "I must say, Anatoly, you are the most inquisitive photographer I have ever met."

Ha! Anatoly had just blown his cover, big-time! I, on the other hand, was playing out my role perfectly.

"I'm actually a photojournalist. It's a job that requires a certain amount of inquisitiveness."

And he had recovered. Damn it all to hell.

"I see. Anatoly, the political world is a small one. I may

not have had the chance to converse with Eugene personally, but I certainly am acquainted with a number of people
who have. Everyone knows about Eugene's selective adoption of biblical ethics."

"'Selective adoption of biblical ethics'?" I repeated. "I'm
not sure I know what that means."

"It means that he had a reputation for being very dedi-
cated to his wife, or at least to his marriage vows. However,
he doesn't pay any heed to Jesus' suggestion that we refrain
from throwing stones at one another."

"Maybe he didn't think he lived in a glass house," I suggested.

"We *all* live in glass houses, Sophie," Anne said with a tone
that hinted at a superiority complex. "If you can't see inside
it's because the glass is tinted, but if you pound on it with
enough force it *will* break."

"That's very true," Anatoly agreed, "and eloquently stated.
I wonder, do you think O'Reilly was the only one responsible
for leaking the reports about your supposed infidelities? What
about the reports of your previous drug use and the abortion?"

"That was a long time ago," Anne snapped.

"I am well aware of that," Anatoly said soothingly. "As far
as I'm concerned your ability to kick an addictive habit is a
tribute to your personal strength and courage."

Wow, he was laying it on thick.

"But I was just trying to figure out if Mr. O'Reilly might
have had help in his attempts to slander you."

"I'm sure Fitzgerald encourages his team to share any information that could potentially hurt my campaign, but I
have a hunch that Mr. O'Reilly was the only one who made
a career out of it."

"I see. And before he died…do you have any reason to believe that he was trying to expose anything other than all of your past affairs?"

"*All* of my past affairs? I've had *two*. That's it! They were a long time ago and I've apologized for them!"

"Forgive me, I misspoke. I'm just trying to get a handle on how low Fitzgerald is willing to go in the name of winning."

Anne leaned forward and lowered her voice to a kind of growl. "Fitzgerald would do anything to win. He may like to pretend that he's the perfect Christian, but I guarantee you he's not a kindhearted man. If I was the one who had been shot instead of Mr. O'Reilly, Fitzgerald would have offered the gunman a job on his campaign."

When the interview was over, Anatoly snapped a few pictures of Anne standing next to her campaign volunteers and talking on the telephone to a nonexistent person. Unlike some people, I didn't feel the need to play both photographer and journalist, so I stood aside as they did their thing.

"What is this for?"

I looked up to see a pleasant-looking salt-and-pepper-haired man looking down at me inquisitively.

"It's just a photo shoot for *Tikkun* magazine."

"*Tikkun?*" The man released a low whistle. "Impressive. I'm surprised they're interested in a small district race."

"It's an article about how political campaigns are conducted. I'm Sophie Katz, the reporter. Who are you?"

"Sam Griffin, Anne's husband."

"You're kidding!" I shook his hand enthusiastically. "What

an unexpected surprise Mr....I'm sorry, what did you say your last name was?"

"Griffin. Anne kept her maiden name. It's more liberated." There was a note of resentment in his voice. With everything I had read about Anne it seemed to me that her unwillingness to change her name was the least of his problems.

"Do you help Anne with her campaign?" I asked.

"She has my full support, but I'm nowhere near savvy enough to be a political consultant. I make a living as a doctor."

"Oh? What do you specialize in?"

"I'm a nutritionist. Perhaps you've read my book, *Broccoli for Life?*"

That's right, the gas guy Johnny was talking about. "It's on my must-read list."

Sam Griffin nodded and looked at his wife admiringly. "She's beautiful, isn't she? She was born to be in front of a camera."

I followed his gaze. Anne wasn't unattractive, but "beautiful" was a stretch. Then again maybe I would see her with different eyes if I didn't suspect that she had killed a man.

"How long have you been married?" I asked.

"Two years."

"Practically newlyweds," I said with a smile. I had uncovered news reports revealing that Anne had divorced the father of her teenage son, but I had found very little written about her latest union.

"I think we'll always be newlyweds," he sighed. "She's such a remarkable woman. I completely adore her."

"Really?" I quickly realized how that sounded and tried to adjust my tone. "I mean she's obviously worthy of adoration, but most men don't fully appreciate the women in their lives." *Like the one currently photographing your wife.*

"There's no way to be with Anne without appreciating her. She's amazing."

Sam was beginning to annoy me. I gave him a discreet once-over. He didn't *look* like a freak. He was wearing a pair of dress slacks matched with a tasteful sport coat. He wasn't buff but he wasn't out of shape, either. He was the kind of guy who was attractive enough to show off to friends but not so gorgeous that you had to worry about him outshining you. The perfect husband for a woman who was running for office.

"Sam!" Anne waved at her husband as Anatoly put his camera back in its case. "You're right on time for our lunch date." She walked to his side and linked her arm through his. "It's hard finding quality time to spend with your spouse when you're in the middle of a campaign," Anne explained, "but Sam and I always find a way to do it." She batted her eyes at him. *Literally batted her eyes.* Who does that? But judging from the way Sam's chest puffed up it was clear that he enjoyed it.

"I have all the photos I need." Anatoly crossed to my side and smiled at the sickeningly happy couple. "Thank you so much for your time."

"No, thank you." Anne smiled. "I have an enormous amount of respect for your publication and I am honored to be featured in it."

The quintessential politician. I managed not to gag and bid both Anne and her brainwashed husband goodbye. I didn't say a word to Anatoly until we stepped outside. "How did you find out about the interview?"

"How many times do I have to remind you that I'm a private detective?"

"So what does that mean? Do you have my phone tapped or something? Because it's not like I posted my meeting with Anne on the Internet."

"I know you, Sophie, and I know that you wouldn't invite me to lunch at a restaurant that doesn't have a full liquor license unless you weren't planning on showing up."

"Very funny."

"I'm not joking. You told me that you pretended to be a journalist when talking to Fitzgerald, so I put two and two together and I called Brooke's campaign headquarters claiming that I was your photographer and needed to double-check the time of the interview. Just like that they confirmed my suspicions."

"Just because you figured it out doesn't prove you're a good detective," I grumbled.

"That's exactly what it proves," Anatoly said with a smirk. "Now that we've finished the interview, there is nothing left for you to contribute to this investigation. I'll take it over from here."

"I told you once and I'll say it again—I'm not leaving this whole thing to you."

Anatoly scowled. "Why do you care so much? Why is it so important to you that you personally investigate this?"

I swallowed and looked away. "I'm using the experience to enhance my writing. I'm going to use this tragedy as a basis for a fictional novel that will touch people's lives."

Anatoly burst out laughing.

"What's so funny?"

"You're going to touch people's lives? Sophie, don't you read your own books? Adam Sandler movies have more depth."

"That is so not fair! My books are often very touching!"

"Hardly…although I will say that some of your sex scenes may prompt readers to touch *themselves.*"

"Cute. You know, you're in no position to question my motives. At least I'm not bilking Melanie for thousands of dollars up front. And don't tell me you're not. I see the evidence." I gestured to his Harley that was parked not far away. Obviously it had been fixed.

"Melanie is the one who set the price for my services," Anatoly said. "I told her she was offering me way too much, but she insisted. *Somebody* told her that ten thousand dollars is what I normally charge, and considering who I have to deal with I don't think I'm being overpaid."

"Listen, Anatoly, there is no way in hell that Melanie will let you work on this case alone."

Anatoly's eyebrows furrowed. "Funny you should say that. When Melanie first contacted me, she and I agreed that you shouldn't be involved in this. Suddenly she's changed her mind. Why is that, Sophie?"

"Simple, she realized that I've already dug up a lot of valuable information and she wants me to continue to build on my leads."

"I got the feeling it was more complicated than that. Tell me, why is it that during our conversations Melanie now refers to God as a 'higher power'?"

I bit my lip and tried to think up a response.

"Did you tell her I was an addict of some kind?" Anatoly pressed.

Just then I heard my cell phone ringing in my handbag. Literally saved by the bell. I grabbed it and pressed it to my ear, not even bothering to check the caller ID. "Hello?"

"Sophie, is that you? It's Johnny, as in Fitzgerald's Johnny. Wait, that sounds wrong. I didn't mean anything by that— I'm not Fitzgerald's Johnny, I'm your Johnny. Wait, that sounds bad, too…"

I squeezed my eyes closed. This was almost as bad as talking to Anatoly. Almost, but not quite. "Johnny, are you calling because you set something up with Maggie Gallagher?"

Anatoly raised his eyebrows at the name and I gave myself a mental slap for clueing him in on a lead.

"Um, yeah, I mean no. Maggie's being really squirrelly about being interviewed. I asked Fitzgerald if he would talk her into it and he said he'd try. I don't really get that. Fitzgerald's the boss, he shouldn't have to try. He should just tell her to do it and then she would. She works for him. It doesn't make sense to me. Does it make sense to you?"

"Not really," I admitted. Just then a large truck went by. I turned my back to the street to avoid getting dust in my eyes.

"Was that a car?" Johnny asked. "Is this your cell phone? You didn't tell me this was a cell phone number. That's great! That means I can reach you even when you're out! Do you even have a home phone? Because a lot of people just use cells these days."

"I have a home phone number, too," I admitted, secretly glad that I had only been stupid enough to give him one of my numbers. "If you haven't been able to get me an appointment with Maggie, then why are you calling?"

"I wanted to invite you to a party. Do you like parties?

Who doesn't, right? I'm having a dinner party on Thursday night. It's a housewarming party to celebrate my recent move to El Cerrito."

"Who else did you invite?" I did *not* want to go to this party, but if Eugene's coworkers were going to be there, I probably should.

"Lots of people, friends, people from work. Rick's gonna be there and I think he's going to ask Mary Ann. Did you know they talk on the phone all the time? And I think they went out to dinner again, too. They've really hit it off. Maybe we could do another double date in the city sometime."

Anatoly was studying me, clearly trying to piece together the conversation from my end of it.

"You want to have dinner with me again?" I purred, purely for Anatoly's benefit.

"Yeah, of course!" Johnny gushed.

"I see, well I think I can make it to your place on Thursday. I'm kind of in the middle of something right now, but I'll call you back and get the details."

"Great!"

"Yeah, great. I'll talk to you later, Johnny." I hung up and grinned at Anatoly.

"Who was that?" he asked.

"*That* was a man who is head over heels in love with me."

"And you're meeting him at his place?"

Was that concern in his eyes? Jealousy, even? Oh, this was too good. "He's cooking me dinner."

"Maggie Gallagher is Fitzgerald's media person. How does this Johnny person know her?"

Oops, I had forgotten that he had overheard that part, too.

"Johnny is Fitzgerald's personal assistant," I confessed. "He's really nice and not just a little bit cute and he *loves* me."

"Just how far are you planning on going in order to get information about Eugene?"

I held up my hands as if trying to physically grasp what I thought he was implying. "Do you actually think I'm planning on sleeping with some guy just so I can get a little more information about Eugene and his former life? Is that seriously what you think?"

"I *think* that murder investigations are very dangerous and that you are risking your life just so you can make me angry. I *think* that you are capable of doing some very stupid things."

"Let me explain a few things to you. When I sleep with a man, I do so in order to get off, not to get information. Secondly, one of the *stupid* things I'm capable of is solving the *stupid* cases that you can't!"

Anatoly took a step back. "Excuse me?"

"Let's face it, Anatoly. You stink at your job. Once upon a time you were determined to figure out who killed Alex Tolsky, but I'm the one who figured that out. Granted, I didn't work it out until the killer was actually standing in front of me and threatening my life, but that's still more than you can say."

"I would have been able to figure it out if you hadn't had me thrown in jail for a crime I didn't commit."

"Now you're just making excuses," I said with a dismissive wave of my hand. "I'm a better detective than you and I'm not walking away from the case."

"Want to bet?"

"Never bet against me, Anatoly. You will always lose."

"That's because you cheat."

"All's fair in love and war."

Anatoly took a step forward and he tilted his head to the side. He studied my face with the attention of a sculptor being introduced to his next model. "Funny," he muttered, "I don't think this is about war."

For a moment there was total silence. Sure, we were standing on the sidewalk and cars were driving past and the wind was rustling the trees that lined the street, but all of that faded away as I tried to absorb what he had just said.

And then he turned around, walked to his newly repaired Harley and drove off.

This is why I hated Anatoly. He would drop these little bombs and then walk away without dealing with the emotional chaos he had just created. Did he just tell me that he loved me? Was he just messing with my head? A comment like that needed to be immediately followed by a serious discussion or sex, but to say something like that and then just hop on a motorized phallic symbol and ride off wasn't acceptable.

"I'm done with this," I said aloud. "I'm done with obsessing and overanalyzing every comment. I'm just done."

A woman pushing a toddler in a stroller walked by just as I finished my mutterings. She gave me a frightened look and a wide berth. I guess people on the streets of Livermore didn't talk to themselves as much as those on the streets of San Francisco.

I sighed and started for my car. I would show Anatoly up and then I would wash my hands of him. I didn't need him or his ambiguous endearments or his hands, which were strong and just a little rough.... There had been one time when he had lifted me up with one hand while the other one gently worked its way up my shirt. God, that had felt good. Would it be so awful to let those hands touch me again?

Yes, it would. I jumped in the driver's seat of my car, eager to get home and take a cold shower.

The first thing I noticed when I got home was the folded-over piece of paper taped to my front door.

I pulled it off and examined it. It was written with letters cut out individually from magazines and said, *My private life is my business. Stay out of it or else!*

It was signed with a child's sticker depicting the Pink Panther.

Unlike the phone message this was clearly a threat, but for the life of me I had no idea what I was being threatened with or why. And how had this note gotten on my door? My building consisted of three flats, and you needed a key just to get into the lobby. The people who lived on the bottom floor were out of town (as they always were). That just left Nancy on the second floor and me on the third. I glanced toward the stairs and considered stopping by her apartment to ask if she had admitted anyone, but then quickly thought better of it. Nancy and I didn't get along…at all…and the reality was that if someone rang her place and told her that they wanted to leave a threatening anonymous message on my door she probably would have buzzed them right in. I stared at the note again and then finally let myself inside.

Mr. Katz greeted me by swishing his tail in my direction before disappearing into the kitchen. I got the hint, but my cat would have to wait a few minutes for his meal.

I crossed to my phone and dialed Marcus's cell.

"What's up, sweetie?" Marcus asked. "Have you turned Anatoly into an alcoholic yet?"

"I got another message from Darth Vader, at least that's who I think this is from—but this time the message is in written form," I said slowly.

"Darth Vader wrote…hold it, are you talking about the Darth Vader who left the message on your machine?"

"That's the one."

"Shit, so what does it say?"

"The note just tells me to stay out of his private life or else."

"That's all it says?"

"Yep. The message is spelled out with letters cut out from magazines."

"My God, it's like a bad 1980s TV drama. How do you know it's from Vader?"

"Because there's a picture of the Pink Panther on it."

"Steve Martin?"

"No, not Steve Martin, the animated Pink Panther, the one they always show during the opening credits. It's in keeping with his last cat comment."

"I see," Marcus breathed. We were both silent for a moment and then Marcus broke in again. "I take it back, I don't see at all. Have you been sticking your nose into the personal affairs of the Pink Panther? *Does* this relate to the last movie? And if so, are you Beyoncé?"

"I don't think so. I'm nowhere near blond or curvy enough. Should I call the cops?"

"And tell them that Darth Vader had teamed up with everybody's favorite bumbling French detective to send you a message?" Marcus asked.

"Yeah, it doesn't exactly scream emergency situation."

"Hardly." He paused before adding, "This is just more evidence that the person responsible for all this is Anne Brooke."

"I don't know, Marcus. I'm not even sure this has anything to do with Eugene or politics."

"Of course it does. The note is a bit harsh, but the picture of the animated character softens it a bit. It's a vague threat bundled inside a mixed message…sounds just like a Democrat."

I rolled my eyes. "Goodbye, Marcus." I put the phone back in its cradle. Better to hang up on him than admit he was right.

8

Without the lies I am uncomplicated and uninteresting. My bullshit gives me depth.
—*C'est La Mort*

I SPENT THE NEXT MORNING DOING MORE INTERNET RESEARCH ON ALL the players. I had started by gathering information on Fitzgerald, Brooke and the top members of their teams. They were nothing if not consistent in their behavior. It seemed that when Fitzgerald wasn't speaking at some pro-life rally he was in church praying for a more homogeneous and intolerant world. Brooke, on the other hand, was all about the seven deadly sins. But really, who wasn't? Spend one afternoon of lying around eating Oreos, fantasizing about Brad Pitt in a toga, and you were guilty of three. The problem was that Brooke always took things a step too far. She didn't just drool over the eighteen-year-old kid her former hubby had hired to paint their fence, she actually slept with him.

I ended up spending much more time reading about Anne than Fitzgerald. Not just because I thought she was likely to be Eugene's murderer, but because she was much more fun to research. Which article would you rather read? "Fitzgerald Urges Teens To Practice Abstinence" or "Brooke Dirty Dances With Distressed Foreign Dignitary"?

I was actually printing up the latter article when my phone rang.

"Hello?"

"Sophie, it's Melanie. Is this a good time?"

"It's a fine time," I reassured her. "What's up?"

"I haven't been able to reach Anatoly today and I was just wondering if either of you were able to get in touch with that boy's family."

I straightened my back as I tried to make sense of her words. "That boy's family?"

"Yes, I know Anatoly thinks I shouldn't worry about it, but the whole thing is very upsetting."

I felt my hands clench into fists. *What* boy? Anatoly hadn't told me anything about this! "Anatoly's right, Melanie," I said slowly. "You shouldn't worry about…um…oh shoot, what's the boy's name again?"

"Peter Strauss," Melanie supplied. "And I'm not exactly worried about him, not that his death wasn't a tragedy, but at least he's with God now."

Little bells started to go off in my head. Peter was the guy who jumped to his death just months after he had begun working for Brooke's campaign.

"But I'd be lying if I said that I wasn't up all last night thinking about that letter," Melanie continued.

"Right, the letter. Do you really think the letter was all that important?" I asked.

"You don't?"

"I don't know," I said. What I wanted to do was scream in frustration. If this were a movie Melanie would have answered my question by giving me all the information I needed to know about the letter and this Peter person. Instead she was answering me with vague, two-word sentences. Of course, I could have told her that Anatoly had neglected to tell me about this, but I was afraid that if I exposed the communication problems between Anatoly and myself, Melanie would decide that she didn't want me on the case after all. So I took a breath and tried again. "What part of the letter was responsible for giving you insomnia?"

"Every part of it!" Melanie's voice was shaking, although it was unclear which emotion was causing the tremble. "Why would this boy be writing my husband in the first place? And what did he mean when he wrote that Eugene 'had the power to not only destroy political careers but also his life and the lives and families of other well-meaning people'? Does this mean that Eugene had information on Anne Brooke that would have ruined her? Even if that was true, why would a twenty-two-year-old campaign worker be so distraught over that? Is this why he took his own life? Is it possible that my Eugene was culpable in the death of another person? Is that possible, Sophie?" The last sentence was more of a hysterical scream than a question.

"I don't know. I'm sure Eugene didn't want Peter to die, but maybe he didn't know that Peter was the kind of guy who would jump out a fifteenth-story window in order to avoid a little scandal."

"Perhaps," Melanie said. Her voice had dropped a few notches in volume but it was a ways from being calm. "I do think Anatoly was on the right track when he suggested that he contact Peter's surviving family. They may be able to shed some light on all this. Has Anatoly gotten through to any of them?"

"Not yet. They haven't been answering their phone and there hasn't been a machine. I'm beginning to suspect that Anatoly transcribed the number incorrectly. Could you give it to me again?"

"I never gave it to him in the first place. Anatoly said he could get it himself."

Hate him. "I'll just ask him again, then. And I'll try calling…um, I'm sorry, I just blanked out on Peter's parents' names." I was getting less subtle by the second.

"Anatoly did tell you about all this, didn't he? Because from the nature of your questions you appear to be a tad out of the loop."

"I'm totally looped. Trust me. I'm just a little tired. Look, I really do have to get going, but I'll get back to you with some answers really soon."

"How soon?"

"Soon, soon. It's my top priority, so try to relax and leave the worrying to me. Take care, Melanie!" I hung up before she could ask me any more questions.

It took me two more hours of searching the Net before I was able to track down the phone number of someone related to Peter. His obituary gave the names of his parents and a sister. His parents were unlisted, but I struck major pay dirt with his sister, Tiffany Strauss. As luck would have it she worked in the city as an esthetician at Mojo, a day spa on upper Haight that was all the rage among the seriously hip and moderately budget-conscious.

I clutched the phone in my hand and sat cross-legged on my bed. Getting in touch with this woman would be a cinch, but what was I going to say? *Hi, I think I may need to talk to you about your brother and I was hoping you could help me figure out why?* For some reason I doubted that would work.

No, the best course of action would be to book an appointment with her for one of the services she offered and pray that she liked to get chatty with her clients.

I leaned over and peered at Mojo's Web site. According to the site Tiffany was considered to be one of San Francisco's best waxers. I was perhaps the last woman in the western world who didn't wax. Yes, I tweezed, shaved and used Nair, but I drew the line when it came to ripping out hair follicles with a strip of hot wax.

Fortunately Tiffany didn't just wax, she also gave facials. I'd never had one of those, either. I didn't have any wrinkles and rarely got more than one pimple a month, so the service seemed like an unnecessary extravagance. The Web site claimed that the facial Tiffany specialized in was a "fully relaxing experience" and that clients would leave the salon with "the famous Mojo glow." I could deal with that.

I dialed the salon and told the perky receptionist that I wanted a facial with Tiffany.

"Sure thing," the woman said. "It looks like her next available appointment is in a little over three weeks on—"

"Did you just say three weeks?" I asked. "But I needed to see her sooner than that!"

"I'm really sorry, but she's majorly booked this month," the receptionist said sympathetically. "She did have a cancellation for tomorrow at five but—"

"I'll take it."

"Wait," the woman said, giggling at my desperation, "that appointment is only for twenty minutes. That's enough for a waxing but not for a facial."

"A waxing?" I asked weakly. "Um, could you hold on a moment?" I covered the mouthpiece of the phone and took a deep breath before turning my gaze on Mr. Katz, who was peeking out at me from under the bed. "I can do this. After all, I'll just be getting rid of a few hairs."

Mr. Katz blinked at me. He was very attached to his hair.

"I can do this," I said again. But which body hairs should I sacrifice in the pursuit of justice? Definitely not pubic hairs. I couldn't have an intimate conversation with a woman while she was in the middle of giving me a Brazilian. However, I *could* allow her to dispense with my leg hairs.

I brought the phone back up to my ear. "Is twenty minutes enough for a leg wax?"

"It should be. But if you want to see someone else I could get you in for both a wax and a facial in two days."

"No, Tiffany was recommended to me. Just put me down for the waxing appointment with her tomorrow."

"Will do," the girl chirped. I gave her my phone number before hanging up.

I looked down as Mr. Katz crawled out from under the bed and brushed up against my leg. "So that's done. Now, do you have any ideas on how I should go about getting a complete stranger to talk to me about what was undoubtedly one of the most painful events of her life?"

Mr. Katz turned away from me and positioned himself in a full-body stretch with his head near the floor and his tail straight up in the air.

"Got it. If all else fails, show her my ass. We'll see how that works for me."

Five o'clock Tuesday evening came way too soon. I lay on the padded table within one of Mojo's intimate rooms surrounded by cream-colored walls and Keith Haring prints and studied Tiffany's back as she stirred scalding-hot goo in a stainless-steel pot. What had I been thinking when I had scheduled this appointment? I couldn't question her about her brother now. I was too freaked out to talk. Plus, I felt nauseous. Of course, that might have something to do with the five Advil I had taken an hour earlier in anticipation of this moment.

I took a deep breath and tried to calm myself. I couldn't think about the pain I was about to endure. I needed to keep my eye on the ball, and in this case the ball was the tall blonde with the 1980s-style hairclip who was about to torture me.

No, no, no, I wasn't going to think about my impending torture! I forced myself to tear my eyes away from the pot with the hot wax and lowered my gaze to Tiffany's green cowboy boots instead. Who the hell wore green cowboy boots? Tiffany was an attractive woman and her skin had the kind of radiance that women always hoped to get when they're pregnant (and never do). She wasn't excessively overweight, but the skin-tight pants she was wearing made her look at least three sizes bigger than I was sure she was. Under her apron she wore a bright red sleeveless mock turtleneck sweater, which made her selection of the green cowboy boots all the more bewildering.

"It's Sophie, right?" she asked in her soprano-pitched voice. "Not Sophia?"

"I think the last person to refer to me as Sophia was the clerk who wrote up my birth certificate. How 'bout you? Do you always go by Tiffany?"

"Almost never. I prefer Tiff." She turned away from her evil potion long enough to give my legs a visual once-over. "This is great," she enthused. "First-timers usually make the mistake of shaving just days before they come in. It's nearly impossible to wax stubble, but I see you haven't shaved in quite a long time."

"I wanted to make sure you really had something to grab onto." The truth was that I had stopped shaving my legs around the same time I had stopped having sex, which was just over two months ago when Anatoly and I split. Of course, I had bought a new razor so I'd be prepared for the next man who entered my life. I had even bought a package of condoms, but so far I hadn't met anyone interesting enough to test them out on.

Tiff came up and examined my face. "I can see it's been a while since you've done your brows, too."

"Well, I guess it depends on what qualifies as doing brows. I tweeze them."

"Yourself?" Tiff asked. From her expression you would have thought that I had just told her that I did my own Pap smears. "I can neaten them up if you like. You have such great brows. If you let me shape them a bit, it will really bring out your eyes."

"I'm kind of on a budget," I fibbed.

"I won't charge you for it. Consider it a free gift with purchase for first-time clients."

She turned back to the wax as if the issue had been decided. She was going to put wax on my face. My face! That was so not okay with me!

"We'll start with the legs, all right?" she asked.

I rolled my eyes skyward and swallowed the rising bile. I had been threatened by murderers on more than one occasion, so why was I so terrified of a friendly esthetician? But I knew the answer. My last college roommate had gotten her upper lip waxed shortly after she had begun using Retin-A for acne, and the combination of the two beauty treatments had cost her a few layers of skin and given me a phobia to last a lifetime.

Tiff freed what looked like an oversize Popsicle stick from its plastic wrapper and dipped it in the wax. *Okay, I just need to remember why I'm here: to solve a case. I can do this.* "I'm so glad the receptionist was able to fit me in so quickly. I really needed to treat myself to a day of pampering."

"Have things been stressful lately?" Tiff asked innocently as she layered the warm wax onto my leg.

"That's an understatement. My older…*holy fuck that hurt!*"

Tiff smiled benignly. "The first time's always the worst. Just relax, breathe and try to think about something else. What was it you were just about to tell me?" she asked as she spread more globs of wax onto my skin.

"What? Oh, right, I was about to say that I just recently lost my older sister." Leah was my only sister and she was two years younger. The only time I had ever lost her was at one of Nordstrom's half-yearly sales.

"You mean she passed away?" Tiff asked, briefly looking up from her task. "I'm so sorry! When did it happen?"

"A few months ago, but I don't think it has really sunk in yet. We weren't that close, but you know...Susie was still my sister." Susie? Was that really the best name I could come up with? The pain must have been hampering my creativity.

"I know exactly what you mean," Tiff said sadly as she carefully applied more wax with the Popsicle stick of pain. "I lost a brother not too long ago."

"You're kidding! What hap—*oh my God!* Where the hell did you learn to do this? Abu Ghraib?"

Tiff laughed politely and began to apply more wax.

I swallowed hard and tried to keep my mind on my objective. "I was just about to ask you what happened to your brother."

Tiffany hesitated. "He was sort of in an accident."

"That's terrible! Susie's death wasn't exactly an accident, although I think she was trying to make it look like one."

A little gasp escaped Tiff's lips. "You mean she committed suicide?"

I nodded, and then gritted my teeth as the next strip of hair came off. At the moment suicide didn't seem like such a bad idea.

"How'd she do it?" Tiff asked softly.

"Drove her car off a cliff. It was awful, no one in the family saw it coming."

"Yeah, I get that…no one saw it coming with my brother, either."

"But his was a real accident, right?" I prodded.

"Not exactly." Tiffany's shoulders slumped and her attention dropped from my legs to the ground. "Not at all. Peter threw himself out a fifteenth-story window. He wanted to die."

I felt a pang of guilt that rivaled the physical pain that was currently being inflicted on me. Tiffany was clearly still very upset about the loss of her brother, and why wouldn't she be? He had died less than two months ago. And here I was prying information out of her with false claims of empathy. I was a truly dreadful person.

On the other hand, Tiff's brother wasn't the only person who was dead. And unlike Peter, Eugene hadn't wanted to cut *his* life short. If Tiff had information that could lead to the arrest of the responsible party, then I owed it to Melanie to get it.

"Losing a sibling to violence, even when it's self-inflicted, is just so incredibly tragic," I said carefully. "The weird thing is that in Susie's case no one even knew she was depressed. What about Peter, did he show any signs at all?"

Tiff sighed and removed the last bit of skin…er…hair from my right leg and then moved to my left. "I've gone over the conversations we had during the months before his death a thousand times," she said. "There was nothing abnormal about them…well, at least they weren't abnormal for him."

"What do you mean?"

"Peter was *different*." She emphasized the last word and then laughed self-consciously. "I'm making it sound like he was some kind of weirdo, but that's not what I mean. He was just kind of a loner. He didn't have many friends and the ones he had were kind of…well, *geeky* would be a good word for them. He was smart, but he didn't have a lot of direction and he never liked school, although he did like to take part in the school sporting events."

"He was an athlete?"

Tiff shook her head and applied more wax. "A mascot. He was the school cougar in high school and the bear when he went to Berkeley. He took it really seriously, too. He used to go to other schools' games just so he could see what stunts the other mascots were pulling. I figured he must have had some kind of secret urge to do theater, but he would never agree to audition for anything or even take a drama class. I suppose it's less humiliating to act like a goof when you have a big hairy mask over your head."

I didn't say anything. I couldn't imagine anything more humiliating than dressing up like a giant jacked-up circus animal.

"He never even had a girlfriend," she continued. "I'm not even sure if he ever wanted one."

"Maybe he was gay."

"You know, I asked him about that. I would have been okay with it and I think my parents would have been fine with it, too. We're all very liberal about that kind of stuff. But he told me he wasn't, and I'm pretty sure he was being honest."

"It doesn't sound like he had any reason to lie."

"Exactly. So I just assumed that he didn't have a very strong sex drive." Tiff yanked out a few more hairs and then started vigorously rubbing some mercifully cool lotion into my calves and thighs. "Is it weird for me to be talking about my brother's sex drive?"

"No. It just sounds like you knew your brother."

"I wouldn't go that far." Tiff walked to the end of the table that was supporting my head, pulled out a large magnifying glass and studied my forehead with a look of earnest concentration.

"Don't tell me, you've discovered a new bacteria currently unknown to science."

"What? No, no, I was just trying to figure out how to go about this. I don't want to make your brows too perfect, it would detract from them. I think I'm just going to shape them a little and emphasize their natural arch. Is that okay?"

"Yeah, sure, it's fine. What do you mean you 'wouldn't go that far'?" I asked, bringing the conversation back to a subject that was moderately less terrifying. "You don't think you knew your brother very well?" I saw her wince at my question so I quickly added, "I only ask because Susie was always a mystery to me. I loved her dearly but I never could figure out what made her tick."

"See, I totally relate to that," Tiff said as she applied the wax to the bridge of my nose. *God help me!* "I'm not sure *anyone* really knew Peter. It wasn't that he completely shut me out, but he never fully let me in, either. There was always a little part of himself that he wouldn't share with anyone, but what that part could have been is beyond me."

"That's exactly how it was with—*oh my frigging God!*—Susie." I blinked back the tears of pain. "Do I still have skin?"

Tiff laughed gently. Bitch thought I was joking! "Maybe what Peter was hiding *was* depression," she whispered as she continued to peel off my face. "Isn't lack of a sex drive or desire for companionship a sign of depression? I guess what bothers me the most is that I'll never know the answer to those questions."

I released the breath I'd been holding as she put down the wax applicator and pulled out a pair of tweezers. *That* I could handle. "Susie didn't leave a note," I said. "What about Peter?"

Tiffany smiled, but it was tremulous. "It was addressed to my parents and me. They found it on Peter's desk. He said he was sorry. He asked that we try to remember his good qualities and not to dwell on the things about him that we might find disturbing."

I thought about that for a second. A few years ago I had helped prove that a movie producer who had supposedly committed suicide had actually been murdered. He, too, had left a note, but his note was addressed to his estranged wife. He had written that he couldn't live without her. Although the police had initially assumed that message supported the theory that the producer's death had been a suicide, the note had turned out to be nothing more than a plea for reconciliation. But Peter's note sounded different. From Tiff's description he hadn't spouted clichés like "I can't live without you," which everybody says and nobody means. He was asking to be remembered in a positive light. I couldn't imagine anyone writing something like that unless they planned on imminently dying, and since most people don't have the time to write a farewell note before being pushed out a window, it seemed logical to assume that he really had jumped.

"What was it about him that you and your family might find disturbing?"

"Beats me." Tiff tweezed a brow growing in a place where brows were never meant to grow.

"I'll never know why Susie did what she did, but I can't

stop torturing myself about it," I said. "I keep trying to pinpoint what exactly was so awful about Susie's life that made her feel like she needed to end it. The only thing I can come up with is her job. She worked for a charity foundation, so you would have thought that her work environment would have been all warm and peaceful, but instead it was absolutely toxic. There was all this backstabbing among the employees, then Susie had to make everything a thousand times worse by sleeping with her married boss. That affair ended a little while back, but there's part of me that will always wonder if that relationship wasn't partially responsible for breaking her spirit, you know what I mean?"

"All too well." Tiff put the tweezers down and rubbed her eyes as if she were tired, but I'm fairly sure that what she was really doing was wiping away a tear.

I had made her cry. Wonderful. I was like an undercover Barbara Walters. I pushed aside my guilty conscience and forged ahead. "Did Peter like his work?"

Tiff hesitated. "Peter actually had two jobs. He worked the ticket counter of American Airlines, which he hated, but it paid okay and it allowed him to travel a lot. His other job was at a political campaign headquarters, which he loved, although I'll never understand why. He was managing phone campaigns for seven dollars an hour." Tiff scrunched up her face as a way of expressing exactly how she felt about that. "He was a peon at both places. I know that would have bothered a lot of people, but not Peter. He liked to keep a low profile, and he didn't deal with stress very well so he learned how to avoid it. I have a real hard time believing that he would have gotten himself involved in an office romance that had the potential of blowing up in his face." Tiffany held up a hand mirror to my face. "What do you think about your brows?"

"Oh, my God, Tiff! I mean, wow!" I didn't even know that brows *could* be gorgeous. *This* is why people suffered for beauty, so they could look like a Bond girl, one of the bad Bond girls, too. They were always sexier than their more innocent Bond-girl co-stars.

Tiff looked up at the clock. "I usually work until eight-thirty on Tuesdays, but the client that was coming in after you canceled earlier today, so now I have this hour-long window. I was going to use it to catch up on my reading, but the receptionist told me that you had originally wanted a facial. If you want, I can do it now."

"Seriously?" So I hadn't needed to get a waxing after all? I had gone through all that pain for nothing? *Not for nothing,* I reminded myself. *I now look like a badass Bond girl.* Still, I couldn't help but feel like I had been tricked into allowing myself to be tortured.

I watched as she gathered some products from the wall shelves, apparently taking my *seriously* as a *yes.* "You know, you said Peter didn't seem to have a lot of direction, but most people who work on political campaigns are pretty passionate about their causes."

"Peter just became politically active a few years ago," Tiff noted. She started rubbing my skin with something that looked like crystallized snow and felt like cool grains of sand. "He became fanatical about certain issues, although I can't say that he was very loyal to either of the two major parties."

"Really? What was he registered as?"

"I think he registered as an independent. I never once

heard him state his position on taxes or anything like that, but he loved animals. I think he was part of some kind of environmental group, like the humane society or something. He was always going to these conventions that he said were for animal lovers. He was also a big advocate for the right to privacy and he abhorred the idea of 'big government.'"

"That sounds kind of Republican."

"Not really," Tiff said as she gently stroked my face with a damp cloth. "I'm not all that political, but it seems to me that when the Republicans say they don't want big government what they mean is that they don't want the government interfering with commerce, but they're totally supportive of laws that require citizens to abide by a certain moral code. Like if the government says that gays can't marry and women can't have abortions…well, isn't that big government? See, that's the stuff that set Peter off. He thought the government should stay out of people's personal lives. He was also pretty passionate about curtailing discrimination as much as possible. The candidate he worked for once proposed this ridiculous plan that would make it illegal to discriminate against ugly people. It was so stupid. Who in their right mind would humiliate themselves by filing a complaint claiming that their employer was being mean to them because they had too many blackheads? But Peter thought the whole plan was great. Save the Gays and the Ugly People, that was his motto."

"You already told me he wasn't gay, but was he…um…?" How could I phrase this delicately?

"Ugly?" Tiff finished for me. "No, not gorgeous, but not ugly. He had this great smile, kind of crooked and impossibly sweet, and he had the rosiest cheeks you've ever seen.

People used to ask him if he was wearing blush." She started to laugh but it morphed into a strangled sob. She turned away from me and faced the wall. "I haven't talked about this with anyone. My family is far away and my friends…" Her voice trailed off and she shrugged while still facing away from me. "You know how it is. People don't know what to say to someone who's lost a loved one to suicide. It's like they don't know if they should comfort you or distract you or what. It never occurs to anyone that all you really need is someone to listen." She turned back around. "I'm sorry, I'm used to playing therapist to my clients, but this is the first time a client has played therapist to me. I think I owe you a big discount."

"Don't be ridiculous," I said softly. "I know what it's like to lose someone you love. I was a total daddy's girl, and when my father died my college English professor took me under her wing. She was there for me when no one else really was, so the way I see it this is just my way of taking care of a karmic obligation."

"What about when you lost Susie?" Tiff asked. "Was anyone there for you then?"

Shit, for a moment there I had totally forgotten about Susie. "Sort of," I hedged. "It helps to hear you talk about your brother, it makes me feel less alone." God, I was going to have so much to atone for on Yom Kippur.

Tiff grabbed a Kleenex from a box sitting on the shelf behind her and dabbed at her nose. "Peter and I weren't even that close, but I miss him. I miss him so much."

"Family's like that," I said. "We never want to deal with them until they're no longer around to deal with."

"So true." Tiff tossed the tissue in the garbage and set back to work on my face. I waited until I thought she was composed before continuing my interrogation.

"So you can't think of anything that might have pushed Peter over the edge." I was getting desperate. Pretty soon my appointment would be over and Tiff had given me nothing useful—apart from the killer eyebrows.

"As far as I know Peter was doing fine. In some ways he was the healthiest one in the family. He was the only one of us who was able to conquer his fear of flying."

"Yeah? Was Peter afraid of flying when he got the job at American?"

"Totally. It was initially my mom's phobia, but with a little effort she was able to instill her fear in her children. As far as I'm concerned, humans are land animals and we need to stay true to our nature."

I flashed Tiff what I hoped was an understanding smile. In the past year and a half two people had tried to kill me and four people I knew (albeit casually) had been killed. As far as I was concerned, human nature was something that could use improvement. "So as far as you know there was no straw that broke the camel's back."

"Not that I'm aware of," she confirmed. "But you have to remember, I didn't even know there was a camel…the camel's supposed to represent his depression, right?"

"Sure, why not." I suppressed a heavy sigh as Tiff began to spread some thick green gunk all over my face. This interview was going nowhere. If there was a link between Peter's death and Eugene's it was likely to remain a mystery forever.

I let the subject of Peter and the fictitious Susie drop.

Instead we chatted about other important issues, like if it was really true that French women don't get fat or if Halle Berry really used the drugstore cosmetics she endorsed. Somewhere along the line Tiff told me that she needed to lose twenty pounds and I resisted the urge to tell her that the bulk of her figure problems could be solved with a straight-cut pant and support bra. But fashion faux pas aside, I found myself really liking Tiff. She was open, unpretentious and just a fun person to hang with. I briefly reversed that opinion when I looked in the mirror after my facial, but Tiff assured me that the splotchy red face she had given me would transform into a perfect complexion by the next morning.

I was about to leave when it occurred to me that there was one more question I should ask. "I probably shouldn't bring our siblings up again, but Susie was a big traveler, too, and I was just wondering if they went to any of the same places."

Tiff wrinkled her pert little nose. "What if they did? Why would it matter now?"

"It wouldn't—it just seems like Susie and Peter had a lot in common, and I just wanted to know if that extended to their preference in vacation destinations."

By her expression it was clear that Tiff still didn't understand my reasons for wanting to know this (which is something the two of us had in common), but she took a stab at answering. "Let's see," she said. "He's been to Denver, Orlando, Portland, Des Moines—"

"Des Moines?" I repeated. "He took a vacation to Des Moines, Iowa?"

"I've never been," Tiff admitted, "but he said that there's some cool stuff there. Like there's the Iowa Hall of Pride, which he said was kind of neat, and he couldn't say enough about this shop called Gung Fu Tea. Peter was a big tea drinker."

"You're serious? He flew halfway across the country for tea?"

Tiff laughed. "What can I say, he had his eccentricities. Actually, I think there might have been those humane society gatherings in some of those places. His next trip was supposed to be to Eureka."

"Eureka, huh? That's um…sounds like it would have been fun." The only way I would vacation in Eureka was if my only other option was Des Moines. I grabbed my purse off the matte silver hook on the wall. "Thank you so much for everything, Tiff. I'll definitely make another appointment with you."

"Great. You know, Sophie, I'm really glad we met. It's so rare to talk to someone who's coming from the same place as I am."

"The hand of fate I guess." I carefully avoided her eyes.

"Maybe we could go out sometime, for lunch or something. We could just hang out and talk."

I actually would have loved to add Tiff to my list of friends, but the lies I had told her made that impossible. Ironically that reality necessitated another lie, which I forced myself to say. "Sure, I'll give you a call and we'll set it up."

Tiff beamed, making me feel a thousand times worse. "Great! Maybe we can go to someplace nice. I so rarely get to treat myself to a good meal."

"Sounds great," I said with as much mock enthusiasm as I could muster. I went out to the front desk and decided to deal with my guilt in the American way: I left her a huge tip.

Intellectuals have an excellent grasp of the abstract and intangible. If I have questions about God and mysticism, I talk to them. But if I want a clear and simple solution to an everyday problem, I seek advice from the uncomplicated folks at the church.

—*C'est La Mort*

I DON'T KNOW WHAT OTHER PEOPLE LOOK LIKE RIGHT AFTER GETTING A facial but I looked like the "before" picture on a makeover show. A night on the town was out of the question. There were only two guys I felt comfortable enough to be with when I looked this bad, Mr. Katz and Hitchcock. Mr. Katz was waiting for me at home, but I was going to have to make a detour to get my hands on my buddy Alfred.

I drove over to the Inner Sunset and parked my car a mere block and a half away from Le Video. If there was a cult flick, documentary or silent movie you wanted to see you could always count on Le Video to have it in stock. I found the Hitchcock shelf among the other dusty displays and ran my fingers lightly over the bindings. Was I in a black-and-white mood or was I craving some color…

"Sophie?"

I turned to see Mary Ann standing behind me. Why is it that when you don't want to be seen you run into everyone you know? Is that just God's way of being funny?

Mary Ann flashed me a stunning smile as a way of greeting. "What are you doing here?"

"Hitchcock," I said, gesturing to a *Rear Window* VHS. "I'm a little surprised to see you here. You're usually a Block-buster girl."

"This is the second time in my life I've been here," Mary Ann admitted, "but I've been spending a lot of time with Rick lately and he's really into old movies. His favorite actor is Errol Flynn, and I wanted to see one of his movies."

"So you figured you'd go to the only video store in the city that you knew *would* have it," I said.

"Exactly." Mary Ann and I both looked down at her right hand, which was clutching a copy of *The Adventures of Robin Hood*. "Do you think this is a good choice?"

"It's supposed to be one of his best, but since I've never actually seen it I can't vouch for it."

"You want to watch it with me tonight?"

"No, I want to watch Hitchcock tonight. I want to see something that is more frightening than my face."

Mary Ann bit her lower lip. "I was going to ask but I didn't want to be rude…did you get a facial?"

"It's that noticeable?"

"You kind of look like you've been exfoliated and steamed. And your brows look fantastic. Who'd you go to?"

"I saw this girl named Tiff who works at Mojo."

Mary Ann nodded vigorously. "Some of the girls I work with go to Mojo. They say it's great." Mary Ann looked down at her video again. "If you watch this movie with me, then I'll watch a Hitchcock movie with you."

I was about to say no but then quickly reconsidered. My initial goal had been to hide my face from anyone who would recognize me, but that hadn't worked out, so why not take Mary Ann up on her offer? I liked Errol Flynn in the few movies of his that I had seen, and I felt that the reputation he'd had as a hot-tempered, sex-crazed alcoholic bonded us in an abstract kind of way. I pulled out *The Man Who Knew Too Much* and tucked it under my arm. "Your place or mine?"

Less than a half hour later we were in Mary Ann's large studio apartment on Lake Street getting ready for our impromptu movie night. Dena, Mary Ann and I had a "movie night" tradition. Every Monday the three of us would get together at my place and watch a video. But we had let that lapse over the past several months, and besides, this was Tuesday night and Dena wasn't there. I was actually a lot closer to Dena than Mary Ann, partly because Dena and I were in the same grade together in high school and Mary Ann was a full two years behind, which at that time made her barely fit to speak to. But there was more to it than that. If I was asked to describe Dena to a stranger, lots of words would leap to mind: *strong, outspoken, fun, abrasive, dynamic, loyal, intelligent, entrepreneurial, nymphomaniac*—I could go on and on. But if someone were to ask me to describe Mary Ann, only one word would come to my lips—*sweet*. That single word seemed to sum up all of her qualities from her heart-shaped mouth to her generous nature. And it was Mary Ann's simplicity that kept me from seeking out her company as frequently as I sought out the company of her cousin.

Mary Ann was taking a moment to water the plants while I went through her cupboard looking for microwave popcorn. I found one box, Orville Redenbacher's Sweet 'n Buttery. How Mary Ann remained a size two was beyond me.

"I don't suppose you have any vodka on hand?" I asked. I have found that after one cocktail, calories became much less of an issue for me.

"No vodka," Mary Ann said distractedly as she fed her ficus a few drops of plant food. "But I think I might have a baby bottle of wine in the cupboard.

"What's a baby bottle of wine—oh wait, do you mean this?" I pulled out a mini bottle of white zin produced by a winery that I was fairly sure I never wanted to become familiar with. Most of the label was covered up by another, makeshift label that read "Elaine and Dave's Wedding 1994."

"That's it," Mary Ann said. "You can have it if you want it."

"I don't." I put it back and reached for the popcorn. I'd rather feel guilty than get drunk on cheap wine that had aged too long.

"So what made you decide to get a facial and an eyebrow wax?" Mary Ann asked as she put the plant food away under the sink.

"Long boring story. Why don't I just pop this and you can put the movie on."

"Please, Sophie? I'm so curious."

"Fine," I said as I placed a bag in the microwave. "That Tiff girl who worked on me? Well, she's the sister of the guy who killed himself in Brooke's headquarters."

"Peter Strauss? Rick was telling me about him the other day."

My eyes widened. "Really? What did he say?"

"He said…" Mary Ann looked down at her slender hands and her curls hid her face. "He said that his death was the first of a lot of negative news stories about Anne and her campaign staff. Rick didn't think that was fair because, well, none of us really knows why Peter Strauss did what he did, but it probably didn't have anything to do with his politics. Rick thinks that the media's attempts to somehow link his death with the congressional campaign is sort of disrespectful and ghoulish…that's the word he used. He said the press was kind of 'ghoulish.'"

"I can see his point," I said, not at all sure that I did. I went on to recount everything Tiff had told me, right down to the details of his vacation destinations.

"He went to Iowa?" Mary Ann asked with unexpected enthusiasm. "Rick *loves* Iowa. He says it's beautiful in the wintertime."

"Why was Rick in Iowa?"

"There was some political convention or something that Fitzgerald needed to attend."

"The caucus?"

Mary Ann looked at me blankly.

"The caucus is…you know what? It doesn't matter. So Fitzgerald took Rick to Iowa, huh?"

"Mmm-hmm." Mary Ann was now picking at her cuticles. She *never* picked at her cuticles.

"Mary Ann, are you keeping something from me?"

"Not really." Mary Ann still wasn't looking at me. "It's just that it was during their trip to Iowa that Rick found out that he and Fitzgerald didn't agree on as much as he used to think they did, and, well, Rick told me a bunch of really personal stuff that I really can't talk about it. I promised I wouldn't."

I hesitated a full minute before articulating the horrible thought that was forming inside my head. "Mary Ann," I said slowly, "is it possible that Rick had something to do with what happened to Peter?"

"No!" Mary Ann exclaimed, making eye contact for the first time since we got on the subject of her new man. "That's not what I meant at all!"

"Then tell me what you do mean." I guided her to the couch and sat down next to her. "Come on, since when have we ever kept secrets from each another?" That last question was a gamble, because if Mary Ann stopped to think about it she would recall that there had been several occasions when Dena and I had kept things from her. The secrets never lasted very long; we all talked too much to be discreet for any length of time.

Mary Ann scooted farther back onto the sofa and pulled her knees to her chest. "He's beginning to question whether or not it was a good idea to take this job with Fitzgerald. This isn't Rick's first campaign, but he thinks that Republicans are kind of different now than when he started. Rick says that in a few years he might register as a liberator."

"A liberator? Wait, do you mean Libertarian?"

"Yes, that's it." Mary Ann nodded enthusiastically. "But I guess the big problem right now is that Rick thinks that Fitzgerald is trying to become one of the new different Republicans, but that in his heart that's not who he is. He thinks Fitzgerald's kind of confused."

"How is he confused?" I asked, feeling a little befuddled myself. I would have thought that the "new different Republicans" would have been the Rick Santorums of the world: religious, conservative and morally righteous, and that "old school" would have been more like Nixon and the Rockefellers. But if that was the case, then Fitzgerald wouldn't have to *try* to be new and different. You didn't get more morally righteous than Fitzgerald. So who were these new different Republicans that Rick was talking about?

Mary Ann shrugged. "It's just Rick's opinion. He thinks Fitzgerald isn't as traditional as he tells everybody. He thinks he's just too afraid of what people will think if they find out that he's open-minded."

"Fitzgerald's open-minded?" I asked skeptically.

"Again, it's just what Rick thinks. Sophie, he would kill me if he knew I told you all this. Fitzgerald is his boss and he's totally loyal to him. Rick says that if Fitzgerald gets elected he could be a great friend to have, even if Rick does do the whole liberation thing."

"I won't tell a soul. And it's *Libertarian*."

"Libertarian, you just told me that, too. I'm so stupid sometimes."

I rolled my eyes again and reached for the DVD/VHS remote. "Come on, of course you're not stupid."

"Please, Sophie," Mary Ann said in a voice barely above a whisper, "I never lie to you."

I froze, seriously disturbed by the direction this conversation was going. "Mary Ann…"

"No, I'm serious. I am so tired of people lying to me just to make me feel better about myself. I know I'm not smart."

"Where is this coming from?"

"Did you read last month's *7x7?*"

"Are you kidding? Marcus bought me eight copies." *7x7* is a San Francisco magazine. Last month they'd named Marcus as one of the Bay Area's top ten hairstylists.

"When I saw what they said about Marcus I was totally happy for him," Mary Ann said wistfully. "He really deserves to be recognized for his talent."

"Marcus would agree with you on that."

"I know this is awful," Mary Ann continued, "but I felt a little jealous. You're a bestselling author, Dena owns her own business and now Marcus has been named one of the best hairstylists around. What am I? Just a makeup artist at Lancôme who had to struggle just to graduate high school with a 2.8."

I dropped the remote and took a deep breath. "Mary Ann, I lie to a lot of people but never to you, Dena or Marcus. So you're just going to have to trust me when I tell you that you're not stupid. Stupid is investigating a murder when you're not even an investigator. Stupid is going out of your way to argue with a former boyfriend you're trying to forget about. Believe me, Mary Ann, I'm an expert when it comes to being stupid and you've never even come close."

Mary Ann smiled weakly. "Now you sound like Rick."

"You had *this* conversation with Rick?" Mary Ann was one of those people who always assumed that her problems weren't important enough to burden others with. The heart-to-heart we were having was a little out of character, but the very idea that she had talked about this with someone she had known for less than a decade was downright shocking.

"Sort of. He's just so complimentary, telling me how thoughtful I am and what incredible people skills I have. He makes me feel important."

"You are important."

Mary Ann shrugged but for once she didn't protest. "I tried telling Rick that I'm not as great as he thinks I am but he won't hear of it. He says my humility just proves that he's right about me."

"I think I like Rick."

"You and me both," Mary Ann said with a grin. "Okay, enough about me, what's bothering you these days?"

"You mean other than the fact that my mentor's husband was shot to death thirty seconds after I left his company and that I have now put myself in the position of having to spend an exorbitant amount of time with corrupt, obnoxious and possibly murderous politicians, not to mention my ex-lover whom I'm trying really hard to hate?"

Mary Ann winced. "That was another one of my dumb questions, huh?"

"No, no," I said quickly. "There actually is something else. I was talking to Tiff about her brother and for some weird reason I started thinking about my dad."

"You started thinking about your *dad*," Mary Ann asked carefully, "or about how hard it was to lose him?"

Maybe there was more to Mary Ann than sweetness. She was by far the most perceptive airhead I had ever met.

"About losing him," I admitted. "Jeez, how long has it been…I'm thirty-one now so I guess it was twelve years ago. God, I'm getting old!"

Mary Ann smiled sympathetically. "It's not how old you are that matters. It's how much Botox you get."

I laughed and got up to retrieve the now-popped popcorn before rejoining her on the couch. "Do you remember how my dad and I used to fight?"

"You two were always arguing about something and it was always something kind of…weird."

"Yeah," I agreed. "Like who was a better physicist, Albert Einstein or Stephen Hawking. I still think Hawking wins the prize."

"Really weird stuff," Mary Ann muttered, grabbing a handful of popcorn.

"I think we just liked debating, but the problem was we both really liked to win, too. I can't tell you how many times we'd get into a major blowup over some subject that neither of us really cared about. We once went an entire week without speaking to each other because he insisted Shakespeare didn't write his own plays and I refused to accept that. I mean really, who cares who wrote *Hamlet* as long as I don't have to watch Ethan Hawke massacre the play on screen?"

Mary Ann nodded and kicked off her shoes. "I always felt bad about not being there for you when your dad had his heart attack."

I shrugged. "You were in L.A. trying to make it big as a makeup artist to the stars. It wasn't your fault that you weren't here."

"But you were alone! Dena was off at UC Irvine and you

didn't even know Marcus yet. Of course, you had other friends, but you never seemed all that close to them."

"I wasn't," I admitted. "And my mother and Leah were predictably a mess. I tried to be strong for them, but I think I just made things worse when I…well when I made the biggest mistake of my life."

"You're talking about Scott now, right?"

I winced. I hadn't been kidding when I said I was an expert when it came to being stupid. What kind of woman runs off to Vegas to elope with her womanizing boyfriend just so she could avoid dealing with her grief? Couldn't I have done something a little more healthy, like get a therapist or start abusing illegal narcotics? I'm fairly sure a heroin addiction would have cost me less money than my ex-husband and I *know* it would have been easier to kick.

"I didn't know Scott very well," Mary Ann said carefully, "but he didn't seem like the kind of guy who would be good at doing things like…well, like listening."

"He was awful at listening. He was awful at a lot of things—academics, fiscal responsibility, sobriety, fidelity—but he *was* good at making mixed drinks. I think I married him for his lemon drops…or maybe I married him because I drank too *many* of his lemon drops."

Mary Ann eyed me suspiciously. "Were you really that drunk when you got married?"

"No, my blood-alcohol level wasn't high enough to account for my decision to enter into unholy matrimony, although I do blame it for our choice in officiants."

Mary Ann giggled. "I forgot about the female Elvis impersonator. I kind of wish I had been there to see that."

"She actually looked a lot like the male Elvis impersonators wandering around Vegas, only she was a little more butch."

"So what was the real reason you married Scott? I always wanted to know but I was afraid that if I asked it would sound like I didn't approve or something."

I leaned my head back against the sofa and pondered her question. I had been divorced for almost ten years now and I still wasn't a hundred percent sure why I had specifically chosen to marry Scott. Maybe it had been the fact that making cocktails was just a small part of a greater talent that Scott rightfully laid claim to. That talent was for escapism. Scott knew how to distract a girl. Sometimes it was with a spontaneous vacation, a wild party or an even wilder lovemaking session. Regardless, you could always count on him to support you in your quest to avoid dealing with anything that was too unpleasant or too real. On the other hand, maybe I had just married him because he was there and willing.

"I don't know why I married him," I admitted. "I just know that it didn't help me deal with the loss of my dad."

"How did you end up coping with that? You would never talk to me about it."

"That's another long story," I said with a laugh. "As you know, I was attending USF, and while I was doing pretty well in all my courses, I was the absolute *star* of my creative-writing class, if I do say so myself. But after dad died, my work began to suffer. Eventually my professor asked me to stay after class. I thought she was going to ream me for handing in a paper a day late, but instead she just sat me down and looked at me for what felt like forever. Finally she just said 'Tell me.' And just like that I fell apart. I was crying and talking all at the same time, which probably made it difficult to understand what I was saying, but she never once stopped me to ask for a clarification. She just passed me the Kleenex and listened."

"Wow, your professor must have been an incredible person. Is she still teaching at USF?"

I shook my head. "I'm talking about Melanie Allen... now O'Reilly."

"And now you're helping her!" Mary Ann exclaimed. "That is so neat!"

I studied a brown color variance on Mary Ann's hardwood floor.

"Sophie? It is neat, isn't it?"

I remained silent. I hadn't really thought about that moment for a very long time, but now I could see it unfold in my mind's eye as clearly as I could see the popcorn I was now shoving into my mouth. There I was, sitting in Melanie's office shedding enough tears to fill one of the Great Lakes and she was just nodding and listening. And then I had stopped crying and I let my inner bitch slip out and my bitch was *pissed*.

"I want to make someone pay for my father's death," I had hissed. "If only there was a doctor who screwed up, or an ambulance that didn't arrive in time, or...or...a company that was knowingly distributing products that increased people's chances of having a heart attack. I just want a villain that I can rip apart."

Melanie had sat back in her chair and regarded me thoughtfully. "How would you go about ripping apart this villain?"

"I'd kill him," I said without hesitation. "But not before

making him suffer in the most horrible ways imaginable, and I'd be sure that the whole world knew what an asshole he was. Hell, maybe I wouldn't even have to kill him. By the time I was done mentally and physically tormenting him he'd probably want to take his own life!"

What I was saying was more than a little dark and incredibly insane. That's why I hadn't voiced those thoughts before. I didn't want people referring to me as "that dark crazy chick." Yet there I was confessing my most evil and whacked fantasies to a woman who wore a gold crucifix and had a silver Christian fish attached to the back of her car. I reluctantly made eye contact with her, expecting to see evidence of her horror and disapproval, but instead she just looked thoughtful. Eventually she took a deep breath and said the most shocking thing imaginable: "Do it."

"Excuse me?" I had asked.

"Destroy a villain. Get your revenge." She reached into her desk drawer and pulled out a three-and-a-half-inch floppy and handed it over. "You're a writer, Sophie, so write it up. Create a bad guy. Make him responsible for whatever you want him to be responsible for and then make him pay the way you see fit. It's your story and no one is going to be grading it, so you can make up any rules you want. You're the one in control of this."

"You want me to make up a fictional character for the sole purpose of killing him?"

"If you think he should pay for his crimes with his life, then yes. But be sure to make it into a story. Any story that has a good villain deserves a good hero…or heroine." She gave me a meaningful look. "Be sure that you thoroughly develop your protagonist. Give readers a reason to root for her. She doesn't have to be perfect, just human. If she's troubled, then provide insight into what those troubles are and how they originated. Explain the source of her anger and her motivations for going after the villain. That part's important, Sophie," Melanie had said, her tone getting sharper, underscoring her point. "Readers need to understand a protagonist's motivations even if the protagonist herself doesn't."

I had gone home that day armed with the floppy disk, and for the first time since my father's death I had turned down Scott's offers of distraction. Instead, I had sat down at my computer and started typing. I created Alice Wright, a journalism major with an enormous amount of emotional baggage who was investigating her father's homicide. The killer was a horrible man, although I had stopped short of making him pure evil. I didn't want this to be a cartoon villain; this story was too important for one-dimensional characters.

Then a funny thing happened. While creating my fictional world I found less desire to escape the real world I lived in. I don't want to say that I became more centered (that sounds a bit too Taoist for me), but I did feel calmer and I was ready to cope with my life—even if Dad was no longer a part of it. Every week or so I would take my newly written chapters to Melanie, who offered me advice and constructive criticism, and after two years of writing and rewriting I had finished my first novel. I also had a divorce decree, so there were two milestones to celebrate.

I never did try to get the Alice Wright book published. I

couldn't give some agent or editor the opportunity to reject something of mine so deeply personal. Instead I stashed the disk in a safety deposit box and spent the next year writing yet another book. It was about an investigative journalist named Alicia Bright. In that book Alicia had to track down this lovable but slightly deranged murderess who took pleasure in castrating and killing bartenders who specialized in making lemon drops.

If I hadn't had Melanie to talk to back then I would have exploded. Now Melanie was asking me to save her, and how had I handled her request? I had made it about me and my feelings regarding Anatoly. I bit into my lower lip and replayed Melanie's words one more time in my head. "Readers need to understand a protagonist's motivations even if the protagonist herself doesn't."

I was the protagonist in my own life story and I had totally misread my motivations, or rather I had been right the first time around. This wasn't just about besting Anatoly (that was just a really great bonus). The truth was that I wouldn't be doing any of this if a big part of me didn't feel compelled to do everything in my power to put Melanie's mind at ease. If *that* was the goal, then I needed to get past the pettiness and start working with Anatoly a little better, even if he wasn't working well with me. I would call him tomorrow and tell him about my meeting with Tiff and then we would find out who had killed Melanie's husband.

"Sophie? Are you okay?"

I pulled myself out of my contemplation and forced a smile. "I'm fine. Let's just start this movie before all the popcorn's gone."

10

In the Andes there's an entire order of monks who have taken a vow of silence. They spend their days in peaceful and cooperative coexistence. If nothing else, this proves that communication is overrated.
—*C'est La Mort*

WHEN I LEFT MARY ANN'S IT WAS NEARING ELEVEN O'CLOCK, AND IT WASN'T until I was sitting at a stoplight on Geary that I remembered I had turned off my cell phone while being pampered by Tiff and had neglected to turn it back on. I corrected the problem and cursed under my breath when I noted that I had two missed calls, both from Melanie. I tapped the button for voice mail and put my phone on loudspeaker.

"Sophie, it's Melanie. Could you call me when you have a moment? I think it just hit me that Eugene's not coming back. I'm alone and…he's not coming back. You're already doing so much for me and I have no right to burden you with more, but I need to talk to someone...well, if you aren't too busy could you call? I'll try your home number."

Then the second message: "I just tried your home and you're not there. I didn't leave a message." Then a strangled sob. "I know this is simply a panic attack. But I'm alone, Sophie. I'm sixty years old and I've lost the only man who ever loved me. I loved him, too, but I treated him so appallingly. I'll be all right, but I do need someone to talk me through this. Call me...*please*."

Shit. My phone told me she had placed that call five hours ago. I had just promised myself that I was going to be there for Melanie, but when she had needed a shoulder, where had I been? At Mary Ann's, watching Errol Flynn redistribute wealth in Sherwood Forest. I punched in her number but only got the answering machine. Great, she had probably cried herself to sleep.

When I got home I changed into something more comfortable and then plopped down on my couch, Mr. Katz curled up next to me. "I really wish I had gotten that call earlier," I whispered to him. I checked the time again, eleven-twenty-five, way too late to call. I called, anyway.

"Hello, you've reached the O'Reilly residence. Please leave your message after the beep."

"Melanie, it's Sophie again. You're probably asleep right now, but if you're awake, could you pick up? I'm worried about you."

Nothing. I hung up the phone and stared at the wall. I had this vague feeling that something was wrong, and that it was more than just Melanie being upset about Eugene. But this feeling was based on nothing. Melanie probably *was* asleep. She might have even taken a sleeping pill, which is what I would have done in her position. I just needed to relax and call her tomorrow. I clicked on the television and flipped through the channels until I got to Comedy Central. Laughter and sleep is what I needed tonight. I could be a good friend tomorrow.

At exactly 8:00 a.m. the next morning the shrill ring of my phone jarred me out of a very nice dream involving both Johnny Depp and George Clooney. Without opening my eyes I fumbled for the phone and pressed it to my ear. "This had better be good."

"It's not good," Anatoly growled.

"You."

"Yes, me. When were you planning on telling me about your meeting with Tiff Strauss?"

"Right around the time you told me that Melanie had found a letter written by Peter Strauss to Eugene."

"I was going to tell you...right after my interview with Tiff."

"Uh-huh. Next you'll be trying to sell me the Brooklyn Bridge. And what's the deal with you calling me at 8:00 a.m.? Do I need to add passive-aggressive to your list of character flaws?"

"Passive-aggressive people try to upset those around them in subtle ways. I'm not trying to be subtle."

I hung up the phone.

Two seconds later it rang again. "I wasn't done," he snapped when I finally answered.

"I was." I hung up again.

The third time he called I let the answering machine pick up. "Sophie, I know you can hear me. Pick up the phone!"

I put a pillow over my head.

"If you don't pick up I'm going to come over, and this time I'm not going to pretend that you look good without your makeup."

I snatched up the receiver. "You used to tell me that I looked sexy in the morning!"

"You do, when you're naked. I don't suppose there's any chance of that now, is there?"

"I'm going to hang up again…."

"Don't. I talked to Tiff last night and we need to compare notes."

"I won't compare notes or anything else until I've had at least two cups of coffee. You know that."

"So we'll meet at Starbucks. I'll even buy the first round."

"Of coffee? Am I supposed to be impressed by that?"

"I'll meet you at the Starbucks on Polk in one hour," Anatoly said, ignoring my last comment.

"Make it three hours. I have to finish up with Johnny and George and I don't want to feel rushed."

"Johnny and George?"

"The men who were entertaining me when you called." Let him think I was having ménage à trois. That should be enough to screw up his morning.

"Are you talking about Johnny Depp and George Clooney?" Anatoly asked with a laugh. "Are you still dreaming about them?"

"Shut up. I'll see you at eleven." I slammed down the phone, squeezed my eyes shut and tried to reconjure the dream. Three seconds later my cell phone rang. I snatched it from my bedside where it had been charging without even bothering to check the number on the screen. "Why can't you just leave me alone!"

There was a moment of silence and then a very tiny, very wounded voice. "Are you mad at me?"

"Johnny," I breathed. Not Depp, the other, much less appealing Johnny. "No, I just thought you were somebody else."

"Nope, just me," he said with a little more self-assurance. "Is someone giving you a hard time? Is there anything I can help you with?"

"No, I've got it covered. Look, I don't mean to be rude, but it's still early for me. Could we talk later?"

"Sure, sure, but the thing is I thought you might want to talk to Maggie today."

"You got me an appointment?" That news was enough to get me into a sitting position. "Does she want to meet me in Pleasant Hill? When?"

"Actually, she can meet you in San Francisco. She and Rick are going to meet with Carl Pearson, you know, the guy who's been on all those news shows speaking out against stem-cell research. They want him to endorse Fitzgerald, and I guess he lives in Sausalito or something, so they're meeting in Frisco—"

"It's *San Francisco*," I said.

"That is so cute the way you defend the name of your city like that! I can just see you with your fists all clenched up and your nose wrinkled. Do you wrinkle your nose when you're mad? You seem like the kind of girl who would. You have an adorable nose, did you know that?"

I give up. "Johnny, when do I get to meet Maggie?"

"Rick wanted to take Maggie to Neiman's to meet Mary Ann. All he does is talk about her, 'Mary Ann this and Mary Ann that.' She met him after work for drinks the other day—Mary Ann, that is. I ran into them in this little wine bar. I hung out with them for a while but I kind of felt like a third wheel so I split. Besides, Rick was so absorbed with Mary Ann he barely noticed that I was there at all. The guy's seriously in love. So anyway, yesterday Maggie went up to Rick and said, 'Hey, when am I going to meet this Mary Ann person?' and Rick said, 'Well, why don't we meet her after our morning meeting with Carl Pearson?' and Maggie thought that was a great idea so…"

I pulled up my knees so that I could use them to support my head. This conversation was going to kill me. Seriously, if I had to listen to Johnny go on like this for another hour I was going to flat-out die.

Hey! Maybe Johnny killed Eugene! Surely someone capable of being this annoying was capable of all sorts of other sordid things. Maybe he killed him because…because Eugene wouldn't chat with him at the watercooler?

I was pretty good at convincing myself of things but that one was a stretch.

"…so they called Mary Ann and they're all going to have lunch together at the Rotunda. It's supposed to be just social and Maggie doesn't like to talk to media people when she's trying to be social, but if you just show up coincidentally, you know, to see Mary Ann or something, then I bet they'd invite you to eat with them. You're Mary Ann's friend after all and so Maggie's really nice and…"

"Johnny, what time should I show up at Neiman's?"

"One o'clock, at the Lancôme counter. Can you make that? Because if you can't maybe I could—"

"I can make it."

"Good, because I know you wanted to talk to her and she's not going to be able to attend my dinner party tonight. You're still coming though, right?"

I brought my fingers to my temples. I had completely forgotten about the party. If I met Maggie for lunch, did I really need to go? Probably—there could be other people there who knew Eugene and had useful information.

"I'll be there tonight," I interjected as soon as he took a breath. "I appreciate your inviting me, since we're *just friends.*"

"Of course I invited you. I always think it's best for men and women to start as friends because then when the relationship grows into more they have a strong foundation. What do you think?"

"Goodbye, Johnny." I hung up quickly. How did Fitzgerald deal with him?

I rolled out of bed, plodded into the bathroom and looked in the mirror, and that's when I really woke up. I looked great! My skin, which I've always been reasonably content with, looked *incredible,* and with the new eyebrows…I mean *damn!* And I was going to see Anatoly! How often does one get to meet up with their ex when they're looking their absolute best? The day was looking up—until I remembered Melanie. God, how could I have forgotten about her hysterical calls last night? I retrieved the phone and dialed her home.

Answering machine.

Melanie had once told me that she liked to get up early.

She even claimed to take the occasional stroll at sunrise, a habit that I believed to be indicative of some kind of mental illness, but whatever. The point was that her not being home early in the morning didn't mean anything.

So why didn't it feel right?

I shook my head in an effort to expel my budding concerns. It was good that Melanie was out, better that than hiding under the covers attempting to treat her anxiety with bon-bons and Montel Williams. I could talk to her later.

Shortly after trying to reach Melanie I called Mary Ann, who quickly agreed to include me in her lunch plans. So far so good. I strolled into Starbucks at twenty minutes after eleven and discovered, to my immense irritation, that Anatoly hadn't arrived yet.

I walked outside and looked up and down the street, then stood outside the door to wait. Eventually he came walking around the corner at a pace that suggested he was in no major rush to get anywhere.

"You're late!" I snarled as we both walked into the café.

"You can't convince me that you've been here for more than five minutes."

"That's not the point I…you're glowing."

Anatoly looked away quickly. "I don't know what you're talking about."

"Your skin looks great! It's almost as smooth as mine and…Tiff gave you a facial last night, didn't she? You were her last client!"

"Grab that table over there," Anatoly said, steadfastly avoiding my eyes, "and I'll get us some coffee…."

"Don't change the subject!" I reached out and stroked his cheek. "Damn, Anatoly, it's like a baby's butt!"

"Shh!"

"So did she apply a mud mask?" I said, raising my voice so those around us could hear. "Or did you just ask her to exfoliate? Oh, my God, she waxed your eyebrows, too, didn't she! Look how pretty they are!"

"Go sit down at that table before someone else takes it," Anatoly growled.

"Aren't his eyebrows pretty?" I asked a blond man sitting by the window.

"Fabulicious," the man agreed with a rather pronounced and undoubtedly cultivated lisp. "Who do you go to?"

"He goes to Mojo," I answered before Anatoly had a chance. I nudged Anatoly in the ribs and said in a stage whisper, "See, I told you the guys would be into it."

"Sophie, sit down at the table now or I'll tell the barista to pour you a decaf."

I skipped to the table knowing I had achieved my goal; now there were three guys in the place actively checking Anatoly out.

"So what did Tiff tell you?" Anatoly asked when he returned with our drinks. He had been thoughtful enough to get me a Frappuccino without my having to ask for it, but nonetheless I tasted it carefully.

"It's not decaf, just regular," Anatoly said, reading my mind. "At least it's as regular as a Light Espresso White Chocolate Mocha Frappuccino with extra whipped cream can get."

I gasped. "This has been my new favorite drink for the past month! How did you know?"

"Deduction. I figured out what was the most complicated thing I could order and got you that."

I smiled. He was so not over me. The specialty Frappuccino was a token of his affection.

"You never answered my question," Anatoly said as he sat opposite me. "What did Tiff tell you?"

"Basically she told me that her brother was a freak but in a nonoffensive kind of way." I recounted Tiff's tales about her brother's previous passion for being a mascot, his frequent vacations to conspicuously nonexotic locales, his interest in politics and the way he championed the rights of ugly people. I also told him about my impending lunch date and dinner party. Anatoly took notes the whole time.

"So now I've given you the rundown," I said after taking a long sip of my drink. "What kind of dirt did she share with you?"

Anatoly shrugged. "Basically the same thing."

"If that was true you wouldn't have had to take notes just now. Seriously, tell me what she said to you."

"Not much."

"Damn it, Anatoly, will you stop holding out on me?"

"Sophie, she didn't tell me anything. I had planned on getting her to talk by making up a story about losing a parent to suicide, but as soon as I tried that she started going on and on about how amazing it was that she had met two different people who had lost a family member to suicide in one day. Every time I tried to get her to talk about Peter she would bring the conversation back to how incredible the coincidence was. I couldn't get her off the subject."

"Oh." I leaned back in my seat. "So I got more information out of her than you."

"You could say that, yes."

"In fact, of the two of us I'm the only one who got any information at all."

Anatoly scowled into his coffee.

"One might say this proves I'm a better investigator than you."

"One might say that," Anatoly snapped. "But then that 'one' would be wrong. You undermined my interview by showing up two hours before me."

"Excuse me, but you held out on me first."

Anatoly looked liked he was about to argue, but then stopped himself. His expression softened considerably. "Sophie, I never said you were bad at getting information out of people, but you're not careful. You have a habit of making everything worse right before you make it better. That may work in your day-to-day life, but not when you're dealing with murderers. I have no idea why I care about you, but I do."

"Seriously?" I felt a rush of warmth that filled up every inch of my body. "You care about me?"

"I never said I didn't."

"You said you didn't want to be my boyfriend."

"I'm not comfortable with that title."

So much for the warmth. "How about commitment-phobic rat bastard?" I asked. "Are you comfortable with that title?"

The spark of amusement lit up Anatoly's eyes. "I also worry about your temper."

"Humph."

"Let me at least go with you to this party," Anatoly said. "Together we'll be able to get more information out of more of the guests."

"You can't come to the party."

"Sophie, I've agreed to work with you, but you can't keep me out of the loop."

"I'm not trying to."

Anatoly gave me a withering stare.

"Okay, I *was* trying to, but not anymore. You're looking at the new and improved Sophie Katz. This model is more cooperative and has better skin. But as I said before, Johnny has a crush on me and so far that's worked in my favor. If I show up with a guy on my arm he might stop being so helpful."

Anatoly's jaw stiffened at the mention of Johnny's infatuation, so I laid a reassuring hand over his. "You're being silly, Anatoly. It's a party, not an intimate night alone. I'm not going to agree to one of those until I've gotten to know him a lot better."

Anatoly muttered something in Russian that sounded suspiciously like a curse.

"Was that a curse?" I asked.

He just glared at me.

"Tell you what, why don't you come to lunch at Neiman's?"

"I can't. I've been looking into Eugene's FBI days. David Espinoza was one of the men he put away. Thanks to Eugene the guy did ten years. He has a history of violence and he's been working for his brother's construction company in South San Francisco for the past six months. He's agreed to meet me in an hour."

Now it was my turn to glare. "You weren't going to tell me about this, were you."

"If I wasn't going to tell you, I wouldn't have told you. I'd even invite you to come with me, but you have another appointment."

"Okay, fine, I'll give you that. But I want to know what you find out from this guy."

"What time is your lunch at the Rotunda?"

"One o'clock. It won't be more than an hour because it's during Mary Ann's lunch break."

"I should be able to get back to San Francisco by two. Why don't I meet you at Neiman's and we'll compare notes."

"Yeah, okay. Meet me at the Lancôme counter. Maybe we could find you an eyebrow pencil to help emphasize your new look."

"Let's talk about Tiff," Anatoly said, ignoring my last comment. "Do you think you established enough of a bond to arrange to meet her socially, or do you need to make another appointment?"

My playful mood flew out the picture-glass window. "I could probably get her to have lunch with me, but I'd rather not."

"Why's that?"

"I feel bad about lying to her during my appointment, but at least in that context I was just a client. You're asking me to pretend to be a friend."

"You don't have to pretend," Anatoly suggested. "You could actually be her friend if that would make it easier on you."

"I don't lie to my friends."

"You lie to me all the time."

"Again, I don't lie to my *friends.* That would be morally wrong. Lying to an ex-boyfriend is totally within the confines of acceptable behavior."

"I was never really your boyfriend."

"Like hell."

Anatoly chuckled and shook his head. "I would like to know if Tiff's brother left her anything or if she had a chance to go through his apartment. I would also like to know a little more about these trips of his. Did he say anything about these animal-lover conventions? Was there a political tie to either Brooke or Fitzgerald? You've obviously established a rapport with her, but if you don't want to meet her outside of Mojo, then make another appointment with her. Surely you can think of something else she could wax." His eyes fell to my lap, and I smacked him on the arm.

"Get your mind out of my pants. I'll find a way to talk to Tiff, but in the meantime you need to explain to me what this letter Melanie found is all about."

Anatoly's expression became more serious and he rested his forearms on the table. "I haven't seen the original, but Melanie scanned it and e-mailed it to me. It's a little cryptic. Peter simply wrote that people had a right to privacy, even public figures. He implored Eugene not to expose his secret, claiming that doing so would not only ruin political careers but families as well."

"You think he was having an affair with Anne Brooke?"

"It's possible."

I clucked my tongue. "Voters never like it when their elected officials commit adultery, but if an affair led to the death of the person they were sleeping with…well, that would be a tough one to recover from."

Anatoly shrugged. "It hasn't been a problem for the Kennedys."

"Touché. Still, if I were Anne I'd be worried."

"You might be right, but it's still too early in the game to limit ourselves to one theory." Anatoly glanced at his watch. "I should get going." He finished up his drink and started to leave, but hesitated. "You've done a good job."

"Excuse me?"

"The connection you made with Tiff and the information you've gathered so far. I'm impressed."

I couldn't have been more floored if he had dropped to his knees and proposed marriage.

Anatoly smiled when I didn't immediately respond. "Don't tell me that my compliment left you speechless? That is a first. Would I be overdoing it if I added that you looked incredibly beautiful today?"

"I like it when people overdo things," I said, once I managed to find my voice. "Moderation is for wimps."

Anatoly laughed gently and leaned over so close that I could smell the faint fragrance of the soap he must have showered with that morning. "Do you think we might prove the old adage to be true?"

"What old adage would that be?" I asked in a whisper.

"Will politics turn us into strange bedfellows?"

"Not a chance."

Anatoly's lips curled into his little half smile. "We shall see." I watched him as he walked out the door. I wanted him..

He was like a shot of espresso: strong, dark and addictive, with the ability to keep you up all night long.

I was in major trouble.

My yoga instructor says that when I'm feeling stressed
I should close my eyes and go to my happy place. But
how am I supposed to drive to Neiman Marcus with
my eyes closed?
—*C'est La Mort*

AFTER GETTING MY CAFFEINE FIX I HEADED TO UNION SQUARE WITH THE
intention of stopping at Cody's Books before meeting
everyone at Neiman's. I needed to pick up a new copy of
the book I borrowed from Marcus. I hadn't told Marcus this,
but there was a passage in that book involving a lusty rabbi
that had me laughing so hard that I had inadvertently spit
coffee all over his copy.

As I wound my way up multiple stories of the Ellis
O'Farrell Garage I mulled over Anatoly's request that I speak
to Tiff again in the near future. What service could I hire
her for this time? It would be a month before I had enough

regrowth on my legs or brows to wax them again, I was blessed with a relatively hairless upper lip, and there was no way she was getting near my bikini area. That only left underarms. *Underarms*—my God, that sounded painful. I squeezed my Audi into a spot between a Lexus SUV and a Hummer and then admired my brows in the rearview mirror. Tiff certainly knew what she was doing, and it would be great not have to shave my underarms—that would save me a good, oh I don't know, thirty seconds every day. I took a deep breath and called Mojo. As luck would have it, Tiff was standing right next to the receptionist when I called and usurped the phone.

"Hi there!" she said cheerfully. "I was just thinking of you. You'll never believe this but an hour after you left I had another new client and it turns out he lost a family member to suicide, too. It was kind of disturbing, but I feel like it's a sign. I'm just not sure of what."

Maybe it's a sign that you're being manipulated. "That *is* weird. I was actually calling because…" *Tell her you want your underarms waxed. You can do it, Sophie!* "Because…because…I was wondering if you would like to get together sometime since we do have so much in common and we could obviously both use a friend to talk to." Oh God, I was a horrible, horrible person, but at least my underarms were safe.

"I would *love* that. Do you want to get together Saturday? I never work past four on the weekends."

"Yeah, Saturday would be great. Name the restaurant."

"You know, I've always wanted to go to Michael Mina, although it's seriously expensive. I should probably save my money. Or we could go to—"

"We'll go to Michael Mina. My treat."

"Seriously?"

"Seriously." I was fooling myself if I thought one expensive dinner was going to make up for what I was doing, but I was very good at fooling myself.

"Hey, that is so nice of you. Okay, why don't we meet there at six."

"Beautiful, see you there." I hung up and immediately dialed Melanie's number, hoping that by providing Melanie with a sympathetic ear I'd both comfort her and convince myself that using Tiff was an act of necessity, not cruelty.

Melanie's answering machine picked up. I hung up without leaving a message. "So she's not answering her phone. So what?" I whispered to myself.

I got out of the car and headed to the elevator, determined not to pay attention to the knot that had taken up permanent residence in my stomach.

I love Neiman Marcus's Union Square store. It's just impossible not to. The actual building rivals the beauty of the impossibly fabulous items it contains. It often takes tourists a few minutes to realize this. They get caught up in their quest to find Donna Karan's new fragrance or whatever. But eventually they look up and they are rewarded with a vision of the beautifully designed stained-glass domed ceiling that is protecting them from the cool San Francisco drizzle that they failed to pack for. Not being overly fond of tourists, I don't get to Union Square all that often (despite its close proximity to my apartment), so I took a moment to admire my surroundings before approaching the Lancôme counter.

And there they all were. Rick was standing at Mary Ann's side as Mary Ann carefully applied eye shadow to Maggie Gallagher.

Rick saw me first and offered a halfhearted wave. "Hello, Sophie. Mary Ann was just saying that you would be joining us. I'm so glad you could come."

Funny, he didn't sound glad, he sounded put out.

"Hi, Sophie," Mary Ann said. She sounded glad to see me, although she hadn't really seen me yet since all her focus was on applying shadow to Maggie's naked eyelid. "Have you two met before?" she asked.

Maggie, currently unable to meet my gaze, smiled vaguely. "I saw you at Eugene's funeral, but we've never been officially introduced. I'm Maggie Gallagher."

"Sophie Katz. I've actually been wanting to talk to you for a while."

Now Mary Ann pulled her brush away and Maggie opened both her eyes. Several of her red curls, which she had tried to restrain inside a bun, were rebelliously popping out in various directions. "I am sorry about not returning your calls. Fitzgerald actually asked me to make myself available to you, or rather to the *National Review*."

Had that been a hint of sarcasm in her voice? Johnny had said that she didn't like to hang out with journalists during her free time; maybe she was just irritated that I was there at all.

"I've just been so busy," Maggie continued. "The election is less than two months away and my husband just had back surgery."

"Is he all right?" I asked.

"He's recovering nicely. He should be back on his feet in

a matter of weeks." She looked up at the ceiling to allow Mary Ann to apply some mascara.

"Our meeting with Carl Pearson wrapped up earlier than expected," Rick explained, "and Maggie thought it might be fun to have Mary Ann give her a makeover."

Mary Ann finished up and handed Maggie a mirror. "What do you think?"

"Oh, darling, it's wonderful! I can see why Rick's so smitten with you. You're talented, sweet and absolutely adorable." She waved her hand in front of me, showing off a particularly beautiful diamond ring. "Can you believe she actually had the people in jewelry clean this for me while she was doing my makeup? That's what I call service."

"Yes, Mary Ann is one of a kind," I agreed. "She's done my makeup before and—" Mary Ann was looking at me with her mouth wide open. "Mary Ann? Are you okay?"

"Your skin," she gasped. "It's perfect! It's always good but now you have this…this…"

"Mojo glow," I supplied. "Yeah, Tiff definitely knows her stuff. Yesterday I had my first facial," I explained to Rick and Maggie. "I went to see this woman named Tiffany Strauss and here's a weird bit of trivia—her brother was Peter Strauss. You know who I'm talking about, right? He was the guy who worked for Anne Brooke who committed suicide."

Their reaction was incredibly subtle. Rick's Adam's apple bobbed and Maggie's fingers, which had been relaxed in her lap before I mentioned Peter, were now curled and clutching the fabric of her A-line skirt.

"We do live in a small world, don't we?" Maggie said in

an even voice. "It must have been horrible to lose a brother like that. Did you talk to her about it?"

"I did."

"Does she have any idea why he did it?" she pressed.

"Not a clue."

"That's awful," Rick whispered. "Truly awful."

Mary Ann was now busily cleaning her brushes. She glanced at her watch. "My lunch break is supposed to start right now. Is everyone ready to eat?"

We went upstairs and were quickly seated at one of the tables adjacent to the floor-to-ceiling windows. "Can you believe I've never lunched here?" Maggie asked as she admired her surroundings.

"Everything's good." I tapped my fingers on my leg as I watched Maggie study the culinary choices. She was an attractive woman, more so now that Mary Ann had worked her magic on her face. She was athletically built and exuded strength and self-confidence. I wouldn't want to mess with her, but I wondered if maybe Eugene had.

"I was moved by the eulogy you delivered at Eugene's funeral," I said as I casually unfolded my napkin and dropped it in my lap.

"I only said what I felt." Maggie put down the menu and looked at me. "Eugene was by far the most honest and moral man I have ever met."

"I'll second that," Rick said quietly.

Mary Ann placed her hand on Rick's arm. "I really do wish I could have met him," she said. "Anyone you cared about so much *had* to have been a really good guy."

"He was a good guy, better than me." His mouth turned

down, making his face look longer than usual. "I know this is a cliché, but Eugene truly was too good for this world. He was what the rest of us strive to be."

I sat back in my chair. Usually those kinds of compliments were reserved for the likes of Jesus and Bono.

Mary Ann still hadn't let go of Rick's arm and was now leaning into him a bit more, her perfect forehead wrinkled in concern. What exactly was I in the middle of here?

My thoughts were interrupted by the waiter. We all placed our orders, and as usual, Mary Ann, the thinnest of all of us, ordered the most caloric thing on the menu. The woman wasn't human.

"How long did you work with Eugene?" I asked Maggie as the busboy presented each of us with our own popover with a side of strawberry butter.

"I only met him a year ago, when I came onto Fitzgerald's team. Of course I knew him from reputation before then." She leaned forward and added in a hushed voice, "I had heard about what happened on the Bruni campaign."

"The Bruni campaign? Do you mean Edward Bruni? Eugene worked for *him?*" Bruni had run for Congress a while back. Normally I wouldn't know the names of the losers in the congressional races that took place outside of my district, but Edward Bruni had managed to achieve national infamy. He had been in the lead, running on a platform that exalted law enforcement and programs that would encourage teenage abstinence and moral behavior. And then he was caught with his pants down, which might not have been a problem if the person he had been caught with hadn't been a seventeen-year-old girl. She had been a freshman in college at the time, having skipped a grade at some point, but still, seventeen was seventeen.

"You do know how they caught him, don't you?" Maggie asked.

"Maggie." By the way Rick said her name it was clear that he was issuing her a warning.

"How they caught Bruni?" I tore off a piece of my popover and tried to remember the articles I had read about the scandal. "Didn't the police receive an anonymous tip? They broke down the door of some sleazy motel room or something, right?"

"Yes, but do you know who was responsible for the tip?"

"This strawberry butter is wonderful," Rick said quickly. "Maggie, why don't you try some?"

Maggie waved off both the butter and the distraction tactic. "It was Eugene. The general public doesn't know that, but people in political circles do. Apparently lots of people on Bruni's payroll knew about Bruni and his sick fascination with underage girls, but everybody kept quiet. They had all managed to convince themselves that it was acceptable to support a morally reprehensible man as long as he was a Republican. Plus, Bruni had big political plans and a lot of powerful connections. He had promised Eugene that he would recommend him to a certain individual who was planning to run for president. But Eugene turned his back on all of that in order to do the right thing. A lot of politicians didn't want anything to do with Eugene after that, but not Fitzgerald. As soon as he found out about Eugene's actions against Bruni, he offered Eugene a top position on his campaign. He wanted his right-hand man to be like him: a man who practices what he preaches."

"So you like Fitzgerald?" Mary Ann asked. The question was presumably directed toward Maggie, but I noticed that it was Rick she was looking at.

"Absolutely," Maggie said with a nod. "You couldn't ask for a more genuine…" Her voice trailed off and a look of surprise and then severe distress crossed her face. I followed her gaze and there, standing at the host stand, staring right at our table, was Flynn Fitzgerald. And he looked anything but happy to see us.

12

Conspiracy theorists drive me nuts. I'm way too busy plotting against my enemies to waste my time entertaining their paranoid ideas.
—*C'est La Mort*

"YOU WERE EXPECTING HIM?" I ASKED DOUBTFULLY. THE EXPRESSION ON Fitzgerald's, Rick's and Maggie's faces said that this was anything but a planned meeting, but if that was true what the hell was going on? Fitzgerald didn't immediately come to greet us. Instead, he stepped back from the host and started rapidly pressing buttons on his cell. I glanced over at Maggie, half expecting her phone to ring, but her handbag remained silent.

"Well, Maggie, you certainly called it when you said it was a small world," Rick said with what I think was supposed to be a chuckle, but came out more like a whimper.

Maggie finally tore off a piece of the popover she had been ignoring and methodically covered its entire surface with a thin layer of butter. This was a woman trying to buy time to think. "Today is full of amazing coincidences, isn't it?" she finally said.

I had no idea how to respond to that. If Fitzgerald lived in San Francisco I might buy the coincidence line, but he lived a good forty minutes away.

"You must have *some* idea of why he's here," I said. Fitzgerald was now talking on the phone, and even from across the restaurant I could sense his agitation.

"I honestly don't," Maggie insisted. "Rick?"

"Perhaps he…wanted to buy a gift for his wife," he ventured. "Yes, that would make sense. He's always buying her little presents."

"A gift," I said flatly. "He couldn't buy a gift in say, Walnut Creek?"

"We don't have a Neiman Marcus in Contra Costa," Maggie said.

"So?"

"So it's *Neiman Marcus.*" From her tone I could tell that she thought that explained everything.

I glanced back at Fitzgerald. He was off the phone now and heading toward us.

"Isn't this a pleasant surprise," he said once he'd reached our table. The smile on his face was too big and his voice too boisterous. For a politician Fitzgerald seemed to be ill-practiced in the art of faking enthusiasm.

"Are you here to buy a gift for Jan?" Maggie asked, obviously trying to lead his remarks.

"What? No, no, I have a lunch meeting with Robin Striffler."

I lifted my eyebrows. Robin Striffler was another name I knew. She had started a grassroots campaign in Santa Rosa to prevent supermarkets from selling magazines featuring articles inappropriate for children. According to her, that was pretty much all of them. She had become famous by hosting a series of public *Cosmopolitan* magazine burnings in three consecutive weeks. Of course, no one was willing to give her little organization magazines to burn, so she and her followers had to buy them—a lot of them. It had been a banner month for *Cosmo.*

Rick looked even more puzzled than before. "I thought Robin was going to Tennessee this week to take part in a *Maxim* burning."

"She postponed her trip by a day," Fitzgerald explained. "She's spending the night in the city so she can be closer to the airport, and at the last minute she called to see if we could meet here. I think she's planning to endorse our campaign." His shifted his weight back on his heels, and turned his attention to Mary Ann. "I don't believe we've met."

"What am I thinking," Rick said, quickly straightening up. "This is Mary Ann Walker. Mary Ann, this is my boss." He laughed as if he had made a joke.

Mary Ann shook Fitzgerald's hand, albeit a bit tentatively. "It's good to meet you." Was she blushing? "Rick's told me a lot about you."

"I could say the same, but it would be an understatement." Fitzgerald slapped Rick on the back hard enough to make him jerk forward. "Wilkes has done nothing but sing your praises for the past week. If Gallagher here could get the media as enthusiastic about me as Wilkes has gotten us about you I'd have this race in the bag!"

I saw Maggie's shoulders tense. "I was just telling Sophie about what a wonderful, honest and principled man you are, and she *is* the media. She's writing for the *National Review.* But of course you know that. That's why you've been encouraging me to speak with her."

There was an entire coded conversation going on between these two that I was unable to decipher. By the miserable look on Rick's face it was clear he was in on it, too.

Maggie and Fitzgerald continued to stare each other down. "You'll have to stop by my table when Striffler shows up. She enjoyed meeting you the last time," Fitzgerald said.

"Of course," Maggie agreed. She watched as Fitzgerald retreated to his table, a good twenty feet away from us.

"I'm still having a hard time believing this was a coincidence," I admitted.

"I know it's odd, but that's exactly what it was," Maggie said with a shrug. "I'm truly delighted to hear that he's going to be meeting with Robin. Her organization consists of the demographic we're trying to reach."

"Mmm, right. I can see that." I took a long sip of water and silently considered how much nicer our country would be if people had to pass a psychiatric evaluation before being allowed to vote.

I spent the rest of our meal peppering Maggie with questions, hoping to get her to divulge something useful, but all of her answers were predictable and unrevealing. Unlike Rick, Maggie managed to talk about Eugene without exposing him as a "researcher." She talked about the challenges of being part of a political campaign and how Fitzgerald and his ideas about legislated morality made it all

worth it. I could see why Fitzgerald used her as a media consultant. She chose her words carefully and they all conveyed
exactly what she wanted them to, nothing more, nothing
less. What I did find interesting was Fitzgerald's nonexistent
lunch date.

We were in the restaurant for a good forty-five minutes
and Fitzgerald sat there the whole time by himself. The
waiter would periodically try to take his order, but he would
wave him away, most likely claiming to be waiting for his
companion. Eventually he ordered a bottle of spring water.
Every ten minutes or so he would get on his phone, and he
never took his eyes off our table. Rick sent him a few nervous
glances, but Maggie didn't look at him once. My guess was
that she didn't want to bring my attention to him, but her
steadfast refusal to look his way actually made his presence
even more conspicuous. Fitzgerald was the big white Republican elephant in the room.

So maybe it was Fitzgerald who had something to hide,
not Anne. After all, if Eugene was willing to turn on Edward
Bruni, why not Fitzgerald? It was clear from Peter's letter that
whatever information Eugene had discovered, he'd had it for
weeks before he was shot. Maybe he'd sat on the scandalous
tidbit because he was reluctant to hand a congressional seat
over to the Democrats.

Except it didn't make sense at all. Maggie said that Eugene's
betrayal of Bruni was known by everyone in the political
world. If Fitzgerald had a dark secret, why would he hire
someone like Eugene? And if Eugene was sitting on the information, why kill him? Anne was still a more logical suspect.
Still, it was Fitzgerald who was currently creeping me out.

When the waiter presented us with dessert menus, Maggie and Rick both quickly declined without waiting to see if Mary Ann or I wanted something. "We're in a bit of a rush," Rick explained as he handed our server his credit card. "Just put this all on my card and bring me the slip to sign."

"Where are you two off to now?" I asked.

"Walnut Creek," Maggie answered as she pushed her handbag up on her shoulder, clearly wanting to bolt for the door the minute Rick signed the receipt. "We have another meeting."

"Do you think Striffler is standing Fitzgerald up?"

Rick swallowed and Maggie looked out the glass windows. "I'm sure she has a good reason," she said. "I do hope she hasn't been in an accident or anything horrible like that."

Rick signed the receipt before the waiter even had a chance to take his hand away from the leather case that held it. Maggie jumped up from her chair and then waited impatiently for the rest of us. "Forgive us," she said, "but we really are in a hurry."

We all followed Maggie out of the dining room. No one said goodbye to Fitzgerald, who was talking on the phone again, his eyes glued to Maggie's back. "Where are you parked?" Maggie asked as we walked out of the Rotunda.

"Ellis O'Farrell garage."

"As are we. Shall we walk together to our cars?"

"Actually, I thought I'd let Mary Ann sell me some products. Something to go with the new skin Tiff Strauss gave me."

This time Rick actually winced at the mention of Tiff's name. Come to think of it, he was the one who needed cosmetics. His skin tone had taken on a rather unattractive shade of green. Mary Ann had her hand on his arm again, but this time she wasn't so much holding on to him as she was holding him up.

We descended the three escalators leading to the ground floor and stopped abruptly a few feet away from the Lancôme counter. "It truly was a pleasure to meet you both." Maggie shook both mine and Mary Ann's hand. Her palm was damp, despite the moderate temperature in the store. She shot Rick a stern look and he meekly kissed Mary Ann on the forehead before tailing after Maggie. She was on her cell phone before she even hit the sidewalk.

"Mary Ann, what the hell was that?"

Mary Ann avoided my eyes and quickly took her place behind the counter. "I don't know what brought Fitzgerald here." She started tinkering with the free-gift-with-purchase display.

"Why do I have the feeling you're not telling me something?"

"Sophie, I—" Something behind me caught her attention and she stopped short.

I whirled around and there was Flynn Fitzgerald, standing at the foot of the escalator, glaring at me. I've always hated the cliché about shooting daggers from your eyes, but for this instance the expression was felicitous. For reasons that I couldn't even begin to guess at, this man hated me. I could physically feel his detestation from thirty feet away.

And then he looked away and walked out, leaving me with nothing but a hazy sense of foreboding.

13

My boyfriend doesn't understand my need to be the center of attention. That's why I love my stalkers. They get me.
—*C'est La Mort*

I CONSIDERED GOING AFTER FITZGERALD, BUT WHAT WOULD I SAY?
I wanted to press Mary Ann for more information, but as soon as Fitzgerald left, one of San Francisco's most beloved socialites walked in and demanded Mary Ann's services. It was only another minute before Anatoly was at my side.

He gave Mary Ann a curt nod, then placed a hand on my back and directed me out of the store.

"How was South San Francisco?" I asked.

"A waste of time. Espinoza barely remembers Eugene, and why would he? He's been arrested so many times in his life he'd have to have a photographic memory to recall the names of all of the officers who have hassled him. Besides, he was in a halfway house during the week in which Eugene was shot. He couldn't have gotten to Antioch late at night without alerting the police of his whereabouts. How 'bout you? Did you have better luck?"

I filled him in on all the details as we stood in front of the flower stand on the corner of Stockton and Geary.

"So Fitzgerald said he came here to meet with Robin Striffler?" Anatoly asked. "Isn't she the magazine burner?"

"That's the one. He said they had a lunch date scheduled today."

"But he ate alone."

"Exactly. Either Miss Pyromaniac stood him up or Fitzgerald was lying about the meeting."

Anatoly crossed his arms, appearing to ponder this news. "So Fitzgerald came over to your table and told you he had a lunch date at the same restaurant. Why lie about something when you know you're going to get caught?"

I shook my head, not having an answer.

"I'd suspect him of following me, Maggie or Rick, but he was very rattled. The moment he saw all of us at a table, he became agitated and got on his cell phone. I really don't think he expected to see us." I snapped my fingers in the air. "I know! Maybe he was calling the person he'd planned to meet and told them not to come *because* we were all there. Maybe he came all the way to San Francisco because he didn't want anyone he knew to see him!"

"No," Anatoly said dismissively as he pulled me back a little so as not to block the steady stream of tourists and homeless people who were trying to make their way down the sidewalk. "That's not it, either."

"How can you be so sure?"

"Sophie, if you wanted to keep a low profile, which table in the Rotunda would you request?"

"Oh, I see your point." His point was that there wasn't a single table in the Rotunda that wasn't completely visible to all the other tables in the restaurant. Round restaurants didn't have corners to hide in.

"Maybe we need to start looking at Fitzgerald a little more closely."

"Why?" I snapped. "There's obviously something going on with Fitzgerald, but it's not like he would kill his own adviser."

"Researcher," Anatoly corrected.

"Whatever. The point is that they were on the same team and it was a *good* team. Eugene dug around in Anne's past, Anne's poll numbers dropped. Fitzgerald had no reason to kill Eugene. Anne did."

"Why are you so reluctant to look at other possibilities?" Anatoly asked.

"Because I don't want to make this more complicated than it needs to be." A few tourists did a double take as they walked by, probably hoping that my rising voice was the precursor to a photo-worthy violent fit. "Every time I blink there's another twist, another goddamned turn. First it's my old mentor asking me to seduce her husband, then there's a murder—somebody shot Melanie's husband!" Now the tourists were really interested. We were attracting a small crowd. "I'm dealing with politicians and suicidal mascots, and you! We broke up because I couldn't deal with the complications you brought into my life and now I'm dealing with you every day!"

"You chose this for yourself, Sophie, and we broke up because you wanted to make our relationship *more* complicated," Anatoly retorted.

"You are so wrong. I wanted to *simplify* things by giving you a title."

"Husband," Anatoly said quietly.

"What? Where?" I searched the crowd, suddenly afraid I'd find my ex-husband there.

"That's how it works," Anatoly muttered, then glanced at the crowd once again. "We *need* to take this somewhere else."

"Fine, I'm going to stop by Ooh La La to give Marcus the new *Drama Queen* I bought him. If you come with me we can talk about all this in the car."

I glared at the tourists and then stormed off toward the parking garage, Anatoly at my side. We didn't speak again until we were in the car.

"Where's the *Drama Queen?*"

I gestured at the Cody's bag by his feet.

Anatoly raised his eyebrows. "I thought Marcus preferred his queens a little bigger than that."

"Marcus isn't interested in sharing his throne with any queen that isn't securely confined between the covers of a book." I drove the car down the multiple floors and then turned onto the street. "Now, what was all that about husbands?"

"You wanted our relationship to progress at a steady rate, correct?"

"I guess so." This was beginning to sound like a story problem. I sucked at story problems.

"So what would have happened after I became your boyfriend? What would you have wanted next?"

Yeah, this was a story problem. At least it wasn't geometry. If the next question was *What is the circumference of my penis?* I'd be screwed.

"Sophie?" Anatoly said, prodding me for a response.

"I'm thinking." I mulled it over for another half a block before answering. "This is a trick question."

"No, the question is very straightforward."

"It's so not. You're asking what I would have wanted if you had agreed to be in a committed relationship with me, but I didn't want anything more than that. There is no *next* for me."

Anatoly scoffed. "For women there's always a next. Eventually you would have wanted marriage and I'm not the kind of man who is cut out to be a husband. If I had agreed to be your boyfriend, it would have been the equivalent of promising you a future that I knew I couldn't deliver."

"Ah, I see. So you couldn't give me what I wanted because you didn't want to disappoint me, is that it?"

"Something like that."

I gave him a sidelong glance before turning my eyes (if not my full attention) to the road. As sexist as Anatoly's remarks were, it was true that most women wanted to get married. I had been married once before and it had been a huge mistake, but that didn't mean I couldn't do it again and do it successfully. Anatoly wasn't Scott. Oddly enough his refusal to commit proved that. Scott didn't have a problem with telling people what they wanted to hear and then breaking his promises later. But Anatoly clearly wasn't going to agree to anything he didn't think he could follow through on. If we started seeing each other again, would I eventually want to marry him?

I thought about my life and the wonderful times I had had with Anatoly during the year we had dated. I had loved arguing with him and laughing with him. And I had really loved sleeping with him.

If I married Anatoly I could have the very things the average girl on JDate dreamed of: a sexy, *tall,* Jewish husband and a mother-in-law who lived on another continent. Did I want what the JDate women wanted?

No. Absolutely not. Some people were meant to be married. My sister was one of them, and I had no doubt that Mary Ann would eventually tie the knot with some Prince Charming. Marriage was right for them. But the very thought of putting on a long white dress gave me hives. It just wasn't me. Right now I didn't even want to live with Anatoly, but that might change given enough time, say five or six years from now when Mr. Katz had gone senile and I needed help getting him back and forth to the kitty-litter box.

We were only a few minutes away from Ooh La La at this point, and it was clear from his glazed over expression that Anatoly thought the conversation had ended, so I probably should have let the whole thing go. But instead I blurted out, "I want to be Susan Sarandon."

Anatoly's glazed expression was replaced by one of complete confusion. "Did I miss something?"

"I want to be Susan, and in a few years I might want you to be my Tim Robbins."

Anatoly gave me a funny look but didn't say anything as I turned the car onto Fillmore. I held my breath, waiting for him to say "Yes! I want to be Tim!" but it didn't happen. I should have known we weren't going to work anything out.

Why had I ever wanted to be with this person? And why wasn't I over him?

I took a few minutes to search for nonmetered parking since neither Anatoly nor I had any change, but I wasn't having any success. Eventually I gave up and pulled into a metered spot on one of the side streets. I leaned over Anatoly to grab the Cody's bag and my hand brushed against his leg. The man could win the Tour de France with those legs. Well-defined calves, solid thighs. I used to love watching those muscles tense when I—

"Having a hard time?"

"Huh?" I looked up at Anatoly, who was smirking.

"Are you having a hard time getting the book? You've been down there awhile."

I grabbed the book and jerked back up. "Just stay with the car in case a meter maid shows up. I'll be back in a minute." I left the keys in the ignition and jumped out, slamming my door a little harder than necessary.

My cell rang right as I turned the corner. The words on the screen read Unknown Number.

"Hello?"

"Hello, Sophie." It was Darth Vader. "I may like to dress up like a koala bear, but I have the temper of a wild grizzly."

"Okay, who—" But before I had a chance to finish my question there was a beep. Someone else was calling me. "Hold on for a second," I instructed, and then clicked over. "Hello?"

"Hi, Sophie, it's Johnny." He sounded much less cheerful than usual.

"Johnny, I'm on the other line right now, can I call you back?"

"Yeah, okay, but I sort of have some bad news. Well, not bad news exactly, but it's not good. I can't believe I'm doing this—I don't want to do this."

"Johnny, what are you talking about?"

"I just talked to the boss man, you know, Fitzgerald. I had invited him and his wife to come to my housewarming party and he had said yes, which is great because it could really help my career if Fitzgerald starts to consider me a friend, I mean assuming I stay in politics, which I might."

"Johnny, can we hurry this up?" It seemed rude to keep the leader of the dark side on hold.

"Oh, sorry. Like I said, I just talked to Fitzgerald and I happened to mention that the woman who interviewed him for the *National Review* was coming to the party and he got all wiggy and kind of mad. He said he wouldn't come if you were there and I know I should stand up to him, but I really need my job, Sophie. The rent on my new place is super high and I just signed the lease and—"

"Johnny, it's fine." Weird, but fine. "We'll talk more about this later, okay?" I clicked over without waiting for him to answer. "Are you still there?"

"You put me on *hooold!*" Darth Vader shouted. Well, he didn't really shout, Darth Vader doesn't have those kind of vocal chords, but his voice box did seem to be on a louder setting. "How could you put me on hold when I was in the middle of threatening you?"

"Oh, is that what you were doing? Because normally when someone threatens you, they don't mention koala bears, or cats. And here's an FYI, if you want to leave someone an ominous note you shouldn't sign it with a Pink

Panther sticker. You know what you need? An image consultant. Who does Cheney use? He always comes across as *really* evil."

"Just stay out of my business, or else!" he said.

And then there was a dial tone.

When I got to the salon, Marcus was walking a client to the door. "Well, well, if it isn't my favorite authoress." He introduced me to his client, Dee Dee something, and then, after exchanging a few air kisses, sent her on her way. "I hope you aren't trying to whisk me away for a late lunch. My next client is in the girl's room as we speak."

I handed him the book.

"You bought me a new one?"

I nodded.

Marcus studied me for a moment. "Why do you seem discombobulated? Is there something else?"

"Darth Vader likes to dress up like a koala bear."

Marcus paused for a beat. "He said that?"

"Yes, but he has the temper of a grizzly."

Marcus toyed with one of his dreadlocks. "Maybe this guy isn't Darth Vader after all. Maybe he's an Ewok with a cold."

"Ewoks are nice."

"Not always. They almost cooked Luke and Han Solo when they first met them."

"You're not helping."

"Sophie, how can I help you with this? This is nuts!"

"It is, isn't it?"

"Um, *yeah!*"

"I've been threatened by a cat-loving Ewok with a cold."

We were both quiet for a minute and then simultaneously

burst into peals of laughter, attracting the quizzical looks of the other people in the reception area.

"I assume you have no idea what number the Ewok was calling you from," Marcus said once the giggles had subsided, "since you are the last person on the planet not to have caller ID."

"I'm not the last person on the planet without it, there's still my mother. Besides, it wouldn't have done me any good. This guy called me on my cell and his number came up as unknown…." My voice faded out as the full significance of what I was saying dawned on me.

"He has your cell number now?" Marcus's smile disappeared and he took a step closer. "Sophie, when you said you got a note from Darth Vader did you mean he *sent* you a note or did you find it somewhere?"

"I found it taped to my front door. He knows my home phone number, he knows where I live and now he knows my cell number." I swallowed and stared down at the Nokia that was still in my hands. "This is one resourceful Ewok."

Neither of us laughed this time.

"Do you think I should report this to the police?" I asked.

"Maybe."

"They won't do anything."

"Not a damn thing," Marcus agreed.

"Do you still think that these threats are related to what happened to Eugene?"

"At first I did," Marcus said, lowering his voice to a near whisper. "But now I'm not sure. Politicians are crazy, Sophie, but they're not usually this kind of crazy. This is more San-Francisco-State-stoner-college-student brand of crazy. I'd chalk it all up to a prank, but the fact that this guy took the time to find out your cell phone number *and* your address shows that he's at least somewhat serious." He put a hand on my shoulder and his face was painted with concern. "Sophie, you may have another stalker on your hands."

I bit into my lip. Last time I had been stalked it had led to a near-death experience. "Why does this always happen to me?"

"I have no idea, honey, but I'm thinking you must have been a serious bitch in a past life."

"Great, Marcus, that's just great." A woman came out of the restroom and, upon seeing Marcus, removed her hair from its ponytail. "I'll let you get back to work," I said, and turned to leave.

"Wait. Do you really think you should be alone right now?"

"I'm not alone. I have my nemesis waiting for me in the car."

"Your nephew?"

"Anatoly."

"Anatoly's with you?" Marcus's tone reflected his relief. I wasn't so sure that I shared the sentiment. Alone I was more vulnerable to attack, but with Anatoly I was just more vulnerable, period.

I found Anatoly and my car exactly where I had left them. I slipped behind the wheel just as he was hanging up his cell phone.

"You're not my koala bear, are you?" I asked.

Anatoly gave me a funny look. "Is that some kind of sexual innuendo?"

I shook my head and started the engine, but before I could push the car into Drive Anatoly put his hand over mine. "Sophie, when is the last time you talked to Melanie?"

"She called me around five o'clock last night, but I didn't get the message until after eleven. I haven't been able to reach her since. Why?"

"She called me several times yesterday," Anatoly said. "She wanted to know what I found out about that letter. I was waiting until I met with Tiff to call her back, but she hasn't been answering her phone. She still isn't."

My hand mechanically clutched at the strap of my seat belt. "How many times did she call yesterday?"

"Four," Anatoly said, "and now she's not responding to my messages...or my e-mails. This visit to Marcus reminded me that one of her messages said that the only time she would be unavailable was between two and three-thirty today because she was getting her hair done at some place called Changes Salon."

"Maybe we should call there."

"I just did. She never showed up."

I was silent for a very long time.

Finally Anatoly cleared his throat. "Would you like to go to her house with me?"

"Yes," I whispered. It was the only word I could manage.

Anatoly nodded. "Why don't we go back for the Harley. It'll get us there faster."

14

I used to be a perfectionist, but not anymore. I finally
realized that it's much healthier to just live in denial.
—*C'est La Mort*

ANATOLY WOVE HIS HARLEY THROUGH THE TRAFFIC ON HIGHWAY 101
while I embraced him from the back of the bike. I was trying to figure out what I was feeling. I wanted to be angry—
angry at Melanie for scaring us like this—but that didn't
work because I wasn't going to allow myself to be scared.
Melanie was one of those people who always sent her Christmas and birthday cards out on time and always returned her
phone calls. Unless she had undergone a personality trans-
plant, there had to be something very, very wrong.

I squeezed my eyes shut and tried to calm myself.
"Wrong" was such a loose term. If Melanie, who had never
indulged in more than two drinks on any given day, had, in
a moment of despair, gotten hammered, she would have

considered that wrong—so wrong she would have likely locked herself in the confessional with some priest to repent. That was the kind of "wrong" I could live with.

I clung to this unlikely fantasy as we rode to Melanie's house. When we arrived, Anatoly waited for me to get off the bike before placing both of our helmets in the saddle bags.

"Maybe she's home from church by now," I said hopefully as I studied her ornately carved double wood door from the sidewalk.

"Church?"

"That's where she's been," I said. "I've decided."

"I see." For once Anatoly didn't sound sarcastic. Worse, he sounded like he felt sorry for me, as if he knew that I was about to be dealt a terrible blow.

But he didn't know any more than I did and I wasn't going to let his pessimism freak me out. I started up the walkway but Anatoly grabbed my arm. "She didn't pick up her paper this morning," he noted.

I swallowed hard and stared at the untouched *Contra Costa Times* that lay on the well-manicured front lawn. "That's because she was a little out of it. This was probably her first hangover."

"Ah, this is something else you've decided?"

I nodded, pulled my arm free and strode up to her porch. I pressed the doorbell and waited a full minute before pounding on the door.

No answer.

Anatoly stepped onto the lawn and pressed his face against her bay window. Then, when he apparently didn't see anything of interest, he went to the garage and looked up at the narrow windows that were well beyond his reach. "Come here," he instructed.

I did as requested and didn't make a peep when he lifted me up so that I could peer inside the windows. "Is her car there?" he asked, his hands firmly gripping my waist.

"Nope. See, I told you she went to church."

"It's Thursday."

"She's very religious."

Anatoly put me back down on the ground. "You could be right. There could be nothing to worry about. She's a grown woman and she's been out of contact for less than twenty-four hours, so it's a little early to alert the police."

"Why the hell would we alert the police? Melanie was upset and she probably decided she didn't want to return her phone calls right away. This behavior is not exactly the kind of thing you call in the cavalry for."

"Not at all. Nonetheless…"

"Nonetheless, what?"

"Instinct tells me that something's wrong. She was anxious to hear if I could make any sense out of that letter. Anxious people don't ignore phone calls that could potentially put them at ease."

"Maybe she doesn't know we called. Maybe she's with a lover."

Anatoly raised an eyebrow. "You know something I don't?"

"No, but as I've told you, I've decided that she got drunk last night, so she might have done something else out of character like pick up some stranger in a bar."

Anatoly gave me an odd look and, despite my distress, I laughed. "Okay, I can't really picture that one, either, but anything's possible." Anything except the thing we were both worried about.

Anatoly looked back at the front door. "She left the porch light on."

I followed his gaze. It wasn't immediately noticeable in the afternoon sun, but he was right, which meant that she either left earlier that day with the expectation of coming home after dark or she had left yesterday and never made it home.

"I'm going to walk around the house," Anatoly said decisively. I considered following him but decided against it. Instead, I sat on the front step and gazed out at the tree-lined street. It was a little after three o'clock and minivans and Volvos were pulling out of driveways presumably to pick young children up from their after-school activities. Were these Melanie's friends? I stood up and cut across Melanie's yard to reach her neighbor's house. A forty-something woman with a perfectly groomed brown bob answered the door. She had a tote-bag slung over her shoulder and her keys in her hand.

"Can I help you?"

"Yeah, I'm sorry to bother you, but I'm a friend of Melanie's and I was supposed to meet her a half hour ago," I lied. "It's not like her to stand me up and I was wondering if you might have seen her today."

"Who's Melanie?"

So much for the friend idea. "Your neighbor." I gestured to Melanie's house with my thumb.

"Ah, right, of course. She just lost her husband, didn't she? No, I haven't seen her. I'm sorry I can't be of much help, but I have to go pick up my kids."

"Yeah, okay." I stepped aside as she breezed past me to get to the Mercedes parked in the driveway. "I don't suppose you know if she's friends with anyone else on the block?"

The woman shook her head as she opened the car door. "I couldn't say for sure, but my guess is no. Her husband was a bit intolerant when it came to the children in the neighborhood, and since most of the people on the block have kids, we kept our distance."

"Intolerant in what way?" I asked out of idle curiosity.

The woman paused briefly, one foot in the car. "He thought they should all act like Little Lord Fauntleroy."

I smiled as I watched her drive away. That did sound like Eugene.

Anatoly came out from behind the house.

"Find anything worrisome?" *Please say no.*

"No."

Thank you.

Anatoly stuck his thumbs through his belt loops and cast another look at the empty house. "Are you still going to that dinner party tonight?"

"Forgot to tell you, I've been uninvited."

Anatoly smiled slightly. "Don't tell me Johnny has fallen out of love with you."

"No, he still loves me but his boss doesn't. He told Johnny he didn't want me there."

Anatoly did a quick double take. "Why's that?"

"I have no idea except…you know, he called Melanie a while back and asked her if I worked at the *National Review*. She backed up my story but not very convincingly."

"Perhaps he thinks you're working for another publication,

one that isn't likely to feature him in a favorable light," Anatoly mused. "If that's the case he'd want to keep his distance."

"True. But no matter what's going on with Fitzgerald I still think Anne's the most likely suspect. Not only does she have motive, but she knew way too much about Eugene when we talked to her."

"Agreed," Anatoly said as he directed me back to the Harley. "Come on, I'm taking you back to the city."

"And then what?"

"And then you're going to stick by the phone and your computer in case Melanie calls or e-mails, and I'm coming back here."

"Here, as in this house?"

"Here, as in Contra Costa County. I'll start in Livermore. I think the time has come for me to start tailing Anne Brooke."

There were no messages on either one of our answering machines. While Anne Brooke worked in Livermore she lived in Lafayette, and Anatoly and I both agreed that in a suburban city known for its manicured lawns and safe family environment a Harley might be a little conspicuous, so he put in a call to Avis. I offered to lend him my car, but as he pointed out, the amount Melanie had paid him for this case was enough to cover the expense of renting a car, every day for a month, if necessary.

For once I didn't ask to tag along. I felt the bizarre need to wait by the phone. The phone that didn't ring. I tried to distract myself by calling Dena, but she was in the middle of an inventory, so I called Mary Ann at the dinner party. She told me that Fitzgerald and his wife were there and that

Johnny felt awful about having to uninvite me. She swore up and down that she didn't know why Fitzgerald had come to the Rotunda earlier that day, and I actually believed her, although I still felt she was holding something back. Eventually I let her off the phone and I brought my laptop into the living room, determined to lose myself in the creation of a new manuscript. But I couldn't concentrate. At nine-thirty I called Leah on her cell. We hadn't spoken since I stormed out of the restaurant in Pleasanton, but that was only because we had both been busy. Leah and I stormed out on each other all the time; we knew better than to take it seriously.

"Sophie, I just wrapped up that retirement dinner at the Marines' Memorial," she said triumphantly as soon as she picked up. "The whole event went off without a hitch!"

"Congratulations. Are you heading home now?"

"I was. I actually didn't expect to be done this early so the babysitter won't be expecting me for another hour. New babysitter," she said, before I could ask, "not Liz-the-lap-dancer."

When Leah had arrived to pick Jack up early after Eugene's funeral she had found Liz sitting on Bruce's lap listening to music. I'll confess that I found this news a little shocking until Leah admitted that Liz hadn't actually been sitting on Bruce so much as she had been sitting beside him with her calves resting on his lap and that Jack had been no more than ten feet away, trying to convince an incredulous puppy to attack a plastic squeaky hamburger. Oh, and the music that was playing was from *The Little Mermaid* soundtrack. Nonetheless Leah had been horrified by the "vulgarity of it all."

"Why don't you stop by and tell me more about the party?" I asked.

"You want me to come over there and tell you about a dinner party I threw for a retiring CEO?" Leah asked slowly.

She knew as well as I did that under normal circumstances I'd rather get a root canal than listen to her drone on about something like that, but these weren't normal circumstances. I needed a distraction and I'd take it in any form I could get it. "Yes," I said firmly. "I want to know all the juicy details."

Leah was silent for an uncharacteristically long stretch of time.

"Leah? Are you still there?"

"Yes, I was just thinking how odd it was that the earth could be warming at the same time that hell is freezing over."

"Hell doesn't have to freeze over for me to be interested in formal entertaining."

"Really? That's news to me," she said with a note of amusement. "I'm only a few minutes away from your apartment, but with parking—"

"I'll meet you at my front door and drive around with you while you look for a spot," I suggested. "That way we won't waste twenty minutes of visiting time."

"Very well, see you in a minute."

I knew my sister well enough to know that "a few minutes" usually meant a quarter of an hour, but Leah surprised me by pulling up in front of my door a mere ten minutes later. I hopped in the passenger seat and pushed aside the few shopping bags that she had placed on the floor of the car in order to make room for my feet.

"So," Leah said as she slowly drove down a side street. "Why am I really here?"

"I told you. I want to hear about the party."

"Yes, and earlier this evening I told an attractive stock-broker that I was twenty-four. That doesn't make it true."

"Leah! You're only twenty-nine! You can't start lying about your age until you're at least forty!"

"But everybody expects you to lie about your age at forty. If you start lying at twenty-nine people don't question you. That way when you reach forty everyone will actually believe you when you tell them you're thirty-five."

"So you've figured out what lies you need to tell now in order to make the lies you will want to tell eleven years from now more convincing?" I asked. "God, you are so organized. I could never plan for anything that far in advance."

"It always pays to think ahead," she said. "Now, tell me why you wanted me to come over. Does it have something to do with this investigation you're doing for Melanie?"

"Sort of," I hedged. I didn't want to tell anyone that Melanie might be missing. There was no reason to alarm everyone until more time had passed and I was sure there actually was something to worry about.

"You figured out why you feel compelled to help her, didn't you?" she asked.

"Yes, that's it. That's why I wanted to talk to you," I lied. "I've finally come to terms with how much I owe Melanie. When I was at my lowest, she was there for me. She helped me find my way and she basically turned me into a novelist. Everything I have, everything I *am* is the result of the deci-sions she helped me make during my college years. Now, with Eugene gone, Melanie's going to have to take her life in a new direction. Maybe by helping her get justice for Eugene I will be giving her the peace of mind she needs to find that direction. I have to at least try to do for her what she did for me." I flashed Leah a proud smile. "So it seems your therapist was right, I was able to figure out my own issues without your spelling them out for me."

Leah made a face but kept her eyes on the side of the road as she continued to look for parking. "I think my therapist would agree that telling you you're still not seeing the big picture isn't so much a criticism as it is a helpful hint."

"Oh, for God's sake." I dropped by head back against my seat. "What do you think I'm repressing now?"

"I'm not supposed to tell—"

"Enough, Leah. Knock off the Freud crap and tell me what's on your mind!"

"Fine." She double parked the car and shifted in her seat so she could look me in the eyes. "Melanie helped you get your life together. She showed you how to channel your anger and do what you needed to do in order to ensure yourself a prosperous future. But if you had stayed in touch with her, as in seen her more than once every other year, she would have started to push you to take the next step, which is to deal with the past. You were a daddy's girl, Sophie. You two had a connection that he and I never had."

"He loved you, too, Leah."

"He adored me," Leah agreed, "but you were his favorite and I'm Mama's. Or at least I was Mama's favorite until I married a slimeball in a church. I'm still making up for that. But as kids I was Mama's princess and you were Dad's pride and joy. And Dad-Dad was your world. You know you've never really said goodbye to him."

I swallowed hard and looked away. "Maybe you should drive down Lexington. Sometimes I find parking there."

"See! You can't even talk about it! Melanie's the only one you've ever really opened up to about Dad. You've shared your innermost feelings with her and now you expect her to play caretaker to those feelings so you don't have to examine them again. It's like you see grief as an object and you just gave yours to Melanie and asked her to put it some-where so you didn't have to look at it anymore. But by doing that you've created a situation that requires you to distance yourself from Melanie, because if you don't she'll eventually make you take your grief back and deal with it."

"If I want to distance myself from her, why am I helping her? I could have left this whole thing to Anatoly."

"Two reasons. At the moment, Melanie's too upset about her own life to make you deal with yours, so it's safe to help her now. The second reason is that she truly appreciates how much you cared about Dad and how much his death affected you and that makes her your friend whether you like it or not. You have never been able to walk away from a friend in need. Oh, and you also want to be around Anatoly—I suppose that's three reasons."

"Are you *seeing* a therapist or becoming one?" I asked.

"Really, Sophie, you know I've always been very good at figuring out what other people's problems are. It's my prob-lems that elude me."

"Join the club," I said. "Everything would be so much easier if we could just run one another's lives instead of our own."

"Well that's why I have a therapist. I'm hoping he'll tell me how to run my life, although he's done an awful job of it so far. He still hasn't told me how to find a husband."

"Maybe you can order one from the Neiman Marcus Christmas catalog."

Leah smiled and started the car again. "You're changing the subject again."

"Yeah, but you let me do it." I looked out at the dark streets and sighed. "A lot of years have gone by since Dad died."

"Twelve," Leah said softly.

"Do you think I'll ever come to terms with it?"

"Maybe. Melanie helped you with it when you were in college, maybe you could talk to her about it again—after you've solved this case, of course."

I understood that Leah had just given my involvement in this case her approval and oddly enough that meant something to me. I was going to take her advice and start talking to Melanie about Dad again. It was time. But what if Melanie was no longer around to listen?

The fear that I had been trying to distract myself from came back with a new force.

"Sophie, by the time I find parking I'm going to have to leave," Leah grumbled.

"I know," I said. "Why don't you drop me off at my door and you can go home and take care of Jack."

My visit with Leah hadn't calmed me. If anything, it had intensified my need to find Melanie. I needed to help her. I needed to talk to her. But most of all, I needed her to be safe.

Once back in my apartment I checked my e-mails in hopes of finding something from Melanie, but of course there was nothing there. I took out a piece of paper and tried to make a list of all the places she might be, but when I couldn't come up with anything I tore the paper up. At eleven I turned on the television but found that even Jon Stewart didn't have the power to distract me from my growing trepidation. At eleven-twenty Anatoly called.

"Have you heard from Melanie?" I asked hopefully.

"Not yet." He didn't bother asking me if I had heard anything. There were lots of things that Anatoly and I were willing to keep from each other, but not this kind of stuff.

I turned off the TV and adjusted my legs so Mr. Katz could make himself at home on my lap. "Okay, so what's Anne been up to?"

"Nothing interesting. She was at the campaign head-quarters until seven-thirty, then she and a few people from her office went out for pizza and now she's home with her husband."

"Scintillating."

"Mmm…but the night hasn't been a total waste."

"How do you figure?"

"Anne may not be doing anything out of the ordinary, but I'm not the only one interested in her. There's another man who's been following her."

"You're kidding me!" I scooted to the edge of the couch, earning a look of admonishment from my pet.

"No, some guy in an old white Dodge Conversion. I'm watching him right now."

"A Conversion? I don't know much about cars, but isn't that a van?"

"Yep, and from the looks of it I'd say it was a model from

the early eighties and hasn't been washed or serviced since the nineties."

"Someone is following Anne Brooke in a white dilapidated van? Isn't that kind of conspicuous?"

"You could say that."

"Do you think Anne has noticed?"

"Hard to tell, but I wouldn't be surprised if she has. Unfortunately that means that if she was planning on doing something incriminating, she's probably changed her mind. On the plus side this guy is making it less likely that she'll notice *me*."

"How totally weird."

"Ah, he's leaving. I'm going to see where he's headed. I'll call if I find out anything important. Otherwise I'll call tomorrow morning—late morning."

"Okay. After you're done chasing Mr. Smog Emissions do you think you could swing by Melanie's place again?"

"I was planning on it."

"And if she's home you'll call me, right?"

Anatoly waited a few moments before speaking. "We will find her, Sophie. I promise you that."

An unexpected wave of relief washed over me. Anatoly rarely made promises, and when he did he never broke them. When Leah was accused of murder he never said "Everything's going to be okay" or "She'll be fine." It had pissed me off at the time, but now I was grateful for it because it meant that this last promise was valid. He felt confident in his ability to track Melanie down.

"Thank you, Anatoly," I breathed. "I think I might even be able to sleep now."

"You're welcome. Good night, Sophie."

"Wait!" I should have let him end the call on a good note, but now that he had given me a taste of reassurance I craved more. "You think Melanie's okay, right? I mean she's going to be fine."

"Try to get some sleep, Sophie. I'll call you tomorrow." No promises that time. And with that he ended the call, along with any hopes I had of a good night's rest.

At nine-forty-five the next morning, Anatoly forgot his promised phone call and showed up on my doorstep instead. Nine-forty-five does not fit my definition of "late morning" but I forgave him because he came bearing muffins and Frappuccinos. I polished off my drink and was halfway through my muffin before I worked up the nerve to ask him what he had discovered the night before. Anatoly and I may have our differences, but we both firmly believe in the Jewish rules of life, first and foremost being that every sweet moment must be balanced with a healthy dose of bitterness. And the fact that Anatoly had brought me a breakfast rich in refined sugar was not lost on me.

"I found out the name of the man who was following Anne last night," Anatoly said after swallowing a mouthful of blueberry pastry. "His name's Darrell Jenkins and he's a private detective."

"What!" I set down my muffin and stared at Anatoly across my dining table. "Are you sure about that?"

"Very sure. After he left Anne's he went straight home. He didn't check his mail, which turned out to be an incredibly lucky break, although from the looks of it he only picks up his mail once or twice a week."

"What was in his mail?"

"Two credit card bills and a notice from the IRS, complete with his full name and social security number. It only took an hour or so on the Internet and a few phone calls earlier this morning to get a fairly complete account of this man's life."

"Give me the Cliffs Notes version."

"He's a high school dropout born and raised in Gilroy. He tried to join the army but was rejected because he didn't have a GED."

"I thought the military had some kind of program these days to help dropouts who want to enlist to *get* their GED," I said.

"That program isn't open to everyone and you do still have to pass the GED at some point, and Darrell failed. So when the army turned him away he got a job as a nighttime security guard at the local Pak'nSave but was fired because he was trying to frisk the female customers. That's when he came up to Contra Costa County. He worked as a bouncer at a nightclub for a long time but eventually he got in a fistfight with one of the owners after that owner reportedly called our president a pussy."

"Well, in Darrell's defense the owner was out of line," I said. "It's been decades since we've had a president sensitive enough to be called a pussy."

"Yes, well, there's that," Anatoly agreed. "Criminal charges were filed, but it was unclear who instigated the physical aspect of the fight and the whole thing was thrown out of court in short order. Soon thereafter Darrell managed to actually pass a test and he got himself a private investigator's license, courtesy of an online training course."

"Kind of puts a chink in the exclusivity of your industry, doesn't it?"

"This from an author of murder mysteries. You don't have to be Shakespeare to get a book published these days."

I groaned and fell back in my chair. "I'm so tired of being criticized for not writing like some guy who died four hundred years ago. I bet when Shakespeare wrote his first sonnet the sixteenth-century critics got out their quills and wrote, 'While the work doest have merit, William doth not compare to the greatness that was Chaucer.'"

Anatoly started to laugh, which was problematic since he had a mouth full of coffee. Once he managed to swallow he said, "Literary greats aside, Darrell Jenkins is not very good at what he does."

"The white van was probably a bad call."

"Yes, particularly when you consider that Anne lives in Lafayette, a town in which most of the cars have German or Italian names and cost about the same as a two-bedroom condo in Arkansas. But his incompetence doesn't stop there."

"No?"

"He advertises in the Yellow Pages."

"*You* advertise in the Yellow Pages."

"Yes, but my ad doesn't feature a five-by-six color photograph of myself. Do you see the problem with exposing your identity to the world when your job requires a degree of anonymity?"

"Yes," I agreed between muffin bites, "that was unwise. Who's he working for?"

"I don't have the answer to that yet, but I will soon."

I nodded and let my gaze fall to my cat, who was rubbing

himself up against the table leg. "I think we need to get to the subject we're both avoiding."

Anatoly sighed. "I rode by her house at 2:00 a.m. and she wasn't home and she didn't answer the phone when I called earlier this morning. I'm going to drive over there again today, and if she's not around I think we should file a missing-person report."

"Shit."

"Unless of course you can think of some place where she might have gone to. Did she have any close friends or special places that she liked to escape to?"

"That's the problem. I don't know those things. We haven't spent a lot of time together over the past few years." I considered telling him Leah's theories about why that was but I stopped myself. The details of my relationship with Melanie were too emotionally complicated to share with a man who wasn't even my boyfriend. But there was one thing that I did need to share with him. I twiddled with the plastic top of my empty cup and tried to figure out how to broach the subject. "Listen, there's something that I've been meaning to talk to you about. I was going to tell you yesterday, but then I got distracted by our search for Melanie. But well, um…someone's been kind of threatening me."

"What?" Anatoly yelled.

"Yeah. I'm not sure who. They left one message on my answering machine, one anonymous note on my door and called my cell once. The cell call came right after the Rotunda lunch while you were waiting for me in the car. I don't know if the caller is a man or a woman because they're using a voice synthesizer that makes them sound a little like Darth Vader."

"Sophie," Anatoly growled, "we are investigating a murder. You have to *tell me* when you get death threats."

"But that's the thing. They're not death threats, I don't think. They're more like…funny threats."

"Funny threats," Anatoly repeated.

I nodded and walked over to my answering machine to play the message for him. While he listened I pulled out the Pink Panther note and handed it over.

For a few minutes Anatoly simply stared silently at the note. "I have to admit," he finally said, "I don't know what to make of this."

"In the last call he told me that he liked to dress up as a koala bear."

"You're serious?"

"I don't think I could make that up."

Anatoly looked at the note again. Finally, he handed it back to me. "I'll think about this. In the meantime I should get over to Melanie's."

"I'm going with you."

"That's not necessary."

"It will be necessary if you need to file a missing-person report. I may not know who Melanie hangs out with when I'm not around, but I will be able to give the cops a lot more information about her than you will. Besides, if you talk to the police you might do something stupid like tell them the truth."

"I don't think I want to know where this is going."

"We can't tell them that Melanie hired us to investigate Eugene's death."

"Sophie, we can't *not* tell them. It may be the reason she's disappeared."

"I promised her I'd keep my mouth shut about that and I'm not going to break that promise just because she's been MIA for a couple of days."

"Sophie…"

"If after a little snooping we find a concrete reason for the police to know about everything, then we'll tell them. Not necessarily that we've been investigating anything, but that Melanie was worried that Eugene's murder might have been premeditated. But if we break Melanie's confidence straight away it could seriously damage my relationship with her, and I don't want it to come to that."

Anatoly met my eyes, his expression somber with a touch of empathy. "Sophie, there's a chance that Melanie is no longer in the position to end her relationship with you or anyone else."

I didn't flinch or even acknowledge the fact that I'd heard him. There were some things I just couldn't deal with. Instead I looked down at the cotton bleach-stained pants that I had pulled on under my nightshirt when Anatoly buzzed my apartment. "Give me twenty minutes to get myself together."

"You're insisting on this, aren't you?"

"Trust me, Anatoly, telling the cops the truth, the whole truth and nothing but the truth is rarely a good strategy."

"How would you know? Have you ever tried it?"

I shrugged dismissively and got to my feet. "I'm getting dressed now." I noted the hungry look in his eyes and added, "You can't watch."

Anatoly smirked. "This isn't turning out to be my day."

Melanie wasn't home. Worse yet, there were now two newspapers rolled up on her front yard. We knocked on the doors of a few more neighbors, but those who were home had no idea where she was, nor could they recall when they last saw her.

The trip to the police station wasn't as traumatic as I had anticipated. For one thing, unlike the SFPD, the police in Walnut Creek were actually nice to me. That was probably because they didn't know me, but whatever their reasons, I appreciated it. They asked us a ton of questions and Anatoly and I managed to keep our lies to ones of omission only. When we walked out, Anatoly put his arm around my shoulders and for once I didn't read anything into it.

"I'll take you home now," Anatoly said as he handed me a helmet.

"What about you? Where are you going?"

"I'm going to visit Darrell Jenkins."

"I'm going with you."

"For a woman who doesn't want anything to do with me, you spend a tremendous amount of time following me around."

I grunted in response. The truth was that I didn't want to be alone. I didn't want to give myself the time and space that would allow me to obsess over all the things that *might* have happened to Melanie.

I climbed on the bike behind Anatoly. If there was one thing that has always kept me from thinking, it's the act of pressing my body up against Anatoly's V-shaped back while straddling the pony-size vibrator he calls a Harley.

Anatoly explained that Darrell's office was in Moraga, not far from Anne's hometown of Lafayette, but since Darrell was following Anne, the first place we should look was in Livermore where Anne's office was. Sure enough, sitting right across from the building that held the Brooke headquarters was a rusted white van.

Anatoly parked his bike around the corner and together we strode up to the van's driver's-side window where a guy with a blond buzz cut and green camouflage gear was sleeping behind the wheel. His head lolled back against the headrest and he was snoring loud enough to be heard through the glass.

Anatoly knocked gently and Darrell Jenkins jumped up as high as his seat belt would allow.

He knocked again and Darrell lowered his window, which I noted was not automatic.

"What the fuck do you want?"

Anatoly folded his arms over his chest and shifted his weight back onto his heels. "Why are you following Anne Brooke, Mr. Jenkins? And who are you working for?"

Darrell's mouth dropped open. "How do you know what I'm doing? And how the fuck do you know my name?"

"We know because we are neither dumb nor blind," Anatoly said simply. "It's in your best interest to be cooperative. The government doesn't like it when individuals stalk politicians."

"Holy shit, are you the Secret Service? I thought you guys only protected the president!"

"Are you kidding me?" I snapped. "We're not the Secret Service, you idiot, we're…"

"FBI," Anatoly said quickly.

"Holy shit!" The little color Darrell had drained from his face.

I bit down hard on my lip. Impersonating FBI agents?

That was so illegal! Then again maybe it wasn't. It's not like Anatoly flashed a badge or anything. Was it really our fault if some guy with an IQ of fifty took a bad joke seriously?

"I'm not a stalker," Darrell said. "I wasn't going to hurt her or even get near the lady! Hell, I'm even planning on voting for her!"

My eyes shot up to his military-style haircut. "You've never voted for a Democrat in your life."

Darrell's eyes grew about an inch in size. "How'd you know I was a Republican?"

"Voting records," I said curtly.

"Voting records? But aren't those private?"

"Not for the likes of you." I was beginning to really enjoy myself. I leaned against the side of the truck and brushed a frizzy curl away from my eyes. "Listen, I'm going to give it to you straight. You were put on the national list of possible terrorists, and now that we've caught you following a senatorial candidate around—" I shook my head sadly "—let's just say it doesn't look good for you, Mr. Jenkins."

Anatoly shot me a warning look, undoubtedly his way of telling me to tone it down, but Darrell was eating it up with a spoon. "Terrorist list! I'm not a terrorist! I'm a patriot!"

"I find that hard to believe."

"No, really I am! You must know that if you've been watching me! Haven't you been wiretapping my phone and shit?"

"We were going to, but the ACLU has really been up our ass about that stuff lately."

"Oh, oh, oh!" Darrell said enthusiastically. "I hate the ACLU!"

"Really?" Anatoly pulled a small notebook and pen out

of the inside pocket of his leather jacket. "Is that why you've been following Anne Brooke around? You knew she was a member of that organization and you wanted to hurt her in order to make a point?"

"What? No!"

"Then perhaps you were just going to bomb her campaign headquarters," I suggested.

"I wasn't going to bomb anybody!"

Now even Anatoly was amused. "Perhaps we should take you in for questioning."

"You gotta listen to me!" Darrell pleaded. "I'm not a terrorist, and I don't mean Anne Brooke any harm. I'm a private detective. You guys know that!"

"We know that's your day job," I said coolly.

"No, no, it's my *everything* job! It's all I do! This is my second case! Some guy wanted me to follow his wife around to make sure she wasn't fucking somebody else, that's all, I swear!"

"Some guy?" Anatoly said slowly. "Are you referring to Sam Griffin?"

"Yeah, that's him, Anne Brooke's husband. You believe me, right?"

Anatoly and I exchanged quick looks. "Have you caught her in the act of doing anything…suspicious?" he asked.

"Nah, but she's up to something. She's nervous as fuck, always looking over her shoulder and shit. It's just a matter of time before I catch her screwing around."

"I see," Anatoly said flatly. "Did it ever occur to you that she was nervous because she was being followed?"

Darrell shook his head. "Who's following her, you?"

"He's taking about you, you moron!" I smacked the side of

the van hard enough to make my hand tingle from the impact. "I take it back, you're way too stupid to be a terrorist. We should get you enlisted in Al Qaeda just to fuck with them."

This time Anatoly couldn't help but chuckle. "Listen, Darrell, this is what I want you to do. I want you to allow Mr. Griffin to believe that you are continuing to tail his wife, but in reality I don't want you to get anywhere near Anne Brooke. Going forward, the only people who will be tailing her will be me and my associate."

Darrell grabbed a chewed-up pencil and started writing down Anatoly's instructions on the back of a Proactiv Solution box that had been on the passenger seat. "Okay, got it. Anything else?"

"No, just remember to stay away from Anne Brooke. When the time's right we'll give you a report to hand over to Mr. Griffin."

"Wait, does this mean that we're working together now?"

"No," Anatoly and I said in unison. Anatoly gestured to me that it was time to leave and I followed him around the corner to where he had parked his bike.

"That was sooo much fun!" I gushed.

"Yes," Anatoly agreed, but he sounded distracted.

"What are you thinking?"

Anatoly turned to face me just as we reached the Harley. "I'm thinking that Melanie might have been right about Eugene."

"About his having an affair or about his having done something unethical that somehow led to his murder?"

Anatoly tapped the handlebars of his bike gently. "Both would be true if he was having an affair with Anne Brooke."

"But what about the letter from Peter Strauss?" I asked. "How does that fit in?"

"I'm not sure yet. It's possible that he seduced Anne under false pretenses."

"You mean you think he was sleeping with her to get information?" I gave a dismissive wave of my hand. "No way, it wasn't his style."

"You only met him once, right?"

"Yeah, but I'm a good judge of character."

Anatoly snorted. "Just because you like to judge people doesn't mean you're good at it."

"I'm telling you, Eugene would never have slept with Anne Brooke, for information or any other reason."

"You'll forgive me if I don't just take your word for that."

"Whatever," I said with a shrug. "Bark up the wrong tree if you like. It'll just give me a leg-up on figuring this thing out before you do."

"And your legs always look so lovely when they're up," Anatoly said with a smile.

"Well, I hope your memories are enough to satisfy you, because you're never going to be touching these legs again."

"I'm giving you a ride home, right?" he asked.

"Of course you're giving me a ride home."

"Then you're going to have to let me touch your legs, aren't you?"

"I hate you." I quickly pulled the helmet over my head before he could see me flush.

15

Every woman knows that she will eventually lose the man in her life. Men leave to pursue younger women during their midlife crises or they die ten years before women due to their weaker hearts. But to lose a girl-friend…that's an unexpected tragedy.
—*C'est La Mort.*

IT WAS TEN-THIRTY AT NIGHT WHEN THE POLICE BUZZED MY APARTMENT. I'm ashamed to admit this, but my first thought was that I didn't want to greet them in the ratty sweatpants I had changed into. But I hadn't been expecting any visitors. After Anatoly and I had gotten back to San Francisco, he'd gone off to the library and the city's public records department to do a little research into Eugene's FBI days. He didn't want to leave any stone unturned. My intention had been to use the afternoon to look into Sam Griffin, but when a quick Google search and a fifty-dollar Internet background check told me that he had been married once before and had no criminal history, I had switched tasks and started working on my next manuscript. Escaping into a fictional universe was the only way I could keep myself from thinking about Melanie.

But maybe if I *had* been thinking about Melanie I would have been able to figure out why the police wanted to talk to me. When I opened the door I saw two plainclothes officers in ugly brown suits holding out badges for my inspection.

"Good evening," said the first officer. He was a tall, thirty-something guy with prematurely gray hair that only served to bring more attention to his youthful face. "I'm Detective Kelly and this is my partner, Detective Stone." He pointed a thumb in the direction of his dark-haired partner, who seemed to be overcompensating for his lack of height with the kind of muscle mass obtained by downing a bottle of Barry Bonds's miracle head-growing vitamins.

"And you're Sophie Katz," Detective Kelly continued. "I recognize you from your picture."

"My picture? You mean on the back of my books?"

"I mean the ones they've printed in the newspaper. You and your sister have often been the talk of the SFPD."

"Uh-huh." I leaned against the door frame. "I'm not really liking the way this conversation is starting out."

"I'm sorry," Detective Kelly said with a smile (apparently Mr. Mini-Universe was the silent type), "I didn't mean to insult you or imply that you were in some kind of trouble, but we would like to ask you a few questions about the missing-person report you filed in Walnut Creek earlier today."

"Oh, okay." I waved them into the room. The Walnut Creek PD had asked for the assistance of the SFPD? Why?

The San Francisco police didn't have time to investigate the crimes committed on their own turf, let alone potential ones that took place a couple of cities away.

The two men walked in and stood in the middle of my living room, taking in the hardwood floors and the coffee table that was partially visible under a pile of magazines and a PG&E bill that I had made the mistake of opening while sober.

"Feel free to sit and make yourself comfortable," I said. Mr. Katz came strolling down the hall, took one look at our visitors and did a quick one-eighty. He had inherited his owner's aversion to authority figures.

The two officers sat side by side on the couch and Detective Stone pulled out a notepad before asking, "When exactly was the last time you heard from Melanie O'Reilly?"

"I don't mean to be rude," I said as I sat opposite them on the love seat, "but I've already given all the information I have on Melanie to the Walnut Creek police."

Detective Stone looked up with an expression that made me rethink my impulse to resist questioning. These guys were serious. I put my hand on my stomach as if that would help alleviate the queasiness that had just overtaken me.

"I spoke to her on the phone two days ago," I said quietly. "She just called to check in. Later, around five o'clock that night, she phoned because she was upset about her husband, Eugene. He was killed in a drive-by shooting two weeks ago and I think Monday night it finally hit her that he was gone for good. My cell was off when she called so I didn't get her message until hours after she left it. You know, you guys didn't tell me what department you're in. Are you normally assigned to missing-person stuff?"

Kelly and Stone exchanged quick glances. Kelly cleared his throat and scooted further forward on the couch. "We work in homicide, Ms. Katz. I regret to inform you that this morning we found a woman's body hidden in some brush by Ocean Beach. She didn't have any identification on her, but when we started calling other police departments we found out that there had been a missing-person report issued in Walnut Creek for a woman who fit the description of the victim."

"You've made a mistake." My voice sounded flat and mechanical even to me. "The woman you found wasn't Melanie. She had no reason to be in San Francisco…."

"We don't think she was killed at the scene," Detective Stone interjected.

"It wasn't her!"

Detective Kelly sighed and adjusted his diamond-patterned tie. "I know how difficult this must be for you, but we wouldn't be here talking to you unless we were sure. You're welcome to come and officially identify the body, but it's not necessary. The body was intact, so we were easily able to figure out who she was."

Who she *was*. He was talking about Melanie in the past tense. I stood up and started pacing. Both Kelly and Stone stood up as well and followed me with their eyes. A little voice inside my head told me that police officers didn't like it when interview subjects became physically agitated, but I couldn't listen to that voice any more than I could listen to what these cops were telling me. I had to figure out how to get out of this nightmare. I had to find a way to turn these men into liars.

"Let me see your badges again," I demanded, finally stopping directly in front of them.

Both men silently pulled out their badges. I reached out and touched the one in Kelly's hand praying that it was a fake. But the badges were made of metal and their IDs looked legit, which meant…

"Oh, God," I whispered, and backed up until I bumped into my built-in bookcase. "Oh, God!"

"Now, take it easy." Kelly took a step closer to me, his voice soft and steady.

"What?" I asked. "What are you saying? Are you asking me to be calm about this? We're talking about Melanie! Do you understand that?" I turned my back to them and leaned my forehead against the sleeve of one of my own murder mysteries. In my life I had seen two dead bodies outside of funeral parlors. Both of them had been murdered and both of them had been acquaintances. I had been the first to find them and the memories of those discoveries would haunt me all my life, but this…this was so much worse.

"Ms. Katz—" I was vaguely aware that it was Stone addressing me this time "—why did you file a missing-person report on Melanie O'Reilly?"

"Because she was missing," I whispered, not even able to summon the energy to point out that his question was amazingly stupid.

"She was missing for just over twenty-four hours when you filed the report," he pressed. "That's not very long for an adult single woman to be out of contact."

"She wasn't returning my calls." I clutched one of the shelves to help me keep my balance.

"Did you think that she was in some kind of danger?"

That was enough to get me to turn back around to face him.

"If I had thought she was in danger then I would have found a way to keep her safe," I hissed. "I would have invited her to stay with me, or vice versa. I wouldn't have let this happen."

Kelly slipped his hands in his pant pockets and released a tired sigh. "There are times when we can't protect our friends."

"Are we done here?" I asked.

Stone shook his head. "Who had it in for O'Reilly?"

"Melanie, her name is Melanie," I said. "Don't talk about her like she's one of your perps. No one has it in for her. She's a good person...." My voice was beginning to shake and I looked away. "I told the police in Walnut Creek all of this. I don't have anything to add."

"Ms. Katz," Detective Stone said, "you don't get to decide when this interview is over."

"We can do this later," Kelly declared, ignoring Stone's scowl. He reached into his coat pocket and handed me a business card. "We'll be in touch soon. If you think of anything between now and then, please give me a call. We'll find out who did this."

I took the card wordlessly and watched as they both exited my apartment. After a few minutes I retrieved my cell phone from my handbag and accessed the saved messages on my voice mail.

Sophie, it's Melanie, could you call me when you have a moment? I think it just hit me that...Eugene's not coming back.

I sat down on the floor in front of my bay windows, put my phone on loudspeaker and listened to the message again, and again.

I must have listened to Melanie's message at least forty times before I finally gave it a rest, and even then I didn't move from my spot on the floor. Perhaps an hour had passed before there was a knock on my apartment door. On some level I was aware that it was rather late for surprise visitors and that if someone was going to come and see me they should have had to buzz my flat just to get admittance into the building. But I wasn't concerned with any of that. I wasn't even interested in finding out who it was. Instead I just continued to sit there, gazing out at the hazy black sky.

I heard the doorknob turn and finally it occurred to me that I was having a 911 kind of moment. I reached for my phone, but before I could press the three numbers the door opened wide and Anatoly stepped inside. "Your door was unlocked."

"The door to the building, too?"

Anatoly hesitated a moment. "Do you recall losing the key to your building approximately seven months ago?"

"Yes."

"I found it."

"When?"

"Approximately seven months ago…in your purse."

I stared at him for a moment. It had been the day Anatoly had driven Mr. Katz and me to the vet. I hadn't realized the key was missing until he was driving us back home. I had spent hours looking for that key, and since both my landlord and Marcus (the only other people who had a key to my place) were out of town, I had been forced to spend three days with Anatoly while I waited for one of them to return. Three days that I should have spent writing that I had instead spent exploring different sexual positions with Anatoly. And all that time he had my key? I should be furious right now. But I couldn't get there. Instead I turned my attention back to the window.

Anatoly quietly closed the door and after a moment in my kitchen joined me on the floor and handed me a vodka and orange-juice. I studied the little floating pieces of orange pulp. "I guess the police visited you, too."

"They did."

I downed half my drink in one gulp. "Did you tell them that Melanie hired you to investigate Eugene's death?"

"No, I kept her confidence."

"Why?" I scoffed. "It's not like she's around to make you keep your word."

"I did it for you. I knew you wouldn't want me to break that promise to Melanie."

I finished my drink in lieu of answering.

We sat in silence for a few minutes as I waited for the alcohol to dull the pain. It didn't seem to be working.

"We have to find out who did this," I said eventually. "And don't tell me to leave it all up to you. I'm going to track this guy down personally. I'm going to be there in the courtroom when they sentence him, and I'm going to be there when they put the needle in his arm. I want this killer to die."

Anatoly gently took my empty glass with one hand while he encircled me with his other arm. I leaned my body against him and squeezed my eyes shut. "He killed my friend," I whispered. "Somebody killed my friend."

I was sobbing now and Anatoly was stroking my hair. He was muttering something comforting, but I was crying so hard that I wasn't able to decipher if he was speaking in English or Russian.

He waited until my sobs had been reduced to pathetic whimpers and then with one swift move he lifted me up into his arms. He didn't throw me over his shoulder the way he sometimes had when he was rushing me to the bedroom. This time he carried me like a princess. I buried my face in his chest as he took me back to my room and laid me down on my unmade bed. Without a word he climbed in next to me and held me close. The tears kept coming until I finally fell asleep in his arms.

16

The best cure for grief is anger.
—*C'est La Mort*

I WOKE UP WITH WHAT FELT LIKE THE WORST HANGOVER OF MY LIFE.
What had I drunk last night? I forced my tired, scratchy eyes
open and stared at my bedside clock until it came into focus.
Only eight-thirty in the morning. I heard a noise in the
kitchen…a cabinet door opening and closing. Anatoly must
have been making himself something to eat.

And then the memory of yesterday hit me like a lead ball to
the stomach. I hadn't gotten drunk last night; this was an emotional hangover. I clutched the sheets and pulled them to my
chin. Melanie was gone. How was I going to deal with that?

But I had to deal with it. I had to find a way to suck it up
and move forward, because succumbing to depression had
never been a viable option for me. In order to be depressed
you had to spend a significant amount of time dwelling on

terrible things. I didn't have the strength for that. However, I'm an expert when it comes to giving in to anger and living in denial. I slowly got to my feet. My legs ached as if I had run a marathon. So did my arms, my chest, my heart...the physical aftermath of a mini-breakdown. I found Anatoly at my dining table reading the paper with a cup of Starbucks and an unopened box of pastries in front of him with the name of the bakery down the street printed on the box. When he looked up and saw me, he quickly folded the paper and placed it on the table with the headline facing down.

I swallowed and reached my hand out. "Let me see it."

"Wouldn't you like your coffee first? There's a Frappuccino waiting for you in the kitchen. A Light White Mocha—"

"Let me see the paper."

Anatoly hesitated, then handed it over. The headline was in the usual black bold print walking the line between gravity and sensationalism: Woman's Discarded Body Discovered Just Weeks After Husband's Murder.

"The police have released a lot of information about this," Anatoly said as I silently perused the article. "They're probably hoping this will jar someone into remembering something. Supply them with a new lead."

"It says that the police are unsure if there is a connection between Eugene's death and Melanie's," I said quietly. "They barely mention Fitzgerald or Eugene's work at all."

"I don't think they believe it's that relevant." Anatoly took a sip of his coffee. "Eat your breakfast, Sophie. I got us dark chocolate éclairs."

I looked over at the pastries. "I don't think I can eat."

Anatoly studied me for a moment, gauging the gravity of

my mood. I never turned down dark chocolate. "Will you drink the Frappuccino?" he asked carefully.

"Oh, yeah, I'll drink the Frappuccino."

He exhaled in relief and went to the kitchen to retrieve my drink. He probably saw my willingness to indulge in caffeine as a sign that I was okay…acting like myself and all that. It was a stupid conclusion to jump to. If a rifle owner loaded his gun before hiking off to the woods, it might mean that he was embarking on his usual hunting expedition or it *might* mean that he was about to kill somebody. I was the gun and the caffeine was my bullet. I needed to load myself up before I hunted down Melanie's killer.

"Anne Brooke is supposed to be meeting with some people from Code Pink in the city this morning."

"Code Pink…they're an activist group, right? Women for Peace?"

Anatoly nodded in confirmation. "I thought I'd hang out in front of the meeting spot and see where she went after that." He gently took the paper from me and dropped it on the table. "Would you like to come with me?"

"You're *inviting* me to join you on a stakeout? Seriously?"

"I don't see this as one of my more dangerous missions."

I stared down at my drink. "I don't feel like going today," I said slowly.

Anatoly blinked. "What?"

"I'm not going."

Anatoly locked me into a staring contest for what felt like five minutes but was probably less than thirty seconds. Finally he asked in a low voice, "Tell me what you're planning, Sophie."

"Nothing."

"C'mon."

"Anatoly…" I placed a hand on his chest both to soothe him and to absorb some of his strength. "I need to be on my own today. I need to process some stuff. You have to give me space to do that."

Anatoly paused for a beat, then cupped my chin and stared into my eyes. "Don't get yourself killed, Sophie."

"I'll do my best to avoid it."

He nodded, and then after studying me for another moment turned around and left the apartment.

For once I had actually been telling him the truth.

Hours later I was sitting in my car gazing at the gray ocean as it reflected the fog hovering above it. This was where she died. Well no, that wasn't right. Her body was found here. No one knew exactly where she was killed. I got out of the car and walked over to the brush a few yards away. The newspaper said that her body was dumped in the bushes and they had featured a photograph of this exact spot. Dumped. Like she was nothing but a bag of garbage. The ocean breeze deposited little droplets of cool water on my skin, but I didn't bother to go back to the car to retrieve my jacket.

Three times in five years. That was how many times I had seen Melanie before she had called to ask for my help with Eugene. I saw my dentist more often than that. How could I be so deeply affected by the loss of a woman whose friendship I had treated so casually? In fact, I had never really thought of her as a friend. A professor, a mentor, even a distant relation, but never a friend…until now. Leah had been right, Melanie had silently agreed to hold on to the grief I had felt in association with my father's death and all this time she had patiently sat back and given me space—just waiting for me to reach a point when I was ready to deal with my feelings. I think she knew I would come to her when that day arrived. But then again she hadn't expected to die so soon. Now I had two losses to mourn and I wasn't sure who I should give my grief to, or if I even had the right to give it away at all. I squeezed my eyes shut and imagined how nice it would be if God gave us all erasers so we could remove the painful events of our pasts. All I could do was get revenge. Get revenge, euphemistically call it justice and hope that it granted me some solace.

"It was that damn bear who did it."

I squeaked in surprise and my eyes flew open. Several feet behind me, standing on the sidewalk, was a heavyset black woman wearing about five layers of extremely tattered clothing and a hat made out of tinfoil. She was clutching a shopping cart filled with what I assumed amounted to her worldly possessions.

"Um…I didn't hear you approach," I said with a little self-conscious laugh.

"I'm tricky that way."

I nodded, not knowing how to respond. "Were you addressing me just now?"

"No one else in hearing distance," the woman snapped.

That was true, but when someone wore a tinfoil hat you had to assume that she might be seeing people you didn't.

"The police were all over here yesterday," the woman grumbled, abandoning her shopping cart momentarily so she could join me in the brush. "Flashing their cameras in everybody's face and asking questions like they're all important." She loudly cleared her throat and then spit what could only be described as a large yellow loogie on the ground.

"They found a woman's body here," I explained.

"I knows what they found. Whole damn city knows what they found here. You should have seen the scene those cops were making. You'd have thought someone killed the damn pope. But that's what happens when a white woman dies. Everybody acts like the world's comin' to an end. When one of us black folk shows up dead we're lucky if they send out a meter maid. And mark my words, they'll be trying to blame one of us. That or maybe one of those Mexicans everybody wants to deport. But let me tell you something. This lady wasn't killed by no black and she wasn't killed by no Mexican."

"No?"

"No," she said with a definitive shake of her head. "She was killed by a bear."

"Excuse me?"

"You heard me. It was a killer bear that did that white woman in. I saw the whole thing and let me tell you, I knew that bear was trouble the second he hauled his pink ass out of that rental truck. Pink bears aren't supposed to be driving no Ford vehicle. Pink bears should be driving pink Cadillacs and Mustangs or one of those Japanese things—they like pink bears in Japan."

"I didn't know that," I said carefully, "about the Japanese and the bears, that is."

"Sure, sure, they like that stuff. 'Specially the gay ones."

"The gay Japanese?"

"No, the gay bears!" the woman snapped as if I was being incredibly dense.

"Oh, right, right," I said quickly. "A pink bear would probably be gay. That makes sense." *Not.*

"The color of a bear's fur don't make him gay. What are you, one of those midwestern bigots?"

"No!" I raised my hands in protest. "I'm sure that all bears are created equal regardless of their color, subspecies or sexual orientation."

"It was the rainbow that made him gay," the woman said.

"Uh-huh." I looked around to see if there was anyone around to help me if this woman became violent, but it was a cold day for the beach and the few people in sight were at least fifty yards away. "So this pink bear you saw was carrying a Gay Pride flag?" I asked.

"He wasn't carrying no flag, the rainbow was on his stomach. Big white tummy with a rainbow."

"Wait a minute," I said slowly, "are we talking about a Cuddly Bear?"

"He wasn't so cuddly if you ask me. He murdered that woman. I seen the whole thing with my own two eyes."

"Are you telling me that you witnessed a woman being murdered by a homosexual bear?" We really needed to do something about the mental health-care system. People who wore tinfoil hats should not be expected to take care of themselves.

"That's right," the woman answered. "'Course, I didn't tell none of this to the police. I don't talk to cops. No police, no bears. Them are my rules."

"No kidding? Those are my rules, too," I admitted. "I do talk to domestic cats, though."

"Cats are okay," the woman said with a nod. "The small ones almost never kill people and they don't go around flaunting their gay lifestyle on their belly. Them cats are discreet."

My mind wandered to Mr. Katz. I had never thought of him as discreet, but compared to a homicidal Ford-driving Cuddly Bear, I guess he was. "Hey, I've got a question for you," I said with a smile. For some reason I liked this woman, and our conversation was turning into an amusing distraction. "How did you know the Ford was a rental?"

The woman let out an exasperated sigh. "Nobody's gonna sell no Ford to no goddamn bear. They got bad credit." And with that the woman turned around and shuffled off.

I felt better after that conversation. I sort of found it comforting. People always say that they find it disconcerting when the world continues to go on as normal after they've experienced an intense personal tragedy. I could understand that, but things were never really normal in San Francisco. They were always…interesting. I took strength from that. It was much easier to lose yourself in insanity than normalcy. Besides, I simply couldn't grieve right now. I needed to be like Scarlett O'Hara and think about Melanie tomorrow. Right now I had to keep my focus on what was important: revenge.

I stopped by the police station that was listed on Officer Kelly's card and asked to speak with him. I knew that if I didn't go to see him he'd come to see me in order to ask the questions he had withheld the night before. I figured I might as well get it over with. He basically asked me to repeat everything I had told the Walnut Creek police. I was embarrassingly ignorant of Melanie's personal life and habits. Of course, I could have told him that Melanie thought her husband's death was something other than a random act of violence. I could have told him about Peter's letter, too. I have no idea why I chose not to. Habit, maybe? I hadn't had a lot of luck with the police in the past and I was reluctant to hand over the entire investigation to them. Maybe I was just indulging my baser instincts by trying to get the vengeance on my own. If I gave the police too much info they would have the power to cut me out of the loop. I was being petty and unreasonable and I knew it, but I couldn't help myself. I wanted to be there when the person who killed Melanie went down.

It was about noon when I got home. As I walked up to my floor I detected the smell of eggs and the sound of a smoke alarm, both coming from my apartment. The alarm stopped as I opened the door and I found Anatoly climbing down off the kitchen counter with my smoke detector in his hands.

"Don't say anything," he warned.

"Why, is there an obvious wisecrack that I'm missing?"

Anatoly looked slightly thrown by my lack of sarcasm. He cleared his throat and handed me a small teacup worth of coffee that he had already poured.

I took it and regarded him curiously. "I thought you were going to be following Anne around."

"I called her campaign headquarters. As it turns out she has meetings all day. After meeting with Code Pink she's scheduled to meet with some people from Greenpeace and then Bay Area Vegetarians and so on. Following her while she woos one grassroots organization after another isn't going to tell me anything, so I found other things to do."

"Like make me eggs."

"You didn't eat the éclairs I got you this morning. I wasn't sure if you would be coming back here any time soon but I took a gamble."

"You realize that the eggs in the refrigerator expired a few decades ago," I said.

"I went back to my apartment to get some food. I don't understand how you live." He gestured in the general direction of my cabinets.

"What are you talking about? I have food." I pulled a box of Cinnamon Toast Crunch off the top of the refrigerator and waved it in his face. "It's made with whole grains now."

"It's not real food," Anatoly insisted as he slipped an omelet out of a pan and onto a plate before handing it over to me.

"What is this?"

"Lox omelet with caviar hollandaise sauce."

My eyes widened. "Seriously?"

"Would I lie about caviar hollandaise sauce?"

I looked from the plate I held in one hand to the cup I held in the other. Carefully I tasted my coffee, only to discover that it was actually a very large dose of espresso. That's when I noticed that his espresso machine was now sitting between my toaster and sink. I put my breakfast down on the white tile partition that separated the kitchen from the dining area and living room. "I know what you're doing," I said softly.

"It's just a late breakfast, Sophie."

"You're trying to lift my spirits, but, Anatoly—" I gently

tapped my fingernail on the edge of the plate "—this is kind of like giving a child an ice-cream cone after they've lost their favorite grandparent. It's just not going to work."

"Are you sure about that?" Anatoly cocked his head to the side. "You've only had one sip of espresso and already you seem better than you were."

I smiled sadly. "Caffeine can only do so much. But I am better. I have to be. I made some promises to Melanie. I can't fulfill them if I'm a hysterical mess."

Anatoly took a step closer and adjusted the clasp of my necklace. "You're a strong woman, Sophie Katz."

I pulled a fork from the top drawer and cut into the omelet. "And you're a great cook, Anatoly Dar—oh, my God! This is sooo insanely good!"

Anatoly chuckled. "I'm glad you like it." He stepped back and retrieved another omelet from the oven, which he had apparently been keeping warm for himself. "I can't say that I'm surprised, though. I've always been able to satisfy your appetite."

I rolled my eyes but decided that eating took precedence over hurling insults. His adolescent sexual innuendos were actually a relief. If Anatoly had continued with the level of sensitivity he had demonstrated the night before, I wouldn't have been able to remain strong or resolved. I would have fallen apart again and on some level I think he knew that. "I love that you brought the espresso machine over," I said with a smile. "That couldn't have been easy."

"Between that and the groceries I had to make three trips." He patted the machine. "I just don't like being without this for long periods of time."

"My God, and they say *I'm* an addict," I scoffed. "We're talking about one meal, Anatoly, it's not like you're moving in."

"About that…"

"About what?" I took another mouthful of the omelet.

"I think I should move in here for a little while," Anatoly said.

I nearly choked on a fish egg.

"Listen," Anatoly continued before I had a chance to recover. "I don't know why Melanie was killed and I don't know why the killer decided to deposit her body in San Francisco. I sure as hell don't know why someone is calling and threatening you with talk of cats and koala bears, but the combination of the three things spell danger. Danger for *you,* Sophie. Someone might have thought that Melanie knew more than they were comfortable with and they may have come to the same conclusion about us. I know you think that you can take care of yourself—" he held up his hand to delay my predictable protest "—but sometimes taking care of yourself means knowing when to ask for help. It means not taking stupid risks. Being alone here in the middle of the night falls into the latter category."

"So what are you planning on doing? Do you actually think you can stay glued to my side until we figure out who did this?"

"No, but I'd like to be as close by as possible. I would be more comfortable if I stayed here for just a little while. I'll sleep in the guest room, of course."

For some reason the last comment pissed me off the most. He wasn't even trying to manipulate his way into my bed! He actually believed this bullshit about my needing a babysitter.

"You can't stay here," I said flatly as I stabbed the remainder of my breakfast with my fork.

"Why not?"

"You annoy me."

"I see." Anatoly moved in closer. "First of all, I don't annoy you, I agitate you." His eyes ran over my figure. "English may be my second language but I do know that there is a big difference between the two things. Second, your high level of agitation isn't going to change my mind about this. If you don't want me to stay here, that's fine. You can stay at my place."

"Ugh." I looked up at the ceiling, which was hard to do with Anatoly looming over me. "That's not going to happen. Your couch is filthier than my kitchen floor, and I *never* clean my kitchen floor."

"Then it's settled. I'll make a fourth trip to my apartment so I can get some more of my things and I'll set up camp."

"At what point did this become entirely your decision? This is my place and my life."

"Sophie, I think that by now even you will have to admit that you need my help in order to solve this case."

"And you need mine!" I snapped.

"If it pleases you to think so. However, I am not as emotionally invested in solving Eugene's and Melanie's murders as you are. I can walk away."

I gasped and took a staggered step backward. "Anatoly, you wouldn't...you know how important this is to me. You can't quit!"

"Let me move in for a few days and I won't."

"You're blackmailing me! I just lost my friend and you're blackmailing me!"

"I'm doing what I need to do in order to keep you safe."

I glanced over at the iron skillet that was still on the stove and considered hitting him over the head with it. "I'm only going to agree to this because you're forcing me."

"That was never in question. So it'll be you, me and—" his gaze traveled to Mr. Katz, who had just entered the room "—kitty makes three."

My anger with Anatoly was pretty much all-consuming. I tried to dig up some superficial information on Sam Griffin while Anatoly moved a gym bag full of stuff into my guest room. I studiously ignored him when he requested that I print up anything interesting I might come across. On the bright side, I was too pissed to pay any mind to the dull pain that had taken up residence in my chest the moment I had learned about Melanie.

At around three o'clock Anatoly stood behind me while I reread the first of two Amazon reviews for *Broccoli for Life*. "I'm going out to do some research," he said.

I pressed my lips together and scrolled to the third review.

Anatoly sighed. "You're not going to ask me what I'm researching."

It was a statement, not a question, which increased my irritation because it robbed me of yet another opportunity to snub him.

"That's fine," he continued. He placed a folded-up piece of paper by my side. "Here's a photocopy of the letter Peter wrote to Eugene. I assume you're still going to meet with Tiff tonight at Michael Mina. That's in the St. Francis hotel, correct?"

I looked at him for the first time in hours. "Anatoly, if I see you anywhere near that restaurant I will write your address and phone number on the bathroom wall of every gay biker bar in the city."

Anatoly winced. "That's actually an effective threat. I'll let you handle this one alone."

"Yes, why don't you *let* me do that?"

Anatoly opened his mouth to say something before changing his mind and walking out. I smiled to myself. Anatoly was tough, but there wasn't a straight man alive who wasn't intimidated by a burly gay guy in chaps.

I arrived at the St. Francis twenty minutes early and waited in the lobby for Tiff to arrive. The only reason I had been able to get the reservation on such short notice was because the floor manager was a fan of my novels. When she still hadn't arrived five minutes after our reservation, I lied to the maître d' and told him that my companion was in the restroom. It was the only way they were going to seat me, and if I didn't get seated soon our table would be given to someone else.

Tiff finally arrived at six-fifteen. Her hair was curled and sprayed and her crossing-guard-orange cotton-Lycra skirt was ankle length with a slit high enough to ensure that her legs received a little more attention than they deserved. She had topped the whole thing off with an unmistakable polyester blouse with a wide ruffled neckline that exposed her broad shoulders. Put a basket of fruit on her head and she could have been Carmen Miranda. Still, her skin looked fabulous despite (or perhaps because of) her minimalist approach to makeup.

"I'm so sorry I'm late," she said breathlessly, apparently oblivious to the looks she was getting from the other more conservatively dressed patrons. "My car's out of commission and I had to take the bus. You know what that's like after five."

I waved off her apology. "The perpetual tardiness of the Muni buses is one of the things that define this city. Just think what San Francisco would be like if it had reliable public transportation, it'd be…well, it'd be a poor man's Manhattan. Nobody wants that."

Tiff laughed softly as the busboy filled her water glass. "I don't usually mind waiting for the bus, I just didn't want to keep you waiting."

"I'll give you a ride home," I offered. "Are you hungry? If so, you should consider the three-course prix fixe menu. It's been over a year since I've tasted their ricotta tortellini and yet I still dream about it."

Tiff laughed again, but her giggles soon turned into a coughing fit when she looked at the menu. "I can't get that! The prix fixe is eighty-eight dollars per person!"

"My treat, remember?"

"But…"

"Please, Tiff, I really want to."

You could tell by the rose in her cheeks that she was flustered by the idea of taking a gourmet handout, but her hunger must have won out and she started studying the menu in earnest.

I looked down at my menu as well, but I was having a hard time focusing on the words. I had decided to tell Tiff the truth about everything. I had told way too many lies in the past few weeks and they were getting hard to keep track of. So tonight I would confess to inventing a dead sister for the sole purpose of getting her to open up about her dead brother. There was no way that was going to go over well. I had actually recommended the prix fixe dinner because I was hoping she would choose the foie gras as her first course. I would feel a little less guilty if I knew that Tiff was the kind of person who contributed to the pain and suffering of innocent geese.

The waiter came to the table. "Would you like to start with a bottle of wine?"

"Absolutely." I lifted the wine list and pointed out an expensive bottle of Austrian riesling. When he offered to take the list from me I asked if I could keep it a little longer. I sensed that alcohol could be the deciding factor on how well the night played out.

When the waiter disappeared, Tiff glanced at the list out of curiosity. "Whoa! They're charging thirty-six dollars a glass for some of that stuff!"

"Some of their wines are very rare," I said. "Have you decided what you want?"

"Um…I guess I *will* get the three-course meal. I think I'll start with the tempura langoustine and chilled ceviche."

"Not the foie gras? I hear it's wonderful."

"No, I could never support that kind of treatment of a goose."

Well, shoot.

Eventually we ordered, and for the first two courses I allowed her to direct the conversation. She detailed all the labor laws that the proprietor of Mojo routinely broke and told me about the increasing demand for male Brazilian waxes. It wasn't until dessert that she finally started talking about her family, and that's when I broke in with my confession.

"I haven't been completely honest with you about my sister," I hedged.

Tiff nodded, almost enthusiastically. "I was reading one of those psychology self-help books and it said that when we lose someone who was important to us we change our memory of them in a way that makes the loss more bearable. So if you lost a husband to divorce all you remember are the bad things about him because that makes it okay to let him go. If someone you love dies, you remember all the good things so you can take comfort in a bunch of warm, fuzzy feelings. Make sense?"

"Yeah, but, well the things I lied about are kind of…different. For instance, my sister isn't older, she's younger."

Tiff cast me a puzzled look. "That *is* kind of an odd thing to lie about."

"I guess. But perhaps the weirdest part of the lie is that she's, um…she's not exactly resting in peace. In fact, she hasn't rested peacefully since the birth of my nephew."

"Excuse me?"

"I only have one sister, Tiff. Her name is Leah and I seriously doubt that she's ever considered suicide. Narcissists rarely do. The girl I told you about? Susie? She doesn't exist."

Tiff put her fork down. She blinked her eyes rapidly as if trying to wake herself up from a particularly bizarre and disturbing dream. "Why…why would you do that?"

"I have this friend…her name's Melanie and she needed my help. Her husband was killed in a drive-by shooting and she's been trying to figure out who did it and why. She found a letter from your brother in her husband's home office and neither of us could figure out what it meant but it seemed like it might be relevant." I shrugged sheepishly. "I took it upon myself to go undercover. I made up Susie because I thought that if I told you I had lost a sibling to suicide then you would tell me a little bit more about Peter."

"That's sick," Tiff whispered.

"I know." I looked down at my half-eaten peanut butter pudding cake and wondered how many of them I'd have to eat to make the empty feeling in the pit of my stomach go away.

Tiff pushed her chair back. "I have to go."

"She's dead, Tiff."

"Who?" Tiff asked coldly. "One of your imaginary family members?"

"Melanie. They found her body yesterday. I don't know exactly how it happened but I do know it was murder." I looked up and met her eyes. "I've been really awful to you. You'd be crazy if you had any urge to help me, but that's what I need you to do. I need you to help me get justice for my friend."

Tiff didn't scoot her chair back in but she didn't get up, either. "What did my brother's letter say?"

I reached into my handbag and took out the photocopy of the letter Anatoly had given me.

Tiff snatched it from me and read it over. "This doesn't make sense," she said, the edge in her voice beginning to dull.

I squeezed my eyes shut. "I was hoping that it would."

"'Political careers are going to be ruined and so is my life?'" Tiff read the quote while running one finger across the line that contained it. "This is way too melodramatic for my brother."

"Is it his handwriting?"

Tiff squinted her eyes. "It's a photocopy so it's a little hard to tell but…yeah, that's his writing. But it still doesn't make sense. What had he gotten himself into?"

"You said before that you didn't think he would have an affair with Anne Brooke or anyone else he worked with, but is it possible that you were wrong? Brooke has an impressive track record when it comes to adultery, and her new husband thinks she's up to her old tricks. Could your brother have been her latest conquest?"

"I almost wish that were true," Tiff said, her eyes still scanning the letter. "That would make him a little more normal. But like I said, my brother never dated." Tiff put the letter in her lap and let her chin drop to her chest. "He was in trouble. He was in trouble and he didn't trust me enough to tell me about it."

"Tiff, you can't shoulder the blame for your brother's inability to cope."

"Then who can I blame?" she snapped. "Can I blame this Eugene guy? Because from this letter he certainly seems culpable."

"Maybe he was," I admitted.

Tiff swallowed hard, and she put the end of a bright pink acrylic nail in her mouth. "I need to look through his apartment."

"Excuse me?"

Tiff looked up, and although her expression didn't exactly convey forgiveness, she didn't seem livid, either. "When Peter died my parents asked if I would be the one who went through his apartment. It wasn't just because I was the one who lived the closest to Danville. They said it would just be too painful for them. But it's painful for me, too. I've picked Peter up at his place before but I've never actually gone inside, and for some reason the thought of going in there now that he's dead…" Tiff shook her head in defeat. "I ended up calling his landlord and he agreed to let me pay him a fraction of my brother's rent until his lease came up in a few months. He thinks I've been slowly clearing the place out, but I haven't even stepped inside the door. I just couldn't deal with it."

"Are you saying that no one has been inside your brother's place since he died two months ago?"

Tiff smiled weakly. "I hope he had baking soda in the refrigerator."

"Tiff, we have to go there."

"We?" she asked incredulously. "Are you suggesting that I take *you* along?"

I toyed with the remainder of my dessert, somewhat appalled by the audacity of my own request. "I'm not suggesting," I said carefully. "I'm asking. It would seem that whatever Eugene knew about your brother was upsetting enough to make him suicidal. But Eugene died a month *after* your brother did, and you still don't know what Peter was hiding, so obviously Eugene didn't rat him out. Maybe someone else was involved in that secret. Maybe that person was not only responsible for both Eugene's and Melanie's deaths but was also responsible for getting your brother involved in something that pushed him to suicide. If you let me come with you while you look through Peter's apartment, then together we might be able to find the clues we need to get justice for all three victims."

"I'll think about it," she said. I could tell by the way her lips were pressed together that this was not the time to push. She glanced at her Swatch. "I'd like you to take me home now."

I nodded and slipped my credit card into the bill our waiter had left for us. If Tiff's judgment was as bad as her fashion sense then there was a chance that she might come to trust me again.

Tiff lived in the Richmond district in a cozy little cottage with a front lawn surrounded by a white picket fence. At least that's how a real estate agent would describe it. I would say that it was a run-down converted earthquake shelter whose only boasting right was a front lawn that doubled as a parking spot for her VW Bug. By the looks of it the picket fence hadn't been white for at least a decade.

One of the nice things about that area of Richmond is that parking isn't just a pipe dream. I pulled my car up right in front and turned off the music that had previously been masking the silent treatment Tiff was giving me. "Thank you for letting me take you out to dinner," I said lamely. "If you decide to allow me to come with you to Peter's place, just give me a ring, okay?"

"Okay." Tiff didn't look at me when she responded but she didn't get out of the car, either.

"Tiff? You okay?"

Silence.

"Tiff?"

"I'm…I'm scared."

"Of what?"

"Of what?" Tiff scoffed. "You just told me that two people have been murdered and that their deaths are all somehow connected to what happened to my brother. *My brother!* That's scary!"

"I see your point."

"Aren't you scared?"

I thought about that for a moment. "You know how some people bring out the worst in others? Well apparently I make them homicidal. In the past few years I've found two dead bodies and been threatened by two different killers on different occasions for totally different reasons. I'm fairly sure that's not normal."

"I'm fairly sure you're right."

"But it does give some credence to the whole what-doesn't-kill-you-makes-you-stronger cliché. At this very moment nobody is trying to kill me and I actually find that comforting. So no, I'm not scared. I'm just a little sad and seriously angry."

"You are so weird."

I smiled wryly. "You should meet my friends."

"That's okay. Walk me to my door?"

"You got it." I took this last request as a good sign. There were two gates, one big enough for her VW to pass through should it ever become mobile again, and one just big enough for people to pass through single file. We went through the latter and climbed the two slightly uneven steps that led to her front door.

"Just stay until I get the lights on."

I nodded and waited as she very, very carefully opened the front door, and even then she only opened it a quarter of the way. She slipped inside and I started to follow her in when she yelled, "No, Chica!"

I jumped back outside. "What! What did I do?"

"Not *you.*" A light went on and I stepped inside again. Tiff was standing in the middle of the living room with a little Taco Bell dog in her arms. "This is Chica," she explained. "She gets a little excited whenever I walk through that door and I didn't want her getting her dirty paws all over this skirt."

As if anything could make that skirt more hideous. "Looks like you stopped her in time."

Tiff looked down at Chica, who was squirming in her arms. "I'll do it."

I ran my fingers through my hair as I took in Tiff's white pleather couch. Above it she had hung an electric landscape picture that when turned on simulated the movement of the ocean.

"Did you hear me, Sophie?" Tiff asked.

"Huh? Oh, were you talking to me? I thought you were talking to your dog. I have conversations with my cat all the time so I figured—"

"I said I'd do it. I'll take you with me when I go to Peter's place."

"Seriously? Tiff, I swear you won't re—"

"Don't jinx this," Tiff said, effectively cutting me off. "I have tomorrow off so why don't we go then and just get it over with. You'll have to drive because obviously my car won't be working by then."

"Tomorrow, perfect. Morning, afternoon? Whatever you want."

"I like to work out on Sunday mornings, so why don't we say afternoon. Maybe one o'clock?"

"One it is. Thank you, Tiff, I think…" I was going to say "You have made the right decision," but that was probably one of those comments that would "jinx us," so I opted for the only safe comment I could come up with. "You have a nice couch. It has a nice…retro feel to it."

"Retro?" Tiff raised her perfectly shaped eyebrows. "I always thought of it as being pretty modern. Can you believe it's not real leather?"

I smiled at this and bid her goodbye. I had just gotten on her good side, and if I allowed myself to comment further on her taste I'd be back on her shit list in no time.

17

All these years I thought I was being the perfect Catholic, but as it turns out there's more to the rhythm method than just having sex on a dance floor.
—*C'est La Mort*

ON THE WAY HOME LEAH CALLED ME ON MY CELL PHONE.

"I just found out what happened on the news," she said. "Are you all right?"

"I'm fine," I lied.

"Do you want to talk about it?"

"No."

She sighed heavily into the receiver. "Who'd you give grief to this time?"

"No one, which is not to say that I'm willing to deal with it right now," I said as I rushed through a yellow light. "I have to focus on finding Melanie's killer."

"Are you absolutely sure you don't want to let the police take it from here?"

"Approximately seventy percent of violent crimes go unsolved in this city," I retorted. "With that kind of track record, why would I leave something this important to the police?"

"Because it's what you're supposed to do! Because some of us would prefer it if you didn't die young. Isn't that a good enough reason?"

"I have to do this, Leah," I said quietly, "for Melanie."

Leah sighed again, but this time it was a sigh of resignation. "At the risk of sounding repetitive, you're like a psychological case study."

"Right back at you," I said with a smile. "And you're not supposed to criticize me until I hang up, which is now." I ended the call and after a long search for parking made my way back up to my apartment.

"Hello?" I hung my jacket up on my coatrack and searched for signs of life. The only response I got was from Mr. Katz, who stepped into the foyer long enough for me to see that he was going into the kitchen, where he undoubtedly expected to be fed. Anatoly wasn't there. "Can you believe that guy?" I snapped as I went to fill my pet's bowl with kibble. "He blackmails me into letting him stay here so he can protect me and then when I come home at nine o'clock at night he's nowhere to be found."

As if in response, my front door opened and Anatoly strode in. "Have a good dinner?"

"Where have you been?"

Anatoly smirked and got himself a glass of water. "You're

upset that I wasn't here when you got home? You haven't forgotten that you don't want me around, have you?"

"No I haven't *forgotten*," I snipped. "But you said you were going to do some research. Obviously I want to know what that was about."

"You didn't seem to care this afternoon."

"You know what, that's fine. Be an asshole. It is, after all, what you do best. I'll just take my laptop into my bedroom and do some writing. I think I'm going to have my character beat her ex-boyfriend to death with the front fairing of his own stupid bike."

"I did some research on Sam. He's been married before."

"Yeah, I found that out, too. That hardly makes him unusual."

"No, but he's not divorced, he's a widower. His wife was killed in a drive-by shooting."

My mouth dropped open. "Oh, my God! We have to talk to this guy!"

"My thoughts exactly. I called Darrell and he's going to set it up."

"But Sam's seen us before. He thinks we work for *Tikkun.* He's not going to be open and honest with a couple of journalists."

"I faxed Darrell a script that he used to explain all that. He's already told Sam that the *Tikkun* reporters he met are actually detectives whom he occasionally calls when he needs help on a difficult investigation. Darrell is also going to tell him that due to a sudden turn in his health, he can no longer pursue this case and that he's handing the whole thing over to us. I had him tell Sam that we are considerably more experienced and skilled than he is, which of course is *half* true."

"What's Darrell supposed to be ill with?" I asked, ignoring the obvious jab.

"Mono."

"That's a stretch. Who would get close enough to Darrell to give him mono?"

"A prostitute?" Anatoly suggested. "I assume he uses them, either that or he's a virgin."

"Okay, so when is this meeting?"

"Tomorrow at four. Anne will be at some fund-raiser for MAC."

I leaned against the white-tiled counter and gave Anatoly a quizzical look. "I only know of two MACs—one makes lipstick, the other makes computers—and neither of them are struggling financially."

"In this case MAC stands for Mothers Against Censorship."

"Are you kidding? I thought mothers were supposed to be *for* censorship."

"Not the ones who support Anne. These mothers apparently want their children to be exposed to depravity on a daily basis."

"Huh," I said thoughtfully. "I wonder if Dena would be interested in hosting one of their events. It could be good publicity for the shop…wait a minute, did you say tomorrow at four? I can't make that! Tiff and I are driving to Danville to go through Peter's apartment."

"She hasn't cleared that out yet?"

"No, she's never even been inside. No one has since he killed himself."

"Really?" Anatoly's tone clearly conveyed his appreciation of this news. "That is a lucky break."

"Yeah, but by the time I pick her up, drive to Danville, search his place and then drive back to San Francisco to drop her off…there's just no way I'll be able to be in Lafayette by four, so you'll have to reschedule with Sam."

"Can't do it," Anatoly said definitively. "Darrell's already called and gotten the whole thing set up and I talked to Sam not a half hour later. He wasn't exactly thrilled with having his case handed over to someone new and I can't afford to further upset him by rescheduling our first appointment. If he decides to go with yet another detective agency, we lose our advantage. Ask Tiff if she can go to Peter's place on Monday."

"I can't ask her to do that! It's taken her months to work up the nerve to go over there. If I try to hold her off she might back out completely. Besides, I'm skating on thin ice with her as it is."

"What are you talking about? She obviously likes you. She agreed to go out to dinner and she even allowed you to drive her home—" Anatoly stopped short and winced.

"You followed me?" I asked, my voice trembling with rage. I pushed myself away from the counter and yanked open my junk drawer by the sink.

"What are you doing?" Anatoly asked.

"I'm getting a permanent marker and then I'm going to a gay biker bar!"

Anatoly came up behind me and held me still by placing a firm hand on each of my arms. "For the record, I did keep my promise. I didn't go anywhere near the restaurant. I simply followed you to the parking garage on O'Farrell, which is where I waited until you returned with Tiff in tow."

"How did I not notice you?" I snapped. I considered pulling away, but there was something rather pleasant about being restrained like this. God, I was as sick as Dena.

"I rented a car again," Anatoly answered.

"What are you, a Hertz Gold Club member or something?" I said, finally finding the will to free myself. I pulled myself up on the counter and sat there, glaring at him. "Why don't you just buy yourself a car?"

"I don't know, Sophie," Anatoly said dryly. "Why don't you just buy yourself a plane?"

"People who eat salmon and caviar for breakfast don't get to complain about financial problems."

"It's how I choose to spend my money," Anatoly said with a dismissive wave of his hand.

"You can't keep following me around town, Anatoly."

"Sophie, I don't think you understood what I was trying to tell you before. There is a killer out there and he may think that you're on to him. I know you want your space but you're not going to get it in a coffin."

I blanched. "That was harsh."

"So is murder."

For a full minute Anatoly and I stared at each other in silence. Mr. Katz seemed to sense the tension and abandoned the meager remains of his late-night snack in order to get out of the line of fire.

"I can't reschedule with Tiff," I said through clenched teeth.

"Fine, then you go with Tiff and I'll talk to Sam on my own."

"But I really want to meet with Sam!"

Anatoly shrugged. "We can't always have what we want." His gaze slipped from my face and took inventory of my more erogenous zones. "At least that's what I've been told."

"You *had* what you wanted. But that's what happens when you don't appreciate what you have, you lose it." And with that I jumped down and left the room.

It had been twelve hours since my last cup of coffee and yet I still found it impossible to sleep. All I could do was lie in bed and stare up at my bedroom ceiling while Mr. Katz used my stomach as a mattress. In the next room Anatoly was using my futon as a mattress and I suspected that was one of the reasons I couldn't sleep.

There was part of me (a part that was nowhere near my brain) that was thrilled by his new sleeping arrangement. He was lying in *my* guest room, undoubtedly wearing nothing but a pair of fitted Calvin Klein boxers and a wife-beater, and the only thing that separated us was a wall and a few square feet of floor space.

Of course, the part of me that wanted Anatoly there was seriously pissing off the part of me that didn't.

I sighed and turned on my side, thus irritating the previously comfortable Mr. Katz. I needed to stop thinking about Anatoly; then again if I did that I would start thinking about Melanie and that was infinitely worse.

Maybe I was in danger. God, if something happened to me, it would destroy my mother. She might actually get that ulcer that she was always complaining about. And Leah would be a mess. Still, Anatoly was being overprotective and I hated that. I had a major aversion to men with white-knight complexes. Of course, Anatoly wasn't really a white knight. He was a bad boy who occasionally experimented with heroism. That's what had made our sex life so exciting. I had never been able to predict if he was going to slowly caress me, sweetly exploring every curve of my body with strong, gentle hands, or if he was going to throw me on the dining table, tear off my clothes and plunge inside of me with the force of a hurricane.

I squeezed my eyes shut. I wasn't supposed to be thinking about that. Come on, Sophie, *sleep, sleep, sleep.*

No luck. I scooted into a sitting position, for which Mr. Katz rewarded me by digging his nails into my skin. I was losing it. I needed someone to calm me down. Dena was good at that. I reached for the phone, but the sight of the red digital numbers on my alarm clock stopped me. It was after two in the morning. Dena would either be asleep or orgasmic right now. Either way, calling her was out of the question. I glanced at the wall that separated me from my nemesis. I couldn't.

Yeah, I could.

I slipped out of bed, the hem of my cotton nightshirt brushing against my thighs as I tiptoed into the guest room. "Anatoly," I whispered, "are you asleep?"

"I was until you snuck into my room."

"I was very quiet."

"I'm a light sleeper."

"You are, aren't you? I had forgotten."

"I highly doubt that you did. What do you want? If it's not sex, then I'm sure it can wait until the morning."

"It's not sex, and it can't wait." I flipped the light on and sat down on the edge of his bed. He was lying on his side with the covers pulled up to the point just bellow his chest. He wasn't wearing a shirt. I closed my eyes for a moment and silently convinced myself not to rip the sheets off the bed to find out what else he wasn't wearing.

"Are you going to tell me what it is you want or are you going to just sit there thinking about it?" he asked.

"You can't stay here forever," I stated simply.

Anatoly groaned and turned away from me. "Good night, Sophie."

"I'm serious."

"I'm not staying here forever. If we can peg Sam as our killer and get him arrested quickly, I won't even be staying for the week."

"Good, I'm glad we're clear on that."

"Can we have sex now?"

"No."

"Then why don't we both go back to sleep."

"That's the problem," I said with a sigh. "I can't sleep and misery loves company."

"If I promise to have a nightmare, will you leave?"

"Maybe Anne was sleeping with Peter and Eugene found out so Peter threw himself out a fifteen-story window to avoid the humiliation of exposure," I suggested.

"The humiliation of exposure?" Anatoly turned back in my direction. "Peter's a single guy and Anne's not a bad-looking woman. No one would have shunned Peter for his role in that kind of affair. If I were in his shoes I would have slept with her—ow!"

I shook my hand to relieve the pain that hitting Anatoly

on the chest had caused me. "Maybe Peter and Anne were having kinky sex."

"Again, how would that be humiliating for Peter?"

"Really kinky sex, not just S and M. Like maybe she had him dress up like Little Bo Peep or something."

"Little Bo Peep," Anatoly said flatly.

"Don't dismiss it so quickly," I snapped. "Dena dressed up as Little Bo Peep one Halloween and it was really sexy. She had a staff, a fitted bodice and this ultra-short little ruffled skirt with matching undies. Oh, and she was carrying an inflatable sheep with a love-hole in his tuchas."

"Sophie, I'm very tired."

"You know what's really funny? At some point in our night of drunken debauchery Dena realized that she was one air-filled animal short of being a shepherdess. Little Bo Peep lost her sheep."

"Sophie…"

"I'm afraid I'll dream of Melanie."

There was silence for a moment and then Anatoly propped himself up on one arm. The sheets fell, exposing more of his torso and making him look like one of those guys in the Versace ads, except straight.

"Listen, Sophie, I know that Melanie meant more to you than you let on in the beginning."

I looked away. I couldn't be flippant about this and I didn't want to expose my pain to Anatoly. Not again.

"I didn't know her very well," he said quietly, "but I got the impression that she didn't have a lot of friends."

"She was active in her church," I said, almost defensively.

"I'm sure she was, but outside of the luncheons and

bake sales, did she ever actually hang out with any of those people?"

I shrugged.

"If she did, don't you think that she would have called on one of them to help her with her problems with Eugene, before and after he was killed? I know you two have a history, but you hardly share the connection with her that you do with Dena, Marcus or even Mary Ann."

"S'pose not," I agreed reluctantly.

"Are her parents still alive?"

I shook my head.

"And she doesn't have children, right?"

"She didn't believe in premarital sex and she married late. I think that by the time she got around to losing her virginity, it was too late." I had actually given this matter a lot of thought. Melanie had married Eugene at fifty. How could anyone remain a virgin for fifty years without exploding in a fit of sexual frustration?

"Sophie? Are you still with me?"

"Huh? Oh yeah, sorry. I was just thinking about Melanie and the...challenges that she was faced with in her life."

"Yes, well that's what I'm driving at. All Melanie had was her husband. Clearly it wasn't a perfect union, but I don't think we have any reason to believe it was a loveless one. Now she has him again. She's not alone anymore."

"You think that's true?" I asked hopefully. "You think when we die we get to spend eternity kicking it with the other dead people whom we loved in this life?"

Anatoly sighed. "Sophie, I'm fanatically agnostic. I don't know what comes next and I'm never going to, not until I'm dead and maybe not even then. But I do think that whatever comes, it's going to be easier than this." He made a sweeping gesture to illustrate that he was talking about life in general. "Melanie wasn't a happy woman. Maybe now she is."

"Is that supposed to be comforting?"

"That depends, was it?"

"Sort of."

"Then, yes, it was supposed to be comforting."

I smiled, despite myself.

Anatoly pushed himself into a full sitting position and I could see the elastic waistband of his boxers. "Anne Brooke and her husband aren't the only people I investigated today."

"No?"

"No, I also checked into Tim Robbins and Susan Sarandon."

"Excuse me?" I scooted back a little on the bed and tried to figure out if Anatoly was delirious from exhaustion.

"I believe you said you wanted somebody to play Tim Robbins to your Susan Sarandon."

"Yeah, I said something like that." I actually had said I had wanted *him* to be my Tim Robbins, but I didn't want to remind him of that.

"I didn't know what that meant at the time, but I did some checking and it seems that Robbins and Sarandon are a couple."

"You didn't know that? Don't you read *People?*"

"Perhaps I should start," Anatoly said with one of his little half smiles. I swallowed hard and tried to keep my breathing even.

"I also found out that, while committed to each other, they have never shown any interest in getting married."

"And they travel a lot individually," I added. "And they have a big place. I think that romantic relationships have a better chance of surviving when they take place in spacious homes."

"If I'm understanding you," Anatoly said slowly, "you're looking for a man who will be committed to you without the legalities of marriage and will give you lots of space. Is that right?"

"And who's willing to take it slow," I said quickly. "I'm not looking to move anyone in here right *now*." Considering the situation, this seemed like an important point to make.

Anatoly laughed softly. It was a low and sensual sound. "I see."

"You see? As in you didn't see before?"

"I can't read your mind, Sophie."

"No one asked you to read my mind. You made a decision about our relationship based on what you thought I wanted rather than what I actually asked for. That's messed up."

"I understand that now."

"Well, it took you long enough," I grumbled.

"Is it too late? Or are you still willing to be my Susan Sarandon?"

I smiled and looked away. "So you're finally willing to be my boyfriend?"

"Sophie, I already was your boyfriend. I just wasn't willing to admit to it."

I shot him a look. "I still don't think you're serious about this."

"What can I do to convince you?"

"Well, you could start by taking off your boxers and showing me some enthusiasm."

And before you could say Bull Durham, Anatoly had his

boxers off and had me pinned to the bed beneath him, his "enthusiasm" pressing into my thigh.

I writhed beneath him as he devoured my neck. His hand quickly moved under my nightshirt and I groaned as his fingers gently pinched my nipple. "God, I've missed you," he whispered.

I tried to respond, but I had now completely lost my ability to control my breathing. Instead, I answered by digging my nails into his back, my excitement heightening as his muscles rippled beneath my grip. He lifted himself up and placed one knee between my legs, spreading them ever so slightly as he yanked my nightshirt over my head. For a few seconds he just stared at me. "I haven't seen you like this for a very long time," he noted. His hand moved slowly down from my neck, to my breast, to my stomach, and then it froze.

"What are you doing?" I gasped. "Don't stop now!"

"Sophie, I don't have anything."

"Yes, you do!" I snapped. "You have a very big something right there!"

"I meant I don't have a condom on me."

"Oh, that." I pushed him off of me and rushed into the bathroom, quickly emerging with an unopened box. I jumped back on the bed and started ripping at the plastic with my teeth.

"You never have condoms," Anatoly said, a note of accusation in his voice. "You always insisted that I be the one to buy them."

"Well, obviously I haven't *used* them," I mumbled as I spit out some wrapping and struggled to open the box. "I just got them after we broke up so I'd be prepared for every eventuality."

Anatoly took the package from me and easily opened it. He raised one eyebrow teasingly. "Magnum extra large?"

I lifted one shoulder in a partial shrug. "It's my glass-slipper test. If it doesn't fit, you're not my prince."

Anatoly laughed and handed me an unwrapped condom. I placed it on his tip and gently rolled it down to the base. Anatoly was a prince among men.

He was touching me again, my hair, my hips, the insides of my thighs…it seemed impossible that he could so thoroughly explore so much territory with only two hands. I fell back against the bed and he immediately pushed inside of me and I almost exploded right then and there. He moved slowly at first, as if he wanted to savor every sensation, and then his speed picked up and my hips rose to greet him. The futon squeaked and rocked beneath us until I finally screamed out his name, the strength of my orgasm making me oblivious to everything else. A moment later it was my name on his lips and then I felt the full weight of his body as he collapsed on top of me. For a few minutes we lay just like that; his breath tickled my cheek and his sweat mingled with my own. He wrapped me back up in his arms, and it wasn't long before I fell into the sleep that had previously eluded me.

And my dreams were very, very good.

18

Bizarre sexual fetishes are a by-product of our overly comfortable middle-class lifestyle. Men don't ask you to spank them in Zimbabwe.
—*C'est La Mort*

AT NINE-THIRTY IN THE MORNING I WOKE UP ALONE, SATISFIED AND pleasantly sore. I inhaled deeply as the scent of freshly brewed espresso wafted into the room. God, how I had missed that espresso machine. Sometime in the near future I was going to have to buy a box full of dark-chocolate-covered espresso beans and recreate our first lovemaking session, but not today. Today I had to accompany Tiff to her brother's old place in hopes of finding something that could make sense of that bizarre letter. If only I could figure out a way to do that *and* accompany Anatoly when he visited Sam Griffin.

I found my nightshirt crumpled into a ball under the futon and had just pulled it over my head when I had a brainstorm. If I was able to find another person with a car to drive Tiff and me to her brother's apartment, that person could drop me off with Anatoly when we were done and take Tiff back to her place in the city. Surely Dena, Mary Ann or Marcus would do that for me. Of course, the trick was going to be convincing Tiff to allow a stranger to tag along during this deeply personal task, particularly since she was still reluctant to allow me to accompany her. I tried to think up some kind of situation that would require the presence of a third person, but then quickly nixed the idea of a cover story. I had promised myself I was going to be truthful with Tiff going forward.

I looked down and spotted Anatoly's cell phone by my feet. Neat he was not, but the phone's proximity did allow me to make the necessary call without getting out of bed quite yet. I punched in Tiff's number (the last four digits happened to be my birthday so I had easily remembered it) and waited for her to pick up.

"Hello, Sophie." From her tone it was clear that I was not yet on her list of favorite people. Asking her for a favor wasn't going to be easy.

"Hey, Tiff. Listen, I just wanted you to know that I've come up with a new lead that I'm going to follow up on."

"A new *lead?* Jeez, you even sound like a detective."

"I try. Anyway, this lead, well, it's Anne Brooke's husband. He seems to think Anne was having an affair."

"With my brother?" Tiff asked with a gasp.

"I don't actually know—maybe. That's what I have to find out, but if I want to talk to him I'm going to have to do it today."

"Wait a minute, are you seriously about to ask me to reschedule our plans? After you practically begged me to include you in this?"

"No, of course not. I know how long it took you to work up the courage to go to your brother's place and I'm not going to ask you to put it off any longer. Would it be okay if I brought another friend along with us?"

"To my brother's place? You want to turn this into some kind of social gathering?"

"Not at all, I just need a third person to drive. Then when we're done my friend can take you back to the city while I talk to Anne Brooke's husband in Lafayette."

Tiff hesitated for a minute, and it suddenly occurred to me that she might ask to meet with Anne's husband as well, and that would not be good. Sam had already been told that his case was being handed over to two people, not three. I also doubted that Tiff would be able to convince anyone that she was a private detective. She didn't strike me as a very good liar.

Finally Tiff spoke. "Would it be okay if this third person just stayed in the car while we went inside Peter's apartment?"

"No problem. They can go out to coffee or something until we call and tell them we're ready to leave."

"I'm not loving this, Sophie."

"I know, but if talking to Anne's husband helps us figure out why your brother did what he did, wouldn't it be worth it?"

Another long pause.

"Tiff? Are you still there?"

"I can't believe I'm going to agree to this."

"Thank you, Tiff. I promise that the friend I get to drive us will be quiet and sensitive to the emotional nature of the situation."

Ten minutes later I was on the phone with Dena. Dena was not one of my more "quiet and sensitive" friends, which is why I called Mary Ann first, but she had to work and Marcus had a wedding to attend, so that left Dena and Leah, and Dena *was* quiet compared to Leah.

"Let me get this straight," Dena said as I rolled on my side so that I could press the ear that wasn't listening to her against the pillow. "You want me to drive you and this chick to Danville and sit around and do nothing while the two of you snoop through her dead brother's place, then drop you off in Lafayette and then take her back to her house in the city?"

"Yep."

"Forgive me for saying this, but that's not exactly my idea of a relaxing day away from the store."

"Dena, I know I'm asking a lot, but I really need your help with this."

I heard Dena groan into the receiver.

"Dena, try to understand, I started this thing because I wanted to help Melanie. I felt I owed her, but now…now things have changed."

There was a moment's pause. "What's changed?"

"Dena, didn't you read yesterday's paper?"

"I almost never read the paper on Saturdays. You know that."

"Melanie was killed." I felt my throat constrict on the last word. "The police don't know who did it, but I think it's connected to what happened to Eugene."

There was almost a full minute of silence before she audibly exhaled. "Shit," she muttered. "Sophie, I'm so—"

"Please don't," I said quickly, forcing myself to suppress the emotions that wanted to come to the surface. "I can't deal with it yet. Not really. But, Dena, I have to get answers. I just can't let someone get away with this."

"Sophie, I'm sure the police are doing everything they can."

"The police have to follow certain rules. I don't."

"The hell you don't! Just because you don't have a badge doesn't mean that you're free to break any laws that you find inconvenient!"

"Yeah, well I don't have a watchdog group hovering over my shoulder."

Dena groaned again but this groan was softer than the last. I smiled to myself. "You're going to help me with this, aren't you?"

"Yeah, I'm going to help you. You owe me big-time, Sophie."

"Dena, I already owe you my life. Any other debt I accrue is kind of like adding twenty years to a hundred-year prison sentence."

"Ain't it the truth. What time do you want me to come over?"

"I told Tiff we'd pick her up at one, so if you could be here at twelve-thirty we'll have lots of cushion room."

"Twelve-thirty it is. I expect you to make some coffee for the road."

"For you, Dena, I'll make espresso."

As if on cue Anatoly opened the door, a small cup of espresso in each hand. Unfortunately he was dressed. I hung up the phone as I accepted my beverage. "So you are awake," he noted. "I thought I heard you in here."

"I was just talking to Dena, who is by far the most fabulous friend anyone could ever ask for."

Anatoly sat on the side of the bed while I explained the arrangements I had just made. "I'd invite you to come along with us, but I think that might be asking a little more of Tiff than I can get away with."

"I wouldn't have been able to make it, anyway," Anatoly said after finishing off his drink. "I'm going to meet with Darrell Jenkins this morning. I want a full account of where Anne went, what she did and who she talked to while he was watching her. I also want to know what Sam told him when he initially hired him. That way when we talk to Sam I'll be able to tell if he's changed his story at all."

"Good plan," I agreed. I peeked over his shoulder. "I'm surprised Mr. Katz hasn't come to find me."

"I fed him this morning."

My heart skipped a beat. "You fed my baby? Thank you!"

Anatoly waved off my gratitude and glanced over at the clock. "I should get going soon."

"Just like that?"

"Is there something else I'm supposed to do?"

"Well, sort of. Where's my goodbye sex?"

"Your goodbye sex?"

"It's like a goodbye kiss but better." I leaned forward and let my finger make an idle trail from his collar bone to the waistline of his jeans. "A whole lot better."

Anatoly grinned and threaded his fingers through my hair. "I think I'm about to learn to love long goodbyes."

At exactly one o'clock Dena and I arrived at Tiff's place. Dena followed me through the picket fence and surveyed the property. "You said she lived in a house."

"This is a house—or at least it qualifies as a cottage."

"This place does *not* qualify as a cottage. If it qualifies for anything it's a demolition."

"Don't be such an elitist," I said while pulling her down the path by the sleeve of her red hoodie. "Not everybody can afford to live in a Noe Valley two-bedroom apartment."

"I'm not saying she needs to live in a place like mine, but why wouldn't she just get herself a nice studio? Or a one-bedroom in the outer Sunset? She might have a little less space, but at least she wouldn't have to worry about being condemned by the health inspector. This place is, what—eighty, ninety years old? Has it been painted since then?"

"I think she likes having an enclosed front yard."

"And that's important because…?"

"Dena, just shut up and be good, okay?" I said as we walked up the steps of Tiff's front porch. "This is going to be hard on Tiff and we need to be as supportive as possible." I pressed the doorbell, but it seemed to be out of commission so I rapped my knuckles against the door.

A moment later it swung open and Tiff was standing before us, smiling nervously.

I heard Dena gasp. I didn't need to ask what it was that she found so shocking. It was Tiff's jeans. Tiff's acid-wash jeans. To make matters worse she had paired them with a leopard-print top with sequin accents. "You must be Dena," Tiff said amiably. "Thank you for agreeing to drive us."

Dena nodded but didn't answer immediately. Tiff noted that we were both staring at her shirt and she looked down at it admiringly. "You like it? Can you believe they don't let me wear this to work? They say that they want Mojo to be one of San Francisco's hippest salons, but whenever I show up in something cutting-edge they make me go home and change."

"Imagine that," I said with a smile. Dena was still shocked into silence.

"Give me one second to get my shoes on," she said, turning away from us and disappearing back inside the house.

Dena looked at me with wide eyes. "I *gasped,*" she whispered. "Sophie, I didn't think I was even *capable* of gasping, but apparently a woman wearing acid-wash jeans and sequins in the twenty-first century is all it takes to completely shock me."

"Dena—"

"Is it a costume?" Dena asked. "Is she in *disguise?* Please tell me there's some kind of rational explanation for that outfit."

"Tiff has her own sense of style."

"That's not style, that's a disaster. Somebody needs to call FEMA immediately!"

Before I could respond Tiff came out again, this time wearing shoes and a cropped black leather jacket with shoulder pads big enough to intimidate any NFL linebacker. She also had Chica on a leash.

"Is it okay if I bring my dog?" Tiff asked. "I don't get to hang out with her as much as I'd like during my workweek so I try to keep her close at hand during my days off."

Dena shook her head quickly. "I don't think it's a good idea. I'm not an animal person."

"Oh, come on, Dena." I gestured toward the little Chihuahua, who was patiently waiting at Tiff's side. "Clearly Chica's very obedient. Besides, she's on a leash and you'll probably only have to see her this one time. If you think about it, it's not much different from one of *your* typical dates."

Dena shot me a dirty look but didn't disagree.

"So she can come?" Tiff asked hopefully.

"Yeah, fine, she can come," Dena grumbled.

Tiff beamed. "Thank you." She picked up Chica in her arms and carried her to Dena's Avalon.

I offered Tiff the front seat but she demurred. She was being incredibly polite, almost too polite. Last I checked she was still rather ticked with me, and rightfully so. What had changed?

Dena popped in a Kanye West CD and drove off toward the freeway.

"Who is this?" Tiff asked.

Dena glanced at her through the rearview mirror. "You've never heard Kanye West?"

"I don't really like rap."

Dena shrugged. I could tell that she had no intention of changing the CD, so I took the initiative and turned off the stereo. Dena shot me another glare, but before she could say anything I whispered, *"Remember, be sensitive!"*

Dena sighed and cast another look in her rearview. "What kind of music do you like?"

"I don't know…I like Madonna, Michael Jackson, Duran Duran…but I'm more into their old stuff. I'm still a big fan of eighties rock."

Dena turned her head to the side so she could once again check out Tiff's jeans. "That doesn't really surprise me."

"Peter liked The Cure," Tiff said quietly. "That's something we had in common."

I shifted in my seat so I could see Tiff, and for the first time noticed that her hands were trembling as she petted Chica.

"Tiff, are you all right?" I asked.

"Going to Peter's place…it's hard for me," she whispered. Chica licked her hand, and for a second I thought Tiff was going to burst into tears. Instead she just blinked her eyes a few times and stared out the window. "I don't feel like talking right now. Why don't you put the music on again? Anything you want to play is fine."

Dena wordlessly switched to Mix 106.5, the only Bay Area radio station I knew of that occasionally played Madonna's early hits. Dena was *not* a Madonna fan so the gesture was extra sweet.

For the rest of the trip the only sound came out of the radio. Tiff continued to stare out the window as she methodically petted her dog, and Dena focused on the road, occasionally wincing when a Kelly Clarkson or Britney Spears song came on.

Eventually we arrived in Danville and easily found a parking spot in front of the somewhat run-down, light green, five-story apartment building that Peter once lived in.

"Oh, God," Tiff whispered, although I'm not sure she had wanted anyone to hear her.

Tiff, Chica and I got out and Dena leaned her head out the window. "I guess I'll just go to that café on the corner and wait for you guys. When you're ready for me just call my…"

"You can come in," Tiff said quickly.

Dena's eyebrows shot up. "Sophie told me that you didn't want me to be there for this."

"You drove all this way," Tiff said softly. "You might as well come up."

"That's really okay." It was obvious to me that Dena would have rather listened to the entire *Like A Virgin* CD than hold

Tiff's hand through this particular adventure, but Tiff didn't seem to be picking up on that.

"Actually," Tiff said slowly, "I was kind of thinking that maybe you two could do this without me. Like, I could go to the café and wait for *you* to call *me*."

I put a hand on her shoulder. "Tiff, you can't put this off forever. Besides, there may be something in there that will explain your brother's actions. You can finally have answers."

"That's what I'm afraid of," she said quietly. "I told you that I didn't know my brother all that well, but what I didn't say was that I wasn't always nice to him. I was always teasing him. I used to give him tons of flack for being a mascot and then when he took that job at American and started traveling, I would tease him about where he chose to go. Like, I would pick on him because he wanted to go to Des Moines but not Cancún."

"Wait, you're saying your brother chose Iowa over Mexico?" Dena asked, clearly taken aback.

"Tiff, my sister and I are *always* giving each other a hard time," I said, ignoring Dena's last question. "That's what siblings do. You don't need to feel guilty about it."

"I used to think it was in good fun," Tiff said, her voice trembling more with each word. "But what if for him it wasn't fun at all? What if I go into that apartment and I find a diary or something that explains why he didn't turn to me when he was upset? Maybe he didn't feel like I accepted him or—oh God, what if he didn't think I loved him?"

"Okay, Tiff, you need to calm down," I said in the most soothing voice I could manage. "All of this is just wild speculation. No one kills themself just because their sister gave them flack for occasionally dressing up like an animal for a football game."

"I can't do this," Tiff said with a quick shake of her head. She pressed the keys to Peter's apartment into my hand. "It's number 342. I'll be at the café on the corner. I don't need the car, I'll walk." She turned and started walking away.

"Wait, Tiff!" I called after her. "Come on, you *can* do this! Besides, that café isn't even going to let you take your dog inside!"

Tiff stopped and turned again. "You're right," she said, and then strode up to me and thrust Chica into my arms. "I shouldn't be around her right now, anyway. She's so sensitive to my moods and I don't want to needlessly upset her. Call me when you're done looking for...whatever it is you're looking for." And with that she turned around and hurried away.

Dena cleared her throat and turned to me. "Your new friend is a little whacked."

"Yeah," I said flatly. "And we're so normal."

Dena laughed. "You got me there."

"You want to come up with me?" I asked.

"What the hell, I'm here, aren't I?"

The three of us (Dena, Chica and I) let ourselves into the apartment building, only to find that the elevator was out of service, so we climbed three flights of stairs to Peter's apartment.

"You say no one's been here in almost two months?"

"Uh-huh."

Dena scrunched up her nose. "The kitchen's yours, and if I see more than five flies or even one small mammal that isn't a pet I'm waiting in the car."

"Fair enough." I opened the door and we both stepped inside. This time it was my turn to gasp, not so much out of shock but disgust.

Dena's eyes perused everything from the stained brown carpet to the yellow floral wallpaper. "Ah," she said knowingly. "So *this* is why he killed himself."

"That's not funny, Dena."

"No, it's not, it's pathetic." She gingerly stepped over a pile of dirty clothes that had been left on the floor. There were actually a lot of things on the floor, from *Time* magazines to dirty socks. I gently put Chica down on a dark green paisley sofa, also covered in clothes, not to mention a few cigarette burns, while Dena tapped the toe of her boot against a waste basket that was literally overflowing with candy wrappers, Kleenex and various other bits of trash. "Not the tidiest guy in the world, was he?"

"No," I said, kicking an empty Diet Coke can away from a coffee table that was a little too big for the proportions of the room. "*Neat* is not a word I would use."

"It's forgivable, though," Dena mused. "The mess draws attention away from the 1970s-style wallpaper."

"Mmm-hmm." I stuck my fingernail in one of the cigarette holes that graced the sofa's armrest. "Do you think he smoked or do you think the couch had these holes when he bought it at…I'm guessing a garage sale."

"He smoked." Dena bent down and lifted up an empty carton of Marlboros she found on the floor. "But not that much because I don't smell anything."

I made a face and turned my attention back to the rest of the mess around me. I personally didn't have a problem with slobs. Housework is both tedious and labor-intensive and I absolutely respect an individual's right to turn on a television rather than a vacuum. But if you're planning on throwing yourself out a fifteenth-story window you should clean up your place first. I mean, was this really the legacy he wanted to leave?

"I don't know where to start," I admitted.

"I'll start with the desk." Dena gestured over to a brown plastic slab that was supported by two three-drawer metal filing cabinets. On it was a computer, piles of mail and other random pieces of paper. "It looks reasonably safe."

Damn, why hadn't I called the desk first? Everything else was bound to be kind of icky. But someone had to go through this stuff, and if nothing else, I knew that if Peter had ever been in possession of the evidence I was looking for he certainly hadn't thrown it out.

Like Dena, I was a little afraid of the kitchen. I lifted Chica off the couch and went into the bedroom. I was relieved to see that it was slightly neater than the living room. Here, too, there were clothes strewn around, but there were fewer Diet Coke cans. The bed was predictably unmade. I went over to the small walk-in closet and found its floor to be covered with several pairs of loafers, tennis shoes and dress shoes. In the back of the closet were a few empty suitcases that Peter undoubtedly used for his frequent trips. Fascinating stuff.

I shifted my weight back onto my heels and lifted my eyes to the clothing racks. Lots of chinos and cotton shirts, one suit that he had probably owned since he was sixteen and a couple of dry-cleaning bags filled with…costumes. I took a closer look. There was a lion costume, and one that kind of looked like a goat. They had to either have been left over from Halloweens past or his mascot days…but then again these costumes didn't look bulky enough to work as a mascot get-up. The goat costume was downright sinewy.

I stepped out of the closet and looked at the bed again. There was something sticking out from under the pillow. I shifted Chica to one arm and lifted up the pillow to find a miniature version of Christopher Robin's favorite bear.

"A grown man who sleeps with a stuffed animal," I said, looking down at Chica. "I guess that's…sweet?"

Chica looked at me doubtfully. Even she understood that males over the age of ten should not be sleeping with a teddy.

On a whim I pulled back the sheets. A little noise of surprise escaped me. The bear had company! There was a bouncy tiger, a donkey and even a mother kangaroo and her joey. I reached down and picked up the donkey. Something about his sad eyes reminded me of Chica. The doll was soft and cuddly except for one spot on his side that was kind of stiff and crusty. Peter must have spilled milk on him or something. I looked down at the animals again and realized that the tiger had a little dried milk on him, too. And so did the bear and the kangaroo and—

"Oh, my God!" I screamed, and threw the donkey across the room, totally startling Chica, who found the strength to wriggle out of my arms. "Ew! Ew, ew, ew, ew, ew!"

Dena appeared in the doorway. "What is it? What did you find?"

"Oh, my God!" I said again. "What—who—does something like this?"

"Does something like what?"

"Ejaculate all over a bunch of innocent stuffed animals, that's what! And I touched it!" I looked down at my hands and then ran to the attached bathroom. I turned on the faucet and ran my hands under the hot water. I looked around for soap, only to find that Peter used the liquid variety and kept it in a soap dispenser that resembled a dog. "Ewwww!" I screamed again. I desperately needed to use the soap, but I was terrified that Peter might have defiled that, too. I lunged for the toilet paper and yanked off about a yard, which I folded up into a thick little square and used to press down on the dog's head in order to get access to the soap.

"Woof, woof, woof!" the plastic dog said as soap streamed from his mouth like clear liquid vomit. I scrubbed my hands raw until I felt certain that I had removed all traces of Peter's germs. Eventually I came out, waving my hands in the air to dry them because there was no way in hell that I was going to use Peter's towels.

Dena was looking casually around the room. "I wonder how much he was paying for this place. It's run-down but it's spacious."

"That's what you're fixating on?" I asked. "He's been sexually assaulting all the innocent animals of Hundred Acre Wood and you're worried about his rent?"

Dena sighed and pointed toward the bear. "I'm not exactly shocked by what happened to this particular honey lover."

"You're not? Why? Do you think he was asking for it by running around in that red little half top of his? Isn't it kind of wrong to blame the victim?"

"Sophie, it's not that big a deal. Peter was a plushy, that's all."

"A whaty?"

"A plushy. He was sexually attracted to stuffed animals."

I held out my freshly scrubbed hand to stop her. "Okay, you are seriously freaking me out. Are you telling me that there are other people who...who use a teddy bear catalog as their porn?"

"That is exactly what I'm telling you," Dena said, clearly bemused by my naiveté. "You know those Weenie Babies that I sell in my store? The little beanbag-stuffed animals with the big..."

"I remember them."

"Well, they're not just gag gifts. I keep them in stock for the plushies. Not very many of them shop in my store, but enough that I make sure to carry a few things that will appeal to them."

I shook my head in horrified amazement. "I can't believe this."

"People have weird fetishes, Sophie. If you think about it, real shoe fetishes aren't that much better than this." She gestured toward the abused animals. "I'm not talking about women who just can't stop themselves from blowing their paychecks on a pair of Manolo Blahniks, I'm talking about the guys who are turned on by a pair of Nine Wests—not the women in them."

"Okay, I am seriously grossed out right now." I pulled on the ends of my hair and looked around the room. "This whole thing is *so* weird."

"What's weird is that he was a furry, too," Dena said.

"Excuse me?"

"Check it out." Dena stepped over to the doorway and gestured for me to follow her into the living room.

I looked down at the floor where the poor, depressed, violated donkey was lying limply at my feet. "I'm not sure I want to be 'shown' anything else in this apartment."

"Don't be a wimp," Dena called out as she walked into the other room. "I swear, sometimes you're as bad as Mary Ann."

That was enough to get me out into the living room. I followed her over to the laptop, which was currently on Peter's Yahoo home page. "Take a look at Peter's bookmarks," Dena said. She clicked the favorites icon and down came a long list of sites. Many of them had to do with Anne Brooke and some of them had to do with newspaper articles with titles like "Supreme Court Weighs in on Privacy Case." But then there were a lot of other site names that were kind of weird. "Click that one," I said, hesitantly tapping a bookmark titled "Furry Fandom."

"You got it." She clicked it and then one of the most disturbing things I have ever seen popped up on the screen. It was a person dressed up as a big fluffy sheep doing it doggy-style with a guy dressed up like the Big Bad Wolf.

I stared at the screen in silence for what had to be a full minute, if not longer. Finally I found my voice. "This is really sick."

"I still don't see what you're freaking out about," Dena said calmly. "I'm actually grateful that some people have these particular fetishes."

"Hello?" I snapped my head in her direction. "I like to think of myself as a fairly open-minded person and I'm even willing to say that people have the right to have sex with toys or to dress up as farm animals as long as everybody, minus the toy, is consenting and it's done in the privacy of their own home. But how can you be *grateful* that this kind of—of—*depravity* exists?"

"First of all, depravity is one of those words that are used by the Christian right. Don't use it again," Dena said. "Second, the people who are into this *are* on the weird side. Every once in a while one will come into my shop looking for a leash for their pseudo-animal love slave and there's something about them that just lets you know that they're a little off."

"I would think that the very fact that they *had* a pseudo-animal love slave would be enough to qualify them as being off."

"No, it's not that," Dena said dismissively, as if such a possession was as common as having a four-slotted toaster. "It's just that a lot of these people come into my store and they'll whisper what it is they want, like they're afraid someone in the next aisle will hear them. They're so intense about the whole thing, it's like they're hiding a habit from their friends and family while they jones for a fix. It's not healthy. But they're only attracted to other people who enjoy dressing up like animals, which keeps them out of *my* dating pool. That's a good thing. And the plushies are some of the most messed-up, insecure people I've ever met in my life. I'm personally grateful that they engage in sexual activities that don't allow them to procreate."

"So this is your version of Darwinian theory?" I asked. "It's not survival of the fittest but survival of the most emotionally well adjusted?"

"Pretty much," Dena confirmed. "Ever wonder why so many antidepressants lower a person's sex drive? Maybe it's

God's way of making sure that we don't populate the earth with a bunch of mopey children."

"Huh." It was the only response I could come up with. I was studying the other titles listed on the favorites bar. There was a site labeled The Horny Unicorn, another called Frisky Puppy Dogs, and yet another titled The Hare Up The Ass. "I can't believe he didn't delete all this before he offed himself," I mused.

"Yeah, that part is a little weird. And then, like I said before, I'm a little surprised that he was both a furry and a plushy. Usually people are one or the other. Furries look *down* on plushies."

"Are you telling me that man on the computer screen thinks his sheep costume makes him superior to others?"

"Kind of. There are different kinds of furries. There are the ones who like to dress up as cartoon characters, but the serious ones wouldn't dream of demeaning themselves by wearing a Danny Duck costume. They want their costumes to look like real animals, or at least like real werewolves and shit. It's like the Trekkies. The New Generation fans do *not* have the respect of the Captain Kirk and Mr. Spock fan club."

"The respect?" I waved my hand toward the screen. "What that wolf is doing to that sheep is *not* respectful."

"Yeah, but that wolf wouldn't even give the sheep the time of day if he was a Cuddly Bear."

"I can't believe…wait, what did you say?"

"I was explaining that serious furry wolves only want serious furry sheep…."

"No, no, about the Cuddly Bear… Oh, my God, Dena."

"What is it?"

"I just figured it out. There was a woman by Ocean Beach. A homeless woman, and I just assumed she was crazy, but she wasn't!"

"Sophie, I have no idea what you're talking about."

"A homeless woman by Ocean Beach saw a pink bear with a rainbow on his belly dump Melanie's body in the brush! Melanie was killed by a pink bear!"

Dena studied me for a moment and then took a deep breath. "Okay, you may be on to something, but you might want to consider rephrasing your conclusion before you go to the police with it."

But I wasn't listening to Dena anymore. I was pacing back and forth, zigzagging around the random piles of clothing. "One of those freaky furries killed my friend! Melanie didn't even approve of lingerie fetishes, and now I find out that she had to suffer the indignity of being killed by a kinky pink bear! I'm going to figure out which one of those freaks did this and then he's going to pay! And…oh, my God!"

Dena jumped. "What now?"

"The threats I've been getting! Why didn't I put this together before? I've been threatened by a furry! That woman stood there and told me that she saw a bear kill Melanie, and just days earlier Darth Vader told me he liked to dress up like a koala bear. How could I not have figured this out! Now I'm going to have to track down a homeless woman whose name I didn't even bother to ask for!"

"Sophie, what the fuck are you talking about? What threats? And what the fuck is this about Darth Vader playing dress-up? Was that in the prequel?"

I quickly told her about the phone calls and the note.

"How the hell do you get yourself mixed up in this kind of shit?" Dena muttered. "All right, I'm not going to lecture you about that now," she continued. "What I'm still confused about is this Cuddly Bear thing. A serious furry doesn't dress up like a pink bear. He would consider that to be humiliating."

"Which makes this worse!" I snapped. "Melanie wasn't even killed by one of the cool furries! She was killed by one of the geeks of the furry world!"

Dena broke into a coughing fit. I knew she was trying to suppress a laugh, and if the circumstances had been even a little different I might have found the whole thing funny, too, but this was Melanie's killer we were talking about. There simply wasn't room in my heart for anything but anger.

"Do you think Tiff knows anything about her brother's eccentricities?" Dena asked, sitting back down in the chair by the desk.

"I doubt it."

"Are you going to tell her?"

I stopped pacing for a moment. "How do you tell a woman that her dead brother was getting busy with a stuffed donkey?"

"I don't know, but I think you may have to find a way. And there's also something else that you may want to tell her."

"What?" I asked warily.

Without another word Dena scrolled further down the favorites menu. She stopped when she got to a site titled STD Fact Sheet.

"Don't tell me," I moaned.

"I'm afraid so." Dena clicked on the site in question.

I leaned over her shoulder and read the information on the page that came up. When I was done Dena showed me a few other bookmarks that she had stumbled across. They all dealt with the same disease. Just as I was digesting all this Chica came out of the bedroom, a kangaroo dangled helplessly from her mouth.

"Chica, no! Drop it," I yelled. "You'll get chlamydia!"

19

A pervert by any other name acts just as freaky.
—*C'est La Mort*

DENA AND I MET UP WITH TIFF OUTSIDE THE CAFÉ A HALF HOUR LATER. WE
had done a little more snooping before leaving Peter's place.
The kitchen hadn't been as bad as either of us had anticipated. It appeared that when it came to food Peter preferred
items that were filled with a maximum amount of preserva-
tives. Say what you like about candy bars and pretzels; the
one thing everyone has to agree on is that they don't rot. I
also found a new box of dishwashing gloves under the sink
and used a pair to go through Peter's garbage. I had been terrified of what I might find, but much to my relief there was
no evidence that Peter ever practiced safe sex while messing
around with adorable inanimate objects. What I did find was
an empty bottle of Zithromax, the medication used to cure
chlamydia. I stuck this in a Ziploc bag and then used a larger

freezer bag to store one of the stuffed animals. It seemed like it might be important evidence, although the idea of bringing the items into my home made my skin crawl.

Tiff greeted us with a half-eaten biscotti in her hand. "It's my fourth one," she said sheepishly as she took Chica from me. "I used to bite my nails when I was nervous, but the owner of the salon gave me a hard time about it so now I eat instead." Tiff sighed and took another bite of her snack. "It's so stupid. You can hide a nail-biting habit with silk or acrylic, but a weight problem is obvious to everybody."

"There's nothing wrong with your body," Dena said. "If anything, you should be showing it off in a new wardrobe."

"Yeah, right," Tiff said with a polite laugh, not picking up on Dena's subtle jab at her outfit. "So, did you two find anything?"

Dena looked at me and I looked at the sidewalk.

"Oh, God," Tiff murmured. "You *did* find something. What is it? Did you find something that makes you think it was my fault? Could I have done something that would have stopped him from jumping out that window?"

"I don't think so, Tiff," I said slowly. "Your brother had a few…issues."

"Issues?" Tiff repeated.

"*Issues* is such a judgmental word," Dena lamented. "Your brother just had peculiar tastes. He liked his sex on the wild side."

"Sex?" Tiff's eyes widened. "My brother was having sex? I didn't even know he was attracted to anyone!"

"Well," I said, "this isn't really about *anyone,* more like *anything.*"

Tiff was looking increasingly alarmed. "What do you mean?" When no one answered, she studied Dena, me and finally Chica, who was the only one willing to return her gaze. "Somebody better tell me what's going on." Tiff's voice had taken on an edge that made me wince.

"You know what? I'm hungry," Dena said. "There's got to be an outdoor café around here. Somewhere we can take the dog."

"Are you stalling?" Tiff asked.

"No, I'm just hungry," Dena said impatiently. "And after snooping around an apartment that hasn't been aired out in more than two months, I would like to sit outside and enjoy the breeze."

Tiff hesitated for a moment. "I guess that would be okay." She scratched Chica behind the ears. "I think I saw a sandwich place with outdoor seating while we were driving over. It can't be more than a few miles from here."

It only took us five minutes of driving around to find the sandwich shop and less than ten minutes to get our food and find a spot at one of the tables that lined the sidewalk. Dena treated herself to a BLT, Tiff got a milk shake and I got a ginger tea that I prayed would abate my queasiness.

"So," Tiff said as she poured a little water into a plastic bowl our cashier had provided for Chica. "Why don't you tell me what you found out about my brother while I still have the courage to hear it? Who exactly was he sleeping with?"

I took a deep breath. "Tiff—"

"You know what my first thought was when I saw you?" Dena asked Tiff, completely cutting me off.

Tiff shook her head mutely.

"I thought your sense of style was beyond atrocious."

I inadvertently spit out my mouthful of ginger tea all over my side of the table.

"Come again?" Tiff asked.

"Your clothes, Tiff," Dena continued. "I hated acid wash when it was first introduced in the eighties and my feelings about it haven't changed since then. And your shirt…you can do animal prints and you can do sequins, but together?" Dena shook her head. "At first sight I considered your outfit to be a shocking, full-scale assault against good taste. I even thought that you didn't have the *right* to dress that way."

Tiff's mouth was now hanging open; mine was, too, for that matter. "Is this your way of distracting me?" she asked. "Are you trying to make me angry?"

"No, I'm making a point. You see, you *do* have the right to wear that stuff." Dena waved her hand towards Tiff's ensemble. "Just because it's not my thing doesn't mean that it shouldn't be yours. Furthermore, somebody *made* that shirt. And then some retailer liked it enough to carry it in their store and dollars to doughnuts you're not the only one who bought it. Yeah, it's different and it freaks me out a little, but obviously there are people out there who think that shirt is *da bomb* and who am I to tell you and your kind that you're wrong?"

"I still don't see where you're going with this."

"Your brother had his own style, too," Dena explained. "I'm not talking about clothes now, I'm talking about sex."

Tiff swallowed, hard. "What exactly did you two find?"

"Your brother had a thing for stuffed animals," Dena said bluntly.

"He had a thing…I'm sorry but I don't understand."

"Stuffed animals," Dena repeated. "The kind you buy in toy stores. Peter liked to have sex with them."

Tiff didn't respond this time. I don't think she knew what to say.

"I know you probably find that shocking," Dena continued. "And maybe the idea of using a teddy bear as a sex toy offends you, but it's not like the guy was hurting anyone. If a person owns a teddy bear, they can do what they want with it, and if what they want is to stick it in their underwear and use it for a little adult entertainment, then who are we to say that's wrong?"

"You…you can't be serious."

"I'm serious. Sophie put one of Peter's stuffed animals in a Ziploc. It's kind of his Monica Lewinsky dress, if you know what I mean. Want to see it?"

"What? No!" Tiff gasped.

"Suit yourself," Dena said with a shrug. She took another bite of her BLT before adding, "We think he also liked to have sex with people dressed up as sheep and shit."

Tiff's eyes were about the size of silver dollars. She looked over at me as I tried to figure out how I could make myself disappear. "She's serious?" Tiff asked me.

I nodded silently.

"So you're saying my brother was a freak."

"But in a nonoffensive way," Dena insisted.

"I don't know how I'm supposed to react to this."

"Well, if I were you I'd feel relieved," Dena said.

"I should be relieved that my brother liked to sleep with sheep?"

"*People* dressed as sheep," Dena corrected. "But, yeah, you should be relieved. My guess is that some asshole threatened to expose Peter as being a furry and a plushy."

"A what?" Tiff asked weakly.

"A furry is what you call people who like to dress up as animals in order to have sex, and a plushy is the term used to describe those who like to have sex with stuffed animals. Anyway, having something like that exposed could really damage a person's reputation, particularly in a puritanical society like our own."

"I'm not sure you have to be a puritan to find this upsetting," Tiff whispered.

Dena shrugged again, obviously impatient with Tiff's more conservative take on the situation. "I'm just saying that I seriously doubt that Peter ended his life because of anything you did or didn't do. You have nothing to feel guilty about."

"Is she always like this?" Tiff asked me, pointing to Dena with her thumb.

"I know she's abrasive," I said carefully, "but she may be right. I think that Peter's furry tendencies played a role in his suicide. We know what he did to his stuffed animals, so I think what we need to do now is figure out if he was actually sleeping with a human furry as well, or if he was just ogling them on the Internet. He did have a couple of animal costumes in his closet."

"They have furry porn sites?" Tiff asked, her voice now a high-pitched squeak.

"A lot of them," Dena and I said in unison.

"We also need to think about who might have wanted to expose…" My voice trailed off as I was struck with a new realization. "Oh, my God, I am so *slow sometimes!* This is what the letter to Eugene was about!"

Dena snapped her fingers. "Bingo!"

"Yes! He wrote that if Eugene went to the media with what he knew, he would not only be destroying political careers but also the lives of—" I stopped short as everything suddenly fell into place. The three of us looked at one another, clearly thinking the same thing.

"Anne Brooke," Tiff whispered, "is a furry! She was dressing up as a sheep and sleeping with my brother!"

"It could have been any animal, not just sheep," Dena said. "But other than that I think you may be on to something."

"No one would elect a furry to Congress," I said quietly.

"Probably not," Tiff agreed.

"So what if Anne Brooke flipped out when she realized that her secret could become public?" I suggested. "She could have gotten desperate. Maybe she decided she needed to do whatever was necessary to shut up everyone who knew about her fetish. And there's only one way she could have guaranteed that was going to happen…."

"Furry politician pushes her plushy lover over the edge." Dena sat back in her chair. "It makes quite a headline."

"Dena, could you talk to some of your furry and plushy customers? Find out if they know Anne, or know someone who knows her?"

"Here's the thing about furries and plushies. Because of the stigma assigned to people who like having sex with anthropomorphic animals, they've had to create this whole underground subculture. It's like a secret club. The only way you're going to get them to talk is if they think you're one of them."

"But you sell them Weenie Babies and leashes!" I protested. "You're their supplier. Surely that gives you an in."

"Nope," Dena said, shaking her head solemnly. "They may buy from me but they'll never trust me. I'm too…tame."

"You're too tame," I said flatly. Tiff blanched and a little chill went up my spine. I was dealing with people who thought Dena, a woman who owned a whip and a drawer full of edible pasties, was tame. I nervously adjusted the clasp on my watch. "Oh, shit! I'm supposed to meet Anatoly in less than twenty minutes!"

Dena confirmed the time on her own watch. "Okay, let's go." She smiled. "I know this is a serious issue but I'm actually glad you got me involved. The furries and plushies are by far my most obnoxious customers. I'm looking forward to throwing one of them to the wolves—pun intended."

20

I don't understand my husband. He says he wants to
grant my every wish, but then he gets mad when I wish
for a night with Matt Dillon.
—*C'est La Mort*

"YOU'RE LATE," ANATOLY SNAPPED AS I BREATHLESSLY BURST INTO THE
Starbucks we had decided to meet in.

"I know, I know, but I've had a really weird day. Listen…"

"We don't have time for me to listen." Anatoly got up and
threw his jacket on before dragging me toward the door.
"We were supposed to be at Sam's five minutes ago."

"But I really need to tell you something! Besides, I haven't
gotten my Frappuccino yet!"

"No time." Anatoly now had me out the door and was
pushing me toward the Harley.

"No time?" I asked incredulously. "Are you actually
asking me to leave a Starbucks without getting a drink?"

"You'll live." He pulled two helmets out of his saddle bags and handed me one.

I made a face and put the helmet over my head. I reluctantly climbed onto the back of Anatoly's bike and gave Starbucks one last look of longing before we roared off. Fortunately Anne and Sam's house was less than five minutes away, so while we were late we weren't excessively so. Anatoly got off the bike and strode toward the front door of the white-and-brown Tudor while I trotted after him. "Anatoly, I really want to tell you about Peter's apartment."

"As soon as we're done talking to Sam," he said curtly before ringing the bell.

Before I had a chance to insist, the door opened and Sam Griffin stood before us, looking sheepish and uncomfortable. "Well if it isn't the *Tikkun* reporters," he said with a forced laugh. "I suppose I should have known that one was a scam straight away. I've never known *Tikkun* to report on a small congressional race."

"Do you read *Tikkun?*" I asked.

"Er…no. I'm not Jewish. Anne and I are Unitarians."

"I see, then I think it's forgivable that you didn't recognize the *Tikkun* thing to be a ruse."

"Right, right." He shifted his weight from foot to foot before it finally dawned on him that he would need to step aside if we were ever going to be able to enter. "Sorry," he said quickly as he ushered us into the house. "I'm a bit nervous. This is the first time I've ever hired a private detective, and I was just beginning to get comfortable with Darrell. Now to have to detail my suspicions to two more strangers…" He released a heavy sigh. "I can't say I'm happy about that."

"I understand your concerns," Anatoly said as we followed Sam into the living room and I took a seat on the couch. "We'll do everything we can to make this transition as painless as possible."

I surveyed my surroundings. The coffee table looked to be hand carved out of redwood, and there was a beautiful dark wood grandfather clock against the wall. Someone had gone to great pains to ensure that the place struck the delicate balance of being both elegant and comfortable. There certainly wasn't anything cutesy about it, no figurines, no stuffed animals.

"You understand that my concerns about my wife's fidelity may very well be nothing more than unjustified paranoia," Sam said as he sat down on an expensive-looking brown leather armchair and propped his feet up on the ottoman. "Darrell has been following Anne for three weeks and he has yet to catch her in the arms of another man."

"You don't say," I mumbled distractedly, still studying the room. "Do you guys have a pet by any chance?"

Sam furrowed his brow and Anatoly gave me a sidelong glance, both clearly confused by my seemingly irrelevant question. "A pet?" Sam repeated. "No, we don't have any animals."

"I see. Does Anne *like* animals?" I asked. "I mean, does she ever talk about getting a dog, maybe a wolfhound or something?"

Now both of my male companions looked completely baffled. "Why a wolfhound?" Anatoly asked.

"I don't know. Anne just struck me as the kind of woman who would have a dog. A really big *furry* dog."

"We don't have a dog, and Anne's never mentioned wanting one," Sam said slowly.

"Okay, I guess I was wrong about that. Anyway, what were you saying before about your suspicions?"

"He was saying that Darrell hasn't caught Anne doing anything incriminating," Anatoly said crossly. He then smiled at Sam apologetically. "I'm hesitant to tell you this because I sincerely like Darrell…"

Bullshit.

"…but he's not exactly a stellar private detective. As uncomfortable as it may be to switch detectives three weeks into the investigation, it's probably for the best," Anatoly explained. "I wouldn't be surprised if Anne knew she was being followed and that was the reason for her chaste behavior."

Sam sucked in a sharp breath. "You think she knew? Jesus Christ, what if she figured out who hired him!"

"She probably just figured it was one of Fitzgerald's goons checking up on her," I said dismissively. "I personally hope Anne wins the election. She seems like a candidate who would really go out of her way to protect the environment. What is her position on the upkeep and funding of wildlife preserves? Is Anne…you know…*passionate* about wildlife?"

"Sophie, we can talk about Anne's politics later," Anatoly said quickly, but now his tone was more bewildered than irritated. "Sam, why don't you tell us what it was that made you think Anne might be being unfaithful."

"Well, I'm sure you're familiar with her history. Everyone is, thanks to Fitzgerald. She did have her reasons for cheating on her first husband. I'm not excusing it, mind you, but she didn't have the connection with him that she has with me."

Oh, so he was one of those she-won't-cheat-on-me-I'm-different types. I sighed inwardly. When will people learn that men and women don't cheat because of the way they feel about their partners? They cheat because of the way they feel about themselves.

"I've never loved a woman the way that I love Anne," Sam continued. "I didn't ever feel this strongly about my first wife, and I did love her."

"You were married before?" Anatoly asked with practiced casualness.

"Yes, when Anne met me I was a widower." Sam coughed out the last word as if it took a little extra effort to say. "Jocelyn was killed in a drive-by shooting when we were living in Oakland."

"That must have been a very hard thing for you to cope with," Anatoly noted. "Did the police ever catch the person who did it?"

Anatoly and I both already knew that they hadn't. Anatoly was feeling Sam out. Trying to gauge his reaction to his questions. Of course, if Anatoly had taken half a second to listen to me, he would have known he was barking up the wrong tree. Anne was the "goddamned furry shit" we were looking for, not Sam.

"They never did." He started fiddling with a corner of a throw pillow. "Jocelyn did a lot of volunteer work, and that night she was in one of the city's poorer areas handing out clean needles, and then some car just drove by and she was shot. No one saw a thing."

Of course they hadn't. No one ever sees anything in the poor neighborhoods of Oakland. Better to suffer from periodic bouts of blindness than be pegged as the person who ratted out a gang member to the cops.

"It was almost ironic that Jocelyn would die because of her own beautiful idealism. She was younger than I and had just received a master's degree in political science. She honestly believed that with compassion, love and reason she could change people. Make them better, more whole. Before she met me she had a habit of dating abusive, controlling men with the hope that she would be the woman to get them to face their childhood issues and become better human beings. Anne would never subject herself to the kind of treatment Jocelyn put up with, not for a second. She knows there are villains out there, men who love war and materialism. Anne lashes out against them. She doesn't try to convince the people who are in power to be good. She fights to give all the power to the good people."

I shifted uncomfortably in my seat. There was a big problem with this strategy. Assuming you weren't talking about people like Mother Teresa and Ted Bundy, "good" and "bad" were subjective terms. If you weren't going to discuss ideas with people who you thought were bad and gave all the power to the people who you alone decided were good, then you were basically advocating fascism. But the dreamy look in Sam's eyes told me that he didn't see it that way.

"Oddly enough, it was my wife's death that brought Anne and me together," he continued. "We met at an anti-gun rally. We were both speakers. She talked about the legislation needed to get guns out of the hands of civilians and I spoke about my personal experiences, driving home the point of why gun control is necessary. We had a drink afterward. We were both going through a difficult time…she was only recently divorced and her son had actually *asked* to go to boarding school—he's still there now. He has less than a year before he graduates high school and Anne only gets to see him on holidays and long weekends. We comfort each other. We only dated six months before she proposed."

"She proposed?" Anatoly asked.

Sam gave him a pitying look. "Anne and I don't believe there should be any difference in the roles of the sexes. She decided she wanted me to be her husband so she asked and I said yes. We went to a locally owned jewelry store that afternoon and bought an engagement ring that was made by Pueblo Indians. It was love. It still is."

"But now you've hired a private detective because you suspect she's cheated. What makes you think that?"

Sam looked so pathetic and sad, sitting there with his legs propped up, picking at the fringes of a throw pillow, that I almost felt embarrassed for him. He lacked both confidence and bravado, two qualities you would expect to see in a killer.

"A month ago I went on a yoga retreat," he said. "I was supposed to be there all weekend, but I wasn't happy with the meals they were serving—can you believe that they were actually trying to serve us cereal that contained high quantities of corn syrup?"

"My God, what is this world coming to?" I asked. Anatoly coughed into his hand.

"My thoughts exactly," Sam continued. "I brought it up with the director and we had a bit of a row so I left a day early. When I got home Anne didn't hear me come in and I inadvertently overheard part of her phone conversation. She was talking about Fitzgerald and speculating on what he was going to do next. It was probably just a business associate—that's what she told me later when I asked. But there was something about her tone that was more intimate than what she usually uses with her staff, and she called the person on the other end of the line 'baby.' I know there are women who use that term of endearment for any person they've known for more than five minutes, but Anne isn't one of them. Lord, I don't think she's called me by a pet name since we took my niece to Disneyland for her seventh birthday!"

I perked up. "You guys went to Disneyland?"

"Yes," Sam said, "but that's not really the point...."

"I just love Disneyland," I said quickly. "What did Anne think of the place?"

"She liked it, I suppose," Sam said uncertainly.

"Did she get really, you know, *cozy* with Mickey Mouse?"

"I'm sorry, Sam," Anatoly said quickly, "but would you mind if I spoke to my partner alone for just a moment?" He stood up, grabbed my hand and yanked me to my feet. "We'll be right back."

Anatoly dragged me out of the house, releasing me as soon as we got to the driveway. "All right, Sophie, what's with the animal references?"

"I think Anne is an animal person."

"So?"

"No, I mean a *real* animal person. As in a person who periodically dresses up like an animal."

"What the hell are you talking about?"

"And when she's dressed up," I continued, "she gets a little frisky."

Anatoly's eyes slanted. "Have you been drinking?"

"I wish, but no. Listen, this is what I was trying to tell you earlier. Dena and I found out that Peter is both a furry and a plushy. Do you know what that means?"

"Evidently, it means that my mastery of the English language isn't a strong as I thought, because I have no idea what you're talking about."

"No, it's not an English problem," I assured him. "You're unfamiliar with furries and plushies because you're a moderately normal person."

"Shall I take that as a compliment?"

"If you choose. Now, allow me to give you an overview of the dark underbelly of the furry world."

I detailed everything I had discovered in Peter's apartment and everything Dena had taught me about furries and plushies. When I began, Anatoly looked skeptical and a bit confused. By the end he looked mildly horrified and a little sick to his stomach.

"He had sex with toys," Anatoly said slowly, clearly trying to make sense of the new information.

"And people dressed up as animals—that's where Anne comes in. Or at least that where I *think* she comes in."

"I suppose that would make sense," Anatoly agreed. "If any of this could possibly qualify as making sense. Eugene could have found out about Anne's perversion…."

"Dena likes to think of those who belong to these groups as eccentrics. She thinks 'perversion' is too judgmental of a word."

"I'll remember that," Anatoly said sarcastically. "But if Eugene did find out and then Peter killed himself, he might have held off for a few weeks before revealing the information out of respect for the dead. Or perhaps he was just waiting for a more opportune time, like a few weeks before the election when Anne wouldn't have much of a chance to refute the charges and the Democrats wouldn't have time to run someone else."

"Either way, it gave Anne time to plot Eugene's death," I said.

"And then she could have thought that Melanie had found out."

"But why would she think that?" I asked. "I'm sure Melanie didn't know about this. This kind of information is way too bizarre not to share. So if she didn't know, why kill her?"

"Maybe Melanie just found out. She could have come across some papers Eugene left behind detailing Anne's fetish. Or maybe Anne just thought she did. She could have taken Melanie's body to San Francisco just to get it as far away from Contra Costa County as possible, confuse the police a little. On the other hand, she could have done it because *we* live in San Francisco. She may have wanted to issue us a warning."

"You think she knows that we've been snooping for Melanie?"

"Anything's possible."

"True." I glanced back at Sam and Anne's house. "So now what?"

"Now we go back there and ask Sam a few questions. But, Sophie?"

"Yeah?"

"The animal questions can wait for another time. If Anne is a fuzzy—"

"Furry."

"All right, if she's one of those, then I doubt Sam knows anything about it. If he does, we don't want to tip him off that *we* know. We may be able to gain a strategic advantage by playing this one close to the vest until later in the game."

"Got it."

When we reentered the house we found Sam sniffing the contents of a small brown glass bottle. "Aromatherapy," he explained. "Cedarwood, to be precise. It has a calming effect."

"Sounds interesting," Anatoly said, clearly disinterested. We sat back down on the sofa and Anatoly cleared his throat. "I'm sorry about stepping out just now. Sophie and I recently finished a case involving animal abuse, and being an animal lover, she's been anxious for any kind of assurance that the majority of people are as fond of our four-legged friends as she is."

Okay, now that was a lame excuse. I waited for Sam to demand that we tell him the truth about what was going on, but shockingly enough he bought it.

"I have always found stories of animal cruelty to be particularly disturbing," he said, smiling at me sympathetically.

"Thanks for understanding," I said. "But none of that has anything to do with why you hired us. Other than that phone call, do you have any other reason to be suspicious of Anne?"

Sam hesitated and then took another sniff of his cedarwood. "There have been a lot of late nights at the campaign headquarters."

"I would think that would be normal," Anatoly said.

"It would be, except...I went by the office one time when she said she would be working late. I thought I'd surprise her with some homemade vegetable juice."

"Lucky her," I muttered. Anatoly jabbed me with his elbow.

"But she wasn't there. I waited in the car across the street for a full forty minutes and she never showed up. I finally rang her cell and without telling her where *I* was I asked where she was and…"

"She said she was in the office, didn't she?" I asked.

"Exactly." Sam chewed on the inside of his cheek. "That's exactly what she said," he whispered again.

Anatoly jotted something down in his notebook and stroked the beginnings of his stubble. "Mr. Griffin…"

"Sam," he corrected.

"All right, Sam, could you e-mail me your wife's schedule? Everything from work-related outings to errands and nail appointments for the next week or two would be helpful."

"I can certainly e-mail you the appointments I know about but…" His chin began to quiver and he whispered, "What if the schedule I have for her isn't accurate? What if she's lying to me about where she's going and what she's doing?"

Anatoly flipped his notebook closed and put it in his jacket pocket. "That is exactly what I plan on finding out. From what you've told us it's clear that your wife has a secret. Now we just have to figure out how dark that secret is."

21

I went to the doctor to see if he could give me something for my anxiety. He told me to simplify my life and then call him in the morning.
—*C'est La Mort*

AFTER WE LEFT SAM, I FILLED ANATOLY IN ON THE EXCHANGE I HAD WITH the homeless tinfoil-hat lady and we both agreed that we needed to at least try to find her. We rode the Harley up and down Highway 1 (which is parallel to Ocean Beach), pulling into each parking lot, looking for the sparkle of aluminum headgear, but no such luck. We turned onto every one of the avenues that were within five miles of the beach and even went into the Sutro Heights park, but there was no sign of her. We searched for three hours before we finally gave it a rest.

When we got back to my apartment I was more than a little exhausted. There is such a thing as too much information, and right then I found myself longing for the time when

S and M seemed avant-garde. Mr. Katz greeted us with an impatient meow, which I responded to by filling his food bowl before collapsing on the couch. "We really do need to keep following Anne," I said. "Eventually she's got to lead us to something."

Anatoly grunted his agreement and threw his leather jacket over a dining chair. "Your answering machine is blinking," he noted before pressing the play button. I shot him a warning look. Being my boyfriend did not give him license to play my messages without asking.

"You have…one new message. First new message."

"Hey, Soph, it's me." Dena's voice filled my room. "Thought I'd let you know that I got Tiff back safe and sound. Also she told me about all of Peter's trips, and I happen to know that there have been furry conventions in each of those cities. Speaking of which, I thought that you might want to check out the furry scene, maybe even catch a homicidal cheetah—" she paused before adding "—cheetahs are actually very popular costumes among furries. Anyway, there's a furry bash at the Chelsea Hotel this Tuesday. I think it's an annual bash or something, so it's getting a lot of buzz among the furs. If Anne Brooke *is* a furry someone there will probably know about it. Anyhoo, I know somebody who knows somebody and it looks like I can score you a couple of invites. If you want them, give me a call."

I glanced up at Anatoly. "We should go."

"Why?" Anatoly crossed his foot over his knee. "If Anne is truly behind all this, she's not going to risk everything by showing up at a large party dressed up as some kind of mutant feline."

"Probably not, but how many people can really be part of this movement? My guess is that they all kind of know one another, so maybe someone will talk to us about Anne."

"If they're wearing masks they might not even know one another's real identity."

"Maybe not, but I think it would be hard to completely hide your identity from someone you're having sex with."

"Rape victims have a hard time identifying their attackers all the time."

"But that's because rape victims aren't expecting to be attacked. These people know what to expect from one another. They're having consensual sex. They have the presence of mind to memorize the kind of details that might help us."

"I still don't think attending this party is necessary."

I studied the protruding position of Anatoly's jaw. "What's going on with you? You know this party could produce leads. Why are you being so obstinate?"

"Just because Dena gets us an invitation doesn't mean that they'll just let us in," he grumbled.

"What do you mean?"

"There will be certain expectations…" His voice trailed off.

"We're going to have to dress up as furries," I said slowly.

Anatoly shook his head definitively. "We'll simply get a room at the Chelsea Hotel on Tuesday and we'll observe."

"Observe what? A bunch of masked strangers wandering in and out of a hotel conference room? Come on, if we want to catch Anne, we have to get into one of these get-togethers and schmooze. Someone's got to know her!"

"I'm not dressing up like an animal."

"Stop being such a wuss. We'll go to one of those

costume-rental places and find you a macho furry costume—
it'll be fine."

"There is no such thing as a macho furry costume."

"Sure there is, like…like that big strappin' bear who
teaches fire safety! Every little girl loves him!"

"I have no interest in little girls."

"Okay, good point. How 'bout King Kong? Come on,
any ape who could win the hearts of Fay Wray, Jessica Lange
and Naomi Watts has got to be an ape worth emulating."

"Sophie, I'm not going to do it."

A sudden burst of fury restored my energy and I was instantly on my feet and in Anatoly's face. "Anne Brooke may
have killed a woman that I truly cared about. And if that's
true, then she also killed Melanie's husband, ensuring that
Melanie's last days on earth were miserable. I'm going to take
this bitch *down*. And if I have to dress up like a fucking pony
to do it, so be it. Now, are you going to help me or not?"

Anatoly hesitated. "You think we'll be able to find a
King Kong costume?"

"I think it's highly possible, yes."

Anatoly grumbled some Russian curse, which I knew was
his way of giving in. I smiled and relaxed back onto the
couch. I had dropped my purse on the end table and took
this moment to check my cell. "Hey, Johnny called me. You
know, the guy who—"

"Loves you," Anatoly finished. "Yes, I remember."

I pressed the phone against my ear and listened to the
message. "He feels awful about rescinding my invitation to
his party," I said, summarizing Johnny's ramblings for Anatoly
while I listened to them. "And he—" I swallowed hard

before relaying the rest of what I was hearing "—he feels awful about Melanie. Fitzgerald told him about what happened on Friday and he's still in shock about the whole thing." I pressed Nine, deleting the message before it was even finished playing. I couldn't stand to hear him blather about Melanie as if he knew her. He may have taken her to church, even introduced her to his mom—but he didn't *know* her. He didn't feel the loss that I did.

Anatoly leaned back in his chair and gave me a quizzical look. "How did Fitzgerald know about what happened on Friday? The papers didn't come out with it until Saturday."

"She was discovered Friday morning," I said quietly. "Maybe the Contra Costa sheriff's department sent someone out to talk to the people who knew Melanie Friday afternoon…or evening." The memory of the police's visit to my apartment on Friday night came pounding into my head like a migraine.

"Maybe," Anatoly mused. "Tell me something, Sophie, what is your opinion of Johnny?"

"If you're still feeling jealous, you don't need to—"

"This isn't about jealousy." Anatoly left his chair and joined me on the sofa, placing my legs on his lap. "We don't know that Anne killed Eugene or Melanie. We just know that she *might* have had a motive. Even if she was sleeping with Peter that doesn't mean he was her only lover. What if she was sleeping with someone else who was willing to kill for her? Someone working for Fitzgerald?"

"Johnny?" I scoffed.

"It's possible," Anatoly pressed. "As a low-level personal assistant his background wouldn't have been scrutinized as carefully as those of the other people working closely with Fitzgerald."

"I have a hard time visualizing him and Anne as being a couple, and if he *does* have a soft spot for Anne he's pretty adept at covering it up. I brought her up when Mary Ann and I went to dinner with him and Rick, and Johnny was not kind. Even *Rick* was willing to cut Anne more slack than Johnny. Besides, Johnny called me during my last conversation with Darth Vader. For a few minutes I had them both on different lines at the same time."

"He could have been calling from a cell and a landline," Anatoly suggested. "It certainly can't hurt to check him out."

I shrugged and I let myself slide into a more horizontal position, my legs elevated slightly by Anatoly's. I didn't particularly like Johnny and I wouldn't be heartbroken if he turned out to be a bad guy, but it didn't seem to fit with what I knew about him. Johnny was too naive and he was way too hyper to be a murderer. The extra adrenaline he would get from killing would probably send him into cardiac arrest.

I stared at our dark reflections in the blank screen of my television. "What if this doesn't come together?" I whispered. "So far we have Eugene, killed in a drive-by shooting, a letter proving that he knew something that Peter Strauss didn't want him to know..."

"That he was a furry," Anatoly interjected, "or at least I think it's fair for us to assume that was it."

"Yeah, we can assume that, but obviously Eugene wouldn't care if some random low-level campaign worker had a thing for cuddly cartoon characters. So it was probably Anne, right? Who else has a reputation that Eugene would want to destroy? But does that mean that Anne is responsible for the threats I've been getting? And why have the threats been so incredibly stupid? Furry or not, these people should be a *little* more adept at being intimidating." I could hear my volume increase with each question, punctuating my aggravation. "Does Sam's first wife's death have any relevance at all or is it totally unrelated? And why did Flynn Fitzgerald show up at Neiman's at the same time I was having lunch with Maggie, Rick and Mary Ann? I mean, when is this thing going to start to make sense?"

"It's confusing," Anatoly agreed. "But we'll figure it out."

"How do you know?"

"I've never failed to solve a case before."

"But most of your cases deal with adultery, not crime."

"An adultery case is still a case," Anatoly said. "And if you remember, I used to do detective work for an insurance company. At that time almost all my cases involved some kind of criminal activity. I've even solved a few kidnapping cases."

"Really? You never told me that." But then again, Anatoly hadn't told me a lot of things. I had gone out with him for almost a year and there was still so much that I didn't know about him, but I was actually okay with that. Dating him was like studying the language of the Ancient Egyptians. He would always be a bit of a mystery to me, but I loved "learning" him.

Tonight, though, I wasn't up for an Anatoly lesson. There were too many other questions floating around in my head. It felt like he and I were chasing down a million little leads, each one taking us nowhere. Anatoly must have picked up on my mood because he stopped talking, and for a good ten minutes neither one of us said a word as we rested on the couch, which was good because my thoughts were so damn loud. Silence was the only thing keeping my head from exploding.

But the silence couldn't last forever. Tomorrow morning I'd have to throw myself into the chaos once again in the hope that I would eventually be able to make sense out of fragments of nonsensical information.

"Whatever you're thinking, let it go," Anatoly finally whispered as he gently started to massage my feet. "At least for tonight."

"How do I do that?" I whispered back.

"Lose yourself in us." His hands moved from my foot to my calf and then continued their journey upward. "Just for tonight. Tomorrow you can let the world in, but tonight the world must do without you."

I sighed as he pulled my jeans down over my hips.

I've always been a sucker for sexy men who are skilled in the art of distraction.

22

When our elected officials make us look bad, we usually give them another chance; but not our hairstylists. We hold them to a higher standard.
—*C'est La Mort*

ANATOLY AND I HAD SEX THREE TIMES THAT NIGHT. IF WE KEPT IT UP LIKE that we would have to start buying our condoms at Costco. But despite the pleasures Anatoly bestowed upon me I was secretly relieved when he suggested that we split up for the day. He had gotten up early to dig further into Sam's, Anne's and Johnny's backgrounds, and when he failed to come up with anything interesting, he drove off to Contra Costa County to put a tail on one of them. At the time he left he had yet to make up his mind *which* one he would be tailing, but he assured me that his decision would be made by the time he crossed the Bay Bridge. My task was to find the tinfoil-hat lady. I truly hoped that I would find her, but regardless of whether or not I did, I would enjoy the breathing room. Some people craved companionship when they were anxious. I craved space.

It was now ten-thirty in the morning and Mr. Katz and I were cuddled up in front of my laptop perusing my e-mail when I spotted one from Sam.

I quickly pulled up the message:

Hello,
I assume you got Anne's schedule that I e-mailed last night…

We had. Anatoly had printed it out this morning.

…but I thought you should know that I just spoke to Anne and there's been a change. Her hairstylist had a family emergency and had to cancel her four-thirty appointment. However, she may reschedule with someone else, even with someone at a different salon if necessary. She's in a bit of a panic because she has a television interview tomorrow morning and she needs some kind of touch-up. She's really not a materialistic woman, but she is cognizant that we do live in a materialistic society that judges women based on their…

I didn't read any more. Instead I just picked up the phone and called the man who was going to help Anne.

Marcus picked up on the fourth ring. "I have a woman under the dryer," he said, "but she only has another five minutes, so whatever it is, make it quick."

"This is quick," I assured him. "I know this is a lot to ask, but I need you to pencil Anne Brooke in for an appointment—a touch-up of some kind, perhaps a cut and highlight. If you're booked all day maybe you could stay late this one night. She has a TV interview tomorrow morning."

"Anne Brooke, as in the promiscuous-politician-with-a-possibly-murderous-ambition Anne Brooke?"

"Yeah, maybe—I'm not one hundred percent sure she's murderous, but I'm positive about the promiscuous-politician part."

"Why do you want me to work on a person you suspect of murder? Do you think she only gets homicidal on bad-hair days?"

"What I *think* is that people talk to their hairstylists. She's not going to sit in your chair and confess to murder just because you've given her killer highlights, but she might drop some useful tidbit if you just subtly quiz her about certain things."

"No, sorry, can't help."

"Why not?" My voice reached such a high pitch that it could have upset the hearing of a dog.

"Sophie, when someone hires me, they are allowing me to alter one of their most prized possessions, *their hair.* You don't take that kind of risk with someone you can't trust. If word got out that I broke a client's confidence, I'd be about as popular as an admitted communist during the McCarthy era."

"You're serious about this? You're not going to help me?"

"Honey," he began, "you know I love you but—"

"Please, Marcus? There's a chance that Anne is responsible for the deaths of two, possibly three, people. If that's true, then there's a good chance she'll kill again." I was aware that I was being hopelessly unfair to Marcus, but I was desperate and I needed to feel like I had an army of friends behind me to help figure this mess out.

There was a beat of silence. "*Three* people?" he finally asked. "I thought this was just about Eugene. How did we get up to three?"

"Well, there's Peter Strauss. He was Anne Brooke's campaign worker and he probably committed suicide, but I think he did it because of Anne and their forbidden affair. And then there's Melanie," and at the mention of her name my voice broke. "They found her body on Friday. Somebody dumped it by Ocean Beach. And right now the bulk of the evidence is pointing toward Anne Brooke. That kinky adulterous parasite probably put on one of her furry costumes and killed Melanie!"

I dropped to the couch and started crying, but I quickly forced my tears into submission. Grieving was a luxury for those who weren't hell-bent on revenge.

When Marcus spoke again his voice was considerably gentler and less playful. "Sophie, sweetie, I'm so sorry. I didn't know."

"Now you do." I reached over for the Kleenex box on the side table and blew my nose as quietly as possible.

"Are you alone right now? Do you want me to try to rearrange my appointments so I can be there with you?"

"I don't need you to be here with me, I just need you to help me."

"I'll help you."

"Really?" I squeaked.

"Yes, really," he said on a sigh, "although I'll undoubtedly regret it. My last appointment should be over by six-thirty. I'll stay late if she wants to come in then."

"Oh, Marcus, I love you!" And I meant that sincerely. I did have an army of friends behind me…actually they were more like the National Guard. Whenever I had a homeland emergency, they came rushing in and they never let me down.

"Okay," I said, after wiping away the few tears that were still clinging to my cheeks, "this is how this is going to work. Her husband's kind of working with me—not that he thinks he's married to a killer or anything, just an adulterer. He's a nutritionist, so I'll just have him tell Anne that one of his patients has an in with you. Hopefully he'll have her calling you within the next few hours."

"Sounds like a plan." Marcus hesitated for a moment before adding, "I may have misheard you, but did you say that Anne was a furry?"

"You know about furries?"

"Of course I know about furries. What, you think I live in a cave?"

I didn't answer. This was kind of like the whole iPod thing. By the time I figured out what they were, everyone and their mother had one. Why was I always being left out of the loop on these important cultural phenomena?

"So I take it that *is* what you said? Anne's a furry?"

"That's what I said, yes." I told him about everything I had found at Peter's apartment. He listened, occasionally breaking into the same kind of contrived coughing fit Dena had when suppressing a laugh.

"So your job is to try to get her to talk about Peter, Eugene and/or Fitzgerald," I continued. "Oh, and there's a furry party tomorrow night at the Chelsea Hotel. Try to fit that into conversation as well. See how she reacts."

"How do I casually bring the subject of a furry party into conversation?"

"Marcus, you're a genius, remember? I'm sure you can find a way to do this."

"I'd need an IQ of 600 in order to figure this one out," he complained.

"Just tell me you'll try, Marcus."

"Fine, I'll see what I can do."

A Cheshire cat grin spread across my face. "I really do love you, Marcus."

"You'd better," he said.

After I hung up I e-mailed Sam and he immediately replied, agreeing to feed Anne my lie. Apparently Anne really was worried about her roots because less than twenty minutes after that Marcus called to tell me she had telephoned to secure the appointment. It probably didn't hurt that Marcus was a well-known hairstylist and most people had to wait weeks if not months to see him. I was about to call Anatoly when it occurred to me that there was one more thing I wanted to check out. I flipped through the Yellow Pages until I found what I wanted, smiled to myself and then got Anatoly on the line. I quickly told him about Anne's impending appointment with Marcus. "Marcus is going to see if he can get any more information out of her," I explained. "You know, when her guard is down, no politicians or so-called journalists in sight."

"Couldn't hurt," Anatoly mused. "Tell Marcus to try to get her talking about Peter."

"Already told him that. But since we know where she's going to be tonight, you don't need to follow her."

"Got it. I'll follow Johnny instead," Anatoly said.

"Follow Johnny tomorrow. Tonight I want you to meet me in the Mission." I rattled off a Mission-district address.

"Is that a residence?" Anatoly asked.

"A retailer."

"What kind of retailer?"

"You'll see…just be there by seven sharp."

"Why do I have a bad feeling about this?"

"Because you're a pessimist. I'll see you tonight."

I hung up and my smile morphed into a full-blown devilish grin. I was actually looking forward to seeing Anatoly's reaction to what I had planned.

He showed up early, undoubtedly hoping to scope the place out before I got there. But of course I had anticipated his move and was there even earlier. The only thing that could have made me late would have been if I had found my tinfoil-hat woman. But despite combing the streets for the better part of the afternoon and questioning at least twenty different homeless people, I had turned up nothing, or rather no one.

I spotted Anatoly walking toward me; at six feet he towered over most of the other pedestrians and his fair complexion was on the lighter side of the wide spectrum of skin tones that were commonplace in the neighborhood. The moment he saw me his eyes went up to the sign hanging above the store behind me. Even from half a block away I could see him wince.

"We have to do it eventually," I said, once he reached my side.

"There's got to be another way."

"There isn't. Come on." I linked my arm through his and led him through the door of Costume Closet. "Let's go find you a King Kong outfit."

Anatoly glanced around at the carelessly placed racks of costumes crammed into the funky little store. "Where do they keep the rentals?" he asked, directing his question to me rather than the disinterested clerk sitting behind the register reading comic books.

"I've decided that we're going to buy. My treat."

"Why do you want to *own* an animal costume?"

"Because," I said, pulling him toward an overstuffed rolling rack, "now that I know what people do in these costumes, I want one that's never been worn before."

"I hadn't thought of that. You're right, we need new ones."

We milled around the store for another five minutes before I finally found something promising. "Here," I said, lifting up a particularly heavy costume. "This can be your King Kong getup."

"That's not King Kong," Anatoly said. "It's just a regular ape."

"What's the difference?"

"King Kong was more impressive than that," he explained. "He was grandiose."

"He was sixty feet tall, Anatoly. I guess I *could* try to score you some steroids and a pair of stilts, but that seems a bit extreme for a furry party."

"I'm not wearing that." His jaw was protruding enough to let me know he meant it.

"Okay, we'll find you something else." I wandered over to the rack against the wall. "Here's one that'll work," I said, holding up another monkey suit. "This one has bigger pecks and a six-pack."

"That's a silverback."

"Excuse me?"

"Look at the back."

I turned the suit around and sure enough it had a gray streak down the middle of its back. "So he's a silverback," I agreed. "That's not so bad. The silverback within a gorilla colony is always the alpha male."

"We agreed that I would be King Kong."

I stared at Anatoly for a few seconds before answering. I had never seen this side of him before. He was this totally macho, irritatingly practical guy who had served in two different armies. Now he was whining like a six-year-old because I couldn't get him the "right" King Kong costume.

"On second thought," I said carefully, "I don't think this is a silverback at all. It *is* King Kong. It's just that he's getting up there in years. I mean, the poor guy was climbing the Empire State Building and fighting off airplanes ten years before World War II. He's entitled to a few gray hairs. It makes him more distinguished."

"Don't patronize me, Sophie."

"Don't patronize you?" I asked, quickly dispensing with the delicacy. "Do you hear yourself? You're upset because this gorilla lacks grandeur! It's a fucking gorilla suit!"

Anatoly pinched the bridge of his nose. "I knew this wasn't a good idea."

"Maybe not, but it's our *only* idea. I think it's fairly obvious that these furries factor into the murders, and if we're going to bust these guys we need to infiltrate them.

You were in the damned Israeli army, Anatoly, you should understand this."

"They didn't ask us to dress up like apes in the Israeli army."

"Fine, don't dress up as an ape, dress up like a wolf, dress up like Kermit the Frog—that way you can lay Miss Piggy. Is that macho enough for you?"

"That depends, are you going to dress up as Miss Piggy?"

Before I could respond, my cell rang. "Marcus!" I said, once I had pulled my phone out of my purse. "Tell me everything."

"That's easy, she confided nothing."

"Nothing?" My disappointment was overwhelming. "But she must have at least engaged in small talk, right? Didn't she say *anything* that I might be able to use?"

"Well, it does seem that we have a mutual acquaintance. Anne was interviewed by a novelist-cum-freelance journalist named Sophie not too long ago."

"Please tell me you didn't give me away."

"Not at all—you actually made quite a favorable impression on her. But other than that tidbit, she didn't reveal a lot. No matter how hard I tried I couldn't get her to talk about Peter or Eugene. She did say that Fitzgerald is a hypocritical hate-monger, but that's it. Apparently she's had a very hard day and only wanted to talk about pleasant things. Like raindrops on roses and whiskers on kittens."

"No white copper kettles or warm woolen mittens?" I asked. Anatoly gave me a strange look.

"She strikes me as the type who prefers stainless steel and cashmere. Anyhow, there's still a chance I'll be able to coax a little more info out of her before she leaves."

"Wait a minute, she's still *there?* Marcus, you shouldn't be calling me now! What if she gets suspicious?"

"Relax, she's under the dryer at the moment. Listen, I may not have been able to get her to say a lot, but there is one question that I have been able to put to rest."

"What's that?"

"Anne's about as furry as a naked mole rat."

"How can you be so sure?"

"She's not the type to dress up as an animal for sexual purposes."

"Forgive me, Marcus," I said as I watched Anatoly sift through another rolling rack of animal costumes, "but I'm not sure that either of us has had enough experience with furries to be able to identify their distinguishing characteristics."

"Maybe not, but I know tons of people who *aren't* furries and it's clear to me that Anne is one of them."

"Why? Because she shaved her legs this morning?"

"Because she's not a minority."

"Oh, give me a break! Being a furry is so not a black thing."

"You're right, it's not. But to become a furry is to willingly become part of a minority group. Furries know that if people find out about their sexual preferences they'll be discriminated against, perhaps even ostracized. A black, lesbian Muslim would have a better chance of gaining societal acceptance."

"So what's your point?"

"Just that Anne doesn't see herself as a minority. Yeah, she's a woman, but my guess is she's spent the better part of her life surrounded by reverse-sexists."

"I still don't see—"

"Sophie, she spent the first half hour of our appointment explaining how much she empathizes with the plight of my people. She just *loves* the blacks and the gays. If I was Native American she probably would've offered to take me out for buffalo burgers. You know the drill. She's one of those liberals who desperately wants to identify with an oppressed group, but she doesn't so she overcompensates by telling anyone who will listen that she's passionate about the issues that are important to the people she's oppressing. You know how people who don't have a lot of sex love to talk about it? Same principle applies here."

"That's a stretch, Marcus." But as I gazed down at my light brown skin I thought about all the people I had met in my life who had never suffered discrimination. A lot of them were under the bizarre impression that they were missing out. It was as if they thought they'd be cooler if they had a glass ceiling hanging over their heads. *Those* were the people who told minorities they barely knew that they understood their so-called struggle. Anne absolutely came across as being one of those people and that didn't really fit with the furry thing.

"I just call them as I see them," Marcus said, interrupting my thoughts.

"Did you mention the furry party yet?" I asked, hoping to find *something* to back up my original theory.

"Yes, I had the receptionist bring me the phone fifteen minutes into our appointment. No one was on the other line, of course, but she didn't know that. I then had a particularly embarrassing one-way conversation about how I wasn't going to be able to make the furry party at the Chelsea this Saturday. If Anne repeats this information to anyone, my reputation as a *moderate* pervert will be forever tarnished."

"Did she ask you about the call after you hung up?"

"No, she just looked at me funny and then she started talking a little faster."

"Aha! So the mention of furries made her nervous!"

"The mention of furries makes everyone nervous, Sophie. Furries are weird."

"But how would she even know what a furry was unless she—"

"*Vanity Fair, Marie Claire,* MTV and a slew of other media giants have run stories on furries," Marcus interrupted. "Brooke would know what a furry was because she doesn't live in a cave."

"She wouldn't have to live in a cave not to know what a furry was!" I snapped. "I didn't know and I've never lived in anything more primitive than a studio apartment!"

"Whatever. Anne was uncomfortable with the furry thing. You can interpret that any way you like. Just keep in mind that if your interpretation is different from mine it's wrong."

"You're impossible," I grumbled.

"Perhaps, but I make impossible cute."

"True." I mulled over the little information that Marcus had shared with me. "Do you really think I made a favorable impression on her?"

"That's what she said, and she seemed to mean it."

"I'm going to stop by," I said impulsively. "I'll pretend I happened to be in the neighborhood and wanted to stop by to say hello to you. Then maybe, just *maybe,* I can talk her into coming out for a drink with me. I might be able to get a little more out of her than you."

"You doubt my skills as an interrogator?"

"You told me yourself that you're not comfortable interrogating a client, and that's bound to affect your performance."

"Okay, I'll give you that. I should be done with Anne in about thirty minutes. Stop by then."

"Beautiful! Marcus, thank you for this."

"You're welcome. You can start to pay me back by bringing me a little chocolate to munch on. I'm having a craving, probably because I'm dealing with PMS."

"You're dealing with PMS?" I asked incredulously.

"Possible Murderous Senator, darling. Just talking to her gives me cramps."

I laughed and said a quick goodbye. Anatoly looked up from the silverback mask he had been studying. "Did Marcus get any information out of Anne?" he asked.

"Not much. He doesn't think she's a furry, but that's just his opinion."

"She'd better be a furry," Anatoly said. "I don't want to dress up like a gorilla for nothing."

"But you *are* going to dress up as a gorilla, right?"

Anatoly sighed and tucked the mask under his arm as if it was his motorcycle helmet, his silent way of saying yes.

I breathed a sigh of relief and told him about my plan to see Anne.

"If you're going to talk to Anne, I'm going with you," Anatoly said firmly.

"You can't, Anatoly. It's one thing for her to coincidentally run into the reporter from *Tikkun* magazine, but it's another thing for her to run into both of us. She'll get suspicious."

"Sophie, this woman could be a killer, and there's a chance

she already knows that you're investigating Eugene's death. You can't be alone with her."

"If we're going to figure this out, we're *both* going to have to take some risks, and you're going to have to find a way to deal with that."

Anatoly grumbled some Russian before relenting. "Fine, I won't be at your side when you speak to her. But I am going to follow you at a distance. It's one thing to take risks and it's another to be needlessly reckless."

"Fine, follow me. I can live with that." I reached into the display rack behind me and pulled out what looked like a generic version of Hello Kitty. It had Hello Kitty's big head and lack of a mouth, but it had longer whiskers, and the bow adorning its ear was purple instead of pink. "This is going to be my costume," I said definitively.

Anatoly cocked his head to the side. "Why that one?"

"For one thing, it doesn't have paws, so I'll be able to use my hands, and second, it doesn't have a mouth, so no one will be able to kiss me or ask me to, you know, put anything *between* my lips."

Anatoly's eyes widened slightly and he looked back down at the large lips of his gorilla mask. "Perhaps I should select a different disguise."

"No, stick with the silverback. No one is going to mess with an alpha ape."

23

As awful as this sounds most of us do not want to live
among the mentally ill. That's why we try to keep them
all in Washington.
—*C'est La Mort*

I DITCHED ANATOLY. HE HAD FOLLOWED ME FROM THE MISSION IN HIS
beige, totally nondescript rented sedan. It was the kind of
car you could sit in for an hour and still not find anything
about it that was interesting enough to remark on. In other
words, it was a perfect car to use to tail someone. Unfortunately Ooh La La was on Fillmore, which was not the perfect
street if you were hoping to park a medium-size car, nondescript or otherwise. I found a spot several blocks away and
Anatoly had signaled to me that I should wait there while
he found a spot for himself. I waited for about two minutes
before getting antsy. God only knew how long Marcus was
going to be able to keep Anne in his chair. Besides, it wasn't

as if Anatoly didn't know where I was going. He would park and find a place where he could watch Ooh La La from a discreet distance and everything would be fine.

When I arrived at the salon Marcus was at the front desk mixing champagne with crème de cassis in a glass flute. The contemporary hip-hop and alternative-rock hits that could usually be heard at Ooh La La were conspicuously absent; in their stead was something that sounded suspiciously like Abba.

"You're the last one here?" I asked in a low voice, craning my neck so I could see the empty room behind him. Marcus's station wasn't visible from the entryway.

"Yes, which means that the task of getting Anne her second kir royale is mine." He held the drink up for my inspection.

"Her second, huh?"

"Yes, and she needs it. Girlfriend is strung as high as a kite." He looked down pointedly at my empty hands. "No chocolate?"

"Oh, dammit. I totally forgot."

"But I have—"

"PMS, I know, I know. I promise to buy you a whole box of chocolates tomorrow, okay?"

Marcus released an exaggerated sigh. "Fine, but I must tell you, I'm feeling very unappreciated right now." With that he turned and led me to his station. "Anne, darling," he called to the back of the woman who was sitting in his chair. "Look who the cat dragged in."

The chair swiveled around and I gasped in surprise. Anne looked gorgeous. Her hair, which had been in a French twist last I had seen her, was now cascading around her shoulders, which were exposed by her pale yellow silk camisole. She undoubtedly had come wearing a blazer, but Marcus always insisted that such things be hung up before he started working, and he had clearly been working on her. Her curls were loose and romantic and adorned with delicate golden highlights that made her look at least five years younger than she was. It was hard to envision this woman putting that head inside an animal mask.

"What a wonderful surprise!" Anne said. Her mouth was curved into a smile, but nothing else about her body language indicated happiness. As I stepped closer I could see that, while lovely, she wasn't quite as put together as she had been during our interview. Her nail polish was chipped, it looked as if she had been biting her cuticles, and her navy skirt needed ironing. She also looked thinner than the last time I had seen her, and she was wiggling her right foot as if she had a nervous twitch.

"Sophie was in the area and noticed the lights were on," Marcus explained. "She knows this is after hours for Ooh La La, so the little journalist stopped by to investigate."

"I'm glad you did," Anne said. "Marcus and I were just talking about you."

"Oh?" I asked innocently.

"Yes," Marcus said with a wicked grin. "We were playing the it's-a-small-world game. Anne found me because her husband is the nutritionist of one of my other clients, and then when we found out that we both knew *you* we realized that we were linked in some wonderful cosmic way." He held up a lock of her hair. "It's like that John Cusak movie, *Serendipity,* except instead of finding the love of her life she found the perfect perm."

"Your hair does look amazing," I admitted. "I hope you're going out tonight to show it off."

"I'm just heading home after this," Anne said. "But my husband will see how I look and that's good enough for me. Besides, physical beauty is not what I'm about. It's what's inside that matters."

Right, that's why you just switched stylists in a pinch and coughed up hundreds of dollars for a perm and color. "When you look that good you should go out," I insisted. "There's lots of cute little bars around here. Why don't we treat ourselves to a glass of merlot?"

The twitch in Anne's foot became more pronounced. "I shouldn't drink any more tonight. This is my second kir royale and I have a long drive home."

Now, that didn't sound like the Anne I had read about on the Internet.

"Then why don't you two go to Bittersweet, the Choco-late Café?" Marcus suggested. "It's just a few doors down and they serve the most amazing chocolate treats you have ever tasted. You might even want to pick up a box for a friend while you're there."

I couldn't help but smile at Marcus's lack of subtlety, but Anne just shook her head. "I really shouldn't…" Just then her cell phone started ringing. Marcus politely retrieved her handbag so she could answer. She took one look at her screen and shoved it back in her purse. "No one I need to talk to right now," she explained quickly. "You know, on second thought, I'd love a cup of hot chocolate."

Less than five minutes later we were sitting right by the banister in the loft area of the Chocolate Café. I was sipping the ChocoLatte and Anne had ordered the Bittersweet, which had to be the most spectacular and decadent chocolate drink ever made. But Anne hadn't touched it, nor had she tasted the dark chocolate macaroons or the dark chocolate truffles that I had purchased. Of course, the small box of truffles was supposed to be for Marcus, but I had already eaten one. I figured I was doing him a favor by consuming at least a few of the excess calories. But Anne didn't seem interested in chocolate. The only thing she seemed to be interested in was the front door of the café.

"Anne, is everything all right?" I asked. "You seem anxious."

"Hmm?" She kept her focus on the exit.

"I asked if you were—" This time it was my cell phone that interrupted us. It was, of course, Anatoly. I held up a finger to indicate to Anne that I would only be a minute.

"Hi," I said after pressing Talk.

"I told you to wait for me."

I laughed jovially for Anne's sake. "I know. I was in a bit of a hurry."

"Here's how this is going to work," Anatoly continued, clearly livid. "You are going to tell me where you are right now. Then I am going to get you and we will walk back to the car that *I'm* driving and then *I* am going to drive us home and *you* are going to leave the rest of this investigation to me."

"Yeah, um…that's not exactly how it works." I covered the mouthpiece and whispered to Anne. "My sister asked me to set up her new DVD player, but I didn't have time. Now I have to walk her through it."

For the first time since her phone had rung, Anne made eye contact. "You don't need to leave, do you?" she asked anxiously.

I blinked in surprise. She wanted me here?

"Damn it, Sophie!" Anatoly yelled, and I pressed the phone tightly against my ear so Anne wouldn't hear his voice. "You don't know what you're doing and you can't follow simple instructions. I'm putting an end to this right now. Where are you?"

"I think you're a little confused," I said into the phone while smiling at Anne. "The system you bought can't be controlled that way." I smiled at Anne and mouthed *I'm not leaving.*

"Sophie, tell me where you are right now," Anatoly growled.

"Listen," I said as sweetly as possible, "you're dealing with a valuable piece of equipment. If you handle it roughly it won't work, and if you try to force it, you might not be able to insert your disk into it ever again. Make sense?"

"No, Sophie, *you* listen to *me…*"

"Sorry, can't do it, but I promise to help you out tomorrow. See you then!" I hung up and put the phone in my handbag, ignoring it as it rang again. "Sisters," I said with an exaggerated eye roll. Anne smiled weakly and toyed with her macaroon. "So what do you think of Marcus?" I asked.

"He's very talented." Her hand went up to her hair. "And very intelligent. I wish I had more time to talk with him."

"About?" I prodded.

"His life. As a gay black man I'm sure he had a lot of hurdles put in his path. My opponent may like to turn a blind eye to the prejudices that are still prevalent in our society, but I see them clearly and I *understand* them. Marcus clearly hasn't let other people's prejudices stand in the way of his success. I think he has a lot to teach people."

"Yeah, it's hard for a gay man to become a successful hairstylist in San Francisco." The comment slipped out of my mouth before I had a chance to check it, but Anne just laughed.

"Well, maybe not in San Francisco. But you'd be surprised, Sophie. There are plenty of people right here in Northern California who seem to think that being gay is like having a contagious disease, and they would never let someone who identified himself as a homosexual get near them, not even to do their hair. Flynn Fitzgerald certainly wouldn't. But then again his problem isn't homophobia, it's pandering. He happily assumes the role of a hate-monger in order to woo the Christian right."

"Yeah," I said after swallowing another one of Marcus's chocolates. "Some people will do just about anything in order to win."

Anne winced, which was…interesting. "Flynn Fitzgerald is not a good man." Her voice was so soft I had to lean toward her in order to hear. "He's a hypocrite and he's dishonest. If he wins, he will not represent the best interests of his constituents. That's why I *have* to win." She put both hands flat down on the table and stared at her mangled cuticles. "If I am elected, I'll be able to do some good, not just for the people of Contra Costa County but for America as a whole. Flynn Fitzgerald won't. If I can stop another opportunistic, unscrupulous conservative from getting to Congress I have to do it. You see that, don't you?" She lifted her eyes to mine, and it suddenly occurred to me that she wasn't really trying to convince me of anything. She was trying to convince herself.

"It's been a hard campaign for you," I noted as I took a sip of my drink. "I read about that guy who committed suicide by throwing himself out the window of your campaign headquarters. What was his name again? Something with a *P*…"

Anne's face instantly hardened. "His name was Peter," she said tersely, "and yes, that was horrible."

"Do you have any idea why he did it?"

"He did it because of people like Flynn Fitzgerald."

I blinked. "Excuse me?"

"Peter was gay, Sophie. He thought he was hiding it from me, but I knew the minute I laid eyes on him. Sometimes you can just tell. To be honest, it's one of the reasons I recruited him. He was clearly a little lost and depressed, and I thought that if I offered him the opportunity to work in an environment where he'd be surrounded by kindhearted progressives like myself, he'd learn to be proud of who he was."

"Wait a minute." I leaned forward in order to make sure I wasn't mishearing anything. "You *recruited* Peter?"

Anne hesitated, then brought the cuticles of her index finger to her mouth. "I did recruit him," she eventually confirmed. "I was taking a trip and had bags to check. Peter was working behind the ticket counter. He was very helpful and sweet and he recognized me from the newspaper. I was looking for someone to help organize my phone campaigns and I invited him to come in for an interview."

"Wow. So you really reached out to him. You said he was depressed, but did you have any inkling that he was suicidal?"

"No." Anne looked down at the liquid chocolate in front of her. There was an awkward silence before she mumbled, "I found him."

"You *found* him?" I repeated.

"It was late and I needed something from the office…my

speech, that was it. I had left a speech I needed to memorize at my desk. I went to the building and there he was. Did you notice that my campaign headquarters is on the top floor of a fifteen-floor building? And the area around the building is nothing but concrete. I've never seen anything so awful. I prayed that I wouldn't have to see anything like that again."

"Hopefully you won't," I offered.

Anne didn't say anything. She just continued to stare at her drink. My handbag was on my lap and I felt it vibrate slightly. Anatoly, no doubt. I pulled out the phone just to make sure.

Not Anatoly. In fact, the only part of the number I recognized was the local area code.

"Sorry about this," I said quickly. "I think it's my sister again." I pressed the talk button. "Hello?"

"It's a shame what happened to your friend. Enough to make your fur stand on end."

It was Darth Vader. He was calling me, taunting me with jokes about Melanie's murder. And Anne was sitting here at my table, staring at her drink, *not talking on the phone.*

"Who is this?" I whispered. Anne looked up at me curiously.

"It's your furry friend. This is your last warning, Katz. Stay out of my life and stay out of my campaign."

The phone went dead.

"What was that about?" Anne asked.

I stared at my phone. My hand was shaking.

"Sophie?"

"Huh?" I looked up at Anne, who was regarding me curiously.

"Who was on the phone?" she pressed.

I swallowed. It was time to gamble with a version of the truth. "It was a prank call," I said. "I've been getting a lot of them lately. They're all from this Darth Vader soundalike who apparently has a thing for animals."

Anne's eyes bulged and she was immediately on her feet. "I need to go." She grabbed her purse and sprinted down the stairs toward the door.

"Anne?" I called after her. I jumped up to follow, but my purse had still been on my lap and I hadn't bothered to close it after pulling out my phone. Everything from my wallet to my ultralight panty liners crashed to the floor. "Shit!" I dropped to my knees and started stuffing the items back in my bag. I ran out of the café, clutching my purse in one hand and Marcus's box of truffles in the other, but Anne was nowhere in sight.

Before I had time to plot my next move Anatoly pulled up in front of me in his beige automobile. "Get in!" he demanded.

I jumped in the passenger seat.

"Sophie, I can't believe you—"

"You can yell at me later, right now we have to find Anne."

"What do you mean *find* her? You were just with her!"

"Yeah, I was but she ran out. Go down Sacramento Street. Maybe we can still catch her."

Anatoly's face contorted into a glower but he quickly complied.

"He called again, Anatoly."

"Who?"

"Darth Vader!"

Anatoly's head snapped in my direction. "You got another threat?"

I pointed at the street. "Keep looking for Anne," I instructed before telling him more about the call. "He said what happened to my friend was a shame. That it made his fur stand on end. And you should have heard the way he said it. It was like this asshole was admitting to killing Melanie!"

"Where was Anne when this call took place?" Anatoly asked.

"Right by my side." I pressed the base of my palms into my forehead. "It's not her. I was so sure it was, but I was wrong. Now I'm totally clueless, *again!*"

"You were always clueless, Sophie. You simply fooled yourself into believing otherwise."

"I'm going to assume that your comment is only referring to my knowledge of this case!" I snapped, then added in a softer tone, "Thing is, I told Anne about the call."

"Told her what exactly?"

"That some guy who sounded like Vader and liked animals had been prank-calling me."

"How'd she react?"

"She literally ran out of the restaurant. That's why we're looking for her. She knows something, but I have no idea what."

"I see." Anatoly was clenching his jaw. "You realize that if you had waited for me I could have started following Anne the minute she left the café. We wouldn't have lost her."

"You realize," I mimicked, "that if you had gotten a small car instead of a sedan the size of a small state, you might have been able to find parking sooner and I wouldn't have had to make the choice between waiting for you and risking missing Anne."

"Marcus would have kept her at the salon until you showed up," Anatoly countered.

"How? By duct-taping her to the chair? She was done, Anatoly. Curled, highlighted and dried. If I had waited longer I would have lost her. Wait, where are you going?"

"Anne obviously got in her car and left. God knows which way she went. I'm driving down to Ocean Beach to look for that homeless woman one more time and then I'm going to take you home and explain to you the meaning of the word *partnership!*"

"Yes, yes, I know. There's no 'I' in team... Oh my God!"

Anatoly slammed on the breaks, nearly causing the Honda hybrid behind us to slam into our bumper. "What!"

"No, no, keep driving...but I have a number this time! It didn't come up as Unknown Number!"

Anatoly pressed back down on the gas pedal. "Are you talking about the threatening call?"

"Yes. What else would I be talking about?" I accessed the numbers of my recent received calls. There it was, a 415 number. I dialed and put my phone on loudspeaker.

Anatoly and I listened with bated breath as it rung three times and then...an awful screeching, never-ending beep shot through the speakers. "What is that?" My hands reflexively flew to my ears in an attempt to block out the sound. "A fax machine?"

Anatoly reached over and pressed End Call. "No, but it is a modem. Whoever called did it from a pay phone. Most of them are set up to go to that kind of modem after they've rung once or twice. It keeps people from calling them all the time."

"There aren't a lot of pay phones left," I noted.

"There's one on California Street, right around the corner from the Bittersweet."

"In front of the Starbucks! Darth Vader was right there! We have to go back and look for him!"

"And how will we know it's him, Sophie? Will he be carrying a light saber?"

"I don't know, Anatoly. Maybe he'll be dressed up like a goddamned sheep. Stop!"

But Anatoly had already seen what I had seen. He yanked the steering wheel to the right, causing the car to pull up onto the sidewalk twenty or so feet in front of the woman with the tinfoil hat.

Without another word we both jumped out of the car and faced her.

The woman hadn't changed her appearance, except this time she was wearing dishwashing gloves. She scowled at me as if I was a middle-school kid who had thrown a rock through her window.

"What are you doin' here?"

"We just wanted to talk to you." Anatoly extended his hand. "My name is Anatoly."

She studied him for what must have been a full minute before she put her yellow gloved hand in his. She didn't shake it, but instead held on to it as if it was one more thing that she wanted to add to her shopping cart.

"I'm afraid I didn't catch your name," Anatoly said.

"I don't want to be givin' up my name to no god-damned stranger."

"Fair enough." Anatoly smiled kindly, still holding her

hand. "I was hoping we could talk to you about that pink bear you saw."

That was enough to get her to yank her hand away. "Don't know you well enough."

"I see. Perhaps you could get to know us," Anatoly suggested. "Ask us anything."

"Are you cops?"

"No," Anatoly and I said in unison.

"Because you gotta tell me if I ask. That there's the law."

"We're not cops," Anatoly assured her again.

"Are you in league with the bears? You gotta fess up to that, too, if you're asked, otherwise you'll be blackballed like dem Pandas."

"Pandas were blackballed?" I asked.

"Yep, for a while there the other bears wouldn't even accept them as one of their own. Said they were raccoons or some shit."

"You're thinking of red pandas," I explained.

"Red pandas? Now, why would I be thinkin' about some red bear? If I'm thinking about anything it's those pink gay bears. Those are the dangerous ones."

Anatoly nodded encouragingly. "Sophie told me about that. Can you tell me a little about the pink bear that killed the woman found here? Did you actually see him kill her?"

"Nope, just saw him carry her out of his rented Ford. Had her wrapped up like a burrito in a big blue tarp. Must of killed her someplace else."

"Blue tarp?" Anatoly asked. "The papers didn't mention that part. Did the police take that with them when they found the body?"

"Nah, I took the tarp."

"You did?" Anatoly grinned. "Do you still have it?"

"Don't be stupid, dem tarps sell for good money in the park. I got three bucks for that tarp."

Anatoly's grin disappeared and I squeezed my eyes closed against the disappointment. That tarp could have been a treasure trove of evidence and it was gone.

"What was this bear like?" Anatoly asked, quickly re-grouping. "Was he trying to be discreet?"

"Now, who ever heard of a discreet pink bear? Those suckers want to be *seen*."

"Ah." Anatoly put his thumbs through his belt loop. "So he made a spectacle of himself?"

"I'd say, what with his waving at me and that grandma with her gran-kiddie."

"Wait a minute." I held up a hand to stop her. "What grandma and what gran-kiddie?"

"He came out of that damn Ford truck and started waving. The only people around was me and some old Chinese lady with some snot-nosed toddler. The toddler was pretty excited about it, too—you know how kids are. But the granny was a sensible woman, like me. She just pulled that little tot along with her and didn't give that bear a second glance. That's the best way to handle 'em—ignore 'em and walk away. If you run they're more likely to eat you."

Anatoly and I exchanged quick looks. Not only had the bear not waited for the coast to be clear, but he had actually waved at a homeless woman and some random pedestrians seconds before dumping the body? What kind of murderer went out of his way to call attention to himself?

"Did he wave again before he drove off?" I asked.

"To me he did, not that I paid him any mind. The grandma and toddler were long gone by then."

"What did the grandmother look like?" I asked.

"Chinese."

"And?" I prompted.

"And that's it. I didn't get a real good look at her. Maybe she wasn't Chinese, maybe she was Japanese, or Korean. I don't know, I was kind of distracted seeing that there was a bear with a rainbow tattooed on his tummy dumping a body wrapped up in a tarp."

"That *would* be distracting," Anatoly agreed. "What about the truck?"

"It was a green Ford."

"Can you tell me anything more about it?" he pushed.

"Nope."

"Wait a minute…" I put my fingers to my temples as if I could touch the memory that was coming back. "Right before Eugene was shot I saw a green truck…or an SUV. It was far away and I wasn't paying a lot of attention, but it was parked in a commercial district, which was weird because all the businesses had closed up, even the bars."

Anatoly took a step closer to me. "Was it a Ford?"

"Anatoly, I can't even tell you if it was an SUV or a truck and you want me to tell you if it was a Ford? Considering my lack of interest in cars, it's amazing I took notice of it at all!"

Just then we heard a ringing. Anatoly looked pointedly at my handbag and I looked pointedly at his jacket pocket. But it wasn't either of our phones. The noise was coming from the shopping cart.

"Damn thing won't shut up," the woman grumbled. "I don't keep it on very much, but every once and a while I do just in case I need to make a quick call. I can't be expected to wait for the damn thing to warm up if there's an emergency, now, can I?"

"You have a cell phone?" I asked skeptically.

"Of course I have a cell phone. Can't you hear it ringing?"

"Where did you get it?" Anatoly asked.

The woman took a protective step toward her cart. "It's mine. I got it as a gift."

"I didn't mean to imply that it wasn't yours," Anatoly assured her. "It's a nice gift. Whoever gave it to you obviously cares about you very much."

"He does."

"May I ask who that person is?" Anatoly asked.

"Jesus."

I raised my eyebrows. "Jesus gave you a cell phone?"

"You got a problem with that?"

"No, not at all," I said quickly. According to my Christian friends, the poor were already going to inherit the earth, so why not throw in a cell phone?

"What exactly does Jesus look like?" Anatoly asked.

"He looks like Jesus," the woman snapped.

"I see," Anatoly nodded solemnly. "Is there any chance that I could see the cell phone?" The woman studied him for a moment before shuffling through her shopping cart and eventually pulled out a top-of-the-line camera phone.

Anatoly put his hand out and waited for her to give it to him, rather than trying to take it from her, but the woman hesitated. "You're gonna give this right back to me, right? I don't know what I'd do without my cell phone."

"I would never steal from you," Anatoly said.

Reluctantly she placed it in his palm. Anatoly immediately flipped it open and started going through the pictures. There were a few of a woman who looked vaguely familiar.

"I've seen pictures of this woman," Anatoly said slowly, clearly addressing me rather than our new friend. "This is Marian Fitzgerald. Flynn Fitzgerald's wife."

I wrinkled my brow. "Why would there be pictures of Flynn Fitzgerald's wife on the phone?"

"Because," Anatoly said as he perused the numbers and names in the address book, "this is Flynn Fitzgerald's phone."

For a moment I couldn't speak. Then all the questions started tumbling out of me, too hurried and frantic to be comprehensible. "How did you get Fitzgerald's phone? Do you know him? Is he the one who gave it to you? Is he the Jesus you're talking about? Does he *know* Jesus?" The woman was looking at me as if I had just lost my mind, and maybe I had. I couldn't make sense of any of this and the pure effort of trying was making me dizzy.

"I told you," the woman said, finally cutting me off, "I got this here phone from Jesus." She snatched the phone from Anatoly and held it tightly in her gloved hand.

"But how did Jesus deliver it to you?" I demanded. "Did it fall out of the sky? Did you find it in a burning bush? What?"

"He wrapped it up in the tarp."

I reached out and clutched Anatoly's arm. "In the tarp? You found the phone in the tarp Melanie was wrapped up in?"

"Is Melanie the woman the bear killed? Yeah, that's where Jesus wrapped it up. Probably should have found different gift wrap, though. It got tangled up in the fabric of that dead woman's skirt. There was blood all over this thing." She waved the pristine phone in front of me. "Took me two days to get it all off."

"To get it *off*? There was blood on it and you cleaned the blood *off*?" I let go of Anatoly's arm and spun around so my back was to both of them. I might be able to resist strangling her if I didn't have to look at her. There had been DNA evidence that would have linked Flynn Fitzgerald to a murder. A tarp *and* a bloody phone. And now it was all gone. Anyone who would pay three dollars to buy a bloody tarp wouldn't think twice about wiping off that blood before using it as a makeshift tent, and even if they hadn't, a few days of exposure to the San Francisco drizzle would have done most of the job for them. Of course this woman was an eyewitness, but as witnesses went she couldn't have been less reliable. And in a city where over a third of the population was Asian, the grandmother with the toddler description wasn't going to help me at all. For once I *wanted* to confide in the police, but thanks to this woman I had nothing helpful to bring them.

"Any chance you'd consider selling the phone to us?" Anatoly asked.

"I don't know," the woman said slowly. "It's special to me, it being from our savior and all."

"Here." I dug into my purse and waved a twenty and a ten over my shoulder, still not trusting myself enough to look at her. "Here's thirty dollars for the phone."

"You really want to pay me thirty dollars for this thing?" the woman gasped.

Finally I turned around. "That's right. Thirty bucks cash right now."

The woman's mouth was hanging open and she stared at the bills in my hand. "Thirty dollars for this here phone."

I nodded impatiently.

"Child, did you not hear me when I said this here phone was a gift from the one and only son of *God?* Wasn't too long ago that some man sold a pancake with Jesus' face on it on eBay for a cool sixty. Sixty dollars for Jesus' leftover breakfast! This here's a Motorola i880 phone! It's got polyphonic ring tones and everything! The pope ain't got a phone this nice! And you think you can buy it off me for thirty dollars? I may be crazy but I ain't *that* crazy."

"But thirty dollars is all I have on me!"

Anatoly already had his wallet in his hand. "I have another ten, that brings it to forty."

"I want a hundred, and that there's a deal. You be robbin' me at a hundred, but I'll do it for you folks since you're anti-bear and all."

"But we don't have any more money on us right now!"

"That ain't my problem. You come back with a better offer, and if I still has the phone, I might still be willing to sell it for a hundred."

"No, no, no, no, no, no." I waved my hand in the air as if I was wiping her words off an invisible chalkboard. "It took us days to find you. I'm not going to walk away and hope that I'm able to find you again."

"Well, you ain't takin' it for no forty dollars and I ain't offerin' no installment plan." The woman glanced toward our car. "What's that there on your dashboard?" She walked forward to get a clearer view. "Is that a box of chocolates?"

"From the Chocolate Café on Fillmore," I confirmed.

"Dark chocolates?"

Anatoly went to the car and took out the box. "It says they're extra dark."

"Tell you what I'll do, you give me the forty dollars, the chocolates and those diamond earrings of yours and I'll give you this here phone."

"Deal!" I shouted. I gave her my money and earrings (praying that she wouldn't realize that the diamonds were about as real as Pamela Anderson's breasts) and Anatoly gave her his money and Marcus's chocolates.

The woman smiled and handed me the phone. Then all of a sudden her hands flew to both sides of her head. "It's him, it's him!"

I spun around expecting to see a pink bear, but there was nothing there. "What are you talking about?" I asked.

"The devil! Don't you hear him? He's coming! He's flying in on that flying pig!"

I searched the sky, but the only thing flying was a beleaguered-looking moth. I was suddenly filled with a deadly sense of hopelessness. I honestly did feel for this woman. She needed help. Furthermore, there was no way to tell what part of this woman's story was true and what was a delusion. Maybe she only *thought* she saw a pink bear, or maybe Jesus really did give her Fitzgerald's Motorola. In a world where people could be sexually attracted to stuffed animals, anything was possible.

The tinfoil-hat woman grabbed the handle of her shopping cart and rushed off, periodically looking over her shoulder. Anatoly and I watched her disappear and then got back in the car. For a moment we just sat there staring at Fitzgerald's cell phone, which I still clutched in my hand. "We could call the police," I suggested.

"We could," Anatoly agreed, but he didn't sound enthusiastic.

"We could tell them that a Darth Vader soundalike has been calling to inform me of his love of animals," I said, "and that a woman who wears a tinfoil hat and thinks that the devil rides on a flying pig had possession of a camera phone that belongs to a right-wing congressional hopeful who may or may not dress up like a pink, rainbow-tattooed bear while dumping the bodies of his murder victims."

We both fell silent. I stared at the phone some more and all of a sudden it hit me. "Get us to Park Presidio and then take a right on Lake Street."

"But your car's right off Fillmore—"

"We're not going to my car," I said. "We're going to see Mary Ann."

24

I always choose the most open and honest people to share my darkest secrets with. I worry that they don't have enough to be ashamed of so I try to share some of my guilt.

—*C'est La Mort*

MARY ANN LOOKED LIKE SHE WAS ABOUT READY TO GO TO BED. HER hair was pulled back in a ponytail and she was wearing a fluffy pale blue robe. "Is everything okay?" she asked as she ushered us inside.

Anatoly sat down on one of her dining chairs but I remained standing. "What aren't you telling us about Fitzgerald?"

Mary Ann's eyes flicked to Anatoly, and then back to me. "I really can't—"

"Mary Ann, I have reason to believe that Fitzgerald might have had a hand in Melanie's death."

"What?" Her hand fluttered to her mouth. "But that's not

possible! Fitzgerald may not be perfect, but he would never…there's just no way!"

"What did Rick say about him, Mary Ann? I need to know this."

Again Mary Ann looked over at Anatoly. She barely knew the man and it was unlikely that she was going to talk with him listening in.

Picking up on this he sighed and got back to his feet. "I'll wait in the car," he said, giving my shoulder a squeeze as he walked out. Now it was just Mary Ann and myself, in a face-off. Mary Ann looking flustered and worried and me feeling seriously pissed.

"Mary Ann, how long have we been friends?"

"Sophie, this isn't about *us*. Rick confided in me, and I really *like* him! I can't just tell you his secrets!"

"Not even if breaking his confidence could save lives?"

Mary Ann looked down at the floor. "I've met Fitzgerald a few times. He can't be a murderer. I would know."

"Mary Ann, I've had the dubious honor of becoming acquainted with a few murderers over the past few years and I've never suspected a thing until they waved a weapon in my face and issued me a death threat."

Mary Ann swallowed but still didn't look up. "Do you really think Fitzgerald is a murderer?" she asked in a small voice.

"Just tell me what you know. If the information you have doesn't fit with the evidence I've gathered, then nothing you say to me will leave this room. But, Mary Ann, Melanie is dead. Eugene is dead. The time for keeping your mouth shut is over."

Mary Ann's eyes got a little wider and I could make out

the sparkling of tears. "It just didn't seem like that big of a deal," she whispered.

"What didn't?"

"Fitzgerald's extramarital affair. It happened while he was at that political convention in Iowa. Rick walked in on him while he was having kinky sex."

"*Kinky* sex?" I repeated.

"A threesome. A woman and another guy."

"That's all Rick told you about the encounter?"

Mary Ann shrugged. "I didn't ask him for details. He just said it was a kinky ménage à trois. Fitzgerald promised Rick that he wouldn't do it again, but there were…complications."

"What kind of complications?"

"Fitzgerald contracted an STD. He was fine, but he passed it on to his wife, and now she can't have any children."

"What kind of STD…oh, my God." Now it was my turn to put my hand to my mouth. "Did Fitzgerald give his wife chlamydia?"

Mary Ann looked up quickly. "How did you know?"

"So what now?" I asked. After interrogating Mary Ann for another fifteen minutes, I had determined that she didn't have anything more of interest to share and Anatoly and I had gone back to my apartment. We were now both sitting on my bed, me cross-legged, him with his feet planted firmly on the floor, knees supporting his forearms. It was probably the first time we had been in a bedroom together without thinking about sex. Well, that wasn't entirely accurate, we *were* thinking about sex, furry sex, which was kind of like thinking about your parents going at it—it shouldn't freak you out but it absolutely does.

"We can't go to the police yet," Anatoly said to the floor.

"That's usually my line."

"Yes, and for once I'm agreeing with you."

"Hmm, I should probably take some satisfaction in that, but the thing is, I'm waffling."

"Ah."

"I just think that if we bring the police a boatload of circumstantial evidence they might actually take the time to sift through it. Right now we have an eyewitness who saw Fitzgerald engage in extramarital sex, a letter from a known furry begging Eugene, who has a history of turning on his bosses, not to use some undisclosed bit of info to ruin both political careers and personal lives. We know Peter had chlamydia, we know Fitzgerald had chlamydia. We also have Fitzgerald's cell phone that someone found on the body of a murder victim and at least one eyewitness, possibly three, who saw a man dressed up in a furry costume dumping that body. This feels like the makings of an arrest warrant."

"Not even close." Anatoly straightened up before falling back onto the bed. "Rick may have confided in his new girlfriend, but we have no reason to believe that he'd agree to talk to the police about it. And even if he did, the witnessed threesome would only help us if Peter Strauss was part of that particular indiscretion. And, Sophie, lots of people have chlamydia."

"You don't, right?" I asked, suddenly alarmed.

"No," Anatoly chuckled, "I've been lucky. Still, chlamydia is a lot more common than say, AIDS or syphilis. As for the homeless woman, she's delusional. It doesn't matter what she saw because nothing she says will be admissible in court. Tomorrow I'll check to see what kind of car Fitzgerald has, but even if it's a green Ford that doesn't help us much because you don't even know if the car you saw on the night of Eugene's murder was a Ford. The only thing we know about the other two witnesses, if they actually exist, is that they're Asian. That leaves us with Peter's note and that's not enough."

I banged the back of my head against the wall. "Then I don't know what to do."

"We start by following Fitzgerald around town. Anne's given us next to nothing, so I'm switching my attention to her opponent. Early tomorrow morning I'll head to Pleasant Hill and I'll stay on his tail for at least another twenty-four hours. When he retires for the evening I'll nap in the car. So at least for one night you won't have to deal with me hovering over you."

"But the furry party is tomorrow night."

"Sophie, this is more important, I have to—"

"Keep your promise," I finished for him. "That's what you have to do. You said you would put that costume on and accompany me."

"I said I'd do that because I thought it was the best chance we had of getting a lead. I no longer think that's true. If Fitzgerald really did leave his phone with Melanie's body, he's getting very sloppy. Furthermore, he's acting like a man who wants to get caught."

"Really?" I scoffed. "Because if that's the case he might want to consider making it easy for somebody to catch him."

"Maybe he has. Every one of those threats that you received made some kind of reference to furries, but until a few days ago you didn't even know what a furry was. Why draw your attention to something that could be so damaging? Why follow you to Neiman's and make up a story about meeting someone for lunch when he knew that you would see him dine alone? And why the hell didn't he cancel his service when he realized that he lost his cell phone?"

"I hadn't thought of that," I admitted.

Anatoly ran his hand over his evening stubble. "If I was vindictive I'd say that your oversight proves that I'm a better detective than you are."

"Yes," I said. "Good thing you're not vindictive. But, Anatoly, this party may be our only hope of finding a reliable witness who will testify to Fitzgerald's furrydom."

"If Fitzgerald's recent actions have taught us anything, it's that he's not adjusting his behavior for the sake of caution. If Fitzgerald goes to these parties, he'll go to this one, which is why I'll be keeping my gorilla suit on hand."

"You will?"

"Yes, if Fitzgerald goes into that party, I'm following him, no matter what the cost to my pride."

"Oh, Anatoly," I said, flinging my arms around his neck, "I love—I mean, um, I, I love working with you."

Anatoly shot me a bemused look. "Since when?"

"Since right now."

"I see." He turned to me and stroked my cheek with the back of his hand. "I love…working with you, too."

"Hey," I said teasingly, "no copying. If you're going to flirt at least say something original."

"Words are your specialty, not mine."

"And what is your...Anatoly, is that your hand?"

"Shh," he whispered, "there's something here I need to investigate."

25

At work they teach us that there is no such thing as a problem, only an opportunity. So I'm very lucky. I have more opportunities than anyone I know!
—C'est La Vie

THAT NIGHT ANATOLY SHOWED ME EXACTLY WHAT HE SPECIALIZED IN. If we hadn't run out of condoms by 2:00 a.m. we might not have gotten any sleep at all. The next morning I let him talk me out of going with him on his Flynn Fitzgerald surveillance mission. He went on and on about how Fitzgerald could be a murderer and he could be on to me, whereas he probably had no idea who Anatoly was et cetera, et cetera. He then insisted that the smartest thing for me to do was to stay home and wait for his call. I smiled, nodded and told him he was absolutely right and he took my agreement at face value, which just proves my theory that there is a positive correlation between sexual satiation and gullibility.

Of course Anatoly could never have guessed what my real plans were for the day. No one could have because what I did was completely out of character.

I went to the police and told them everything. It's not that Anatoly's arguments against confiding in them didn't make sense to me, but we had so many little bits of incriminating circumstantial evidence and I hoped that maybe, just maybe, the police would take what I had and run with it.

But they didn't run, they laughed...and they laughed and they laughed. And when they were done laughing they guffawed.

It was Officers Kelly and Stone whom I spoke to, and to Officer Kelly's credit, he, unlike the steroid-using-moron he was partnered with, did *try* to hide his amusement. I watched as he pressed his lips together so hard they started going white. I noted the welling up of tears in his gray-blue eyes, I saw the slight shaking of his shoulders until finally I had sighed and said, "Oh, go ahead."

And then it was all over. He buckled over, literally clutching the ends of his chair to keep from rolling on the floor in a full-throttle laughing fit.

When he did catch his breath he asked to see Fitzgerald's cell and Peter's note, but Anatoly had both of those with him. Kelly promised to look into my story, but I didn't believe him. Maybe that was because he was giggling when he told me he would. In the end I did go home, but not before buying a quart of gelato and a bottle of Absolut. If anyone had a reason to drink it was me. Besides, between the excessive pacing and the sex-filled nights, I was bound to burn off the extra calories in no time.

I binged until 2:00 p.m., took a long walk and then came home and passed out in front of the TV at four. Two hours later the phone woke me up. I opened one eye and fumbled for the receiver. "Hello?"

"Sophie, it's Rick Wilkes."

I sat up and muted the television. Why was Rick calling me?

"Sophie? Are you there?"

"Yeah, I'm here, um, how are you?"

Rick exhaled in response. "I talked to Mary Ann. She told me about your conversation last night."

"Oh."

"I know you think Mary Ann has been putting me in front of the friendship you two share and I want you to know that's not the case. I unloaded on her and then I pleaded with her not to tell anyone else what I told her. She wasn't comfortable with keeping my secrets, she's still not. She even asked me not to tell her anything else that she couldn't talk to you about."

"Oh." It wasn't just the previously consumed vodka that was impeding my conversational abilities. I honestly didn't know what to say and I didn't know what Mary Ann had said to him. Unlike Rick, I *hadn't* thought to tell her not to share the details of our discussion with others, and the reality was Rick worked for Fitzgerald. If he knew I was on to them that could be problematic.

"I know Fitzgerald is not exactly a good guy, but he's not exactly a bad guy, either," Rick continued. "He is a hypocrite, though," he added more softly. "There's no denying that."

"Why did he hire Eugene, Rick? Maggie said everybody in your circles knew that it was Eugene who called in that tip about Bruni and the seventeen-year-old. If Fitzgerald had something to hide, then why risk exposure by bringing someone like that onto his team?" I was choosing my words very carefully. The key was to extract as much information from Rick as possible without letting on what I knew or suspected.

"Maggie lied."

"She lied?" Mr. Katz raised his head and gave me a quizzical kitty stare. "So Eugene *didn't* turn Bruni in?"

"No, he did, but Maggie and I were two of maybe three people who knew that it was him. We were Eugene's confidants."

"Who was the third person?"

"Melanie."

I bit down hard on my lip. As devastated as I was by Melanie's death, I couldn't help but be a little angry at her. This was the kind of information that could have helped me, and maybe if she had shared it I could have saved her.

"Maggie liked Eugene because he reminded her of her father," Rick went on, "but she never wanted to emulate him. When it comes down to it, she's all about winning. Fitzgerald…he knows who you really work for, and he told Maggie and me not to talk to you. When Mary Ann dropped the bomb that you would be joining us for lunch, Maggie decided that was the time to throw you off the track. She figured that if you thought Fitzgerald was willing to hire Eugene, knowing his history, you wouldn't suspect him of, well, you know…the threesomes and all."

"Wait, back up. Who do I really work for?"

"Sophie, let's not pretend, okay? I want you to know I haven't talked about it with Mary Ann. I assume you've told her that you're working for the *National Review,* and I haven't told her differently. Unless, of course, you told her the truth and she just hasn't told me. She *is* very good at keeping confidences."

"Rick, stay with me here. What are we not pretending? Who do I work for?"

"*Hustler,* of course."

"What!"

"We know all about the article you're writing about conservative politicians and their bizarre sexual fetishes."

"You think I work for Larry Flint," I said flatly. This was the most surreal conversation I had ever had in my life. Even Dena wouldn't work for Larry Flint.

"Look, I believe in the freedom of the press, and *Hustler* is part of the press—a really seedy part, but it counts. I just wanted you to know that Fitzgerald told me he's turning over a new leaf. I wouldn't continue to work for him if he hadn't. "It's not ideal—" I heard Rick inhale a shaky breath "—it's anything but ideal. Like I was telling Mary Ann, politics… being a Republican and supporting my party…has been a huge part of my life. I can see that the party's changed and I know I've made moral compromises that I shouldn't have and I'm going to have to make some changes in what I do and how I do it. But, Sophie, if you come out with this information and reveal that any of it came from me, you could ruin my career. I'll never get a job in politics again. That was a risk Eugene was willing to take, but he was stronger than I am. So I'm asking you for a huge favor. Don't report this to *Hustler.* Please, for me."

"I promise I won't report this to *Hustler,*" I said without hesitation.

"Really? You mean it?" He released a relieved laugh. "Thank you, Sophie. I should have known you would be decent about all this. You *are* Mary Ann's friend after all, and she is a very special woman." He paused before adding, "She's absolutely incredible. I'm so lucky that I have someone to talk to who really understands me and cares."

"Rick, I gotta go."

"Sure, I understand. Thanks again, Sophie. I trust you to keep your word."

I hung up and stared at Mr. Katz. *"Hustler?"*

Mr. Katz blinked at me, the kitty version of a shrug.

I stopped drinking after that. I kept replaying my conversation with Rick in my head, trying to make sense of it. I tried calling Mary Ann, but she was working. I considered calling Anatoly, but I wanted to get a better grasp of what had been said and what it meant before I relayed it. I mean, *Hustler?* I'd rather write for a Furry Fandom Web site!

I spent about an hour chewing on this, and then I finally worked up the nerve to go on the *Hustler* Web site. I had fuzzy memories of Larry Flint exposing the extramarital affairs of politicians years ago and thought it might be a good idea to read the articles. Oddly enough I wasn't able to find any articles on the *Hustler* Web site and I really did try. If Google ever turned their customers' searches into the federal government I'd be humiliated for life.

So what now?

The party, that's what. Rick had never actually said that Fitzgerald was a furry and there was little doubt that he wasn't going to the police with the information, so I needed to find someone who would. I would take a shower and then

I'd put on my big-headed kitty suit and go to a furry party. It was better than sitting at home trying to figure out what it was about me that screamed pornographic journalist.

I was in the shower for almost twenty minutes (the *Hustler* Web site had me feeling kind of grimy), and then after toweling off went straight into the bedroom to put on my costume. I still wasn't entirely clear why Rick had called me. Was it to convince me not to "tell" on him and his candidate? Or had he merely wanted to repair any damage his secrets made on my friendship with Mary Ann? If it was the latter, that was kind of sweet.

I had everything on except for the mask when I noticed that Mr. Katz was hiding under the bed. Understandable, considering the odd attire his owner had chosen to adorn herself in. I might have hidden, too, if I were him. I sat down on the edge of the bed and leaned over so we were face to whiskers. The poor guy looked terrified. "What's wrong, little buddy? Cat got your tongue?"

"No, a dog got it," said a male voice. I slowly straightened up and pivoted toward the doorway of my bedroom. There, standing before me, was a tall man dressed up like a big white dog with black floppy ears and a benign, closemouthed smile. No part of the man in the costume was visible except his hands. Like me, he had found a costume that didn't have paws, which made it easier for him to grip the gun he was pointing at me.

For a second I thought I was going to pass out.

"One of your neighbors let me into the building," it said, because the thing in front of me was more of an it than a he. "She thought I was a singing telegram. There's a bouquet of balloons in the living room. Not that you'll have a chance to enjoy them."

I swallowed, not knowing what to say. Had I not locked the door to my apartment, or had he broken in?

"You talked to the police?" it asked.

I managed an incredibly small nod, and then realizing that this could help me, started nodding enthusiastically. "I told them all about you, Fitzgerald," I croaked. "If you kill me they'll know exactly where to look." *Unlike Anatoly, who was supposed to have been following you.* How could he have lost him so completely? Or maybe Anatoly was close behind, waiting for the right moment to save me. It was possible, right? There was still hope.

The dog-man raised the gun higher. It was pointing at my forehead now. He was tall so he had to cock his dog head to the side awkwardly in order to see me through those fly-like eyeholes.

Wait a minute…Fitzgerald wasn't a tall man.

"Did I say I told them all about Fitzgerald?" I said slowly. "That's not what I meant. I told the police all about Fitzgerald *and* you."

"How do you know I'm not Fitzgerald?"

"Because I know who you are, and so do the cops." But I didn't know. The voice was sort of familiar but also somehow disconcerting and wrong. It was like listening to someone who had always spoken like a hick speak in the tone of a professional newscaster. And then it came to me and my eyes nearly popped out of my head. "Johnny?"

The non-pistol-wielding hand grabbed hold of the exaggerated muzzle and ripped the mask off. Standing before me was my least-favorite spaz-case. But he wasn't spazzing. He was so calm and collected that it was difficult to recognize him even now that his face was exposed. His eyes weren't twinkling, his mouth wasn't twitching in a nervous grin. This man was serious, frightening and perversely fascinating. Kind of like death itself.

"Johnny." I said his name as cajolingly as possible, praying that this was one of those things I could flirt my way out of. "You don't want to do this."

"You're right, I don't." No extra words, no twittering. "But I'm getting sick of this game, and killing you and pinning it on Fitzgerald is the quickest way to finish it. I talked to Rick. I know you've put the pieces together the way that I wanted you to and now you've just confirmed my assumption that you've talked to the cops."

"You and Rick are in this together?" Oh God, what about Mary Ann? Was she being threatened right now, too?

"No, Rick just talks too much, or at least he talks too much to the people he trusts. He has a soft spot for naive, bubbly idiots. It's a role I've got *down,* and it's earned me the honor of being chosen as his confidant. The guy's been desperate for a confidant these days. He's going through an identity crisis and he needs the support of his surrogate little brother." His eyes traveled to my bedside clock. "Is that right? I didn't time this well."

"We could reschedule," I offered. "Would you like to kill me tomorrow instead?"

His smile was amused and genuine, and the gun was still pointed at me. "I could probably kill you right now and it wouldn't make a difference. But if you don't mind, I'd like to wait a little longer. Anne's providing me with an alibi, and if we can hold off fifteen more minutes it'll make it a tad more secure."

"You and Anne are in this *together?*" God, Anatoly had been right. But I hadn't listened to him. I had been so dismissive of the very idea that Johnny was behind the crimes that I think I managed to even convince Anatoly that he was wrong. Now I might have to pay for that mistake with my life.

"Don't sound so surprised, Anne is a very sexy woman," Johnny retorted. "Plus she's Sam's wife and Sam owes me for Jocelyn."

"I don't understand." I had fourteen minutes now. How could I get myself out of this in fourteen minutes?

"No, you wouldn't. You're not exactly a brilliant detective." Johnny sighed as if my ineptitude was a huge burden to him. "That bitch, Jocelyn, left me for Sam. She had no right to do that."

I felt my heart pick up speed as little fragments from my last conversation with Sam danced around in my head. The things he had said about Jocelyn....

She was younger than I and had just received a master's in political science.

Like Johnny.

Before me, she had a habit of dating abusive, controlling men...

"You killed Jocelyn," I whispered.

"She was mine and she betrayed me. She had to pay," Johnny said simply.

"Are you telling me that Anne seduced the guy who killed her husband's first wife? How messed up is *that?*"

"Anne doesn't know anything about my past relationship

with Jocelyn and she didn't seduce me. I seduced her and it was *not* easy. But you know how it is—the quickest way to a woman's heart is through the destruction of her rival."

"I'm not sure that's true…"

Johnny brought the gun a little closer to my temple.

"…of men," I quickly amended. "But you're right, it's definitely true of women. I'm always telling guys that if they want to get with me they need to get rid of my opponents."

"I like you this way, Sophie," Johnny said quietly, "scared and willing to do or say anything to win another few minutes of life. It's a bit like *Taming of the Shrew,* isn't it?"

Yeah, except that even at his drunkest, Petruchio would never have dressed up like something Charles Schulz would have put in a "Peanuts" cartoon. But I didn't say that because he was right about the scared part. I wasn't going to do anything that might expedite the pulling of that trigger.

"I found a few encrypted e-mails between Peter and Fitzgerald," he went on. "Even after I decoded them I found that the wording of the messages was extremely cautious. Still, I had an inkling of what was going on. My next move was to get information out of Rick. As I said, Rick needs people he can trust to talk to, especially after that Iowa furry incident."

"So Fitzgerald did engage in a ménage à trois with Peter," I whispered.

"All three of them in full costume," Johnny confirmed.

"Who was the third person?" I asked.

Johnny shrugged. "Some woman, I never got a name. But I went to Anne with the information and we both agreed that once the media got wind of it Fitzgerald's career would be over. Anne was so grateful she let me do her doggy-style.

It was the first of many compromising positions I've managed to get her in. But Anne and I miscalculated. We didn't accurately predict the media's reaction."

"I'm confused," I said slowly. "I've been doing a lot of research on Fitzgerald and I haven't come up with one article even hinting at him being a furry."

"That's because there *aren't* any articles hinting at that. We called in lots of anonymous tips and you know what response we got?"

I shook my head mutely.

"They laughed," Johnny said flatly. "Everyone assumed the calls were hoaxes. Even the tabloids that regularly feature articles about alien babies turned us down! It wouldn't have been a big problem if Fitzgerald was a Democrat. There are lots of fanatically right-wing publications that will print anything that makes a liberal look like a Satan-loving nympho. Those guys are experts at making speculation look like fact. But they're not so quick to believe the worst about a candidate that they've already endorsed. That's why Anne recruited Peter. We had hoped that he would give us something we could use, but of course he didn't." Johnny shook his head in frustration. His tone was getting harsher and I noticed he was peppering his speech with crude slang and curses. Who the hell was this man? Did *he* even know?

"So then we came up with plan B," Johnny continued. "Anne kept working on Peter and I worked on Eugene. See, Rick told me about what Eugene did to Bruni, so I figured it wouldn't be too hard to get him to take the furry thing seriously. I manufactured a little evidence to get him on the right track and before long Eugene had discovered that his boss was an ass-fucking pervert."

"But Eugene didn't come forward," I noted. Another minute had come and gone.

"Peter got to him. Eugene actually felt sorry for the sicko, and sorry for Fitzgerald, too," Johnny said, clearly disgusted by Eugene's sense of compassion. "Or perhaps he simply hated Anne so much that he thought Fitzgerald's candidacy was the lesser of two evils. Who knows? Whatever his reasons, he was keeping his mouth shut."

"So how'd you deal with that?" *What did I have in my room that I could use as a weapon?*

"Anne became impatient," Johnny continued. "She called Peter into the office after hours when no one else was around and told him point blank that she knew he had been playing barnyard games with Fitzgerald and was taking the story to the press. She was secretly tape-recording the conversation so all Peter had to do was confirm her accusations. That's all he had to do! But you know what that little shit head did, instead?"

I shook my head mutely.

"He sat down at his desk, wrote out a suicide note and jumped out the fucking window, right in front of Anne!"

"Oh, God," I whispered.

"Yes, it almost screwed up everything. Anne was such a wreck that she nearly washed her hands of both me *and* the idea of exposing Fitzgerald. But with a little effort I was able to convince her that it was Peter's relationship with Fitzgerald that drove him to suicide, not her threat to expose him. It never is difficult to convince people of what they want to believe. So then I came up with plan C."

"Plan C?" *Eight minutes and I still had no idea what I was going to do!*

"Yeah, C. By this time Fitzgerald knew Eugene was on to him and the dynamic between him and Eugene had grown noticeably hostile, so I figured I'd capitalize on that. We just needed to make it look like Fitzgerald was trying to kill Eugene. All I had to do was dress up as one of those furry freaks and borrow Fitzgerald's truck for a night. Fitzgerald was always very generous with that truck. I was going to wait until Eugene had too much to drink, something he did regularly, shoot a few rounds at him, miss, and then screech off before he could sober up enough to effectively follow me. If Eugene thought Fitzgerald was trying to kill him he would have gone to the police no matter what he thought of Anne."

"But you missed missing," I said. "You accidentally killed him." God, I was an idiot. None of this had been clear to me before.

"It's very hard to aim and shoot while wearing a large mask," Johnny explained. "I was dressed as a hippo that night. The costume was very cumbersome."

"But what about *Melanie?*" Her name shot out of my mouth like a bullet. But he wasn't hurt by the sound. Didn't even flinch. Her death meant nothing to him.

"I befriended Melanie, thinking she might prove to be useful, but that was *another* miscalculation. When she was at her most fragile she came to my home, unannounced and completely hysterical. Said she just needed a friend to help her through a panic attack. Unfortunately for her, Anne was there."

"You killed her just because she found out you were sleeping with Anne!"

"Now you sound exactly like Anne. By the way she flipped out over Melanie's death you would have thought I had killed her sister, not a woman she had never even spoken to. But what you and Anne don't seem to understand is I have a long-range plan. If everyone were to find out that I'm screwing Anne, then my plan might not be successful. I can't take that chance."

I was dangerously close to hyperventilating. I had six minutes and not one single useful idea. *Keep him talking,* said a little voice inside my head, *that's what you need to do in hostage situations.* "Why did Fitzgerald follow me to Neiman's? Or was he following Maggie and Rick?"

Johnny's eyes narrowed into little slits. "You are the stupidest woman I have ever met in my life."

"Excuse me?"

"Fitzgerald didn't follow anyone to Neiman's. I manufactured a lunch meeting for him so it would look like he was following you. I also wanted you to see him in San Francisco shortly before they found Melanie's body at Ocean Beach. I've known from the get-go that you weren't working for the *National Review.* Anyone who's had the stomach to get past the first page of one of your books could have figured that out. I knew you had to be helping Melanie figure out who killed Eugene, so I made it my business to make it look like Fitzgerald did it. I called Fitzgerald in the middle of your interview with him and told him that you worked for *Hustler* just so he would wig out in front of you. I told you he drove a green truck…and I *know* you saw his truck shortly before I killed Eugene."

"Wait a minute. You told me Fitzgerald drove a sports car."

"A Sportrac! A Ford Sportrac! It's a truck!"

"So the success of this plan of yours was dependant on my knowledge of cars?" I scoffed. "That was never going to work."

"Not just cars, *everything!* And I know that Rick didn't reveal all of Fitzgerald's secrets to Mary Ann, but he revealed a lot." His voice was rising and he was spitting out his words through gritted teeth. "Women like Mary Ann tell their friends everything, so again, why did it take you so long to become suspicious of Fitzgerald? *Why?* Why is everyone so stupid? I stole Fitzgerald's cell phone and planted it on Melanie's corpse! I didn't even cancel the service like he asked me to when he discovered the phone missing, just to make sure that it was that much easier to trace back to him! But still, nobody put two and fucking two together! And what about those threatening phone calls I've been making? It took you *how* long to figure out that this was about furries?"

"Give me a break!" I snapped, my temper getting the better of me. "How was I even supposed to know what a furry was?"

"You didn't know what a furry was?" Johnny scoffed. "Do you live in a cave?"

"That's it! I've had it!" I screamed. "Lunatics are always trying to kill me and I'm sick of it! I am a good person, a smart person, a reasonably politically savvy, generous and fashion-conscious person, and while I might not be familiar with every sick sexual fetish known to man, I am not a wide-eyed Pollyanna! I don't deserve to be visited by the Snoopy of Death! And if you absolutely have to kill me, the least you can do is let me change out of this furry suit. I want to die in a Vivienne Tam!"

"You're hysterical," Johnny snapped.

"Of course I am! That's what happens to people when they are forced to look down the barrel of a gun!" I started crying. It was the last thing I wanted to do. I wanted to be strong while facing this madman but I didn't feel strong. I felt like a woman who was about to die in the wrong outfit. People would whisper, *Did you know she was killed by an anthropomorphic dog while she was dressed up like a generic version of Hello Kitty?* And my mother—my crazy, neurotic and wonderful mother—would have to listen to people laugh about the death of her child. I simply couldn't let that happen. I would not have my death posted on the Darwin Awards Web site.

"Shh, hush now," Johnny said, his angry fit replaced by a show of mock tenderness. "It could be worse. In a minute your troubles will be over. Anne, on the other hand, has had to reconcile herself to the fact that she is no longer her own person. You see, I *own* Anne. I've been very careful to hide my involvement in these crimes, but I've also made sure that the full blame could easily land on Anne's shoulders should I want it to. At the snap of my fingers I could tie her to two different murders. If I say jump, she has to ask how high. If I tell her to suck my cock she has to ask how long. She's *mine.* But assuming she continues to play along, and she will, Fitzgerald will be the one to go to jail for Eugene's and Melanie's deaths, and yours of course. Then Anne will win this election by default and in a few years her husband will die in a car accident. Her constituents will feel sorry for her and I'll help her use their sympathy as a tool to repair her reputation. Her political star will continue to climb, she'll marry me when I've decided the time is right, and I will be the man behind the scenes. Every political decision will be mine. People think Karl Rove is powerful? Just wait until they see the shit I have planned."

His eyes moved to my bedside clock. "Perfect, Anne should be at her friend's engagement party now. She's telling everyone that she just ran into Fitzgerald's personal assistant at a café. So now she has lots of alibis, and she's provided me with one as well. You can die now."

"Anatoly will know."

"The man who's replaced Darrell Jenkins as Anne's tail? Yeah, I know about him. Too bad he never decided to tail Fitzgerald, but it doesn't matter anymore."

"Anatoly *is* following Fitzgerald."

Johnny chuckled, "Nice try. Fitzgerald's home alone. His wife's visiting her sister."

"Fitzgerald may have told you that he was going to be home alone, but he's not. He's at a furry party right now. Anatoly's following him. Anatoly called me less than a half hour ago to tell me that he had just called the police to tell them to meet him there. Why do you think I put this costume on? I wanted to go over there and see what was going on without being noticed. The cops are probably questioning Fitzgerald now. You understand what that means, don't you? Fitzgerald has an airtight alibi. You don't."

"You're lying."

"Call Fitzgerald and ask him where he is. Call his house. Call his cell phone—not the one you planted on Melanie's body, but the one he has now. Go ahead, Johnny. Make the call."

Johnny's head pivoted to the right where my phone sat on

my dresser. He was uncertain, I could see that much. The grip on the gun was a little looser. Was it still pointing at me or was I now half an inch out of the line of fire? I was still hunched over, sitting on the bed clutching my knees. Anatoly wasn't coming. No one was. Well, not no one…Mr. Katz had finally come out from under the bed and was rubbing himself against my ankles, giving me a questioning look.

Johnny started to turn back to me. "I'm not going to call…"

But he never got a chance to finish. I had done an unspeakable thing, I had thrown my cat through the air, and he had landed, claws extended, on Johnny's face.

The gun went off, and as it turns out I wasn't a half inch out of range, I was a quarter inch. Now the gun was on the floor as Johnny screamed and tried to get Mr. Katz to let go. But in a panicked frenzy, Mr. Katz was trying to claw his way up rather than down. I charged Johnny with my shoulder like a linebacker, knocking him to the floor, and Mr. Katz finally leaped off and ran out of my room. The gun was within my reach, but Johnny had managed to get one hand on my shoulder and the other on my hip and was trying to push me on my back and pin me.

So I grabbed the gun and shot him in the head.

I killed Johnny Keyes.

I untangled myself and stared down at the man in a dog costume bleeding all over my hardwood floor. I was shaking hard enough to make my teeth chatter and I was overcome with nausea, but I didn't feel any remorse. If there was ever a man who deserved to die in the most humiliating way possible, it was Johnny Keyes, the man who killed my friend. I dropped the gun and dialed 911.

26

I understand that all's well that ends well...but what if it doesn't end?
—*C'est La Mort*

IT TOOK A WHILE TO GET THE POLICE TO START TREATING ME LIKE A VICTIM rather than a murderer. I could see why they were confused. Here I was dressed up like a cat standing over a dead man in a dog costume. It looked like a violent ending to a furry lovers' quarrel.

Fortunately for me, I turned out not to be the only woman Johnny had underestimated. Seems Anne Brooke didn't go to her friend's engagement party. Instead she went to the sheriff's department. She had decided to confess everything, despite knowing that doing so would end her political career and could possibly land her in prison. But after a lot of tears she had decided that anything was better than being "owned" by Johnny.

The police took me down to the station, anyway, and asked me a bunch of questions, but in the end they let me go, and when I walked out of the station Anatoly was there waiting for me. He was standing in front of his Harley, a helmet in each hand.

I walked to where he stood, stopping when we were a foot apart. "I killed a man tonight," I said quietly.

"I heard." He handed me a helmet. "We're going for a ride."

I silently geared up and then straddled the bike behind him. I didn't ask where we were going. It didn't really matter, as long as it wasn't home and I wasn't alone.

He drove through the city streets, up Telegraph Hill until we reached Coit Tower. It was a weekday and off-season so there weren't many tourists. He parked and led me to a spot where we could see the lights of both the Golden Gate and Bay Bridge. "We came here on our first date," he reminded me.

I nodded and tried to lose myself in the memory. It hadn't exactly been a perfect date. It had started off with my car being vandalized by a stalker, but even so, it was better to relive that than recount this night's events.

"I didn't trust you then," Anatoly mused.

"The feeling was mutual."

"That didn't stop me from wanting you."

I smiled. That had been mutual, too.

"There were lots of reasons for that," he continued. "There are your almond-shaped eyes, your full red lips, your bronze skin, the curve of your lower back that brings attention to that incredible ass of yours."

"Anatoly!"

"But there's also your spirit. You're a strong woman, Sophie. You've been through a lot over the past few years but you haven't lost your spunk, or your sense of humor. I love arguing with you because I know you give as good as you get. I can't break you. Nothing can. Not even what happened tonight."

We were silent for a few minutes as I watched the overgrown brush on the hillside bend to the will of the wind. "I don't feel guilty about killing him," I said eventually.

"You shouldn't."

"Still…"

"You did what you had to do, Sophie. There's nothing to regret."

I tapped the toe of my shoe on the sidewalk. I didn't want to talk about this anymore, at least not while sober. "So where did Fitzgerald go today?" I asked, trying to change the subject.

Anatoly's jaw tightened.

"Anatoly? Oh, my God, did he go to the furry party?"

"Yes, he went to the furry party. He went to a hotel in Concord, came out in a costume covered by a trench coat, and switched cars. He took as many precautions as possible, but I was able to keep him in sight."

"What'd he dress up as?"

"A lemur."

"Really? Lemurs are kind of cute. I can't really imagine having sex with one, but I like watching them at the zoo."

"Uh-huh."

"So, if you didn't let him leave your sight, that means you had to go inside the party. Tell me, what did the other furries think of *your* costume?"

Anatoly mumbled something that I couldn't quite hear. "What was that?" I pressed.

"They made fun of me."

"Who did? Wait, you mean the furries?"

"It seems that Johnny's impersonation of a furry was a little off. They don't normally dress up like cartoon animals. They wear costumes that are a bit more sleek."

"Are you trying to tell me you weren't good enough for them?"

"I guess silverbacks aren't their thing."

"Silverback my ass." I stepped in front of him and wrapped my arms around his neck. "You're King Kong."

That night I gathered up my hero (Mr. Katz) and slept over at Anatoly's. I wasn't ready to go back to the scene of the crime. We stayed with Anatoly for a couple of weeks. I kept up with what was going on with Fitzgerald and Anne through the newspapers. The press had dubbed the whole thing "Furrygate" and were having a field day with it. Anne was being charged with "aiding and abetting" and "conspiracy to commit a violent act" or some such thing. Fitzgerald had been exposed as being a furry and had dropped out of the race at the insistence of the Republican Party. It was unclear who was going to be Contra Costa County's next senator, but it was generally agreed that whoever stepped up to the plate was bound to be better than either Fitzgerald or Anne.

Fitzgerald's relationship with Peter was also detailed in the press, and after a little thought I decided to call Tiff. I wasn't sure if she'd want to hear from me or not, but I wanted her to know that I was there for her.

As it turns out she was doing surprisingly well. She had decided to buy into Dena's line about her brother being an eccentric rather than a freak. She had even called Dena and offered her a free facial as a way of saying thank-you for giving her a way to deal with it all. With a little bit of coaxing I was able to convince her to make lunch plans with me for the following week. She was still kind of bitter about the way I had lied to her when we first met, but she figured I had been punished enough for my bad deed.

Mary Ann was doing well, too. I talked to her two days after everything had gone down with Johnny. She apologized for being so reluctant to tell me what she knew about Fitzgerald and told me about how distraught Rick was over the whole thing. He had honestly liked Johnny and he felt kind of sorry for Fitzgerald. But the recent events had helped make up his mind about his political affiliation. As soon as he heard what happened, he went down to city hall and filled out a new voter registration card. He was now officially a "liberator."

I talked to Leah, too. I admitted to her that she was right about my relationship with Melanie. I had entrusted Melanie with my feelings regarding our father's death and then I had avoided her so I wouldn't have to face those feelings again. But despite our lack of contact over the past several years, Melanie had been my friend, and at Leah's urging, I spent most of my time at Anatoly's grieving the loss of that friendship. As for dealing with the grief associated with my father's death—that was something I would have to work up to. But I would deal with it—someday.

Of course I eventually did have to go home. Anatoly

offered to stay with me for my first few nights back but I demurred. I refused to allow Johnny's actions to make me permanently afraid to be alone in my own home. Mr. Katz apparently agreed, because the minute we walked in the door he reverted to his old behavior, pestering me for food and giving me dirty looks when I didn't deliver fast enough.

I fed him (I had upgraded his cuisine to the expensive gourmet stuff) and collapsed on my sofa. That's when I saw the blinking light on my machine. I had been checking my messages so this had to be a new call. I leaned over and pressed Talk.

"Hey, Sophie," a male voice said. "Long time no talk. I've been reading a lot about you these days. Sounds like you're a real-life Nancy Drew. That's good because I'm back in town and I'm in a little bit of trouble. You know me. Maybe you can help me out for old times' sake? There might be a lemon drop in it for you."

I rammed my finger against the delete button. Mr. Katz came out of the kitchen and shot me an alarmed stare.

"I know!" I screeched. "I've just finished fending off a bunch of bears, and anthropomorphic dogs, and now I have to deal with that pig!"

Because really, "pig" was the nicest word I could come up with when referring to my ex-husband.

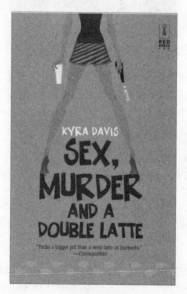